"Delirious thrills."
—*Detroit Free Press*

"Frantic and [...]"
—*Sunday Telegra[...]on)*

"A rolli[...]ad."

"Heartstopping."
—*Kirkus Reviews*

"A slick mystery-suspense tale."
—*Library Journal*

"As entertaining as it is unique...I was hooked."
—*Toronto Star*

THE ULTIMATE RUSH

JOE QUIRK

St. Martin's Paperbacks

This book is a work of fiction and any resemblance to real persons or events is purely coincidental, man. Don't try this shit at home.

Published by arrangement with Rob Weisbach Books

THE ULTIMATE RUSH

Library of Congress Catalog Card Number: 97-29702

ISBN: 0-312-96902-3

Printed in the United States of America

Hardcover edition published 1998
St. Martin's Paperbacks edition / October 1999

St. Martin's Paperbacks are published by St. Martin's Press, 175 Fifth Avenue, New York, N.Y. 10010.

10 9 8 7 6 5 4 3 2 1

FOR JONNA HERVIG
THE MOST BEAUTIFUL HUMAN BEING
I HAVE EVER KNOWN

CONTENTS

Bomb deactivator. Crack dealer. SWAT rifleman. My job will kill you faster than any of these. And it won't just kill you; it'll crush you to a pulpy clot on the streets of San Francisco. It pays fifteen bucks a pop and gets you a rush like no drug ever made.

I am a bike messenger.

On rollerblades.

All my mohawked coworkers snicker at me, but the boss, Mel, says he don't give a damn what I ride, as long as I make the deliveries on time. Which I do. So he keeps me on.

I'm the only rollerblade courier in the city. On any other courier job, rollerblades would be about as practical as snowshoes. But, working off Nob Hill, I got two advantages over those bike dweezels. One, I can thrash where no bicyclist would dare to wheel: up stairs, through backyards, over fences. And two, when the delivery is complete, I can hop the cable car back to the summit, then sit back and wave toodle-oo to my sewer-mouthed colleagues grinding a slow zigzag up the side of Nob Hill.

All of us tattoo punks get an excess of exercise, yet severe ulcers are as common as crushed hips, because we thrash it out paycheck to paycheck on the edge of starvation. Mel Corlini moves through fresh courier meat like a pimp through hoes. Mel creates the hostile environment, then lets a brutal natural selection run its course. Certain personality traits survive.

I work with the type of psychopaths who cut their own brake cables. They hurtle through crowded streets, screaming, "No brakes! No brakes!" Yuppiefolk soon learn to get the hell out of the way. There's nothing scarier than a creature who has no regard for himself and wants the square foot of ground you're standing on. Bike messengers are a despised species, but we Corlini scrubs are particularly vile.

The reason for this is simple. Other bike messengers must carry the fury of the entire city. The eight of us have to carry the fury of Mel Corlini.

Mel Corlini is a coked-up stock market player with rabies. He has three Charlie Brown hairs combed across his bald spot. He is pear-shaped and sweats a lot. A self-proclaimed asshole, so rich he shits chocolate mousse, he is the free market's evolutionary pinnacle, capitalism's Ideal Man made flesh.

I've just completed my fifth delivery of the day, and I'm hungry to make my sixth. I hop off the cable car in front of Mel's office building and skate past four or five stormtroopers who got there ahead of me but are securing their livelihoods, bent over the bike rack like prison freshmen. They scowl at me as I pass. Another advantage to rollerblades is that I don't have to lock them to some rottweiler's urinal. I clash up the stairs and stalk like Frankenstein down the hallway on my platform shoes. I follow the trail of black skid marks along the expensive hallway carpeting to Mel's office and get in line.

Mel, a heart attack waiting to happen, is barking into an innocent phone and chawing a stogie to mulch. Mel always keeps the blue stock market screen turned carefully away from us. He puts meticulous consideration into not remembering our names.

There's only one guy in front of me: blond, tanned, California boy, standing at full attention. His name is either Snake or Spider—I can't remember which. He doesn't look at me. I, a blader ninja in his ranks, am a walking sacrilege.

Even as I try to stand still, my butt cheeks are dancing an impatient mambo. A neon sign is blinking in my brain. It says: MUST MAKE RENT. I'm already two weeks late. Every passing second ticks me closer to the sixteenth and eviction time.

Mel slams down the phone, jabs the disk-eject with his thumb, yanks out a computer disk, and shoves it in a stiff eight-by-eleven. He slaps a seal over the opening, looks up at the bicycle courier waiting for instructions, and makes an outrageous offer.

"If you make this delivery in eight minutes, I'll give you four hundred dollars."

My ears perk up like Lassie spotting a steak frisbee. *Four hundred dollars?!!*

The courier isn't impressed. "Where's it going?"

"Mission and Fifth."

"Forget it."

"C'mon, dammit! It's all downhill."

My colleague laughs. "Yeah, but you can't take it straight down!"

"Five hundred."

The courier snorts and shakes his head.

My tail is wagging, I'm licking my lips, my eyes are darting back and forth between these two bargainers. I know you could conceivably make this twenty-minute run in about a minute-twenty. If you go straight down.

Of course, only a fucking maniac would go straight down. I step up next to Surfer Dude. "I'll do it."

Mel looks stunned, almost disappointed. "You will?"

"Sure."

Surfer Twerp shouts at the side of my face. "You can't get down to flatville in eight minutes! It's a twenty-minute trip, at top speed! And once you get down there, you have to hoof it all the way up Mission to Fifth Street, which is like eight minutes in itself—on a *bike*." He looks down at my skates, then back up at me. "How are *you* gonna do it?"

"Momentum."

He squints at me, confused for a moment. I watch the equation work its way though his face, then he goes white. "Oh, fuck. No way."

I turn to Mel. "Five hundred bucks, right?"

One corner of Mel's mouth is scrunched up in a curlicue. Looks like Genghis Mel wanted one of his peons to tell him it can't be done, so he can have somebody to blame. His face, once incredulous at this courier's refusal, is now suspicious of my acceptance. His eyes scan my surfaces, searching for those telltale tattoo markings that an urban rancher uses to distinguish one courier from the rest of the chattel. He looks at my feet and recognizes me as that what's-his-name on rollerskates all the other punks complain about, and he leans forward on his desk.

"Yeah, five hundred bucks. A guy will be waiting at the front door. But you gotta get it there in *six* minutes now, asshole."

"No problem."

Mel tosses the package at my chest. He points up above my head. "See that clock? Eleven minutes to one. You got to deliver that *before* 12:55."

My back is already to him. I stilt-walk out the door and clatter down the steps, sticking the package in my backpack. Peroxide Man receives his fifteen-dollar assignment and catches up to me as I'm hobbling out the front door.

"Hey, Rollerboy!" he titters, grabbing his bike and running alongside me. "Guess what? If you don't make it, he'll fire you."

"No duh," I say, churning up speed.

"No way," he repeats. "I gotta see this."

I hear his bike pedals clash, his chains lock and grind behind me.

"Hey!" he calls to his comrades. "Rollerskate Boy is gonna take the Cliff! He's gotta be on Mission and Fifth in like five minutes!"

Followed by an annoying chorus of *no way*s, I skate down the short driveway and swing to the left towards the legendary position at the top of Jones Street. Behind me is a small wake of bicycle couriers, sniveling like rats. They pelt me with caterwauls.

"You gonna go straight through the lights? It can't be done, man."

"The streets are too narrow, herpie-head. Swerve to miss a truck, and you're a wall mural."

I skate up to the edge of the precipice and stop dead. I have to catch my breath.

"Whatsamatter, Rollerfag? Chicken?"

*   *   *

Watermelon Hill. So named when some hurtling skateboarder burst his head spectacularly against the curb in front of a hundred witnesses last year. Since then, the spot has inexplicably drawn me. I've taken this hill before, but always from about five blocks down. I've never gone from the office way up on Sacramento Street before.

I have about four minutes. Once I step off this edge, I'll be at my destination in a minute and a half, dead or alive.

Knee pads, check. Shades, check. Helmet, check. Attitude, check.

My eyes reject the view of San Francisco Bay. They are trained like lasers on the five streetlights that curve down the concrete ski ramp below me. I can't budge until the first three streetlights are green, and the last two red. Then I'll push off, and instantly I'll be in my favorite zone, the do-or-die zone, the place where it's too late to turn back.

For dramatic effect, I remove my shades, fog them with breath, and squeak them on my shirt.

My streetwise audience quiets to murmuring when they clue in that I'm serious. One guy finally speaks up with a milliliter of compassion sloshing around in the bottom of his voice. "Hey, dickweed. Don't do it, man. You'll kill yourself."

He's right. If I wipe out on the hot macadam, my knee and elbow pads will protect my tattooed flesh like the candy wrapper in my ass pocket will protect the milk chocolate inside. Be like scraping a strawberry over a cheese grater. I will become a smoking gumbo of bones, gristle, entrails, and blood, slopped and splattered down ten blocks of hand-braked cars clutching to the side of Nob Hill. An entire fire department and a small legion of car insurance bureaucrats to clean me up.

Just the thought gives me a hard-on.

I have to take deep breaths to hold down my Honey Nut Cheerios. The diesel engine in my chest is doing triple flips. My quivering knees hug together to keep me from wetting myself.

I love it.

This is doable once a month, the second Monday of each month. Street cleaning day. On street cleaning day, no vehicles are allowed to park along the right side of Mission Street, so I can hit top speed down Jones and cut the left turn onto Mission without splattering my giblets all over somebody's paint job, and have my oversight immortalized in some new nickname for this hill.

Now they sound like they're talking to a jumper poised on the edge of a building. "Bail out, dude. If this hill got any steeper, you'd be going it upside down. Just come back and let us laugh at you."

"Yeah. So you lose your job! Bladers don't belong on this detail anyways."

I don the headphones. My skull becomes an angry hornet's nest of speed metal riffs. They are shut out.

The first two traffic lights go green. The last two go red. C'mon, c'mon. Then, the third and middle traffic light—green! I'm off!

Instant hyperspeed.

I'm in my zone now: rubber cheeks pulled back and flapping, shins vibrating like jackhammers, eyeballs shaking like ice cubes in a martini shaker. I swear I can hear the rattling of my vertebrae clacking together. My femur and shin bones are pulling apart and snapping together one hundred times per second, playing tug-of-war with my cartilage. All my favorite kinds of pain are humming together in a perfect chord. My body is a harp string vibrating.

I am a comet, leaving two hot parallel streaks in the sizzling tar behind me. My skates are smoking. My fiberglass wheels are starting to get sticky. A couple bugs splatter on my sunglasses, one splats between the teeth of my shit-eating grin.

I rocket past a long line of briefcase trudgers.

"Shwayyyyyt!" I scream—meaning "sweet"—as I reach the most exalted level of adrenaline overdrive.

"Shwaaayyyt! Shwaaayyyt! Shway-yay-yay-yaayyyt!"

I can imagine my voice Dopplering off behind me, the heads of the drones swiveling to gape.

The music is inside me. Bass drums are thudding in my rib

cage, electric guitars shredding blood from my eardrums, bass guitars cracking my skull with each pluck. I am experiencing ultra-face-tuck now. The corners of my mouth can taste my ear wax.

The air friction gradually pulls my headphones off my helmet until they snap away. Now they are flying behind me like a cape. Captain Blader is being garrotted by his own Walkman.

A flock of businesswomen presume to cross my street. I jettison a war cry: standard courier procedure when some ped maggot is about to step in your way. The suits freeze like sheep before the charge of the rabid lion. I tear past and my back gets darted with screechy epithets.

The first three lights, each in succession, turn yellow. I scorch beneath them as each flares red at the top of my vision and bores between my eyebrows like some Hindu implant. The light in front of me flashes green, and the last one beyond that is still red. So far, so good.

O'Farrell Street bump is coming up—not actually a bump but a place where the sixty-degree plummet momentarily levels off for a perpendicular street, then dips down again. My knees take the split-second upward surge like springs. Then—air!

Getting air is like snatching a little piece of eternity. The raucous wheel rattling ceases, the earth melts away, and I am floating. I don't breathe. The only sound is the hum of the tiny rollerblade wheels still spinning on their axes. I am weightless as an angel, free from guilt and shame, a tiny breeze soft as a negligee on my face.

Then I hit street, a hard jolt back to mortality. Knee bones splinter in collision, and I am going faster than when I left the ground. Blader legend says that one second of lost friction increases your speed by ten percent.

The last vibrating red traffic light never turns green as it rockets over my head. Damn, this is too fast.

Still got the Mission Street turn to make. Barreling down in this raging fury, I have to bank it right up against the parking meters on the right side of the street. Coming around the buildings, I glance up Mission, and—

Oh, shit!

Monday! Today is Monday! The second Monday of the month! Right? Street cleaning day!

So then why is there a long line of snugly parked yuppie-mobiles sitting smack in the middle of my safety zone?

Waitaminute! The *first* was a Monday! So this is the *third* Monday of the month!

I'm street spam. Make this turn tighter? At this speed? Im-possible!

Then again, the threat of death has a way of inspiring me.

My right skate is directly behind my left. I snap my right skate around backwards, so I'm skating sideways and my knees are spread-eagled. I raise my elbows up like a figure from an Egyptian hieroglyphic.

I lean, and lean hard. I arch backwards until my spine is retroflexed to the max. I'm trying to bring the back of my skull to my heels, and I can feel sciatic nerves pinching pain-fully. My thigh muscles twist like steel cables as I bend my femurs to the snapping point. I growl in strain, feel my puck-ered face go red hot. Sweat peels off my forehead to the hair above my ears.

I make the turn. The mile-long battering ram of steel passes to my right with a whoosh of air displacement, and I am hur-tling along its side at a squillion miles per second, hearing the steady hum of the parked cars as I pass, an eerie acoustic phenomenon caused by the echo of my wheels. I snap my right leg back around frontwards, get down in a squat like a tubing surfer, and careen along two feet from the car doors like a little cannonball.

I'm in a fetal position, for good speed and in preparation for death, to leave this world in the position I entered it. I'm down below the windows, so a meter feeder couldn't see me even if he glanced over his shoulder.

I zoom up behind a snorting bus lugging its ass up Mission like a crippled hippo. I can't lose the momentum that will carry me to Fifth Street, so I hold my breath as I pass through its black flatulence and wriggle into the narrow steel alley between the leviathan and the parked vehicles. Standard courier maneuver. We call it "chrome sandwich." Keep your elbows tucked close. It looks suicidal, but it's actually pretty safe. Nothing is going to kill me in here, unless—

A car door opens, seventy feet in front of me. It splays its wing like a steel beetle, and out from its armpit steps an Armani shoe. I will cover that distance in one second, with no room to brake or swerve. The car is an open-air convertible with the door window rolled all the way down.

I stand up straight, put one skate in front of the other, and head straight for that door.

The opened door hurtles towards my balls at forty-five MPH. In the half-second I have to act, I see the leathered toe turn outwards, the knee bend for leverage. He is a millisecond from stepping out into my path.

I prance like Baryshnikov, pull my heels into the small of my back, grab my toes with one hand, and—groin muscles be damned—bend them up towards my ear.

Door flashes beneath me. Release toes. Skates clash with perfect precision on the pavement. Bus slips away and shrinks to bunny size. Death is behind me.

As my skates lose momentum and noise at sea level, I hear the cheers of onlookers, who would have been just as thrilled to see me bite it. My chest pistons are thudding out my elation. I want to gasp the whole sky into my lungs. This is the only time I really feel alive.

Twirling around and skating backwards, I can just barely see my innocent motorist sitting frozen in his car with one Armani shoe on the pavement and mouth agape. As I sailed over his leg, I felt the businessman's nose pass within inches of my right buttock.

I cannot tell you how much this immature yet sublime little notion means to me.

I spin, hop the curb, leap a snoozing drunk getting a suntan in the middle of the sidewalk, pull the package out of my backpack, and skid to a halt beneath a street sign. Mission and Fifth. Ten feet from my toes is the delivery site: a Chinese restaurant built into the first floor of an abandoned hotel. A well-dressed Asian man launches out the front door, snatches my package, and skitters back inside.

"Yo! Where's my receipt?"

He's gone. I look at my watch.

12:53.

Fuck if I'm gonna let this weasel gyp me out of my five hundred bucks. I gun after him, barge into the dimly lit restaurant under the prissy gaze of the bourgeois gaping at this sweaty tattoo punk desecrating their snobatorium. My eyes catch the package-snatcher heading through the back kitchen.

"Yo, motherfucker! Hold up!"

The maître d' steps forward. "Can I help you?" he whimpers.

I body-check him aside and skate across the carpet into the bright shrine of the greasy kitchen, dart in and out of shuffling cooks, and just barely notice the gofer scampering through a small green door in the back like Alice's white rabbit.

I got him now. Spitting venom and vitriol, I charge after him.

Just before I reach the small green door, it swings wide, and out steps a gargantuan olive-skinned brute who has to duck to fit through the door. He steps at me and battering-rams my chest with one lead forearm.

My neck snaps forward as the bright tile room crishes to scattering diamonds behind my eyes. Tender lumps instantly sprout on either side of my bitten tongue. It feels like somebody just fired a howitzer off my sternum. I blink and look up into his face, pretending I can still breathe.

I wait for him to tell me I ain't getting in. He doesn't. He's Caucasian, and he's wearing a perfectly tailored suit, with a striped green, white, and red tie, looking about as incongruous in this environment as I do. His slit eyes glow a reptilian green, and he smiles at me. He looks deep into my pupils and espies my innermost animal nature, the ancient part of me that remembers being prey.

Here's a guy who enjoys his job.

Usually in a situation like this, I would be worrying about

preserving my dumbass phallocentric ego. But this mother-fucker is huge. I'll be tough some other day—when a smaller guy bullies me, maybe.

Besides, I can't fight on blades. Believe me, I've tried it. Rollerblades are as crippling as they are empowering. On the move, I am invincible. Standing still, I'm a sheep limping through a lion's famine.

I yank my eyes away from his hypnotic talent and race back through the gawking restaurant, feeling like an Arab who just farted in a synagogue, and hurtle out into daylight. I spy a phone booth across the street and attract a few tire squeals and horn honks getting to it. I pounce up the curb and snatch the receiver from a businessman who is fingering through his wallet in search of his phone card. I look at my watch. Thirty seconds to 12:55.

I fumble through my pockets for a quarter and feverishly stab out the number to Mel's courier line.

"Make your report."

"Yo Mel, man, it's me, Chet Griffin."

"Rollerboy?"

"Yeah, that's me. Hey, the delivery was made, man. Home-boy didn't even give me a—"

"Go home."

"Wha?"

"Go on home. You did good. Now just go home."

"I just want to confirm that I get five hundred—"

Click.

I slam the phone into its stirrup and glare at my watch. 12:55.

I made it.

I breathe deeply, snaking my trailing headphones around my neck. I thumb off the Walkman tape, snipping the clashy whispering of white noise.

The adrenaline high simmers and passes. My heart cools just before its meltdown. The drudgery of safety returns.

I am no longer alive.

Slowly reclaiming possession of me is the incessant agita-tion of my life, the twitching sinews knotted into muscles, the frustration in the marrow of my bones. Damn it all! It always fades! I want one pure experience to wipe the boiling hunger from my blood. I want to catch one crystal piece of timelessness and carry it with me in my pocket. I need to escape this utterly damned existence of mine. I lust for the ultimate rush.

Sound shallow? Fuck you.

New Age bliss ninnies say that life is filled with choices. That's bullshit. There is only one choice: Will you live for comfort or adventure?

The price of stability is drudgery. The price of ecstasy is agony. I don't want the meaning of life. I want the experience of being alive.

Hell, I don't even want the meaning of my job. What is Mel delivering? Is it legal? Who cares. I got no business pondering the upper echelons of the economic structure of which I am a single disposable and semiloose basement screw. On the list of Seven Deadly Courier Sins, ranked right up there with Sloth and Flaccidity, is Curiosity. Succumbing to Curiosity might lead me to break the psychic stone tablets on which are written the Two Courier Commandments:

Commandment I:
Ask no questions

Commandment II:
Never look inside the package

Ravi Shankar and Zakir Hussain are just reaching the frenzied height of their call-and-response parley when I burst in and kick the plug.

"Hey! I was just about to reach Nirvana!" goes my room-mate Denny, shooting himself in the face with an imaginary shotgun.

I yank off my shades and helmet, still sweating from my suicide run. "Where's the phone?"

"I don't know. Check under that pizza box."

I hurl off the greasy cardboard and grab the receiver. "What's Slumlord's number?"

Denny calls forth his superpowers of name and number memorization and tells me. The skills he's developed to make up for his unusual incapacities—like, for instance, the fact that he can't hold a pen—are truly spellbinding.

I punch out the numbers and tap my bladed foot while it rings. A machine picks up.

"Ralph! It's me, Chet Griffin! Don't put my eviction notice up! I have a check for five hundred bucks coming! I'll get it at the end of the week, and sign it straight over to you! This is not bullshit, Ralph. The money is coming. Just gimme till Friday. Okay? Okay!"

I slam the phone down. "Where's the remote?"

He's all, "Why should I relinquish the scepter of power?"

"*Blazing Bladers* is on."

"Of course. How could I forget? God forbid we miss an episode."

"C'mon, man, where is it?"

"Holstered."

Denny sports a utility belt on his wheelchair, where he keeps all his Bat-tools.

"Give it up, homes."

"Bite me. We're watching the business report."

"The *business report*?"

"I heard a rumor, and I want to see if it's true."

I snatch it out.

"Hey, asshole!"

Denny talks like molasses because he has cerebral palsy, but that doesn't deter him from stretching out his already slow sentences with unnecessary profanity.

He unsheathes his spare, and we commence our daily joust of dueling clickers. Feet stomp and calumnies fly while the screen blinks back and forth between a droning newscaster and a tampon spokeswoman doing splits on the beach and sliding down banisters. Then suddenly the screen is switching between two newscasters. Both of us stop clicking.

"What?" I shriek. "What's this nimrod doing in my slot?"

Denny laughs triumphantly.

I point the remote at Denny and hit the off button.

A man wearing a hair helmet is droning: ". . . announced a surprise merger today. Picotex bought all the shares of WordCom, increasing WordCom's worth by three hundred points."

"Did they cancel?" I demand. "Gimme the Bible."

The *TV Guide* splats against my face. "Chill, Chet! They filled the slot with a news show."

"But all the other stations have news! What's become of this world? Don't apathetic people have any clout any more?"

I raise the remote to switch on the VCR.

"Wait!" detonates Denny, stiffly slashing his arm at me and leaning forward in his chair. "I want to hear this!"

I squint at the screen. "Why? Since when are you into stock?"

"They might take over Datavox."

"Where you work?"

"Yeah, now shut up."

The newscaster intones, "Company spokesmen say Picotex

plans to increase its market share by fifty percent over the next three weeks. Buying and selling of stock in small computer companies has reached a furious peak as analysts try to predict . . ."

My five-second attention span is shot by now, and my trigger finger starts to itch as I am overtaken by the absurdity of our posture: two plebeians watching patrician news.

"Fuck this," I go, and raise the remote.

Denny leans back in his chair. "Bastards."

"Whatever," I say, clicking on the VCR.

"*Whatever?* Wasn't it was right after your father—"

"Yeah, yeah, it was right after my father lost all his money in one of those stock market thingies that he went from being an asshole to a sadist. So what? All those white-collar squid-heads got nothing to do with me."

"We could fight this one at CFED, if my compatriots weren't so preoccupied with 'the hot new study group on the deconstruction of socialism in the modern era.'" Denny snorts to himself and maladroitly yanks off his computer headset, hurling it on his desk. "To hell with all of them," he decrees. "I'm going to do this myself. If I can predict which companies are going to be taken over next, I can make it public over the Internet, and mess with the worth of the stock. Do some info-terrorism."

This catches my attention. "How are you going to pull *that* off?" I ask, knowing the answer.

Denny sighs. "The only thing I can think to do is trace their private calls."

Denny is a fallen computer whiz. He used to work with AT&T. He had everything to do with orchestrating its balkanization. He got burned as a result, was fired, banished from his center of power. But he took one tool with him.

"I could use that secret weapon in my own battle, Denny."

"You must earn it, Grasshopper."

"Oh, gimme a break."

"You'd misuse the power."

"How am I going to misuse the power?"

"You can't just smash power centers and create anarchy,

Chet. You have to redistribute power among the citizenry. Revolution is constructive, not destructive. Hatred of authority is not enough to earn you my light saber."

"Whatever you say, Obi One Cannoli." I stand and head for the video stack.

"Don't get pissed, man."

"You can kiss my ass. Keep your damn power sword."

"It's not about power, Chet. Power is only a means, not an end in itself."

"Uh-huh. Deep."

I pull off my shirt, wipe the sweat from under my armpits, and turn my back to Denny to shuffle through the stack of videos.

"Hey, I never noticed that," says Denny.

"What?"

"The thorns in your tattoo form the word ANNA. Who is Anna?"

"My mother."

"Your mother?"

"Yeah. Putting her on my back is the only way I can handle her."

"Handle her? Why do you have to handle somebody who died so long ago?"

"It's not handling *her*, really. It's more handling the way I feel about her."

Denny nods. He knows when to joke, and when not to. "That's cool," he obliges.

I spend the next sixty seconds making a point of not looking at Denny.

Fuck, I hate using the word *feel*. I like to keep conversation at the level of witty repartee. Keeps things from getting too sappy. You know? Kind of like the word *love*. That's another word on my shit list.

I pop in a porn tape called *Sperminator* and lean back in my sweaty skate armor.

"Dude, I'm telling you," Den laughs, "the porn industry is in a conspiracy to keep you celibate. If you finally get laid, they'll go out of business. That's the only explanation. No-body—not even you—could be this pitiful."

I'm like, "Hey, this is a *temporary lapse* in my studhood."

Denny chuckles. Ever since Debbie dumped me, Denny has been gleefully rubbing it in. For a man who has consecrated his life to toiling for the underprivileged, on the off hours he sure is a sadistic motherfucker.

Denny, besides wallowing in the luxury of having a cute female caretaker named Molly cook for him, clean his room, and scrub his naked body, has this gorgeous able-bodied girl-friend named Elana. He met her through CFED, pronounced "see-fed," Citizens for Economic Democracy, a radical politi-cal think tank which he runs mostly through his computer modem. Elana once told me during one of her nitrous stupors that the slow-motion and steady way that Denny laid the pipe brought her to heights of ecstasy no able-bodied man could manage.

Denny is not proud of his disability, he glories in it. Many is the time, when I walk into his room to borrow five bucks and stumble on Molly massaging his back or shaving his face, he looks gleefully at me with an eat-your-heart-out-able-bodied-motherfucker grin on his face. He makes that motor-ized wheelchair of his into a phallic symbol. He loves to speed past his buds who trudge along the street and give them a cheerful middle finger. In every move Denny makes—in every grin, every word, every tilt of his head—there is the implicit message that his mechanized condition is an improvement.

He has two part-time occupations. The first is his true pas-sion: overthrowing the government of the United States. He does radical political work organizing labor and poring through raw data to create graphs and statistics for left-wing periodicals. His enemies call him a socialist. Officially, he calls himself a proponent of a democratized economy. When he's alone with me, he calls himself a shit-stirrer.

Denny's other part-time occupation is as a computer pro-grammer with Datavox. He doesn't actually have to go to work, except maybe twice a week, so he spends most of his time here, writing programs.

Me and Denny have different addresses. Officially, we're neighbors. But, in practice, we're roommates. We live in an apartment complex near Haight Street with twenty apartments and ten bathrooms. One bathroom adjoins two apartments, and me and Denny share a bathroom on the first floor. Most of the time (when nobody is taking a dump, that is) we leave both facing doors open in the bathroom, and call back and forth to each other while we fiddle at our computers. It makes it feel like one big apartment. I get up on Sunday morning and traipse through the bathroom to his apartment and eat breakfast with him. I spend all my time in his place, and keep half my stuff here.

I go into Denny's cabinet, pull out the box of Goobery Grape, and grab his milk.

"Dammit, Chet, you are such a speed freak. You should be banned from sugar."

I've just gotten over my oats and horse-food kick. I used to fill my bowl with muesli that looked like the bottom of a gerbil's cage. It's made from floor sweepings, bird's nests, wood chips, and assorted pebbles and twigs. You can't get more fiber eating a bowl of burlap. Scours out your insides like steel wool. When I finally got tired of giving birth to an endless succession of cinder blocks, I switched back to sugar bombs. I dilute the sugar with another spoonful of sugar, and get slurping.

"Say, Den," I slobber. "Why would somebody pay me hundreds of dollars to make a delivery in eight minutes?"

"*Hundreds* of dollars?"

"Yep."

"Where was it going?"

"This Chinese restaurant built into the first floor of an abandoned hotel."

"Well, there's tons of reasons. Maybe you were delivering crack."

"This was a computer disk."

Denny gasps. "You *looked*?"

"Hell, no. I saw Mel put it in the package before he sealed it."

"So it's some kind of secret info. Some other business wanted to intercept it."

"But with all these faxes and modems and doohickeys we got now, why would somebody deliver a computer disk via human courier? And why would it have to be there in exactly eight minutes?"

"I always wondered why Mel has you guys deliver from the top of Nob Hill. Seems sort of inconvenient."

"Makes for a killer rush, dude. Yo, check this out, man: I made five hundred bucks today on *one run*!"

"Are you serious? Damn! I should get out there on my chair and buzz around! Show you bipeds what speed is."

"Sorry, Den. This job is designed for badass speed ninjas such as myself. Wimpoids need not apply."

Denny's nostrils expand like a bull's. His manhood is challenged. His hand lingers over his holster. My hand hovers over the remote next to me on the couch.

"Your move, pilgrim," says Denny.

The door opens. No knock.

"Hey, circle jerkers."

Denny shouts, "Wassup, baby!"

I turn to see Ho strutting through the door. She kicks her skateboard into the corner and sings in a falsetto Elton John impersonation, "D-D-D-Denny and the Chet."

"Hey, girl!" I go, bounding from my seat. "I ain't seen you in two weeks. How about a hug for your favorite Chet?"

"Denny first," she says, parrying my attempt and striding forward.

She stops dead and looks at the blatant act of fellatio displayed in ridiculous close-up on our tube. "Which one is this?"

"Sperminator."

"Jesus! You guys have seen this one a shitillion times! Don't you have it memorized by now?"

"It's research. I might become the understudy to this guy."

Ho blows a bubble in my face.

I notice Ho's fluorescent green gum exactly matches her tank top and the skate wheel she uses as a hair scrunchie, which puts her hair—blue today—into a kind of postfuturist cheerleader's bob.

No, Ho is not Chinese. Her moms was one of those flower children who was so confident in the immortality of the Groovy Revolution that she named her kid "Ho" after Ho Chi Minh, never foretelling that the word *ho* would soon adopt even more nefarious connotations. Ho refuses to change it.

Today she is sporting the word SLUT magic markered across her bare tummy. Her belly button is pierced with a Roman Catholic claddaugh ring.

Ho, by the way, has a *way* sweet butt. To make things worse, she skates in spandex. She's caused many a traffic accident.

"Anywayyyyy . . ." Ho makes a face at Denny, like, *Too bad you have to live with such a dwid,* and says, "This is a late congratulations Ho-hug to celebrate your promotion at Datavox."

She bends down and embraces Denny. "Ew," she says, wiping her hands on Denny's shirt. "You are just the droolmeister today, aren't you?"

Denny laughs. "Keeps me well lubed."

"Do I have to drool to get one?" I say.

Ho smiles at me, tousles my hair, and we hug.

"How's Megan?" asks Denny.

"We broke up," says Ho, without emotion.

"No!" I say.

"Whoa, shit," says the ever-sensitive Denny.

Ho sighs and puts her hands on her hips. "Yeah. Two weeks ago today."

"Why didn't you tell us?"

She slaps her thighs. Time for Ho to go off. "I just wanted to deal with it on my own for a while! I hate telling the same story me and Megan agreed to tell everybody over and over again. I wanted to hunker down and retrench. Plus I didn't think I could deal with everyone asking me *How's Megan?* like a bunch of pull-string dolls."

"So what went down?" I ask.

"Typical shit. She wanted to go back to her straight world.

Taking flak from her parents about still not being married and all that. Fetus envy—that would be my dyknosis."

"Man!" I go. "What was that? Two years?"

"Three."

"So who moved out?"

"She did. To Idaho."

Our jaws drop. "Not even!" me and Denny chorus.

"Even," says Ho.

"Damn, another Californian bites the dust," I say. But then I notice Ho is holding her breath and tightening her lips, so I shut up.

Me and Denny share a brief glance. This bums us big time. The Gay Pride Parade was just about a month ago, and I still remember Megan and Ho, leading the parade with Dykes on Bykes. It was Megan's first parade. Not exactly *out,* Megan would only go if she got to wear a leather mask, but Ho seemed tolerant. Seeing them straddling the Harley, shouting and smiling together, Megan's arms around Ho's stomach, there had been no hint of a rift. The only thing I remember being crestfallen about was that neither of them had gone bare-chested.

Ho tsks at herself and blinks her big green eyes.

Ouch.

Impulse strikes like a cobra. I reach into my back pocket, pull out my last Hershey's Kiss, and hold it out to Ho, smiling proudly.

She doesn't move. She just stares at it. I look at what I am offering. It's misshapen and greasy with my sweat. My ears flare. Then Ho smiles lightly and takes it.

I look at my toes.

Denny, trying not to hurl, reverses his chair and heads back to his computer.

Ho swallows hard and looks at me. "So why are you home early from fetching sticks?"

"Got off early. Made five hundred big ones today, baby."

"How did you swing that?"

"Took Watermelon Hill in like a minute and a half."

"You're shitting me."

"Nope."

"From way up there on Sacramento?"

"Yep."

"Chet, much as the street surfer in me wants to admire your utter hypeness, as your chum I have to say that is totally the boneheadedest thing you've ever done—and that's saying a lot, for you. You are soooo like gonna be Watermelon Two."

"True, the Cliff claims one fatality, but that was a mere skateboarder." I put my hand to my heart and raise a finger. "*I* am a blader."

"I could expound lengthily upon the idiocy of that comment, but I really must be going." She snags her plank.

"You're not gonna hang?" I ask, disappointed.

"Got to hook up with my skate buds at the Fort Farley half-pipe. Then I got to go rehearse."

"You're performing tomorrow night?"

"Yeah. Coming?"

"Wouldn't miss it for Halloween with Elvira."

I'm starting to feel a familiar agitation. Pinpricks dance up and down my spine. I bend down, shovel in the last of my soggy sugar nuggets, vacuum-slurp up the purple milk, wipe my mouth on my wrist band, and take a deep breath.

Ho slaps my shoulder. "Want to come cool out with me, Chet?"

"No," I say, my face twitching. I stare at my bedroom door.

"Damn, Chet. You're so addicted, it scares me."

"I got it under control."

"If you say so. Catch you later, Denny."

"Peace out, Ho," says Den, not looking up from his computer.

Ho drops her deck, mounts, and soars out the door, trailing a blue mane.

I bust and peel a couple cloves of garlic, cut a slab of cold Velveeta, and throw it all into the blender. I pour in a good tablespoon of Chinese red hot sauce, fill it up halfway with Save-A-Lot eggnog, and hit puree. Then chug. Denny already has his fingers in his ears.

"YYYYEEEEEEEOOOOOOWWWWWW!! WO! WO! WO!"

Red spots blur my vision. I rattle my head and blubber my cheeks. After the shock, I rise to a startling clarity, like when you surface after diving into icy water. Every detail of my surroundings is crystal clear. I can feel blood throbbing through each capillary in my fingers.

"Going surfing?" Denny's voice is so crisp as to be LSD-induced.

"Hell, yeah," I breathe, unable to find my voice box. I wipe the sweat from under my eyes and stalk through the bathroom.

I step into my bedroom, shut the door, and strip naked. I open up my glass case and pull out my five-foot boa constrictor. A long muscular tongue, he wraps himself around my body, squeezing lovingly, stopping just short of asphyxiating me. It's comforting to know he'll take me to the edge and stop. I suppose this is how a woman feels in the arms of a large man. It's trust. I pull the shades and put on John Coltrane's album *Om*.

My room is painted black, and it's papered with H. R. Giger paintings and blown-up images from Milo Minera erotic comic books. On the wall, written in my blood, are the words, "Tranquility is death. Comfort is coma." I was thrashing around the room to "Scentless Apprentice," one of the more agonizing distortion orgies by Nirvana, and I split my knuckle open on the corner of my filing cabinet. In a pagan mood, I smeared blood words on my black wall. They're pretty much invisible now, except when the lamplight hits it right.

My skin is also graffitied. I have many tattoos, each with metaphoric or primal significance to me: creatures whose spirits I want to imbibe, totems I want to carry with me.

A portrait of Ralph Waldo Emerson is on one shoulder, and on the other shoulder is Waldo, his lost son.

I have a scorpion on the back of my calf.

On one forearm is an ancient Incan design.

On the other biceps I have a "perpetual set," which is an optical illusion forming two drawings in one. Look at it one way, and it looks like a peace sign. Blink your eyes and it looks like a swastika. There is blood dripping from the perpetual set and watering flowers, to commemorate the infinite grief of finite living.

But the profundity doesn't stop there. On my back, I have a massive tattoo that opens up to a vision of my skeleton. The spine and ribcage are shattered, and inside is a valentine-style heart, eight inches wide, with a crown of thorns wrapped around it like barbed wire. Each thorn cuts into the meaty flesh of the heart and draws a bright droplet of blood. The thorns form the word ANNA. Anna is my mother's name. She and my father died in a toboggan accident when I was seventeen. This tattoo is on my back, not my chest, in recognition that I have moved on from the grief.

The heart is torn open, and inside is a circular design, sort of like the Yin-Yang symbol, only there's three of them: Yin, Yang, and Yodel. You have to get up close to see the reptile, mammal, and angel devouring each other and making love at the same time.

I conceived the design after I saw a PBS show where this scientist pointed out that the human brain is really three brains stuck together. It's a reptile brain, with a mammal's brain grafted on top of that, with the distinctly human neocortex grafted on top of that. Maybe this is why we humans feel so unintegrated and confused, while reptiles seem so pure. One brain does not evolve into another. They're just scotch-taped on top of each other, filling us with internal contradictions.

All this self-defacement would normally cost thousands of dollars, but I get my tattoos for free. My little brother is a tattoo artist. He's also a crack addict. Last year, when he was fifteen, he went into our old apartment bathroom and didn't come out. I had to shoulder open the door, pushing his co-matose body through a puddle of drool. I stayed up with him all night, pulling strings of vomit out of the back of his throat, changing his soiled drawers. He credits me with saving his life. When he's sober, he cuts a mean tattoo.

I sit on my throne, bedecked in a living reptilian scarf, and flick the red switch. Purring awake, it winds up, revving the cycles of my adjunct mind. I am now entering the only world where I have ever had power. It is a world without place, without form, as immaterial as thought, but it will soon be more powerful than this world. It exists nowhere, yet it is not imaginary. People meet there to do business, have sex, tell secrets, get married, and commit crimes. It is limitless, poten-tially infinite. Yet it will never take up any space here in re-ality. It creates its own space, out of nothing. It is my world, the world of cyberspace.

I am a hacker. In fact, I am a convicted felon.

Phone Fraud, Reckless Misuse of Advanced Technology, Theft of Intellectual Property, Conspiracy to Commit Terror-ism.

I was convicted of these crimes when I was sixteen.

At midnight, on April Fool's Day, my parents' home was raided by the Secret Service, eleven of the 1,900 specially trained elite corps whose sworn duty is normally to protect the President of The United States. My mom and dad were in bed when all the windows on the first floor shattered at once. The front and back doors splintered simultaneously, and armed men in suits raided every sanctum of the house with terrifying swiftness and professionalism. They burst into my parents' bedroom, yanked them out of bed, and cuffed them facedown on the floor.

Alone in my attic crypt, I suppose I heard the commotion downstairs. I suppose I even heard the shoes pounding up the steps. If I had been asleep—hell, even if I had been in a quaalude coma, I would have sat bolt upright, in sudden stunned awareness of the threat. But I was not asleep. I was not comatose. I was deeper. I was in cyberspace. I did not snap out of my trance until the door burst open and the first gun I had ever seen was pointed between my eyes.

They took everything. Or rather, they took only what was electronic, but, to me, it was everything that mattered: my IBM, my printer, my ham radio, my floppies, my phone line, my broken Atari, even my fucking wristwatch. My parents sobbed in their robes in the living room and talked too much. They professed that I was an angelic boy. I had been an altar boy in the fourth grade. I had played basketball, wrestled; I was the youngest kid in my troop to get Eagle Scout. Only recently had my grades been sacrificed to this new obsession. Like most hacker parents, they hadn't the faintest idea what I was up to, alone in my bedroom. When they looked in on me, I was staring at electronic lines of code, not even acknowledging their presence. Hell, it will get the boy a good job someday. At least he kicked that Dungeons and Dragons cult. Let him play. It's harmless, right?

I was advised to plead guilty. At the witness stand, I fessed up that I had broken the codes and surfed the forbidden infozones of AT&T, the IRS, GM, scores of prestigious universities, and, most terrifying to the Feds, the Pentagon. I lived by a strict hacker's dictum: *Look and learn, but do not touch.* I had gained no profit from the information, had crashed no systems, but other kids had. They plugged me for names. It took repeated visits to the court before I could convince them that, yes, though I did spend hours plotting, arguing, and bragging with my hacker cohorts, I had never met one face-to-face. The anonymity of the electronic bulletin board left me no clues as to their ages, their skin colors, their genders. There was only one thing that mattered in the datasphere, and that was skill. I knew who was good, and I knew their handles: "Terminus," "RAMpage," "Knightmare," "Predat0r,"

"><borg," "/\̂\,," "D∗rk$t∗r," and my own handle, "Mac-Hack." I could not, I lied, help them apprehend any other hackers.

I was put on probation for a year, given one hundred hours of community service. I was a minor, a "misled adolescent," who did not understand the power of my unique gifts. Power—electric, godlike power—is intoxicating when you can't even get a girl to go to your junior prom. I was caught before the Great Hacker Witchhunt, when the fascists would start throwing gifted hackers in jail. The judge also commanded me never to sail cyberspace again. He might just as well have told me to stop jacking off.

I stayed off the illegal freeways for a while. But the temptation has always lurked like a tumor in the back of my brain. The challenges of mere programming are stiflingly boring to a true hacker. Steadily, like a patient lizard coiling up my brain stem, the dangerous, government-shaking lust has crept back. In the last year, it has once again taken control of my impulses. I have returned to my kingdom, reborn with a new handle: "Snakebyte."

Because, as only we few hacker warlords understand, the shimmering corridors of electronic code in the finest computer systems can be things of exquisite beauty. Once you have tasted the Platonic, crystal world of cyberspace, mundane reality becomes a purgatory you must return to, to satisfy the eating, sleeping, shitting animal you are leashed to.

I scale the heights and depths of GM. I know how to shut down the electrical system of L.A. I have access to dangerous military secrets. I can incapacitate the IRS. At a flick of my finger, riots will begin, planes will crash, factories will go berserk. I can plant a virus that will shut down half the free world.

I recognized four months ago that I have reached the point of no return. I will, one way or the other, be caught, and go to jail. But I can't stop.

I check my first Underground bulletin board system, the one run by the Gibbon, called Chaos, Ink. It took me a long time to trade enough illicit info and perform enough tricks to earn the respect of Gibbon. Finally, he has given me the access code to this secret meeting place.

When I call it up, I find the entire system has crashed, and this is what I get:

ATTENTION BITHEADS: I HAVE JUST ZORKED ANOTHER RODENT. THE GIBBON IS MINE, THE COURT DATE IS SET, AND GIBBON IS SQUEALING ON ALL YOU PUNKS. HACKERS BEWARE. MP PHRED IS ON YOUR ASS. I AM THE COWBOY IN THE WHITE HAT ON THE NEW FRONTIER OF CYBERSPACE. ONE BY ONE, I WILL BRING YOUR SCRAWNY LITTLE TEENAGE ASSES TO JUSTICE. ALWAYS REMEMBER, PHREAKS, I AM PAID BIG BUCKS TO EAT YOU FOR BREAKFAST. YOU WILL NEVER DISCOVER MY SECRET SUPERHERO IDENTITY. KEEP BREAKING AND ENTERING, ZOIDS. IT GIVES ME SOMETHING TO DO. IN THE MEANTIME, I'M POUNDING ANOTHER RUBBER-STAMP BITHEAD ON THE SIDE OF MY TERMINAL.

Right in the middle of an Underground bulletin board! What gall! He's hacking the hackers!

Mother Phucking Phred, otherwise known as MP Phred, has earned the fanatical wrath of the most powerful group of teenagers on the planet. If they find out who he is in reality, they'll shut off his home power, distort his tax records, erase his bank account, wipe all evidence of his even existing off the face of the electronic world. We have declared the hacker's equivalent of a fatwa upon Mother Phucking Phred.

MP Phred is commonly considered a Fed. A zany anomaly, he has the dark gifts of a true hacker overlord, with the Wonder-bread-and-skim-milk ideology of a straight. He hires himself out as a hacker tracker. He blocks our break-ins, throws off our scents, even traces us back to our addresses and calls the pigs. Which means he has technology the rest of us don't have, technology most of us bitheads would sell our mothers to get. But MP Phred is not one of us. If he had sold his mother to acquire his toys, he would be cool. But he did something worse. He sold out the Hacker Ethic.

The name Mother Phucking Phred plays directly off our slandering of him. When we first detected a vigilante in our midst, everyone was typing about "that motherfucking Fed." So on he came, going public with us, calling himself "Mother Phucking Phred." The use of "ph" in cyberspeak plays off the legendary proto-hackers, the Phone Phreaks, the original out-law pioneers. (Excuse me while I remove my hat.)

I'm not even off the board when a plethora of former Chaos, Ink members are leaping on and frothing at the key-board, cursing MP Phred and his terrorism against terrorists with some extremely creative blasphemy. Hackers, who live to trespass on Establishment systems, are the most outraged when some Establishment heathen desecrates Underground property. After an hour or two of gnashing their teeth and casting hexes, they will set about working through the elec-tronic trickery that MP Phred doubtlessly used to booby-trap his message.

But I know how MP Phred plays. Somewhere in the ruins of that bulletin board is a software bomb that will go off in an hour or three. That cybernazi didn't just find the rat nest and exterminate it. He discovered it days ago, released a virus in its belly that would crash all the hard drives of everybody downloading from the system at the exact moment his timed software bomb hiroshimizes Chaos, Ink. Can you imagine the rage of a pimply teenager who, in the middle of a tongue-lashing tirade, finds his precious bulletin board zipped out of existence and his entire hard drive suddenly swamped? Ooooog, I can't watch.

I would log on just to warn the poor little varmints, but I can't risk catching MP Phred's electronic bug, and I don't want to leave behind any evidence, even evidence that will self-destruct within the hour.

You see, I fear MP Phred.

I've been around. I know a stellar hacker when I see one. And MP Phred is fucking cosmic. A regular Darth Vader, he's been hovering invisibly above his Death Star, zapping us helpless hackers like we were bunnies in a barrel.

There is a lot of speculation among the Underground that he is a legion. But I know he is just a man. Yes, not a boy, not female (rare in Underground cyberspace), but a man. I can tell by his messages. He uses perfect grammar, and he never says "awesome." He's probably gone to MIT, worked for the big boys, been busted as a young hacker, then hired by the straights to protect their systems from his own kind. Culturally, he's not a Fed. Feds don't say, "Attention, bitheads, I am on your ass." They say, "Disperse. This is an unlawful assembly," and then they give you the section and code of the particular statute you are breaking. No, MP Phred is not a Fed, but he works for them—*them,* the very FCIC, the Federal Computer Investigations Committee—Evil Incarnate.

MP Phred's nightstalker hit-and-run image is expertly calculated. Hackers, a high-strung lot in the first place, given to quaffing six-packs of Jolt and amphetamines, are as jumpy as lice, and, at the slightest threat, will skip paranoia and leap straight into hysteria. Sometimes, after weeks of submerged silence, MP Phred pops up in sacred Underground temples and issues threats. "Lex Luthor! You're next! Ha! Ha! Ha! Ha!" This leads the voluble hacker community to instantly believe that the expert techoid MP Phred is working on a scheme to bag one of the biggest boys of them all. But I know this is bullshit. Obviously, if MP Phred wants your ass, he's going to want you talking and leaving evidence all over the bulletin boards. An open threat will only cause his big game to duck and cover for a while. No, he won't let the gun report unless he's going to take you down with one shot. If he's just idly firing, he wants to scare somebody who he knows is too big and too damn good to tackle. MP Phred ain't got shit on Lex Luthor.

But he hasn't threatened me. Which means he might have a bead on me.

I know that if anyone will bring down MP Phred, it will be me. Snakebyte, the Unseen Lord of the Underworld, will meet the rough-riding vigilante. The two granddaddys of cyberspace will do battle for the soul of the Internet.

And, already, I think I have something on him. Something I dare call a clue.

There is one thing I find particularly curious about MP Phred. Every two-thousandth word or so, MP Phred types the entirely wrong word. The mistake is especially strange highlighted so strongly against the backdrop of perfect spelling and grammar. You'll be reading one of his messages, running thusly:

GREETINGS, RUNTS. JUST POP-POP-POPPING ON TO LET YOU KNOW I'VE DISCOVERED YOUR UNDERGROUND CUT-AND-PASTE SHOP, AND I'M AIMING MY LAWMAN'S RAY GUN DOWN YOUR MODEM LINES. WHEN THEY LOCK YOU IN THE HOLE, SAY CHEERIO TO THE HACKER INMATES FOR ME. YOU DARE TO SIDESTEP MY WRATH? I HAVE MORE THAN ONE QUEEN IN THIS GAME OF CHEESE.

Game of *cheese*? What the hell is he talking about? I thought I was hip on all the hacker lingo, but this one really throws me for a loop. Then I realize, Oh, he meant "chess."

But that doesn't really qualify as a *spelling mistake,* does it? So then what the hell is it?

At first you think he's playing word games with you, but

you can't help noticing that they appear at odd times and with no humor value whatsoever.

I keep a small file of these catachreses and the contexts wherein they reside. So far, I have discovered no discernible pattern. But I'm certain this is the key to understanding the Dark Angel of Cyberspace. And bringing him down.

I'm fucked.

I had my damn alarm set on P.M. instead of A.M. I'm reaching the top of Nob Hill a whole hour late. Mel does not tolerate lateness. Hell, he doesn't even tolerate promptness. My first day, I showed up a half hour early, just to be eager and spunky, and found the office already packed with couriers. I soon learned that "six o'clock," in Mel parlance, means five-thirty. If you show up "on time," he gives you all the scuzzy runs for the rest of the day.

A frenzy of piranhas snapping in my blood, I somehow ride the cable car to the summit without spastically chucking people off to save on weight. I leap off before it stops, clatter on 'crete, cut a hard right, and use the momentum to carry me right past a couple bicyclists. I don't even have time to gloat about yesterday.

I stalk into Mel's office. Mel takes one look at me and burps into the phone, "Hey, I'll have to call you back, Gina," then snarls, "Hey! This is business! I'll explain later!" and slams the receiver down. He waves his hands like Moses and commands the parting of the spandex sea. All the weasels reluctantly slink outside and shut the door. Then I discover that, yes, Mel Corlini does indeed have legs. He audibly detaches his suction-cup ass from the leather chair and comes around the desk as if to take a swing at me.

I can't help but take a step back. What's going on here? This is not how Mel fires people. He usually just looks up from his stock market chart, barks over the phone, "You're fired, asswipe," and gets back to what he's doing.

Then I finally interpret the expression on Mel's face. It took me a while because it's so oxymoronic, like a chicken blowing a kiss. Mel Corlini is smiling.

He grabs my shoulder and manfully shakes my hand. "Hey, kid! Heeeyyyy! Chet Griffin, right?"

Okay. He knows my name. This sounds good.

His palm feels like paper. I disengage my hand and raise it to my face. Five one-hundred dollar bills.

"Cash?"

He spreads his arms and walks back around his desk. "Hey! You don't need to worry about taxes after a delivery like that!"

Now he's keeping promises. What's going on here?

Mel leans back in his chair and puts his hands behind his head. "Five minutes, you did it in! I told you six, and you gave me five! Pretty goddamn amazing, Chet!"

I guess I'm not going to have to throw myself on my knees and beg for mercy after all. But I almost feel less comfortable with this dynamic. When a man like Mel Corlini gets friendly, you can't help but crave the old stability of being treated like a maggot.

I struggle to respond, but then I realize Mel is not interested in what I have to say. He stares up at the ceiling, where some grand design must be spinning.

"John Chen was pretty damn happy with you. When he found out I had sent a courier *after* I had called him, he called me up and told me he was gonna kick my ass. I'll tell you, Chet, I was quaking in my boots! Ha! Ha! But before he even got off the phone, there you were, arriving *early*! Woo-hoo! He didn't know I had a secret weapon, a fucking cannon! And that's Chet Griffin!"

I vaguely remember the guy I delivered the package to, an Asian stiff in an expensive suit who met me at the front door of a restaurant, snatched my package, then ran back inside.

Whoever that dude handed that package to must be a pretty powerful man. I didn't know Mel was subservient to any entity in this universe, including God, but it sure sounds like he would beg to get down on his knees and kiss this Chen guy's ass.

"You know what, kid? That's what I'm going to call you!

All you couriers have code names, right? Hedgehog and Twinkie and all that? They probably name you after some bug, right? Spider?"

I blanch with horror that he could make such an association. "No, that's another dude."

"Well, drop the bug name. From now on, I'm calling you *Cannon!*" He bites his stogie and puts his hands behind his head, grinning like he's just conferred a knight's title upon me.

I fake a boyish smile that Donny Osmond would have killed for. What the hell. It's better than Rollerfag.

"You know why I'm calling you Cannon?"

. . . he's waiting. Not rhetorical. "Why, Mel?"

"Because you're going to be my secret weapon!"

Is there a skip in the record here? I'm smiling so hard I've damn near sprained my face. "Wow," I manage.

"Whenever I need an extra-special delivery—and I mean *extra*-special—" he winks, "I'm gonna call out my Cannon."

"Wow," I repeat. I guess there are skips in both our records.

Oh God. Is he expecting me to make five-minute deliveries every day? How can I explain to a patient man like Mel Corlini the second-Monday-of-the-month thing?

"To give you an idea how important these deliveries are: Guess how much I'm going to pay you!"

"How much?"

"About three times as much as everybody else."

Fuck the second-Monday-of-the-month thing.

"Wow," I say. I think the verbal section of my brain is stuck in an infinite loop.

"Dr. Chen has dealt with my couriers for some time. It's a miracle if a bicyclist gets the package there in fifteen minutes. Somebody told Dr. Chen the five-minute delivery was made on rollerskates, and he just went ape-shit for this new technology. I told him that's why I hired you, because rollerskaters are the fastest things going nowadays."

"That's really neat," I articulate. I keep waiting for the Energizer Bunny to come winding across the desk.

"Dr. Chen wants rollerskates, my boy! And you're my little

Cannon on rollerskates! So you need to run them things up stairs, down fire escapes. Hell, we want you to skate down the marble hallways if you can. I don't want some bike speedster with a giant contraption he has to carry around or lock to a fire hydrant for this detail. Them rollerskates are perfect."

"Actually, they're rollerblades."

"Whatever. In my day, we called them rollerskates. The point is, we need speed. I'm talking kickass speeds. God damn, if you make a twenty-minute delivery in five minutes, I figure you go four times as fast on them things. So I expect you to risk your fucking life out there. That's why I'm offering you so much money."

Cut through the bullshit time. "How much money are we talking about here?"

"You're going to be the first courier in history to get paid a flat salary: fifty bucks a day above and beyond your deliveries. And I'm taking you off the payroll as of today, so it will be tax free. Plus I threw an incentive in there. You get thirty bucks for a fifteen-minute delivery, forty bucks for a ten-minute, and fifty bucks for a five."

"Whoa! That comes out to—!"

"Don't get too excited. You only make one or two of those kinds of deliveries a day. The rest will be the normal fifteen-dollar deliveries. I'll be using you off and on all day, but I'll mostly need your speed skills between twelve-forty and twelve-fifty-five. That's when I'll really need you to blow it out."

Just because I'm licking my chops does not mean I don't know the unspoken part of this agreement, which is: If I fuck up, I'm fired. Of course, that has always been an item in the long list of my job hazards. But then again, there is great potential for fuckupitude in every detail of this deal. Does he think I am so shallow that I would sacrifice my already uncertain job security for the immediate gratification of a bucket of money?

"Mel, I got to tell you: I didn't make that run because of my skates. I made that run because I experienced a temporary lapse of sanity due to my economic situation."

"Whatever. You did it once. I want you to keep doing it."

"Waitaminute. Are you trying to tell me you want me to *risk my life* for another hundred bucks a day?"

"Will you?"

"Of course!"

"Good. Here's your delivery for today. Take this to Point E. Ask for Mr. Levy."

Mel unpeels a special sticker from its backing paper and seals the package. He tosses it to me.

"Mel, I just have one question."

"Couriers are not supposed to ask questions, but, under the circumstances, I'll let this one slide. What's your question?"

"Why?"

"None of your damn business."

. . . okaaaay . . . not much I can say here.

Mel has no patience for meaningful pauses. "Just be the courier, Chet. And kiss my ass like it's the hem of the Virgin motherfucking Mary. Don't make me regret I chose you. There are other rollerskate fags in this city, you know."

"Yes sir, Mr. Corlini, sir."

"That's better. Now wipe that brown stain off your nose and tell those assholes they can come back in."

I march towards the door.

"And Chet?"

It's weird to hear him call me by name. I have to be the first peon in history whose name Mel Corlini has memorized.

"Yes, Mel?"

"Don't brag to your fellow punks. Just keep this between you and me. If I hear any whining about who deserves what, I'm gonna do a mass firing."

"My lips are sealed."

"Good. Now piss off."

Trying to contain myself, I skate past the bike dorks, jump down the steps, and clatter on 'crete, my body shaking.

Holy shit! Not only will I be able to make rent, but I will also be able to *eat*! From here on out, life will be gravy! I can buy a new razor! I can finally replace that broken lightbulb! I can pay *somebody else* to cut my hair! I'll be able to afford *lubricated* condoms! Yippeeeee!

And Band-Aids, I think, peeling my face up off the street. I'll definitely have to get some Band-Aids. Mental note: Never, *never* try to click your heels in rollerblades.

I skate to point E, otherwise known as Wozniak and Levy, a big shitkicking building that contains some kind of special bank for hoity-toids only. Crunching down a celebratory packet of grape-flavored Pez, I push through the revolving doors and glide the unnecessary expanse of polished marble to the front desk. I power slide to a stop behind three wealthy-looking personages as the first woman I've seen all day stares at me like I'm desecrating some sacred dress code. Before I can open my chalky mouth, she calls over the desk, "Are you Cannon?"

The aristocrats turn and gape at me in horror. I nod and grin my purple grin.

"Come with me," she says, and abandons the waiting nabobs. I follow smiling. This is rad.

She ushers me to one of the many elevator entrances crowded with about ten people each. She maneuvers to the front of the line, saying, "Personal delivery for Mr. Levy," and everyone lets her cut to the front. I in my sweaty shorts and rollerblades follow in loyal attendance. Before the elevator doors enclose us, I quickly flip the bird at the gawking straights. The elevator does not stop until it reaches the top floor. We get out, and I am shown through a sea of foul-mouthed suits snarfling handfuls of potato chips beneath blue stock market screens swollen to Godzilla size. People are throwing cigarettes and papers and munchies onto the pristine carpeting. The secretary, very intimidated by these big-bellied movers and shakers, uses her smile as a shield to ease her way through them and leads me to an imposing door. She knocks, an icy voice says, "Enter," and I am left to walk in and meet His Heavenly Highness. The secretary closes the door behind me, clipping off the noise that followed me into the room. The lights are off. The walls are utterly soundproof. In the silence,

I can hear the executive flick off the power on his speaker-phone. He stands up and comes around his desk and leans back on the polished surface with an affected casualness. The air-conditioning chills me.

Jesus. Dante would have had a field day with my morning.

The man is thin and frosty-haired and handsome in a Claus-Von-Bülow-as-played-by-Jeremy-Irons sort of way. He looks like he carries the weight of the world on his shoulders. I am certain his skin has never been hit by a single ray of California sunshine.

The man clears his throat. "May I have the package, please?"

I step forward and hand it to him. He places it behind him on his desk. He seems uncomfortable with his sudden close proximity to my unshaved face, so he changes his position.

He looks at my blades, which are probably scuffing up his floor major big time. "Are these the shoes I'm told can travel very swiftly?"

I choke, flabbergasted at this display of dweebulosity. "Yes," I go. "They're called rollerblades. You see them all over the city," as in, *Excuse me, Mr. Zombie, have you ever, like, left this building?*

He nods awkwardly and turns his back and wanders over to the giant window, which I'm just noticing is completely hidden by ten-foot drapes. This seems oddly paranoid. He can't really look at the view like he planned, so he has to adjust his calculated movements. He puts his hands behind his back and gazes at a painting. He's seen it a thousand times, and it's dark.

"You're going to be making deliveries straight to me," he instructs, "and, even more importantly, you're going to take deliveries back to your point of dispatch. These are very private deliveries, and require the utmost secrecy. You are not to talk to the secretaries or anyone. Just tell inquirers you are Cannon making a personal delivery for Mr. Michael Levy, and everyone will let you through. Bankers in this building often use personal couriers during the business day, so this should all be taken as a matter of course."

The silence pounces back in on our conversation.

"That's nice," I say.

He turns and faces me with sudden urgency. "I am told that couriers are not to be concerned with the contents of their packages. Is that correct?"

"Hell, yeah," I say. "We make so many deliveries a day, we don't even think about it." Searching for a fulcrum into levity, I tack on, "I'll bet crack dealers use us couriers all the time, and we don't even notice."

He does *not* roll around on the floor in hysterics. He just blinks a couple times.

"Don't let anyone else accept the package for me. My secretaries have been instructed to refer you straight to me. If you don't find me, wait. You'll be paid for waiting. Then I will hand you a package, and you will deliver it back to Mel Corlini. This is the longest you and I will share company. From now on, just deliver, pick up, and go. We don't even need to exchange words."

That's a relief. Skippy opens a drawer and takes out a manila envelope. "Here's your first package."

He hands it to me, leaving a little damp spot where his palm touched the package. It's sealed with a special sticker exactly like the ones Mel uses. His blue eyes look directly into mine.

"This is a personal arrangement between Mel Corlini and myself, and no one else need be involved. I look forward to a civil relationship with you. Good day."

Overcome by his wit, I shake his icicle hand and break out into a smile. "Hey, Belushi," I say. "We have *got* to party some time."

When I burst into my apartment, Denny and Ho are listening to Nine Inch Nails and playing Ms. Pac-Man (the only video game Denny has the joystick coordination to play). The little yellow tennis ball with the bow in her hair gets gang-banged by the purple monsters, somersaults, and disappears. Denny yowls with rage. Ho jubilates.

Ho leaps to her feet and grabs her board. "It's about time! Let's bolt!"

"Hey, I want to talk to you guys about my job—"

"No time for that!" erupts Ho. "We got to get over to the Padlock for my show!"

"But—"

"C'mon, man! You said you'd come."

Ho grabs my arm and drags me towards the door, calling over her shoulder, "C'mon, Denster. We need some mega-towage."

So Denny gives us a tow. Denny's motorized wheelchair is rigged to go at illegal speeds. When he's towing just me, I can grab the two hand-grips like handlebars and get wigged out velocity. But when there's two of us, there's no room to street-ski, and the both of us can't really hang on with one hand each. But that's no problem. Me and Ho just jump up onto the motor at the base of Denny's ass and get a free ride. We're quite a sight in this circus formation, but, in San Francisco, where townsfolk walk around in Batman and Robin costumes and chains connecting their nipples, no one blinks an eye.

"Hey," shouts Ho over the wind and the electric buzz of Denny's wheelchair. "I'm glad you broke up with Debbie, so I can finally tell you I hated her. Can I go kick her ass now?"

"No, you may not. And Debbie broke up with me, remember?"

"It just goes to show that straight women—"

"Wait, wait, wait! Did you just say you hated her? Why did you hate her?"

"Well, I guess I didn't *hate* her, I just think she didn't appreciate you." Then she says, as if to diffuse her previous statement, "Besides, I hated that Malibu Barbie giggle of hers. Hee! Hee! Hee! Hee!"

"I thought her laugh was cute."

"Ugh!" Hanging on with one arm, she grabs me in a head-lock and gives me a noogie. "Chet, your taste in chicks is even worse than her taste in dudes."

"Hop off, motherfuckers," shouts Denny. He's wearing ridiculous Elton-Johnesque wind goggles. "I got to go around back and use the garbage exit. This is where I make my turn, and I ain't slowing."

I leap off, hurdle a fire hydrant, and scull past Denny. Ho, to show me up, grips the right handgrip with one hand, braces her feet against the motor, and bends her ass to the street. She waits for Denny to swing a hard left and uses the momentum to slingshot herself straight past me. It happens so fast, I hear more than see her feet clatter on her board. I have to hoof it good to catch up.

"Oh, you think you're so slick!"

She ollies a curb and smiles back at me in her shades. "So when are we going to have the Great Street Olympics Clash of the plank and the sissywheels?"

"Ho, don't pass off your surfing ineptitude to the stone-age technology at your feet. We both know it would not be a clash of the skateboard and the rollerblades, but a clash of superior athlete and inferior athlete. And you, my pet, do not take humiliation well."

"Sissywheeler."

"Sideways winder."

"Humph!" We both fold our arms and look the other way as we skate side by side.

I like to think of myself as an open-minded sensitive wimpy liberal. I respect all nations, races, and all six genders. But I hold one particular prejudice close to my heart, and that is against skateboarders.

I've held signs at Denny's rallies, protesting the death penalty, torture, genocide, but I always put a little asterisk on my sign, and down at the bottom, in teeny-weeny writing, I always put, "except in the case of skateboarders." It's inconsistent, I know, but I only go to rallies to meet chicks anyway.

Bladers and thrashers hate each other. Those damn plankers, heading into life sideways, instead of head-on like we cool rollerbladers do, they make me sick. They wear loose clothes; we wear tight clothes. They can do acrobatics, but we can dance disco.

I rationalize hanging out with Ho because she makes a point

of transcending categories. So I guess that makes her semicool, at least. I mean, what plank punk wears *spandex*?

In a moment, the kinetic energy that began in Denny's battery has carried us up the hill to the Padlock. We both stop against the horizon, chug our water bottles, and wipe our foreheads on our wristbands.

In a flamboyant mood, I stand against a billboard with snowy mountains and cop my best pose. I shake my shorts to simulate a breeze.

"Who would have thought," I declare, "that my technological ancestor, the short-skirted rollerskate waitress at the drive-in, would evolve into such a badass as I?"

"I guess you can always tell a badass by his open fly."

"Oops! Thanks." Zip! "Anyways . . . where was I?"

"You are the ultimate badass."

"Yes, I am the ultimate badass, sizzling the streets, rarely seen as anything but a blur until I arrive, glistening for the comely temps, making mere plank skaters such as you cringe with jealousy."

"Mm-hm. Chet, let me ask you something. Have you been skating around San Fran all day making deliveries with your fly open?"

"Of course not! Surely I would have felt my manhood dragging on the 'crete and whipping behind me like a meaty cape."

"You should wear a jock for protection. I think they sell in thimble size."

"C'mon, now. The wind is blowing. There's quite a chill."

"It's also eighty degrees out."

"It doesn't matter. Wind makes even the most massive bratwurst cringe like a spooked turtle."

"Don't worry about it, John Holmes. I'm used to clitorises anyway, remember? Even *you* can beat that!"

"Ho, everyone knows the plural for clitoris is clitorides."

"Well, not everyone fantasizes hopelessly about the presence of multiple clitorides like you do, Chet."

"Speaking of multiple clitorides, what time is your show?"

"You mean you're not attending for the pure joy of experiencing my unique artistic expression?"

I smile deviously.

She laughs. "Not for another hour. We already did the sound check this morning. C'mon, I can get you in for free. Let's go inside and get a couple beers."

"Ho, as you well know, sculpted human machines such as myself do not imbibe any—"

"Excuse me, a beer and a kiwi-guava drink made from only the freshest ingredients and the dew scraped from dandelion fuzz."

"That's better."

We go inside.

Ho spits her fluorescent green gum like a lightning bolt into a short metal trash can. Ptoong! it echoes. The bald and bearded hamhock at the door nods to her and doesn't ask me to pay the six bucks. We strut over to the bartender with a bone through his nose.

"Bud, please," goes Ho. "Bottle."

I'm all, "What do you got with the highest sugar content?"

"I can do you up a Shirley Temple with extra syrup."

"Hit me," I say.

We grab our drinks, throw our bills on the bar, and saunter over to a table. Ho is slapping fives with every color of the hairdo rainbow. I try to look cool. Ho picks out a table and straddles her chair cowboy style, with the chair facing backwards and her forearms leaning on the backrest. I sit across from her and cross my legs like a lady. To the chagrin of the nearby grungesters, I pull off my malodorous skate boots and pull my sneakers out of my backpack.

"I *risked my life* yesterday, Ho. Do you know why? . . . That wasn't rhetorical, Ho."

Ho spins away from drooling at a redheaded meter maid who stopped in for a tequila shot. "Wha? I'm sorry. Gleeps, Chet! Why on earth would you risk your life?"

"For five hundred bucks."

"Your life for five hundred bucks?" Ho sips her beer, frowns in thought. "That sounds about right."

Ho goes back to scoping chicks.

"Ho?"

She grabs my hand. "Yes, darling?"

"Be serious."

She scowls like a cartoon character.

"I mean *really*."

"Okay."

I sigh.

Ho holds both my hands. "What's the matter, bud?"

I shrug, staring at my reflection in the table surface.

"You're not buggin on your family again, are you, Chet?"

I wince. "No, it's got nothing to do with all that."

"Well what, then?"

I sigh and smooth back the porcupine quills that surround my emotions. "There's something wrong with my job."

Just then Denny bursts in from the kitchen with his usual aplomb, waving his arms and regally announcing his presence. All heads turn. He wheelies around the bar firing wisecracks and sizzles across the dance floor towards us.

The bartender shouts, "Can I get you any mind-altering beverages, Denny?"

"Nope. Got to keep my head clear."

"Driving?"

"I'm always driving."

Denny grinds up speed, then skids to a stop on the slippery barroom floor. His stomach stops four inches from the edge of the table. What a show-off.

"What am I missing?" he asks, slapping us a pair of awkward cerebral palsy fives.

"Chet is buggin off something," goes Ho.

"Let's hear it," says Den.

Ho squeezes my hands and looks into my eyes. "So what's up?"

I sigh. "Mel was so impressed with my suicide run yesterday, he made me Extra-Special Delivery Courier and tripled my pay. I got two hundred bucks in my pocket right now."

"What a tragedy!" erupts Ho, shoving my hands away.

Denny's mouth falls open. "Chet!" he gasps. "That's great! Why aren't you celebrating?"

"As in, buying our drinks?" goes Ho.

I shake my head. "Something just ain't kosher. I'm thinking it might be dangerous."

"I thought Blader Boy lived for danger!" says Denny.

"I'm talking it might be illegal." I lower my voice. "A conspiracy, even."

Ho and Denny lean forward like children at a campfire.

After a melodramatic pause, I continue. "Mel is having me deliver all these top-secret packages. None of the other couriers are allowed to deliver them. Just me. One guy who seems to be in cahoots with Mel is this really freaky banker."

"A *banker*?" interrupts Denny.

"Shh!" hisses Ho, slapping Denny on the shoulder.

"But they communicate through phones and computers!" goes Den. "Why would they use a courier?"

"That's exactly what I'm wondering about. Before my suicide run, I saw Mel putting a computer disk in the package."

Ho shrugs. "So?"

"So if all they're relaying is information, what's so secret about it?"

"Maybe they're not trying to hide info from cops," suggests Denny. "Maybe they're trying to hide it from competing business interests."

"And there's another thing," I go. "If most of Mel's priority deliveries go to the Financial District, why does Mel rent an office way up on top of Nob Hill?"

Denny scratches his chin. "I been thinking about that one. Maybe, since he specializes in lightning-fast delivery, he wants gravity on his side. It's like a speed ramp. Couriers jamming down that hill get maxi-momentum for the cruise along Market. I bet a courier starting from the top of the hill would blow right past a courier starting from the bottom."

"Very true," I go, always willing to concur with attestments to the utter hypitude of my profession, "but then deliveries going back to Mel always take extra long because of the brutal incline. Why should the deliveries going back to him be so much less important?"

Ho and Denny look at each other and shrug.

"And that's not all," I continue. "Mel also has us make desperate deliveries to points all over the city, not just the Financial District. And some aren't even major businesses.

They're like home and even apartment addresses, tiny businesses, police stations. Sometimes we make a delivery to a guy standing by a phone booth or waiting in his car. After a while, it dawns on any courier with a clue that there are two kinds of deliveries: the standard legit deliveries made for clients, and the special deliveries made for Mel. The special deliveries are mixed in with regular deliveries, so it's hard to tell. For weeks at a time, the special deliveries will peter out, and you'll decide you were imagining things. Then, all in a day, every single package seems to have personal significance to Mel, and you're certain there's something sinister going on here. But the next day, the desperation falls back to normal levels, Mel is in his version of a good mood, and we return to business as usual. My only purpose seems to be to make lightning-fast last-minute deliveries between twelve-forty and twelve-fifty-five. Twelve-fifty-five is this magical cutoff period that Mel is always trying to beat. What's so special about twelve-fifty-five?"

"Can't you just look inside the package?" asks Ho.

"Not without getting fired. In fact, it's against the law for me to peek. Plus Mel always seals these particular packages with this, like . . . special seal. If I ever deliver it with a broken seal, my ass is toast."

Ho shrugs, wanting to get onto another subject. "Yeah, like, whatever!" she quips.

I sigh. "Looks like I'm just going to have to carry the secret in my hand day after day and never get to see it. Even if I can get at the disk, I can't read it unless I'm skating with a computer strapped to my back."

Denny queries, "What would Mel and a banker and a Chinese restaurant have to do with each other?"

"The only thing they all have in common is these big blue screens they're always reading."

"Waitaminute," says Denny. "What's this banker's name?"

"Something Levy."

"Michael Levy? Of Wozniak and Levy?"

"Yeah."

Denny slaps his forehead. "Oh, my God! That's it!"

"What?" me and Ho chorus.

"The stock market! Levy and Mel must be trading information on stock deals like that WordCom thing!"

"What?"

"Those blue screens are called Quotron machines. It gives stock players all the stock information they can legally trade on. But Wozniak and Levy is an investment firm. Some of the information that Levy is privy to is bound by law to remain a secret. But illegally trading on that information can bring you huge profits. Levy can't send the illegal info over the Net without being detected. So he sends the illegal information to Mel through *you*."

"So what?"

Denny blinks at me, mystified. "Chet, this is a call to action! Do what is right! Workers get screwed by those hostile takeovers!"

I'm like, "Chill out, Denny. I'm just the courier in this arrangement. It's my boss's crime, not mine. If I say no, then they'll just find some other peon to take the money. It's none of my business who those rich dwerbs are screwing."

"They're screwing me! You're being paid by the guys who might buy Datavox!"

"So this is about you."

"It's about everyone! Chet, your father was ruined by the same type of guys you're working for."

"Who cares?" I shout too loudly. "I don't give a shit about that!"

"Oh. I forgot. Daddy's not graced with a spot in your tattoo. What about the way he treated you and your brother after he got screwed?"

I feel my lip hitch up in a wolf's sneer. "Denny, I recommend you back off from this subject."

Ho touches Denny's arm. "Lay off him, Den."

But Denny will not be dissuaded. "Chet, these stock fuckers use blue-collar families as trading chips every day! They break up good companies, sell the parts as scrap, and put thousands of laborers out of work!"

"So what am *I* supposed to do about it?"

"Jesus! You're the one with a fucking Thoreau tattoo on your arm! Just don't cooperate."

"It's *Emerson*, Denny!"

"Yeah, real important detail. What are you going to do about the working families getting screwed by your boss?"

"What is this? You get a cushy promotion, and all of a sudden you're judging us peasants."

"Chet, all you have to do is—"

"I know what *you* would do, Cesar Chavez, but some of us are strapped for cash. I'm not becoming homeless to help your poor little besieged workers. You're the political activist. I'm not. So stop judging me."

"I *will* judge you, Chet, and what you're doing is wrong."

I fold my arms. "Psht! Reverend High and Mighty is going to get all preachy again. You're getting a little too hot and bothered over this, Denny. What are you so defensive about?"

"*I'm* not the rollerblade courier in this scheme! If I was, I'd—"

I snort a laugh. "What *you* would do on rollerblades, Denny, is irrelevant."

"Oh? And why is that?"

"Because you're in a wheelchair."

Denny's face twists. "What's that got to do with it?" he demands.

"Chet can skate. Denny can't."

"Denny can function in a relationship. Chet can't."

My chair cracks against the floor and I am on my feet. *"What's that supposed to mean?!"*

The bar is silent. My fists are clenched. I can feel the muscles in my face twitching. Everything is red. Some barely reasoning part of my mind reminds me that I am preparing to punch the piss out of a disabled man. My best friend.

Denny has never shown fear in his life. If he can face down nazi cops in full riot gear, he can face down me. He slowly wheels around the table, leans close to me, and whispers:

"I'm only crippled on the *outside*, Chet."

He turns away and wheelies around the bar.

I'm left struck dumb, more stunned than if a rubber bullet

had just struck me between the eyes. A roaring ocean of red filling my eyeballs, I watch Denny's twisted back as it disappears out the door to the garbage exit.

Then the dewdrop touch of Ho's fingers on my arm. Red is flooded with blue.

"C'mon, hon. Sit down. Let's just chill for a sec."

Ho uprights my chair. Slowly, as if in a nightmare state, I sit. Folks get back to conversing and drinking and selling Ecstasy. Some look disappointed they didn't get to see some action, so they could vicariously exorcise their own demons.

I breathe deeply and gulp my Shirley Temple.

"I hate this," I confide. "Every time something comes along that makes good money, it's illegal or immoral or something. Everybody wants to live a straight life, but sometimes you just can't afford it."

"I know. We're all economic casualties," says Ho, and I can see she wants to draw us to a more neutral subject. "Even Megan the Marketer. She's the daughter every parent prays for. She makes three times as much as you or I do, yet her job requires a good car, great clothes, buying lunches for big shots, paying school loans, plus rent—so she saves nothing! And look at us. If you or me default on our school loans, we'll never own a house. Chet, if you weren't saddled with debt, you would work two days a week, and bungie jump the rest."

My bowels start to float on a wave of melancholy. "You know, I meet a suit like that Levy, who is like total dorkamundo, and I act like I'm all way hipper than he is. But the reality is that Levy owns me."

"Hipness is invented to justify powerlessness," avers Ho. "We act like we choose this lifestyle. But if somebody offered me Levy's job . . . ?"

I give Ho an incredulous look. Her ruminative expression promptly springs into a grin.

"You'd—"

She joins in chorus with me: "—tell em to fuck off!"

We burst into laughter and snap our forefingers together. "Damn straight!" exults Ho. "You know it, homes! How can anyone in their early twenties be expected to think about pension plans? Might as well go pick out good grave sites." Ho swigs her bottle and snorts to herself. "I should ask the moms if she's *foreseen* anything exciting in my future."

Ho occasionally takes a swipe at her hippie moms, who maintains a career as a psychic.

Ho silences and becomes as momentarily depressed as I am. We both know she's rationalizing our lifestyle. Sure, we have more fun than the nine-to-five cradle-to-gravers, but we pay a heavy price. Ho glances at her tiny kingdom, the stage columned with black amps, amphitheater to nihilism.

She sighs. "I'm already sorry I quit at the daycare center. I went back today, just for a visit, just to hint that I'm ready to come back."

"I'm sure the slander spraypainted across your belly set them at ease."

"Well, now that I don't have Megan to borrow from, I have to make sure I have a steady income. I don't know how long performing will continue to carry me."

"You think your increasing class differences had anything to do with your breakup?"

She snorts. "As *if*! Honey, that was the *least* of our problems."

Not quite brazen enough to pry further, I just say, "The fundamentals, huh?"

"Well, we certainly had a sexual problem." So sayeth Ho.

I clear my throat. If I play this right, I may be able to hear intimate details about lesbian sex. "Well, that's pretty fundamental."

"For me it is. Just between you and me, Chet, I want to do the nasty all the time. It's the primary way I express love. But, to Megan, it was pressure. And it got to the point where every time she saw me getting aroused by how she washed the dishes—she would do it in this really sensual way—she would totally wig out on me. Like that's all I care about. And it's not true. I just express caring through sex sometimes. I hope it levels off when I get older, but Megan is ten years older than me, and she says she's had the exact same drive since puberty."

Debbie's litany is echoing in my mind: *Chet can lust. Chet can't trust.* I realize I'm drifting off into my own problems, and this looks like one of those moments when I should listen. Good time to toss out a platitude.

"Sex isn't everything," I lie, and gulp my drink.

"Of course not," says Ho. "But I'll tell you, man: One thing I really missed was a cock."

I spit my syrup in a sneezy spray. *"What?"*

She cracks a grin and wiggles her nose. "C'mon, stud boy. You know I had a pretty active life before I met Megan."

"But I thought it was all with—!"

She shakes her head and sucks her bottle. "Uh-uh. No way. I do boys, too."

I do a Yosemite Sam yadda-yadda-yadda. "So you're bi?"

"I don't exclude people from my love based on gender, if that's what your bullshit category means."

My heart is doing backflips. And we're both newly singl-ized. To gain my composure, I busy myself with napkining up my puddle of spray.

"After the breakup," says Ho, "I was going through this unbearable anxiety. But it passed. And now, here it is, two weeks later, and I feel pretty amped. Don't get me wrong, I don't want to diminish my feelings for Megan at all. But, after all that fear and anxiety, now that it's finally done, I know it was the right thing. I guess I just couldn't face it."

I look at the table surface. The wetness distorts my reflec-tion. "Couldn't face it," I mutter.

"You let someone get that close, there is no lying. No mat-ter how hard you try, you just can't fake it. Eventually you have to face the fact that loving somebody does not make you want to be with them forever. I was just not facing where my feelings were taking me."

"And where was that?"

"Away."

I look at her inquisitively. "Towards?"

She looks at me and smiles lightly. She sips her drink. "No. Just away."

Shit. Was I fishing too hard? I'm not very good at these things.

She scratches her nose ring and chews the skate tape on her two middle fingers in thought.

"Fuck, I'm really pouring my heart out to you, ain't I, cuz?"

"It's an honor, Ho."

"Shut up."

"No, I mean it. It's cool that you trust me that much."

"Well . . . I do."

A voice calls from the stage, "Yo! Ho!" Her bandmates call to her like the Seven Dwarves. "The bass amp is all fucked up! It's got that buzz again! Can you dezork it?"

"Dammit, Chugger!" Ho slams down her bottle, causing a golden geyser to spurt up and drip down her hand. "I told you twerds not to slam that shit around in the van! That's what causes the buzz!"

Chugger shrugs. "I'm sorry! Chill!"

"Sorry, Chet. Gots biz."

I lean back in my chair and kick my sneaks up onto the table. "Go do your thing," I say.

She stands, stomps the tail of her board, snags the nose, and hollers, "Where are my tools?"

Somebody points her to a toolbox, and she throws her plank into a locker and gets to work.

Ho is the only one in the band with even a sparse knowledge of gadgets. She's the one who fixes guitars, takes buzz out of amps, resplices wire without electrocuting herself. No one ever taught her. She just picked it up while teaching herself how to play bass in high school.

I smile. An hour with Ho is like grabbing the kite tail of a comet that rockets ahead, carrying me to new skies as ever-changing and colorful as maps of the former Soviet Union. Ho is my kind of gal. She's like me.

. . . except, instead of being alienated, Ho is grounded in

herself. Everywhere she goes, Ho is always at home.

Everywhere I go, I'm lost.

I realize after Ho leaves that I should have said something. Something about myself.

An hour later, I watch my fellow wage slave climb the stage to the sound of cheering.

The tables have been moved, the lights are down, and the place is packed with hot flesh and musk. Ho's punk band, Spit, is doing last-minute tuning and dial-turning on stage. Like so few rock bands, they are going to start on time. No opening acts. No encores. No pause for applause. Just two hours of solid jam.

Ho hefts her bass, Pink Testosterone, thuds out the first chords, and the boys join in for a good thrash-swing number I've never heard before. The audience immediately perks up and starts jumping. The walls shake with the simultaneous stomps.

Over the steaming heads and arms of the mosh pit, I can see Ho the rainbow woman quite clearly. I smile at her, though she has no idea where I am in the sea of heads, and has probably forgotten me. Minus the helmet and shades, she's still in her skating outfit, complete with elbow pads and spandex.

Ho holds her ax down below her waist like a holster, and thumps the granite strings with a pick. She stomps both black-booted feet and shakes her blue hair around. There is no posing here. When she plays, she can't hold still. She rehearses the same way.

She's sparse on riffs. She prefers a driving thunderous beat that is surprisingly macho. Five feet tall, she is the most aggressive up there, both musically and visually. The lead guitarist, the *real* musician of the band, tends to concentrate very hard on subtlety. The rhythm guitarist/lead singer is stuck at his microphone, and his playing only sounds good if he's plugged into enough machinery. Ho, her strident sound una-dorned with effects, stomps around the stage like a Viking marauder. Her eyes occasionally meet those of Chugger, the muscular drummer, and the both of them smile in secret sim-patico, so comfortable in the rhythm section, unenvious of the melody spinners.

But then she displays a startling musicality during the cho-ruses. I think the whole thing becomes magical when Ho puts her lips to the microphone and lays a soaring vocal over the harmonies of the two guitarists. That's the yeast that makes the biscuit kick, in my opinion. You don't hear harmonies over the grind anymore.

Call me a caveman, but I can't help but gnash my teeth with pugnacity when Ho turns her little cupcake bottom to the crowd, and I see every dude's eyes go wide. I've seen her still the mosh pit with a wiggle. I want to make a P.A. announce-ment: *She's* my *dyke! Back off!*

Things are going great for Spit. Her band, after playing together a year and a half, suddenly took off within this last month. Some mysterious bursting point was reached in the unpredictable rock democracy, a chemical reaction even the psychic marketing scientists do not understand, and suddenly thousands of SF kids wanted to see Spit. The band had to move their act to bigger venues. Now they've hit in Berkeley. As of four weeks ago, Ho started making plenty to live on, and things are definitely not stopping.

So she quit her daycare job to devote herself to music full-time. She asked me to borrow the band's van from Chugger and come pick her up on her last day of work, because she said she might not be in a condition to drive. I was like, What the hell kind of daycare is this? I waited in the Spitmobile long after our arranged meeting time, figuring they were having a champagne party. I finally got pissed and marched in. I found Ho on her knees in a circle of preschoolers, hug-ging and rehugging and weeping uncontrollably.

You'd never know it seeing her now, standing defiantly among all those baggy-panted male fans stage-diving into the heads bobbing like buoys. Her name here is "that cool chick on bass." Ho thumps that thing like it's her cock.

Ho would make a great guy.

I turn around and look at the rocking tumult of illuminated sweaty faces behind me. They are not in a trance of celebrity worship. They are in an orgy of slam-dancing or closing their eyes to listen. You almost have to slap yourself: My God! Sincerity! Genuineness! An honest response to nonmarketed music! There is something undeniably magical going on here.

But when I close my eyes, plug my ears, I know none of this matters. This experience, unrepeatable and unpreserved by high technology, means, ultimately, nothing to the future of the band. The Spit phenomenon, an honest groundswell in a world controlled by public relations firms, will reach its point of atrophy and pitter out. It will not continue to grow without widescale advertising, without big executives paying media experts to generate rapid-fire Spit imagery flashing in our subconsciouses.

Pretty soon, Ho will have to quit and find another day job. Economics will prevent her from pursuing her passion.

Okay, I've pontificated plenty. Now it's time to soak in this moment.

I slam a teenager next to me. He slams me back. We smile at each other.

After the show, I pull on my skates and plow the skin sea. Normally, I'd have to wrestle my way through, but the height that the rollerblades give me has great psychological effect. Ho, to my joy, has been looking for me, and when she sees me, her face beams like a lighthouse in the fog. She has her helmet on and is using her plank to wedge open the bodies. Ho has absolutely no height effect whatsoever. She meets me in the center of the floor, toting a small paper bag, and we push our way to the front exit.

I can't tell you how tedious it is to rub up against all those squishy mounds of female flesh. I am suddenly shoved backwards into Ho, and my eyes roll back in my head as her nipple ring rubs across my back.

"You know, I'm like you," I blurt. "Sexually, I mean."

"What?" She sounds surprised.

I feel my ears redden. Too late to turn back now. The noise of the crowd blaring in my ears, I take a deep breath and forge ahead. "My dream mate and I would see fucking as a serious part of our lives—I mean, like a part-time job. We could set the morning alarm for an hour earlier, hit the bed right after *The Simpsons* . . . you know . . ."

Ho doesn't say anything. I'm afraid to look at her. I plod onward.

"But I just wanted to tell you, you know, because I wish I had before the show. You were being like so sincere and all . . ." My beet of a head is flashing out like a ruby distress signal. "Because we're friends. That's all. So let's just forget it."

She smiles and punches my arm. "Ba-da-bing," she says.

"Ba-da-boing," I say.

Fuck it. I'm never trying that again. From now on, I'm keeping my shit to myself.

We can't talk anymore, because every rock dude in the place is personally thanking Ho for kicking his ass.

Ho is still flying off that sockdolager of a finale. Spit always ends with a galloping instrumental during which Ho the Human Pogostick leaps around the stage in transcendent spazhood, her knees thudding her chest and her skin pissing sweat. Everybody in the band plays something interesting except Ho, who thuds the same note over and over. Which looks fine with her.

The hamhock doorman stops us as we leave.

"What's with the dude?" he asks Ho. "Are you going straight on us?"

"Never. Though I might fuck the occasional guy."

"So what's his tag?"

"This is the Barnacle. He follows me everywhere I go, and I can't shake him."

"He looks like a disco stiff to me . . . What's up, Barnacle?"

I shake his rump roast of a hand—standard Euroshake, without the fancy variations—and follow Ho out into a dazzling San Fran night.

"Dammit, now I've got another nickname. Barnacle, Cannon, Rollerboy. Why doesn't anybody call me what I want to be called?"

"What's that?"

"Ultimate Badass!"

"Oh, gimme a break."

"I've earned the title!"

"Okay, that will be our wager. If you win the downhill race, I'll call you Ultimate Badass. If I win, you call me Princess Leia. Okay, Mr. Barnacle?"

"Deal."

She looks at me conspiratorially and I notice she's got one hand behind her back. "Guess what I got for you, Punky!"

I smile. Ho loves surprises and gifts. "What, Mom?"

Like Bugs Bunny, she pulls the paper bag from behind her back and extracts two Ben and Jerry's ice cream cups.

"Cool! Where'd you get those?"

"Scammed them off my buds who work in the scoop shop behind the Padlock."

"Gimme some! Gimme some!"

I'm jumping up and down in my skates. Ho is holding me back with her arm.

"Weeeeellll, since you were so good today . . . okay."

She hands me my cup and spoon, and I commence snarfing.

"Man!" I say. "What was that? Three hours without my sugar fix?"

"You're getting better."

"It's my only vice."

"Except masturbating."

"That's a virtue."

Concentrating on our yum-yums, we continue to badminton back and forth our soft darts of exchange as we skate languidly through the neon Haight Street night. Then Ho stops. I turn and look at her.

"Where you going?" she asks.

"Home to Denny."

"Your wife can wait. Don't you want to come to our after-show party?"

"Nah."

"C'mon. You can pretend you're in the band. Pick up a groupie. You're up for a little statutory action, aren't you?"

"Actually, I was thinking of doing a little hackage."

Ho lolls the last morsel of Chunky Monkey around in her mouth, crumples the cup, and hits a three-pointer in a nearby trash can. "A'ight, blood. I'll see you tomorrow."

"Cool."

She smiles. "Later, dude."

Her smile is irresistible. I smile back. "Later, dudette."

We jackhammer fists, slap hands, and part ways.

I watch Ho ride off into the splintered mockery of color. Her hair of blueberry cotton candy seems to leave a comet's tail behind her. It's as blue as a bruise, blue as a hickey, blue as B. B. King, blue as the toe cuticles of wine makers, blue as the squiggly lines that palliate the red lightning bolts in the hemorrhoid commercial, blue as the depths of a blue whale's womb, blue as a newborn polar bear's eyes, blue as the hottest center of a teardrop-shaped candle flame, blue like the blood scuttling back to the warmth of your heart. Her hair is about as blue as anger isn't.

I resurface after a timeless plunge. Coltrane is stuck in the last scratchy groove of his LP. My boa has been so still, I can't distinguish where his muscles end and mine begin.

I flick the red switch, and my mighty cyberworld zips backwards like a glow-in-the-dark tissue taped to the screen and then sucked up at the middle by a straw. A pinprick glow, then fade. A shaman snaps his fingers and you arise from your hypnosis, blinking. The old verities—table, chair, wall—return with hulking substantiality. All my power, vapor.

For a good half-minute, I'm as blind as a mole. My eyes have become so accustomed to focusing on electronic symbols, all I can make out is my clock radio.

It's 2:28 A.M. I have to get up in two hours. I'll don my armor, consume vast quantities of sugar, and book over to Mel's all in an hour.

I turn over the record, push the *Where's Waldo?* books off my bed, and lie back with my snake.

My python does not have a name. A pet name would diminish him. Language is irrelevant to his essence. I like him because he is alien. Our common ancestor probably goes back to the tropical fern, yet we can reach across phylumspace and make a mysterious connection somehow. He does not apply to my world, and I don't apply to his. Yet he is what I aspire to be: calculated, true, untainted by conflicting emotions, acting with the precision of the machine.

I pull my green, white, and red quilt over us, spool myself up until we are both cocooned in the blanket. Once inside our larva, I feel his tail coil around my stomach, and I become conscious of a need. I can't tell whether the hunger is his, or mine.

I stand with the blanket around me and look inside my small habitrail, the plastic prison where I keep the mammal. Whiskers twitch. Eyelashes blink at me.

To me, it is not a feeling creature. It is a five-dollar investment, immediately reducible to its number value.

I lift the fat hot rat and drop him in the snake cage. I uncoil the python from my body, and place him beneath the hot sun lamp with the rodent. I wrap myself in the blanket and stare, listening to Johnny C. interpret mortality, infinity, God.

The serpent snaps into a knot, its muscles squeezing the rat like Grendel's fist. The tiny black eyes of the rodent bulge out of its head. Then something changes about the eyes. There is no color change, no shape change, yet I can perceive when the rat ceases to be a being and becomes a thing.

The python patiently repositions himself around the corpse. His jaws unhinge, his mouth expands forever, and he sets his maw around the dead rat's head. Slowly, the muscles of the endless throat work and undulate as the rat moves into the boa's body. Finally, the long hairless tail is dragged down the tunnel to the Underworld.

I lay a cover over the bright snake cage, and my room disappears. I lie back and let go. Spread-eagled on the bed, I grind my teeth to the hammer in my chest.

I am blind to all of existence except that shimmering ruby boring like a hot drill into my forehead. I blink, and the Hindu urna dot separates into three magical numerals. They hover, marooned in darkness, flaming like the pupils of Satan. Three digital eyes: 2:33—until the right eye blinks. 2:34.

$$234$$
$$+256$$

Fifteen years later, I still have the problem memorized.

My father stood behind me and announced, "Every time you make a mistake, you get a smack."

I was trying to focus my eyes through my burning tears,

trying to focus my mind through the haze and heat. He hollered, *"C'mon! The next one!! Hurry!!"*

I had this method where I wrote the remainder at the top of the column, but added it last. My father saw inefficiency in this method, and said I should start with the remainder and add the other numbers to that, so there was less chance of me forgetting to go back to the top.

I said, "Four plus six is ten, carry the one. Three plus—"
Smack!

His hand blasted against the back of my skull, sending all my brain cells swimming.

He would not tell me what I had done wrong. I had to figure it out for myself. I'd regain my senses, choke back my sobs, and retrace my steps. It must have been in the first column, because he never even let me get to the second one. I started over.

"Four plus six is ten, carry the one. Three—"
Smack! Harder this time.

Still, he didn't say a word. Quickly, I went over the problem in my head. Four plus six is ten, right? It had to be right! Keeping my hands on my pencil and paper, I secretly counted on my fingers.

"Four plus six is ten, carry the one. Thr—"
Smack!

I broke down and started begging. His chair cracked against the floor and he was on his feet. He hollered that I never figured anything out by myself and that whenever there was a problem I always went running to him like a big baby! Now, talking himself into a fury, he raised his fist and bellowed for me to figure it out *right now*.

In a complete panic, I looked at the problem. My machine's eye detached itself from the quivering guts of my fear. Then— as if magically—it all became clear to me.

"Four plus six is ten, carry the one. One plus three is four, plus five is nine. Two plus two is four. Four-ninety."

It was that damn remainder! I was still doing it my old way.

"Do the next one," he said.

* * *

Nightmares tormented me. I'd wake up in the middle of the night and shriek like a demon. My pajamas stuck to me with sweat. I'd hear my mom's voice from the bedroom: "Jesus Christ! Again?"

My father would come—not rushing, but pacing stolidly—and sit down on the bed, while I would scream hysterically that there were Snakemen behind him, and he would get up and check the closet for me and show me that it was only a dream.

He told me he wouldn't leave. I told him to promise. He said he was my father, he didn't need to promise. He laid a giant down quilt over me: green, white, and red. The flag of Italy, he told me. His Italian mother gave it to him when he was a boy. His big deep voice was gravelly with sleep. I would lie down, feel his great weight beside me on the bed, and my breathing would slow and my eyelids would flicker and close.

Every five minutes or so, every time I felt myself lapse into a deeper stage of sleep, my body would tense reflexively, and I would sit up in panic, shouting, "Daddy! Don't leave!"

"Sh," he would husk.

He had not moved. He was always there. Night after night, no matter how many times I sat bolt upright and tried to catch him leaving, he was always there, sleepily watching me do what he wanted to do.

In all those nights, he never once let me down.

My brother Bobby was born when I was six and a half. I used to go into the nursery and look at him, fascinated by his china hands, his little yawning mouth, his eentsy-weentsy pinky toenail, the size of a ladybug.

When he would wail at midnight, I believed he had inherited my nightmares. My father would go to him. A few minutes later, the baby would quieten. My father knew some magic my mother didn't know. One night, I crawled out of bed in my Spider-Man pajamas with the plastic feet and chuffed across the hall to the dark nursery. The shadow of my father was bent over the bassinet. Below the dwindling sound of my baby brother humming like a little bee, I could hear a small patting noise.

I must have stood behind them for five minutes before a slight shift of my weight made a board creak, and my father spun around violently, his eyes flaming red in the darkness.

I cringed and shielded my face, but he merely glared at me and turned back to the baby, who had stirred.

After a long minute, curiosity overrode my caution. I stepped up next to my father, stood on tiptoes, and peeked in at the baby. Father was patting his diaper, his big hairy hand covering a good third of the baby's body.

"This is how you put a baby to sleep," he growled softly at me. "Here."

He took my wrist. He placed my hand on the baby's diaper.

"Pat his bottom as gently as you can," he rumbled, and I could hear the tiny metal rings on the bassinet reverberate with his voice. "A little firmer. Still gently, though. Do it slower, like I was doing it. Do it like your heartbeat. Here."

He took my other hand and placed it on my chest like I was a doll. A twist of his hands could snap me in two. He quietly stared off into space for a second, then his eyes met mine. "Feel it? Just like your heartbeat."

I concentrated. I admitted, "I don't have a heartbeat."

He placed my palm on his hot hairy chest. I could instantly feel the power, the blood gushing through his fat heart. I could smell his musk, like a bear's. Each throb vibrated down my right arm, out my left arm, and triggered a gentle pat on the baby. My patting became one with the drumbeat, and the baby fell asleep.

"Now you can do it by yourself," he said, and left.

Dad and Bobby trudged back up Strawberry Hill with the toboggan, elated, their red noses spurting white smoke like Big and Little Steam Engine. Mom was up top with me. Eleven-year-old Bobby was tugging Dad's arm, salivating, "Again! Again!"

Dad always put his face too close to mine when he addressed me. "C'mon, Chet. I'll take you this time."

I looked at my toes, shook my head.

"C'maaaaaaan! You gotta be kidding me! You just saw your little brother go! He's not dead, is he?"

I was determined not to look at him, pretending I was smart, not scared. "He don't know any better. You could hit that big oak tree."

He circled me, leaning into my face like a drill sergeant. His hot breath scalded my face.

"Look at you. Sixteen, and you act like a baby. Little Bobby has more man in him than you."

I was seventeen.

"You can hold on to my shoulders. You can hide your eyes like a girl if you want."

Of course he always had to steer. He was the type of man who hated rollercoasters, but loved skiing. He needed to be in control. I'd never seen him sit in the passenger seat of a car in my life.

Mother was in her incessant pose, looking somewhere else, blaring a smile at nothing.

After a moment, he snorted and turned his back. Now my eyes bored between his shoulder blades like hot red lasers. I could stare him down with all the confidence of a crusader when his back was turned.

"Okay," he said, and he looked over his shoulder at me, his eyes flashing red. "I'll take your mother then."

Mom and Dad boarded the toboggan, Mom giggling, Dad smiling over his shoulder at her. I watched, wracked with shame, wondering if I should give it a shot next time.

Dad shouted at me through a wide boyish smile, "Chicken!"

Mom slapped his shoulder flirtatiously. "Stop, you."

"Dad!" screamed Bobby, probably figuring I was out of the special circle that had been created by the shared experience of the rush. "Can I go with you after Mom?"

Dad didn't reply, or he didn't hear. Mom and Dad slid over

the edge of Strawberry Hill smiling, caught in a rare moment of romance, a rarer moment of intimacy.

When the toboggan splintered against the tree, I screamed, then hid my eyes for a full minute.

When I opened them, Bobby had already run down to see.

When I arrive at work the next morning, Mel calls me
straight to the front of the line. I step past my scowling com-
petitors, my eyes ching-chinging with little dollar signs.

"My other priority deliveries have already heard about you
and want to check you out. Take this to Mission and Fifth.
The same place. Dr. Chen. No rush. He wants to meet you."

I sail to Mission and Fifth smiling like a clam and singing
the ever-evolving "Chet Is So Cool" song. The same Chinese
dude is waiting at the front door of the restaurant, but this
time he has the unhurried smile of a grandfather who has a
Christmas present hidden behind his back. He leans close and
whispers confidentially: "*You* are going to see Dr. Chen!"

I emit the appropriate squeal of glee. He leads me back
through the bustling Chinese restaurant, takes me through the
noisy back kitchen full of waving skewers and spurting towers
of fire, opens the small green door, and—surprise, surprise—I
am standing in a giant lobby on a polished marble floor with
six or eight armed guards in suits standing around. Each of
them carries a majorly phat cellular phone. Most of them are
Asian. Two are Caucasian, in expensive and tailored pin-
striped suits, with more mousse in their hair than in Alaska.
They both wear identical ties with green, white, and red
stripes. The polished floor is a striking paradox to the rundown
exterior of the building. I also notice they have retrofitted a
PA system into this old place.

It looks like this Chen dude bought this abandoned hotel
and built a restaurant into the first fifty feet of the lobby. My
attendant leads me across the spacious slippery floor to the
very old-fashioned elevators and pulls a lever. As we wait, I

can't help noticing that all the fire exits are chained shut. The only way to get back here is through the restaurant and that single small green door.

My chaperon pulls a noisy crank, and the iron meshwork gates rattle open. As we ascend, I can watch through the grate as floors two, three, and four pass identically like a TV with a bad V-hold. All three are unused and rank-smelling, with fallen plaster littering the floors. I can hear construction going on somewhere, and the effect is made complete when a rat scurries across the fourth floor as if on cue.

The bleak slide show suddenly opens up to a beautiful, well-lit fifth floor, peopled with well-dressed Asian men and a smattering of Italians with those green, white, and red ties.

My escort pulls the crank and pushes open a veil of Chinese beads that hangs over the elevator door. They clack together pleasantly. We step out into a hallway of lush carpeting, professional lighting, paintings on the walls, Muzak played at the gentlest possible decibel level.

This place is remarkably free of females.

I am joined by a small cortege of bodyguards and escorted to a large office. As we step in, they separate from me and line the walls with a heptad of other well-dressed men standing around like waiters. Again, everybody is Asian except for two Caucasians with flag-of-Italy ties. They gesture for me to step into the middle of the half-circle. A middle-aged Asian man is leaning on a mahogany desk, whispering orders very quietly in Chinese to two men who lean close in rapt attention.

He picks up a newspaper. Then, for the apparent benefit of the Italian guys, he raises his voice and switches to English. "See here? This what I talk about. This article in the *Chronicle:* 'When a blind man fell in front of a BART train yesterday, a commuter jumped down onto the tracks and pulled him back into a narrow passageway beneath the passenger platform. "I didn't think," said the man, who declined to give his name. "I just acted." ' This the kind of initiative I speak of—"

When he looks up from his paper, he spots me, and he waves the fawners aside. He spreads his arms like a Venus's-flytrap. "Ah! Chet Griffin!"

He approaches as if to hug me, but stops short and folds his hands prayerfully and bows like a praying mantis. "I am Dr. Chen!" he proclaims as if he's just stepped off a flying saucer. I want to pound my chest and say, *I am Dr. Chet!* "We were very very impressed by the swiftness of your delivery Monday!"

I manage a half-smile. I can tell that nobody was impressed but him. But kingpins are entitled to use the royal *we*.

He bends down very humbly to inspect my footwear.

"These are the rolling shoes, yes? Very impressive. Very impressive."

"Actually, they're called rollerblades," I say. "New technology."

Everybody in the room does the kind of excruciating wince you can't see or hear, but you feel it like a zillion needles in your spine. The two Italian dudes smirk. Guess you're not supposed to correct Dr. Chen.

But Chen is not offended. He nods and smiles with an ecstasy worthy of a Doublemint commercial. "Roller*blades*! I see! How interesting!"

He bubbles a grandfatherly chuckle. All the Chinese toadies, to the notable exclusion of the Italian guys, spring into laughter. I'm not quite sure how to react. I smile and nod as profusely as Chen does. I look at all the other suits and giggle girlishly.

Chen says, "You be making deliveries to us from now onwards. You see him?"

He points to one of the Italian penguins. I nod, still giggling like a moron.

"You deal directly with him! From now onwards! You go with him, and he show you. Very nice to meet you."

He bows and then gives me a wet-fish handshake.

He calls to the Italian dudes, "Time him on the stairs!"

My adjunct abruptly takes my arm and shepherds me away. Dr. Chen gets back to whispering orders in Chinese. The office is large enough that I can be taken to the side and introduced to the pasta-vazools without being overheard.

My usher speaks. He has a thick Chinese accent. "This

Spock. This Data. We call you Cannon. You deliver to them. You don't come up here. You deliver to them."

I nod, like, *Yeah, I get it. Chill.* Then I look into the eyes of the Italian toughs and find myself shaking like a deer caught in headlights.

Nobody steps close enough to shake hands. Spock and Data don't reply, but they do give me the most frightening eye-balling I have ever gotten in my life. They each have what looks like a black hairy caterpillar mounted on their faces: Spock has a moustache, and Data's eyebrows connect.

Spock is shorter and his cunning eyes scissor through me. At first glance, his face looks crooked, as if his jaw, cheek-bones, and forehead have each slid off-kilter like shelves of stone after an earthquake. But this is an illusion. It's not his face that zigzags; it's his broken nose.

Data is linebacker-sized and has no blink reflex. Data's marble face looks blank and nirvanic, like a statue of some antediluvian Eastern god. Beneath his single eyebrow, his eyes glow a reptilian green.

The Chinese tagalong and Spock nod to each other, and the mosquito steps away. Data continues to look at me as if I am a painting of a rollerblader. I realize I have been so mesmerized, I have not yet spoken. When Spock suddenly adopts human characteristics and steps forward to touch me, my veins go cold. He wraps a hot predatory arm around my shoulders and pulls my face into his tie.

"Come on out here, kid."

He leads me further up the hall and down a short flight of cement stairs to the fourth floor. We enter a large, dank, cob-webby room with a blue stock market screen identical to the one Mel has. Sitting at a computer is a skinny guy with a white shirt and tie. He is definitely not Italian. There are no windows.

Spock has still not taken his arm off my shoulders. His voice tickles my eardrum. "When you come with that delivery, you come straight inside, you run up these stairs as fast as you can, count one, two, three, four floors, and come into this room and deliver your package to me or Data here. You messenger guys like receipts, right? Well, forget the receipts. We do things old-fashioned around here, like a family. You trust us; we trust you. A receipt insults our relationship of trust."

I suddenly jump when the electronic voice of God detonates, *"Kirk! Report to Dr. Chen immediately!"*

The guy at the computer jumps up and scurries up the stairs without a word. Above the door is one of those retrofitted PA speakers, looming like a telescreen.

Spock grabs me by the front of my shirt and wiggles his finger in my face with a smile about as sincere as a ticking black bag. "You a courier, right? You know not to ask questions, right?"

I nod obediently. I get the feeling he would prefer I didn't talk at all. He slaps me on the shoulder and takes my package from me, which I had completely forgotten I was carrying. He hands it to Data, who puts it on the desk next to the blue stock market screen.

Spock coils his arm around my shoulders again and moves me like a pawn on his chessboard to a crusty stairway. "You see this here? This leads down to a fire exit that we're going to unlock especially for you. When you come with that package, you come down the alleyway between this building and the abandoned building next door. Okay?"

I nod.

"All right, we're going to time you on the stairs," he says.

Data waits upstairs while Spock corrals me down the cement steps to the first floor where we meet a dude who has been waiting down there to unlock the chains to a fire door. Out from under Data's looming presence, I feel the scared-bunny effect wear off. When we step outside, we are in an alleyway. I can't help staring at the Mercedes and Lincolns parked in a red zone at the mouth of the alley. There are no tickets. Nobody has been towed.

Spock knocks his knuckles on my helmet. "Hello? Pay attention, Einstein. This ain't a fucking music video."

I wag my tail and try to look spunky.

"That's better," Spock says. "Now, when I shout *Go!* up those stairs, Data is going to hit his wristwatch. So you better drive your ass up them steps and make good time. You got to go all the way to the fourth floor. Think you can handle that on them fucking things?"

"Fuck, I can handle forty floors on these things."

Spock looks at the guard and they guffaw. "Listen to this punk!" he yells. "Kid's got sack." He sneers a grin at me, his eyes aflame behind his nose as crooked as a scoliotic potato. "All right, ball sack. Get ready . . . *You ready, Data?*"

From the top of the stairs a voice without quality says, "Yeah."

So Data is not a mute after all.

"Okay, Cannon. Let's see you cannon your ass up there." He calls up the stairs. *"Ready? Set! Go!"*

I jet through the door and chop up the stairs as fast as I can. My clattering urethane wheels echo loudly on the cement stairway. I turn the corner and surprise Data, who hits his watch a little late. For a moment, I stand beneath the shelf of his great unibrow, hypnotized by his spiraling green eyes.

Wait. I remember this dude. After my suicide run—when I was chasing that package-snatcher through the downstairs kitchen—this is the guy who stopped my berserking charge with one iron forearm.

"What's going on, Data?" shouts Spock. "I can't hear him anymore! Did he fall?"

"He's up," says Data, without pulling his eyes from mine.

"He's up?" They laugh. "What's his time?"

"Little more than eight seconds."

The meatheads downstairs break out into laughs and *holy shits*. "Get your ass down here, Cannon!" shouts Spock, still laughing.

Eager to get the hell away from Data, I take the steps three at a time and spring out on them, which causes them to bust out into hysterics.

"What are you? Speedy Gonzales? Don't tell me you're a spic."

"Nope. I'm your average white dude." (One quarter guinea, in fact.)

They guffaw. Everything is funny to these guys. "Okay,

dude. You got the job." He turns to his cohort. "What did we say was the elevator time? Fifty seconds or some kinda shit?"

The guy laughs. I can tell he knows the exact time, but he doesn't want to upstage Spock, who I get the feeling is the only one who's allowed to make hilarious jokes. "Something like that," he says, leaning on his shotgun and stretching out his chortling too long.

"Okay, Cannon. You don't use the elevator. You use the fucking stairs. All right?"

"You got it," I say.

Judging by the reaction, this is the funniest thing I have ever said. Spock takes me by my arm, bids adieu to his boot-lick, and teases me as we schlep up the stairs. I act appropriately brainless. He has to let up on his brilliant witticisms as he begins wheezing by the fourth floor. The urge to kick the living shit out of him dissipates as I step beneath Data's shadow. My old Chinese appendage is there. Now I recognize him. The same package-snatcher I chased through the downstairs kitchen Monday.

"Hey, kid," gasps Spock. "You're smart enough to keep mum about our arrangement, right? All them other rollerskaters hear about this, they'll all come clamoring after your job. Right?"

"Couriers never talk."

"Good man." He puts his arm around me in a near head-lock, pulling me within kissing distance of his frog's-butt face. "This fire door will always be opened for you. You sprint your ass up here and deliver this to me or Data. Then we might give you something to take back, or we might not. Either way, you leave immediately. Follow?"

Under the manacle of Spock's arm, all I can do is nod. Spock pinches my cheek, slaps my face, and releases me.

"Hey, Mu Goo Gai Pan!"

"Mong Pan," corrects my escort.

"Fried Rice or whatever the fuck your name is. Escort our new friend here outside."

Spock and Data follow as my duenna takes me onto the

elevator and pulls the crank. Data stares after me, looming like a side of beef hung from a hook.

Spock calls through the beads and grating, "See you later—*Cannon*! Ha! Ha! Ha! Ha!"

"Okay! Ha! Ha! Ha! Ha!" I say, as Spock's leather shoes disappear into the ceiling. "Ha ha motherfucking ha, you biscuit-head, I'd like to slap your fat face, ha ha ha."

I turn to Mong Pan to see if we can bond and chuckle over what I know to be a shared dislike for Spock. Mong the Granite Face doesn't even look at me.

Have fun much?

We step off the elevator into the lobby. A man in a green, white, and red tie boards the elevator as we exit. He's carrying a crate bearing an insignia that catches my memory. I spin and watch him. He turns and faces me to press his floor. Just before the doors close, I see the logo clearly. It's an enlarged version of what I've seen in miniature a hundred times. A black spider.

Bobby's favorite brand.

I am covered with the scars Bobby has indelibly etched on me with all the ache of love without hope. He carved the grief of our mutual loss into my flesh, both of us weeping, both of us knowing I will outlive him.

Used crack vials littered the floor. They crackled beneath my sneakers when I entered. My tearing eyes fell on one vial, and the tiny stencilled black spider was grotesquely swollen in my vision. Then it broke and ran like watercolors.

Sweat dripped down Bobby's emaciated face; he held off the urge until the last thorn was painted, the last drop of my blood wiped away. Then he put down the needle and picked up the crack pipe with the same motion. He closed his eyes and was gone.

I picked up my shirt and left. We've never spoken about our parents since. Words are feeble. The tattooing ritual was enough.

I tried to give the ratty green, white, and red blanket to Bobby once, but he rejected it.

Now I can't find him. Every week or so, I go hang out at Bobby's old digs: the bars, apartments, and porch stoops he used to haunt. None of his junkie contacts will tell me where he is. The cops haven't got any record of him being arrested or killed. He might be homeless.

Or lost.

Mel does not even use my perceived speed skills until 12:45, when suddenly I'm handed a desperate special delivery that has to be in before 12:55. When I grab it, I figure it's going to one of the big shots like Chen or the bankers, but when I read the address, I see it's going to some laundromat owner.

I'm a little miffed that I only got to make three deliveries so far today, but when I come back at 1:30 for a fourth, Mel slaps another $150 in my hand and tells me to go home. He holds my shoulders and looks paternally into my eyes. "If I had the back for it, I'd bend down and kiss them rollerskates of yours."

I cruise to the library and spend the afternoon reading about stock market crimes.

I skate down my street after a long afternoon of squinting at Wall Street books. Ho is thrashing the cement steps of a municipal building with two of her fellow skate rats beneath a sign that says NO SKATING. Faith No More's "Surprise! You're Dead!" is thudding away. The three hairdos representing the three primary colors swirl and figure-eight like lightning bugs in a Dr. Seuss book. Ho, the blue Who from Whoville at the top of the stairs, pretends she doesn't see me, and nails a caveman rail slide. She slams her plank across the railing, mounts, and slides down a flight of about twenty stairs until she banks off the end, kick-flips the board beneath her, and lands at my feet. We both skid to a stop.

"Oh! Chet!" she gasps, looking very radiant in her new hairdo. "I was so busy being totally fly, I didn't see you! How *are* you?"

Ho has got it goin *on*! She has shaved three inches off both sides of her head and given her blue mohawk purple highlights. Her high cheekbones and shaved sides made her look Eskimo, somehow. Pretty badass for a chick.

Around her neck she wears a spiked dog collar with a one-foot leash hanging at various times down her shoulder blade or her clavicle. Her bare arms converge on a black leather vest. Below this is a pink frilly skirt that swishes girlishly as she struts. Black nazi boots.

"Yeah, right. I guess that's *sort of* a cool trick—you know, if tricks are what you're interested in—at the sacrifice of speed."

"Hey, get me on a downhill with you, and I'll burn your

ass. Your only advantage is on the straightaways. And we have buses and bicycles for that."

"Bite your tongue."

She smiles. "So what's up?"

"I got something serious I want to talk to you about. Privately."

Without another word, she turns to her partners in crime. "Hey, bros! I'm gone! Catch you later!"

"Later, Ho," they chorus.

We start skating towards my apartment and I notice a road rash on her wrist. "What happened here?" I ask.

"I McDoinked it on an acid nose pick. Total wilson."

"Chalk it up as a battle scar."

"Do you have a tissue or anything?"

"No! Let it drip! It looks wicked!"

"I can't get any more wicked than I already am. You just want to be seen with a bleeding chick."

"You got to admit, bleeding is definitely one of the dopest things you can do." I stick my thumbs in my armpits. "It's right up there with rollerblading and being the official Cannon of Mel's Speedy Delivery. In fact, that's what I wanted to talk to you about."

"You're still tripping off your job?"

"I'm certain I'm into some foul shit."

"What makes you so certain?"

"I went to the library and read all about stock market trading."

"Get out!"

"Hey, I can read."

"So commence whining."

"Why are you going that way? Are you going to listen to me, or what?"

"We have to go get Wily. It's time for his walk."

"Aaaaaarrrrrgh!"

There is no entity on this earth I despise more than Wily the Rottweiler.

Imagine if somebody put the following ad in the newspaper:

Wanted: Roommate with completely furnished apartment. Here's the deal: I pay no rent, do no housework, clean no dishes. I have no job. I am a retarded sex maniac. I communicate by shouting the same word over and over until you guess what I want. I have unpredictable behavior, I steal food, I vandalize your possessions for no apparent reason. You must serve my meals and help me go to the bathroom. Otherwise, I will relieve myself on the carpet when it suits me. I may have sex with any random creature I meet, so don't be surprised if I come home stanking. I also barf in corners and don't tell you. I take no phone messages. I can't open doors. I don't turn off the lights after I leave the room. I *never* grow out of it. I make up for all these deficiencies by being cute. Would you like to live with me?

P.S.: I didn't write this, because I can't read. I can't even hold a crayon.

Ho is one of the millions of masochists who consider this a swell deal. Last year, when Ho went to tour L.A. with Spit, I agreed to allow this creature into my home for a month. I would have done just as well to sign up for boot camp.

For two weeks, that thing humped my dates, assaulted my guests, chewed my possessions, drooled on my neck, devoured my pizzas, shat on my couch, vomited on my bed, howled at sunrise, and, for a grand finale, lost a tussle with a skunk and immediately rolled around on my furniture. Then Wily the Rottweiler raped Fifi, the local show poodle, immediately after she got back from her buffing and preening appointment. When I invited Fifi's hysterical owner over to apologize and talk her out of a lawsuit, the smiling mongrel had the nerve to park himself on the floor and suck, lick, and nibble the very assault weapon in question. While I was trying to serve CostCo microwaved hors d'oeuvres, no less. It took me an hour to calm Mrs. Crepbopple down, but, the next day, when she saw me dustpanning the mauled remains of a squirrel into the garbage can, she demanded that I have the misunderstood doggie "put to sleep" before the next day, or she was calling her lawyer. I had the phone in my hand, making an appointment with Dr. Death, and was just asking how much it would cost to have him deballed first just for good measure, when Ho abruptly came back two weeks early and asked how her wittwe shnooky puppy was doing.

I'll never get my deposit back on my apartment. The way I see it, Ho owes me five hundred bucks. She says it's my fault because I didn't give him enough love.

As we style down her street, I start my Dick Tracy shtick. "I have to be at work by six in the morning, and things always slow down at one. That's because Mel is working me on eastern time, nine to four, the seven hours the New York Stock Exchange is open. And the main reason he hired me as Extra-Special Gofer Boy is for those last-minute runs right before one o'clock."

"I always figured what your boss was doing is illegal."

I do a double take, surprised that she has been thinking about this. "What made you think that?"

"Chick's intuition. Plus, why else use you couriers?"

"Maybe he wants it done fast."

"Chet, I would never question your badassedness, but even the wimpiest most el-lame-o electronic impulse can go faster than you."

"Meaning?"

"Meaning he can use a phone. There's no reason he has to make stock market bids by courier. He can call up his broker any time he wants."

"Right," I say. "So it's not stock bids he's making. It's something else."

We climb her steps. I can already hear the scratching and sniffing at the base of Ho's door.

Ho asks, "So what's your theory, Miss Marple?"

"I've said before that information should be free. Well, I was thinking like a hacker, not a stock trader. Stock traders definitely do not want takeover information to be available. I bet you my skates Mel has access to illegal information that gives him the lowdown on hostile takeovers, and he trades that info with other bandits. He must routinely triple his money."

"Fuckin A."

Ho opens the door and Wily leaps with all four paws spread-eagled like a flying squirrel from Hell.

"Hi, shnooky puppy!"

"Down, boy! Down! Eeeeeww! Nasty!"

"He loves you, Chet! How can you reject this innocent face?"

Ho claps Wily under his hanging chops, making a distinctive *chlurp* sound.

"Christ, he is ugly. He drools worse than Denny."

"Awwwwww!" Ho holds Wily's face in both her hands and gyrates his cheeks, getting good *shlurp, chlurp, shlap* going with Wily's salivary glands. "Don't wisten to him, my wittwe wove puppy. Yeeaaaah."

They French-kiss, then Ho goes to her bedroom, leaving me to fend for myself.

She calls back, "So you think Mel is selling this illegal info to other folks?"

"Down, boy! Down! It's got to be something like that."

"So where would Mel get access to this info?"

"The inve—ouch! Shit!—the investment bankers, obviously."

"Well, where would they get it?"

"Get a clue, Ho! Investment bankers deal with inside information on stock mergers every day. That's what they do."

"So the FBI is gonna come down on their ass, or what?"

"Not the FBI. The SEC. They specialize in this stuff. A whole government department devoted to punishing insider trading."

I'm having trouble forming coherent sentences, because I'm waving my hands and sashaying my hips, as Wily is performing expert flanking maneuvers in an attempt to give my testicles a snort.

Ho comes back with a leash. "So does Mel use you couriers

because he thinks these SEC guys are bugging his phones, or what?"

"Not his, but he probably deals with people whose phones are bugged. Investment firms have super-tight security, because they deal in secret information about upcoming take-overs every day. Since they're privy to this knowledge before it goes public, the SEC scrutinizes them like crazy. If they trade stock based on that secret information, they go to jail. Levy doesn't want to use the firm's phones, so he sends the illegal information out through courier, which is the only conduit that cannot be monitored electronically."

"Wow," she says. "Cool. It's like you're some kind of rollerblading espionage samurai."

"Damn straight. Check this out." I reach into my back pocket. "It's a newspaper story about this firm getting busted."

I hand her a library printout of an old newspaper article. "Yeah," she says. "I remember this. That big scam that went down last year. I didn't realize it was Wozniak and Levy."

"It wasn't Wozniak and Levy themselves, but some underlings in their firm who got busted."

Ho walks around behind me, puts her chin on my shoulder, and points to a paragraph. "Look at this. These guys got a couple months in a federal prison where they watch HBO and take correspondence courses. It mentions here that Wozniak and Levy themselves paid for some kickass lawyers to represent their busted employees."

Wily thrusts and I parry, so he darts around behind me.

"Well, what's wrong with that?" I say. "Isn't that to be expected?"

Ho crosses her arms, frowns, and pokes out one hip. I love it when Ho gets intellectual. Brings out her babeliciousness in a most killer way.

"Chet, does the word *duh* mean anything to you? Think about it. You're running one of the biggest, most respectable investment firms in San Francisco. Suddenly, your trusted arbitwhozzitz—"

"—arbitrageurs—"

"—arbitrageurs are busted for using your secret info to

make themselves rich. They've jeopardized the standing of your whole firm. Why would *you* volunteer money for hotshot lawyers to represent these criminals?"

"Well, I—whoop!" I yelp, as Wily manages a backdoor crotch sniff. "Dammit! I swear he ices that nose before I come over."

"Answer my question."

I shake off the chill going up my spine. "To keep blame from going to the top, I guess. You're saying that if the firm paid for the legal defense, Wozniak and Levy themselves must have been somehow culpable."

"Right. I mean, technically, these barbie ragers stole about a hundred million dollars from legitimate stockholders."

"And it looks like they're still doing it," I say. "I can't believe their balls. They're continuing right under the noses of the SEC. How do they do it?"

"Greed churns our brains a thousand times faster than the pursuit of justice. But if the stock cops are scrutinizing things so closely, how can they let couriers go in and out of the building?"

"That's the tragic flaw of high-tech crime fighters. They think high-tech. After securing phone lines, quadrupling security access codes, shredding documents, watching bank accounts to see who makes a lucky guess, it never occurs to them to check some punk courier making deliveries in and out of the building every day. No one would guess that information would be conveyed that way. It's stone-age slow in this age of modems and faxes. But it leaves no paper trail, which is key if you're a bad guy."

Things are getting too quiet, so I look around to locate the beast. So strong was Wily's scrotum suck, his skull nearly imploded when my testicles plugged both his nostrils. Wily is walking in unsteady circles and blinking his eyes. I got the willies like you can't imagine.

"So it looks like you got everything figured out," says Ho.

I shake my head. "Not by a long shot. There's this Chinese guy named Chen who is surrounded by all these armed guards. He's set up some kind of majorly hairy operation in this unused building on Mission and Fifth, behind this restaurant that is obviously a front. They keep the doors to the building locked, everybody has cellular phones and guns. I can't see how this Chen guy fits in."

Ho pensively chews the six-inch leather leash hanging from her neck. It matches Wily's.

"Obviously Chinese mafia," she says, then looks into my eyes for assent.

My brain is blank. For some reason, Ho's leash is giving me a half-hearted erection. God gave man a dick and a brain, but only enough blood to run one at a time.

"Chet? Hello?"

"Yipe!" I pipe, as Wily leaps forward, snorts my anus, and darts away.

"Chet, would you leave Wily alone and talk to me?"

I sigh. "But we're talking about white-collar crime here. What's with all the armed guards? And the Italian dudes? And the restaurant built into a recently abandoned hotel? And why the hell are they all named after *Star Trek* characters?"

"There's obviously a lot we don't know about. Chen is definitely some kind of wild card."

Wily, satisfied he has left no Chet-crevice unperused, hurls himself on Ho like the mongrel extension of my own fantasies. Ho and Wily trade a wet-nosed kiss. My stiffening cock instantly deflates.

Never, *never* would I have dreamed that I would ever be jealous of Wily. But here I am, burning green. I swear the beast is smirking at me.

After smearing Ho with sweat and snot, Wily, amateurish at best as a biped, falls over backwards, kapows his skull on the floor, and lies there stunned for a moment. Ho, utterly charmed, scratches his tummy and snaps the leash on him. Wily's brain probably ruptured, but none of his major organs are damaged, so he is on his feet in a second, his eyes rolling in his head, his legs unsteady, but his disposition unshakably cheerful.

"Wily, go play in traffic."

"Don't listen to him, Wily!"

"Why do you always act like he knows what we're saying? He doesn't even know his own name!"

"Just keep smothering him with love, Wily. You'll win him over someday."

"It'll never happen, Ho."

"I guess that worm of yours is much more cuddly."

"He's not a worm! He's a snake! And Wily is about as cuddly as a porcupine!"

"Actually, you guys have a lot in common."

"If I meet a buddy on the street, I don't sniff his balls, I shake his hand. To establish boundaries with Denny, I don't need to piss down the middle of our bathroom. And when I meet a creature I find attractive, I determine what gender and species it is before I try to fuck it."

"Trivialities, Chet. We pity you—don't we, Wily?"

Wily rubs some ear wax on Ho's thigh and flaps his tongue spitefully at me. Whiskers twitch. Eyelashes blink at me. Ho opens the door and Wily drags her down the stairs. I follow.

We step out onto the street. I leap out of Cerberus's leash range. The sun is setting. I breathe deeply.

"I got to hand it to Denny: He was right. Mel has only hired me on as Extra-Special Carrier Pigeon for the time it takes Picotex to wolf down enough smaller companies. And he took me off the payroll so he can fire me instantly when the feast ends. Somehow I thought Mel was paying me under the table out of the goodness of his heart. Now I know he's paying me under the table because he wants to implicate me in something illegal so I won't go blabbing to the authorities about this suspicious job I had. And he doesn't want records of me working there while Picotex is gorging itself. So fuck him. I'm going to quit."

Ho strokes Wily. "I don't know, Chet. I'm not down with all this."

"You doubt my analysis?"

"Not your analysis, your motive. Your motive just doesn't seem sincere. I can't believe Denny convinced you to take a stand on this stuff."

I spread my arms. "Hey, worker solidarity and all that noise."

"But the workers get screwed regardless of whether you cooperate. The hostile takeovers happen anyway, right? The same number of workers get laid off whether Levy and Mel make a profit or not. This is just rich guys screwing rich guys. Why should a blader punk like you care?"

I sigh, turn, and look Ho in the face. Ever since she spilled her guts about Megan, I've felt compelled to level with her.

"When I was leaving Chen's old place, I saw the spider logo."

Ho's face ossifies and she slowly nods. "Bobby's brand."

Her green pupils flame, and she tries to look into my eyes, but I turn my back and stride ahead of her. "The dealers who are killing my brother are in on this whole thing. No way in hell I'm being their ho. Let somebody else be their ho. I'm— oops, sorry about that."

"Don't sweat it." She slaps me on the shoulder. "C'mon, cuz. Skate with me to the corner."

Ho mounts her board and does a tail slide along the curb. Wily pulls her like a sled dog. Skating through the traffic, I'm struck by how liberating it feels for my balls to hang free of nasal molestation. There are some things in life you just take for granted.

"I'm not taking this money. I'm going to quit."

"Then what are you going to do?"

"I can get a job with the grunge couriers. Take a pay cut."

"You can't do that job on blades."

I turn the corner and skate off. "I'll buy a bike."

"You don't have money for a bike!" she calls. "Not if you pay Ralph his rent! And neither me or Denny has anything to lend!"

"I'll think of something!"

Two bicyclists meet eyes with me as I pounce off the cable car and shred up Mel's driveway. They bolt towards the stairs, but I jam past them. As I climb the first flight, one of them grabs me by my waistband and pulls down my shorts. As he's mesmerized by my gleaming white cheeks, I elbow him on the bike helmet and chop up the steps. They are right behind me as I canter down Mel's hallway. Nobody but Mel is in his office, and I jump in and shut the door in my associates' faces.

Sunshine looks up from his Quotron machine. "What the fuck are you doing, asswipe?"

I pull off my helmet. "Mel, it's me. Cannon."

"I repeat: What the fuck are you doing, asswipe?"

My comrades are pining like mewlings outside the locked door. Better talk fast.

"Mel, I've stumbled upon a moral quandary."

His face scrunches up. "What? What the fuck is that?"

I suppose it makes sense that he would not know. "What I'm trying to say is, I'd like to go back to my old job. I—"

"Fine."

"Wha?"

"Fine," he says, decapitating his bottle of hypertension pills. "I decided I need a whole legion of you sissyskaters. I don't care who it is. I need that high-technology speed. So that will be your first new job. Train somebody else to ride them rollerskates. I'm giving you a week. Then you better find another job."

"*Another job!?* Why? I'm a great courier! Can't you just bump me down a peg?"

"I guess you forgot, Einstein," snaps Mel. He pitches four

pills into the back of his throat and speaks with his mouth full. "I took you off payroll Tuesday. You don't officially work here anymore, remember? You're getting paid under the table." He swigs from a hip flask, winces, and burps. "So I'm giving you a week to train another one of them fuckers, and then I can't use you any more. You don't like it? Quit now. But if you want to work here another week, train somebody else. Open the door."

Stunned, I open it. In leap four bike messengers.

"I need a courier!" shouts Mel. "What's another bug name? Where's that Spider guy?"

"Here I am!" shouts Spider, prancing forward.

Great. My bosom buddy.

"The rest of you assholes get the fuck out."

They file out.

"Shut the door," barks Mel.

They shut the door.

"All right, you two homos, listen up. Spider, lose the bike."

"You got it, Mel," says Spider, not having the slightest clue what's going on.

"Cannonball here is going to teach you how to ride roller-skates today."

"Great, Mel," says Spider.

"Here's three hundred bucks. That should be enough. Buy some top-notch rollerskates and pads and bring me back the change and receipt. Spider, we're training you to rollerskate and giving you a motherlode of a pay raise. So I want to see ass-kissing, lots of ass-kissing."

"I'm on my knees right now if you want it, Mel."

"Save it. Get out there with Cannonball and deliver this package to Chen. Show him the ropes, Cannonball."

"I thought it was Cannon."

"Shut up, Cannonball. Then take him over to the Financial District and jerk those guys off for a while. Teach Spider everything you know, Cannonball, and you'll get a little good-bye bonus at the end of the week. If he comes back at the end of the week, and he don't know his shit, you're both fired, and *you*, Cannonball, *you* don't even get your pay."

I bristle with a Cub Scout's indignation. "You can't do that, Mel! That's illegal!"

"You're not even paying taxes on your earnings this week, douchebag. *That's* illegal! You don't want it? Walk out right now."

Damn. I can't walk out now. If I quit now, I won't even make PG&E, much less next month's rent.

"I'd be delighted to do your bidding, Mel."

"That's Oh Great Benefactor to you. I want to see some love between you two. Hand-holding and everything. Spider, you'll be my new Cannon by next week, right?"

"You got it, Mel."

"All right," says Mel, wincing and digging four fingers into his terror-breeding ulcer. Couriers whisper about the percolations and festerings of Mel's ulcer like they're the cycles of biblical plagues. "Deliver your package."

"Mel," says Spider adoringly. "Thanks for this chance."

"Fuck off."

Spider waits until he is outside to open up his tender feelings to me. "You cocksucking rollerfag!" he roars, grabbing me by my tie-dye. "What did you tell him?"

I shove him back. "Hands off! You'll be pleased to know I'm fired in one week! He wants bladers because he thinks— excuse me—*knows* they're faster. You're lucky as shit he chose you, because you're going to get a tasty pay raise."

"But I don't know how to ride them sissywheels!"

"So you can take the three hundred he gave you and flee like the bicycle pansy you are, or you can spend the week with me learning how to burn blades. Frankly, I don't give a fart, because I'll just march back in there and tell Mel you stole his three hundred bucks and that I'd be prancing with joy if he let me train somebody else."

He makes a fist as if to hit me. I watch his face move through purple, red, orange, and pink, and then he exhales.

"Okay, fucko. Where's the nearest rollerblade store?"

Spider, now known as Eggs Benedict, after Mr. Arnold, is now included in my Untouchable caste. But he's sacrificing his honor for more money. That's a courier for you. Makes me proud to be of his ilk.

All the couriers know something is up. It's not hard to figure out that the King of the Bad Boys must be getting quite a pay raise to wear sissyskates. Spider, quivering around like a newborn fawn on those tiny wheels with his patented pissed-off face, looks like a Hell's Angel on a tricycle. But wearing the courier's equivalent to the Scarlet Letter brings him to no stoic heights of silent dignity. In fact, he can't shut up. When his ex-friends remind him to wipe off his chin and adjust his knee pads (implying certain untoward favors for Mel), he counters passionately that Mel sought him out because, as he says, "I'm the best."

I smirk. What utter bullshit. Mel called in Spider because it was the only bug name he could remember. His fellows, having been present when Mel made his pick, cackle with hysteria.

This sort of treatment is old hat for me, so I can afford to be amused as Spider absorbs most of the jeers that are normally reserved for yours truly. I feel something of the cafeteria geek's satisfaction at seeing the school's Golden Child get squirted with a mustard pack.

I share my first laugh with my fellow couriers when Spider, in the midst of a passionate but inarticulate retort, slips and lands on his ass. Then I savor the exquisite glee of actually *helping Spider up*!

For the first time ever, I'm actually enjoying my job.

"You have to get a center of balance, dude," I say. "It's a yin-yang sort of thing."

He pushes me away, yells, "Get the hell off me!" and lands on his keister again. Cackles abound.

I have to work another week on this job, so I can save up and buy a bike. See, this is the trouble with never having more than two hundred bucks in your bank account and living on potatoes and beans. I can't temp, because it takes a month to go through the red tape program before they get you a six-dollar-an-hour job. I can't switch to bike messengering, because I need about five hundred bucks to get a decent bike. If you live paycheck to paycheck, and you get laid off, you're cast instantly into the abyss.

But I'm a college graduate, dammit!!

Big deal, shmucko. So is everybody else.

So I'm putting off acting on my principles. Get me another paycheck's worth of dirty money under my belt, and *then* I'll quit because it's immoral.

"Here, Twinkletoes," I say, holding Spider's arm like he's my grandmother. "Let's skate away from your fellow assholes and learn this in peace."

"Whoa, whoa, whoa, motherfucker! This is a fucking hill! I don't like hills!"

"I know that, but badasses are supposed to overcome their fears. Now follow my lead, Mr. Benedict, just like I'm a waltzing gentleman."

Spider is quivering as I turn him downhill. "Shit, man! How do you stop on these things?"

"I'm showing you how to control your speed. This is called slaloming. Back and forth. Back and forth. Like a snake. See?"

"Just don't fucking let go."

"Now this is called swizzling, or skulling. Watch my legs. Like a figure eight. You can get that with practice."

"Okay . . . okay, I think I got it," says Spider, duck-walking like a dork.

"Now, the way you'll stop for now is to use your heel-brake. Later, we'll teach you the power slide. For now, do a T-stop like this and drag your heel."

"Like this?" he says, jabbing down his heel-stop, pirouetting out of my grip, and falling on his face.

"Good! That's called a faceplant. I was going to show you that next."

"Up yours."

I try to help him up, but he pushes me away. So I just stand back and watch him scramble around like Fred Astaire with his pubic hairs caught in an electrical outlet. He fumes in his native Fuckspeak and flails about for a full minute before he regains his equipoise.

"I'll definitely have to teach you how to fall."

"Are you messing with me?"

"Knowing when to bail is a basic part of in-line skating."

"I'm a natural on the straightaways," he professes. "I used to rollerskate in gym when I was a kid. I just can't handle any of this downhill shit."

"You know, Mel promoted you because he wants you doing radical downhills like the one I nailed Monday."

Spider's face goes pale, but he folds his arms and resolves like a grade-schooler, "I can learn it. I know I can."

I give him a look. "In a week? It'll never happen, dude. Face it, Spider, we're both toe cheese."

Spider looks at his toes and bites his lip. He pinches the skin between his eyebrows and stands there breathing irregularly.

"You okay, Spider?"

"Fuck!" he suddenly shouts. His macho mask collapses into an avalanche of blubber. "I got to do this for my baby girl," he sobs. "Her moms is a fucking crackhead and can't take care of her. The Child Protection Agency comes to my apartment every week, man. I lose this job, they take my baby girl away from me. You don't know what it's like when crystal comes into your family, so you can't judge me. I can't afford to lose this job. I can't. I can't."

There's that sharp pain inside my chest, like I just pulled a muscle, like somebody is carving a tattoo inside my sternum.

I step forward and clap Spider on his big shoulder. "Hey, don't bug out on this, man. It's no biggie. You'll definitely learn this by the end of the week."

He looks at me. "For real?"

"For real," I lie. "It's hard the first day, easier the second—but after a week of being taught full-time by an expert like me? Shit, you'll be styling with the best of them."

He takes a deep tremulous breath and reaches up under his sunglasses to wipe his eye with his finger. He faces down the deadly plummet of Watermelon Hill.

He clears his throat, tries to look manly. "I can hack it," he says.

"Good man." I slap his ass. "All right. Right now we have

to truck on over to Chen's. We're gonna hitch a ride on this cable car that's going by. It's called skitching, and it's illegal, but bitchin bladers do it anyways. Take my hand."

He takes it.

"Jesus," he smiles. "I hope nobody can see this shit."

"Spider, my boy, that's the advantage of sitting in Chet's Circle of Shame. You can't get any less popular than you already are."

As the trolley passes, I canter up some momentum to give Spider a little tow, then swing him around in front of me. He's spinning his arms like a hummingbird.

"You have the grace of a swan, Spider. Now, believe it or not, I have to put my hands on your ass."

"What?"

I get down low and push him into the slipstream of the cable car. People standing on the outer ledges watch us. Nobody bitches as Spider manages to grab on to the back. I've lost momentum pushing his weight. The cable car is slipping away from me.

"Grab my hand, man!" I yell.

Spider grips the cable car by one hand and stretches to me. Our fingers barely curl together, we clasp hands, he pulls me forward, and I grab the bar next to him. We smile at each other.

"Rad!" cheers Spider.

THE SHIT KICKS IN

"Can I go down this last part by myself?"

"You can't go straight down this!"

"Why not? What am I going to hit?"

"Orphans! Pregnant ladies! Nuns! Pregnant nuns!"

Spider guffaws and spews an incoherent fantasy about pregnant nuns.

I shake my head. "Spider, somebody should cut out that foul tongue of yours."

Spider is getting giddier as the morning goes by. It's nine o'clock by the time we get to the bottom of the hill, but he's already mastered the basics. He's right, he *is* a natural on the straightaways. He's not only asking frequent questions, he's eagerly picking up on blade terminology.

"So if you don't feel like chopping up the hill, but a five-oh is scoping, you can actually draft along behind a bus or something?"

"Dude, you're forgetting. You only need to draft on downhill rips. On uphills, just take the fucking trolley."

His face lights up. "That's right! You take the cable car!"

"You'll never have to grind up Snob Hill again, my man." I wrap my arm around his shoulders. "Now your bicycle chums will *really* love you!"

He gives me a sly grin. "Cannonball, you are brilliant."

I fold my hands prayerfully. "You learn quickly, Grasshopper. Master say: What seem at first to be lame might actually be pretty hype shit."

"This pay raise gets me family medical, dude! We're talking *daycare*, motherfucker!"

"I'm telling you, man: When it comes to downhill delivery,

rollerblades are the future. Here, let me show you the secret
entrance to Chen's place."

I take him down the alley to the fire door that is held open
for us by an armed doorman, who clangs it shut and locks it
behind us. We reach the top of the echoing stairs and enter
the cement room where Spock and Data are waiting for us. I
immediately notice the new tile work that has been put up
since I was last here.

"What's up, boys?" says Spock, spreading his arms lovingly and coming forward. "Is this the new guy you're teaching to rollerskate?"

"Yeah," I say, handing him the package. "How did you
know?"

He slaps my face and points his finger at my left eye. "I
thought couriers didn't ask questions."

I smile meekly and struggle not to rub my raspberry cheek.
Guido turns his back on me. The urge to give him a wedgie
is almost overpowering. He waddles over to Goliath at the far
end of the room.

Spider steps forward protectively and whispers, "What's
that dude's problem?"

"Don't fuck with him," I whisper. "Don't even talk. Just
do as he says."

Spider shrugs. "Okay, bro."

"Got anything for us?" I call.

"Nope," says Spock. "You guys are supposed to go uptown
and visit the big boys today. You know what I'm talking
about?"

"Yup," I say, about-facing and clasping Spider on the
shoulder. "C'mon, Spider. See, you always ask if they have
anything for you to send back. That way—"

"Hey hey hey, waitaminute, fellas!"

We stop, turn.

Spock's face is blank and serious, like how a cop looks
when he's just caught you peeing in the parking lot. He holds
open the mouth of the envelope. "Why is this package open?"

Spider raises his hands obeisantly. "Hey, man—"

I jump in, "We're sorry, man! We didn't even notice it was

open! Mel must have forgot to seal it! We were in such a hurry to get it here, we didn't even look at the package."

Data states quietly, "Corlini sent this package hours ago."

My Adam's apple swells and clogs my voice. After a frozen second, Spider speaks up. He acts as if his pride is hurt. I don't think it's even an act.

"Hey, I been working with Mel Corlini for seven years, dude. Call him up. He'll say I never fuck with a package." Spider puts one hand over his heart and raises the other like Ollie North. "I would never, *never* besmirch the Sacred Courier Code."

I blare a smile. "Fuck honor! We would lose our jobs! Ha! Ha!"

Spock and Data's faces are as cold as statues.

I swallow and try to tie up the loose ends of the joke. ". . . that is, if we were to make a habit of peeking inside our delivery packages. I mean, we being professionals and all."

Silence. Me and Spider are smiling as widely and stupidly as we can. Both of us can sense a subtle yet momentous shift in the paradigm. You know the difference between the way a butcher looks at a cow and his pet dog? Well, somebody just noticed Spot and Fido have udders.

Spock tsks to himself, looks at Data, and says, "Well, looks like we'll just have to waste them."

"Shit!" growls Data. "This is gonna fuck everything up! Chen will be pissed!"

"He said if security is breached, we go to code red!"

"But then we have torch the whole operation!"

"Those are his orders! If the envelopes are tampered with, we go into code red! So let's go!"

"We'll have to start over from scratch! We'll be stuck in California another six months! I promised my gramma I'd be back in New York by her birthday, and she—"

"Data, you see those two idiots with their mouths hanging open?"

"Yeah."

"Well, that's called the scared bunny effect. Shrinks call it denial. It usually lasts about ten seconds, and then they start running. So let's get these guys murdered while they're easy targets and get going."

"I don't want to hurt all Chen's new tile work."

Spock puts his hands on his hips and makes an are-you-fucking-stupid face that is rather humorous. This conversation is so casual, you'd think he was reciting a carrot cake recipe. "Screw the tile work! We got to torch the place anyways! You got your popgun with you?"

"Sure."

"Well, what are you waiting for? Them to start running? Kill the fucks."

My cheeks are getting charley horses from hoisting up this ingratiating smile. I turn to Spider. "Waitaminute," I whisper. "When they say they're going to kill us, does that mean they're really going to *kill* us?"

Spider smirks at me. "They're just kidding," he says, and jokingly punches me in the chest, propelling me backward.

My relieved giggle is shattered by a gunshot that rips past my eardrum and shatters against the tiles where my head just was.

"Shit!" we scream at each other.

It's strange, that reflex to allude to fecal matter at the most acute moment of angst, whether it's dropping your bagel butter-side down or getting shot at with a .357 Magnum. This is the maddeningly pointless observation that hovers with eerie stability in a brain that is otherwise behaving as if it has just been dropped into a spinning Cuisinart. Me and Spider are tearing down the stairs, crying and blubbering, a smoking exhaust of tile dust trailing off our powdered shoulders.

A godlike echo rattles down the cement steps after us. It's Spock's laughter. Past my ringing ears, I hear him jeer, "Nice shooting, hawkeye!"

"Don't worry about it," laughs Data. "Where they gonna go?"

"Turn on the PA."

I jam down the last flight to the fire door, but Spider grabs me by my collar and drags me through a doorway to the open lobby. He just saved my life a second time. I forgot the guard standing at the bottom of the stairs.

Of course, now we're attracting the attention of all the armed guards in the lobby by scrambling across the marble floor like a pair of giraffes on ice when a commanding voice brittles over the loudspeakers. "Attention! We're going into code red! This is not a joke! Kill the rollerskaters before they leave the building!"

We blast through the green door and knock down Chinese cooks like bowling pins. Many a fancy breakfast plate is churned up by the wheels of our scrambling rollerblades and smushed into the holes of the black rubber floor mats. Out into the dimly lit restaurant we hurtle, sending the maître d' over somebody's laden table, flooring many a well-dressed patron, and tracking goop across the rug amid the screaming and the violently swinging paper lanterns.

We slam straight out the front doors as some kind of siren goes off. Skating past the parked Mercedes and Lincolns that will soon be filled with professional killers, we careen out into the extremely public Financial District of San Francisco.

We both immediately discern a perfect series of obstacles to put between ourselves and the gunmen: innocent pedestrians. We weave in and out of baby strollers and lovers and grandmas, who flinch and curse us as we pass. Spider, skating awkwardly but trying his damnedest, falls in behind me and tries to follow my lead. The streetlight straight ahead is yellow. We have to get across before it turns red.

Spider yells, "Don't slow down for me! We should split up! You go that way, and I'll go this way!"

"We're gonna die!!" I scream. "They're gonna kill us!!"

"Not me!" roars Spider. "No way!" He shouts back at the gangsters, "Hey, assholes!"

I look over my shoulder and have to blink several times to accept what I am witnessing. Spider puts this thumb to his nose, sticks out his tongue, and *plbb*s a Herculean raspberry at the gangsters darting into their cars. I face frontwards just in time to hurdle a leash that connects a woman and a squirrel-sized dog, and careen into the street.

"Spider!" I shriek. "Watch out for that—"

I hear the unmistakable splat of a high-velocity wipeout. Spider's holler is snipped off in the middle and ends in a glottal gurgle. I leap the curb, spin around, and focus my eyes as the light changes and Spider and I become separated by walls of grinding traffic.

The first thing I see is the unharmed little dog, yelping and doing what every little dog does when it gets excited: running in circles. This brainless activity has the inadvertent effect of hog-tying Spider by his ankles.

Then I see Spider's face.

Spider did a swan dive. His chin is on the 'crete. Blood leaks between his teeth to form a pretty puddle on the street. He gets up on his knees, holds his throat and chin, and dribbles chewed cherries. He begins to yell.

His sunglasses are gone, and it's the first time I've ever seen his eyes, which are as wide as silver dollars. On the merciless concrete before him, something bright red is flopping around like a fish, exposing a purple, veiny underbelly. It's muscular and pumping. Did this dude just cough up his own beating heart? It flops once, splats in the crimson puddle, and stills: a twitching human tongue.

I've hurled myself a full block before I realize I have not yet inhaled since I began that bloodcurdling scream a block back. One thing about horror, it gives you a supreme unleaded adrenaline rush. I'm foaming like I have a mouth full of Alka Seltzer. Judging by the faces of the innocent pedestrians clutching their children, I must look like the First Rollerblader of the Apocalypse.

I hear a car shriek to a halt back by Spider. I will not turn around to witness what I know is about to happen. I want to save my shattered mind from any more horrible perceptions. But ears, unlike eyes, have three-hundred-sixty-degree spherical reception. I hear Spider shout something, tongueless and bloody mouthed, a name—I think, "Ariewa!" or something. Then erupts the incredibly loud report of a gun, much louder than in the movies. The noise enters my consciousness in a gruesome three-part harmony: the *crack crack crack* of the discharge, the *squelch squelch squelch* of something soft bursting, and, vibrating beneath my feet, the *ponk ponk ponk* of the street absorbing lead.

The crowd stampedes in every direction at once. Packages burst, purses get tangled in limbs, Big Gulps are spilled, kids are knocked down and crying. Well-dressed people dive under vehicles that have recently skidded to a stop. People huddling against walls fight and shove to take cover behind each other. Folks who I'm sure are normally quite neighborly don't hesitate to use trampled human faces as gymnastic springboards.

I collide with a three-hundred-pound woman in frantic pursuit of a giggling toddler. My momentum is no match for her bulk; imagine a hummingbird hitting a cement truck. She bowls me over and her heel stabs into the soft spot below my sternum. Ten different shoes trip over me, and I am buried in screaming bodies. I cover my face and wait to die.

No more shots are fired. The goons must have gotten back in their goonmobiles and disappeared. Right now they're probably yelling at the Guido who shot Spider in the street before they had us both. *We'll never catch that other twerp now! Who's gonna tell Dr. Chen?*

Weepers keep humping the sidewalks for a time, until slowly, in scattered fragments at first, then as a group, people stand. Everyone breathes. Fathers pretend they had thought to protect the wife and kids with their bodies. Mothers suffocate their kids with hugs. Cops remember their uniforms and start acting like cops. They brush the street dirt off themselves and do their real jobs: taking statements and directing traffic. Everybody with a mouth is telling a conflicting story about what happened. Those few seconds, suddenly so much more important than the whole previous workweek, are relayed again and again to other people who were just there and don't need to hear about it and want everybody else to shut up so they can tell their own versions. This is the only time they really feel alive.

A cop tries to rope off the bloody homicide site.

I better get out of here before the news cameras come. They always arrive before the ambulances.

*   *   *

"Mel!" I scream into the phone. "Don't give them my name!"

"Why? What's wrong? Did you get it there?"

"Mel, they're Chinese mafia or something, I swear to God! They murdered Spider right on the street! They're gonna call you! *Please* don't give them my name!"

"Okay, Chet, relax. Where are you?"

"At a pay phone."

"Where?"

"Down Mission."

"Okay, stay right where you are. What's your cross street?"

Oh, my God.

"Chet? Are you there?"

He knows. My God, he knows.

"Chet? Waitaminute, kid. Don't panic."

I hang up.

Jesus H. fucking Christ. I wipe my soaking hands on my shorts and look around hysterically, my eyes unable to check every dark corner fast enough.

I'm taking deep breaths. Okay, if I call him back right now, the line will be busy, because at this moment he is telling Chen I called from a pay phone down Mission Street, and to be ready, because he thinks I just realized what's up. They know I know. Now I'm all the more valuable as a corpse. Cellular phones are ringing. At this moment, they are tearing down Mission with knives and guns, looking for me. They are blocks away, all converging on this point.

I don't have time to think. I just have to pick a direction and plow.

West. I head towards the Castro District.

I'm churning in a fury, all the engines of the Indy Five Hundred are rattling around like pinballs in the contained canister of my skull. My brain is stuck in overdrive, my thoughts shooting out in all directions at once. I should go left! No, right! The trillion atoms of my thoughts contradict each other so often, it creates a stabilizing effect that keeps my body on an even course.

I spot a straight couple exiting their apartment house. An impulse seizes me and I go with it. I careen a hard right, vault a car hood, spring up the stairs, zip past them, and catch the door just *after* it closes.

Shit!

I spin around. My voice quivers. "Hey, man. Can you open this door for me? I forgot my key."

"Sorry," calls the fellow over his shoulder. "You'll have to use the buzzer," and hustles his lady into a car.

"But—"

It's pointless. They see the look on my face. I'm a maniac. I turn and stare down a matrix of four hundred buzzers.

I hit 1A.

Nobody answers in one second, so I hit 1B.

Then I slam both hands against about forty buzzers.

I look behind me. A Lincoln is meandering up the street too slowly.

It stops two houses down. An Italian guy in a suit steps out. My heart explodes in my chest and clogs my voice box. He reaches back into the car and pulls out . . .

. . . the hand of a four-year-old girl.

"Hello?"

"—ub, yeah! I wonder if you could let me in . . . pal?"

"Who is this?"

"Uh . . . Joe, your old buddy."

"Fuck you, Joe."

I bang buzzers. Five cars in a migratory birds' V carve around the corner at high speed. They stop at a red light. They haven't seen me yet.

"Okay!" erupts a staticky woman's voice. "Calm down with the buzzer already!"

"Hi! It's me! Can you buzz me in?"

"Who is me?"

"I forgot my key!"

"Who is this?"

"I can't hear you very well! Can you hit the buzzer for me?"

"Lance! It's over! Just accept it!"

I look over my shoulder. The streetlight turns green. The five cars inch forwards.

"Hello? Hello? Fuck!"

A thousand shards of hard lead are about to strafe my body. I hurl my shoulder against the glass door. It doesn't even crack. My poor shoulder absorbs all the force of my panic attack. I scream and fall to the floor and curl into a fetal position like a potato bug.

No bullets come. The phalanx of cars passes.

I stand, gasping. Man, talk about attracting attention. More expensive cars head up the street. These happen to be filled with heads and visible firearms.

It's them! *It's them!*

I slam more buzzers.

"Hello?"

"Let me in!! Let me in!! For the love of God, let me in!"

"I'm sorry. I'm house-sitting. You'll have to come back when the owners return."

I look over my shoulder. The light remains green as the four cars filled with faces and weapons glide towards me.

I slam my fists and forehead against all the buzzers at once.

Without the antecedent of a voice, I hear a piercing buzz and yank open the door.

Legs churn. I spiral up an endless cataract of stairs until I kiss a door. Jesus. I'm so pumped with panic, I went all the way to the roof.

I try the door. It opens. I jump through onto the roof. There's no way to lock it from the outside. I frantically scan the roof for something to jam it with. There's a lawn chair, some beer cans, sunscreen, empty tar buckets, somebody's bike. I grab the lawn chair and wedge it underneath the door handle.

Okay. Okay. I put my hands on my head and walk in tightly wound circles beneath the open sky, catching my breath and my sanity. A beach of white pebbles scrunches beneath my blades. I'm too afraid to go near the edge where I could be spotted. It looks like there are four outhouses up here, or four brick telephone booths. Each has a door leading downstairs.

Each doorway faces a different side of the building. None of the doors are lockable from the outside.

I lie flat on the pebbles to peer over the four sides. I see there are only two fire escapes, one on either side of the building. Neither reaches the roof. The top fire-escape tier is an eight-foot drop.

Okay. I'm safe. I repeat it over and over in my mind. I am safe. I am safe. I am safe.

But wait.

Did they see me before I got through the front door?

No! I'd hear them thundering up the stairs by now. I'm sure they drove right past!

But what if they *did*?

I'd be cornered up here!

Hmm . . . maybe I'd better open the door and just peek down the stairs. Just to be sure.

I tiptoe to the door and place my ear against it. Not a sound. I gently place my hand on the doorknob, reach for the lawn chair, and . . .

. . . the knob twists beneath my palm.

My hand recoils as if it touched a hairy tarantula, and I stare in disbelief as the doorknob slowly turns. Then the door thuds outwards and strains violently against the bending lawn chair. Spock's voice whispers, "It's stuck."

The door is shrinking, I realize, because my feet are running backwards. No, it can't be them! It can't be! There's no way!

I'm knocked back into another form of insanity when my heels strike the parapet and the shrinking door wheels beneath me and is replaced by a wheeling sky; the world is upside down and I am falling. Something clangs against my skull, my chin stabs into my chest, and my toes clash a metal surface on either side of my head, gonging both my eardrums. Then my heavy feet swing back the way they came and my heels chuck against brick.

I blink away the dancing spots and see blue California sky. My back is latticed by a grating. My brain is functioning at about Wily's level right now, but I manage to figure out that

I am lying on my back on a fire escape, with my ass set against the side of the building and my legs going straight up the brick wall. The ledge I just fell over is eight feet up. I bend my knees back towards my chest, find my blades too heavy for me, and give up.

To my confusion, my feet very loudly melt straight through the brick wall—and then find no floor. The weight of my swinging blades acts as a pendulum to sit me up. I am sitting on a windowsill, covered with a frosting of broken glass, looking into an apartment at an old man and a muscular stud, both naked, in bed, clutching each other, and staring at me.

"I did not order a delivery!" shouts the old man.

"You couriers are a menace!" shouts the studcake.

I think I have definitely entered Oz.

I hear the door on the roof crash open, and somebody yells, "He's got to be up here! Check behind the chimney!"

My feet are on the carpet. I simply stand up. I wipe the glass off myself and adjust my beeper and backpack—and my helmet, which recently saved my life.

The lovers stare as my eyes slowly uncross. "Mind if I just hang here for a while?" I ask.

The white-haired man looks dreamily at the studcake. "Oh, Bruno, you devil!"

"I didn't *arrange* it, Michael!"

Ten seconds of blinking silence. Then I hear Spock's voice out the window, coming from about ten feet up. "There's broken glass on the fire escape! He must have jumped down there and crashed through to the apartment right below us! C'mon!"

I try to crunch across the glass towards the door, but I'm zigzagging like I just got off a tilt-a-whirl. I hear an abrupt thud on the fire escape behind me. It creaks like it's going to yank its bolts from the brick and come crashing down. I snatch the swirling door handle with both hands, use it for balance, and look behind me.

The drapes are parted and a face the size of a pot roast smiles at me. Data.

I scream, yank open the door, and jump out into the hall. I turn and clatter down the hall, turn the corner to the stairs—

The stairs are going up. Why are the stairs going up?

I ran the wrong way down the hall.

I hear Goliath's footsteps pounding across the apartment.

I scramble up the steps. One flight, and I come to a door. I stop.

Spock's voice in the hall below: "Data! Where the fuck did he go?"

"He ran out here!"

"The stairs! C'mon!"

"No! He ran to the other stairs!" says Data.

"Those stairs don't go down! They go to the roof! He'd trap himself!"

"That's where he went! C'mon!"

Footsteps pound towards me.

I try the door. It opens.

I'm back on the roof again. The lawn chair by the other busted door is a twisted paper clip. I grab the bike and wedge the seat underneath the door handle, kick the back tire to make sure it's wedged good. I run to the parapet, throw one leg over, and look straight down.

Into emptiness.

Where the hell is the fire escape?

The door I just blocked is shoved.

"Data! Bust down this door!"

I turn and look at the other busted open door, and find it is facing perpendicular to me. *I'm on the wrong side of the building!* I race across the pebbles as a mastodon smashes himself against the door, crumpling the bike like origami.

"There he is! Shoot him!"

I reach the parapet, leap, *then* look. Then shit. My right rollerblade is pointed down at the fire escape, my left is hanging over an empty chasm of space.

That means the railing is heading straight for my—!

I swing my left foot inward, catch the railing with my hip guard, and interface once again with the rusty grating. My Walkman plummets ten floors and splatters on the pavement. My brain jostles in its fluid like a yolk in a game of egg toss. The old guy and the beefy boy pulling on their trousers are now looking more confused than ever. I jump to my feet and race down one fire escape level as I hear footsteps clattering across the roof like a giant tap-dancing centipede.

There's a window. It's closed.

It's amazing how I never stop finding new uses for these rollerblades.

I kick in the glass. A woman spoon-feeding her baby in a high chair looks over her shoulder at me and freezes. The baby smiles at me and slurps the pureed peas off the spoon. The mother's face is blank. In the movies, people scream. How come nobody has screamed?

I clamber in, saying, "Two windows, and not even a paper cut," as a long posterboard of coffee cups hanging from a nail gets knocked by my helmet and comes crashing down on my head.

Me and Mom both stare at the shattered ceramic. The woman looks up at me.

"Sorry about that," I say.

"Don't mention it," she says blankly.

The fire escape above me thuds again. Somebody yells, "Shit!" A handgun bounces down through fire escape grating and plummets to the pavement below. Heavy footsteps descend. I stumble across her kitchen and throw myself against her front door. It's locked. I reach to unlock it and find—

Ten locks.

"Why are there so many locks?!" I scream.

"To keep intruders out," says the woman, as Data climbs in through the window.

I shred my vocal cords and fumble to undo all the locks at once.

"No!" shrieks the woman, intuiting that this man is about to eat my pancreas. "Only one was locked! You just locked half the others!"

"Waitaminute. Which ones did I just lock?"

The baby starts wailing as Data the Face of Death churns up tremendous speed and rockets at me in a flying tackle designed to snap my spine in half. I scream and hit the floor. Data sails over me.

When I stand up, the door is gone.

I step through and run *up* the hallway to the stairs.

They are, thank God, going down.

Down I thunder. I hear Jolly Green Giant footsteps at my heels. A gunshot blasts and sends sparks from the metal bannister next to my fingers. I hear the bullet ricocheting down through the stairwell. They're shooting down between the stairway banisters. They are a floor behind me.

Keeping my hands in at my sides, I tearass down through this noisy pinball machine of bullets until I pass through the lobby and slam out the front doors to open air. I run down the first three porch steps and stop dead in my tracks.

At the bottom of the stairs, parked on the sidewalk, is a Lincoln with four armed mafiosi leaning against it and staring at me. One of them points up at me.

"There's the kid!"

The glass door automatically shuts and locks behind me.

I turn right, vault the stairway railing, hurtle eight feet straight down below street level, and land in a pile of boxes.

I stand up and leap out. I position myself directly beneath the stairs.

And then I stand there, frozen, for a full five seconds.

I just cornered myself.

I hear the front door open and Spock and company pattering down the front stairs.

"Where is he?"

"He just jumped down beneath the stairs."

"All right, we finally got him. You guys go that way, and we'll go this way."

I can hear the killers fanning out in formation, taking their time about it, approaching the two opposite stairwells that lead down into this dank trench.

There's a door leading to the cellar. It's locked. I shoulder it with all my might, and just barely crack one pane in the green opaque window.

"Okay! When I give the signal!"

"Wait! Decide who the shooters are! I don't want to get shot up in there!"

"Okay. Geordi! You want to be the shooter?"

"I was the shooter last time."

"Okay, Quark, you be the shooter on their side. Who's going to be the shooter on our side?"

I am about to die.

I lift the lid off a garbage can, heave out the plastic garbage bag, and climb inside. I'm just snuggling down inside when I realize I didn't take the lid with me.

I left it on the ground.

"Waitaminute! Quark! How the hell can you be the shooter with an automatic?"

"Well, this is a scrambling little mother!"

"You chowderhead! You know how much ricochet we'll get down there? Worf! What do you got? A Glock?"

I have no choice but to stand up, bend my waist over the edge, and grab that fucking trash can lid. This I do, making what seems like a concert cymbal crash when I gently place the lid over my head. I'm back in my fetal position again. Appropriately, it smells like corpses in here.

"Ready? Go!"

Church shoes clap down both stairways and converge all around me. I hear something soft banging itself against the door.

"He fucking locked it behind him!"

"Dammit, Uhura! You don't yell *There he is!* when you spot the rabbit!"

"Sorry. I was just so surprised the stupid kid just walks right out in front of us."

"Bones and Spock, stay at this exit! Me and Data and the rest of you guys are going to check around the other side!"

Footsteps clatter back up the stairways.

Silence. I can hear the remaining killers breathing, a luxury I am jealous of at this moment. I'm afraid to even sweat. My eyes are darting back and forth inside my sarcophagus. Where the hell are they?

It's actually not too dark in here. Daylight comes in through scores of little rusted-out holes in the lid.

I hear somebody kick the garbage bag away. I hold my breath, waiting for them to make the connection.

A shadow passes over my lid. My constellation of stars blots out with an ass-shaped eclipse, and I get tiny flakes of rust in my eyes.

Spock's voice reverberates down through my can. "I'll tell you, I'm getting too old for this business. If they don't move me up to bodyguard soon, I'm gonna have a heart attack on one of these rabbit chases."

"Yeah, but then you have to do torture. And that's a pain in the ass, unless you sincerely enjoy it like that crazy Data."

"I just want better medical."

Oh joy. This is just the sort of workforce discussion I need to hear. Even though I heard Spider being killed with my own ears, it hits me with renewed confirmation: These guys are really going to *kill* me. No, I mean *kill*. As in *kill*. Not kick my ass, not give me a wedgie, not give me a good scolding, but *kill*. *Me*.

Excuse me if my power to articulate breaks down at this moment, but I really really really really don't want to be killed.

Fear of death. It's a foreign emotion to me. Not long ago, all I would feel is rage. But something has changed in me.

My life is shit, and I don't have a future. And I know, deep down inside, that there is something fundamentally wrong with me. I'll always be lonely. So why should I care?

It's Ho. The idea of never seeing Ho again terrifies me.

Spock leans back. Oh, Jesus, why does he have to lean back? The center of the lid bends inward as he takes his feet right off the ground. I squint as flakes of rust snow my eyebrows and itch down my collar. The lid compresses the top of my head and smushes me down like a jack-in-the-box. My ass scrunches down and wedges against my calves. My rollerbladed feet are skewed in an excruciating pigeon toe. I have a knee going up each nostril. Which is convenient, I suppose, since I can no longer smell the maggot shit. You always have to look on the bright side of every situation, even if that situation is being inside a garbage can being sat on by a fat man who wants to kill you.

If he farts, I'll know God is personally out to get me.

Long moments pass. My breakfast is percolating in my gut. Certain strands of my hair are actually touching Spock's trousers. Don't they know I'm in here? The sides of the can must be barrel-shaped, but the goodfellas don't seem to notice.

Just when I start to think these guys must know I'm in here and are just having a little fun before they ice me, a voice calls, "Spock! Bones! He's gotta be hiding in a dumpster somewhere around here! Come on up!"

With a grunt, fatass heaves himself off me. My body un-accordions somewhat. My ear pops off my shoulder like a little suction cup. Looks like a chiropractor will be getting a little visit.

The only thing I hear is traffic. I can't help imagining that one of them is sitting on the steps and will shoot me if my head pops up. But I can't stay here forever. I grit my teeth and force myself to stand. Oscar the Grouch emerges.

Nobody.

I'm holding the trash can lid over my head like a Vietnamese field hat. As delicately as I can, I lean over the edge of the can to place the lid on the cement—then lose my balance. My arms windmill for a moment, I whisper, "no! no! no! no!" and fall on my face, making about as much noise as somebody trying to attract attention to himself.

I freeze facedown on the 'crete and listen. No sound of running dress shoes. I pull my legs out, tidily replace the bag and upright the can, and crawl up the stairs.

I have to flex every muscle in my body to raise my head over the sidewalk like a trench infantryman and peek up and down the 'vard.

Nothing. No cars, no people. I jump out and begin briskly blading down the street.

As I step out into the air and begin to move, I feel a chill on my thighs. I feel with my hand. Jesus.

Ultimate Badass has wet himself.

I turn a corner, progress halfway to the alleyway between the buildings, and immediately hear Spock's voice straight ahead of me. Shit! They're down this alley! I jump into a doorway and curse my bad fortune. There's no way I could skate across the mouth of that alley without being seen. And I can't turn and skate back for fear one of them will step out and spot me fleeing down the street. Then it's just a matter of shooting ducks in a gallery.

I can't quite accept how confidently these guys march around in broad daylight looking to whack somebody. They shot Spider in front of a thousand shoppers this morning, ten blocks from here, and now they waltz around like they own the street. What is this? Colombia? Where the hell is a cop when you need one? If I manage to escape, I guarantee you some cop will materialize and give me a ticket for jaywalking.

Shit. My socks are all soggy. When I was doing my yoga contortion in the trash can, the leg openings of my boxers formed two perfect pour spouts that sluiced the urine straight into both my waterproof rollerblades. It probably saved my life, because if my plastic boots hadn't caught the outpour, the puddle of piss forming beneath the holes of the trash can most certainly would have piqued the curiosity of the conversing murderers. My toes are skwishing yummily.

Now I hear major goonage all around me. I think some are on the street I just turned from. Their voices are getting louder. In desperation, I wrench off my helmet, shades, and pads, and chuck them down the sewer, hoping some cop will see me and come arrest me for polluting the bay. I pull off my smelly rollerblades, pour out a golden cascade, and shove them in my backpack.

I see two twelve-year-old kids emerge from a store displaying Pogs and Magic cards. Beavis and Butt-head. One of them is oversized, and he is wearing a faded, drooled-on, lame Metallica T-shirt. I march over in my squishy socks and start pulling his shirt off him.

"Hey! What the fuck?" he yells from behind the shirt I'm pulling over his head.

"Hey, asshole!" yells his friend pugnaciously, taking a few steps back.

I pull off my beautiful tie-dye, toss it at the bare-chested dude. "Here."

I pull his shirt over me, and it rips at the armpits. A tad on the tight side. It'll do. "Sorry, I don't have any money," I say, as if that excuses me, and walk off quickly.

The tie-dye is too big for him, but it's brand new and worth ten of his Metallica shirts. And baggy clothes are in. But this younger generation has no appreciation for anything.

"Hey, man! This thing smells like a garbage can!"

I look back and shrug. When I'm a good distance away, they start in with their *fuck you*s, which attracts the attention of a few nearby gangsters who were looking for someone in a tie-dye shirt.

I turn away and start walking briskly towards the Sixteenth Street BART station. I fishhook around the four-foot brick wall, which faces me back towards the boys, and jump on the crowded escalator. Just before my head sinks below the view of the brick wall, I see the young citizens pointing helpfully at me, and the eyes of the killers focus on me and light up.

My adrenal glands spurt into rapid-fire. I pounce up onto the slippery space between the escalators and attract the kind of yelps and gasps a courier is supposed to get when he's doing his job right. My wet heels slip out from under me, my tail-bone thuds, and I hurtle down the steep metal slide, cleaning it with my butt cheeks and bouncing over the painful bumps designed to deter people from doing this. I get beyond the lip of the ceiling just as the gangsters turn the corner at the top of the stairs. Spock shouts, "Police! Get the fuck out of the way!" People cry out as they are trampled from behind. I splat across the waxed floor, leaving a trail of wet footprints behind me. *Slap slap slap* go my soggy socks. *Boosh boosh boosh* goes my heart.

What is wrong with kids today? In my day, we would have hit up those well-dressed goons for some firecracker money before we gave them any information. Kids don't even *try* to do an honest day's hustling any more.

I leap the toll, attracting a helpful "Hey!" from a BART cop, who belatedly starts to pursue me.

Hey! I'm attracting the attention of the authorities! This could save my ass!

Of course, it could also get the authorities killed.

The BART cop sees the Italian gladiators jumping the tolls, realizes something is up, and wisely gets on a phone. I run downstairs to the Richmond/Bay Point line.

Please let there be a BART leaving right now. Please let there be a BART leaving right now. Please, please, pleeeaaase!

Of course, there isn't. There are, however, about fifty BART commuters standing around, all of whom stop talking and stare. Even the zither player stops in midpluck and gawks at me, jaw agape.

Damn. I have to do something about this crazed look on my face.

The goons won't gun me down in front of all these witnesses, will they?

Yes. As a matter of fact they will.

I sense a deep subterranean rumbling. A faint white light swells along the wall. Wisps of hair begin to flutter. A train is coming. But the pug-uglies are ten seconds behind me, reaching the top of the stairs.

Neurons snap like popcorn in my brainpan. My eyes dart up and down the tracks. I scan the billboards on the other side of the tracks as if they were escape doorways into cartoon worlds. My eyes settle on a *Chronicle* advertisement.

"Hero saves blind man," I mutter.

Then, in front of fifty staring witnesses, I jump out in front of the train.

True to the legend, a three-foot-high concavity, running parallel to the tracks, waits for me beneath the passenger platform. Blowing kisses at the *Chronicle* ad, I duck in there as an expanding white light fills my world.

A bleating, churning behemoth hurtles past me in a blur and pops both my eardrums. A tornado of wind sucks me towards the white hot wheels glowing against my face. My left hand stops about six inches from the searing wheels. The monster slows, stops, and spurts, leaving my senses blasted and my mind in a vegetable state.

Spock's voice, directly above my head: "Has anyone seen a shoeless kid with a black T-shirt? He's got white tile powder on his face, rust on his eyebrows, and Chinese food in his hair."

"Yes," an old lady's voice says. "He just threw himself in front of this train."

I can't imagine what the thugs think of this. I have to act. I feverishly crawl along this dwarf's passageway towards the front of the train. Eventually, the dark passageway ends in a flat wall, and I still have not reached the nose of the train.

I can't stay here.

I hear the passenger doors slide shut. I quickly crawl between the steaming wheels and get beneath the train. One of these tracks is supposedly electric and will kill me instantly if I touch it. I'll have to remember this as a suicide recourse if the goons corner me. The glow of the hot metal reveals that the nose of the train is ten feet in front of me. I scuttle forward like a gecko as I hear cranks shifting beneath the train, signaling its start-up.

My face hits a grate. Oh my God. What the hell is this?

The engine huffs and exhales. The train begins to inch forwards.

I scramble forwards, trying to keep up with the moving grate. The nose of the train has been equipped with a cow catcher designed to move debris like fallen cement and brainless spraypainters. Right now, it is barring my escape.

The speed increases. Behind me, the licking mandibles of underbelly gears start to churn towards my ass.

I dive forwards and grab the bars of the cow catcher and get slowly dragged. Pebbles spurting in my face, I blindly reach out between the spinning wheels and grope up the side of the train. I find a perfect handhold. The speed increases. I let go of the grating and pull myself between the wheels, reach up beyond my first handhold to find a second identical handhold. The wheels sear at my ribs, hungry to saw me in half. The threads in the armpits of my T-shirt pop and rip. Using the hand-over-hand method I learned in gym, I pull myself between the wheels and climb up onto the side of the train. Wind howls and lashes at me. As the train reaches top speed, I see that my convenient handholds were little emergency escape steps for BART drivers.

I push myself into the wind and stretch one leg around the front corner of the train. I stick my soggy toes into the grating of the cow catcher and pull myself around to the front. Then I just lie there with my face against the front windshield.

My lips are smushed attractively against the glass, and I meet the eyes of the BART driver who is wearing a facial expression appropriate for someone finding an egg-foo-yung-smeared tattoo punk in his socks splayed like a Garfield suction-cup doll on the outside of his subway windshield.

From behind him emerges Data with a knife in his teeth.

I try to scream to warn the driver, but no facial expression I can muster can communicate more intensity than the one I am already wearing. Data karate-chops the innocent man across the back of the neck. The man crumples like a butterfly shot through with a BB gun.

Paralyzed, displayed like a hunting trophy, I can do nothing but stare wide-eyed through the glass at Data and wait for him to kill me.

Data puts his hands on his hips to assess the situation. Data the Human Battering Ram has already eaten four doors for breakfast this morning, and he has never been one to let things like walls and windshields stop him from going where he wants to go. He searches around the cockpit for a moment, spies what he is looking for, and wrenches a fire extinguisher off the wall. He steps up to my window, winds up . . .

I swing my body like a door, letting one hand on the ridge above the window and my toe wedged in the grating of the cow catcher act as a pair of hinges. I swing a full 270 degrees. My back strikes the side window just as the front windshield shatters, and I am nearly sucked into the vortex between the wall and the train. My clutching fingers and toes are nearly yanked out of their knuckle sockets. I hear the fire extinguisher get sucked beneath the wheels and explode directly beneath me. I am being peeled off the side of this train like a Greenpeace sticker.

No other projectiles pelt through my back, which must be quite visible through the side window. It takes me quite some time to pull myself back to the front of the train, as the wind is filling my cheeks which expand like the parachutes on the back of a race car. When I finally wrench my weight around the front corner of the train, I am instantly propelled back through the broken windshield and into the control room. I roll across the floor until I smack into something soft and wet.

I push myself up onto all fours amid the windy flurry of train schedules, and look into the cherry-red face of Data, tinselled with a thousand teeny-weeny pieces of glass.

I am at this moment in his arms. But his eyes are squinted shut, and he is not squishing me like a mouse in his fingers. He must think I am the unconscious BART driver.

Very, very slowly, I stand up.

The wind is strong, but I can stand. Data, still squinting, pulls himself up to his knees, takes off his suit coat, undoes his tie, and tries to wipe the glass out of his face and eyes. It is very quiet. Me and a three-hundred-pound murderer are sharing a moment together.

I can't step over him and run back through the cars. I have to go back out the window.

I step up onto the jagged ridge of the window, and stick my head out into the darkness of the tunnel. My head is up above the train now, and looking back along its spine I see nothing but blackness.

I duck and peek back in. Data is rubbing the last of the glass from his eyes. He blinks and looks at me. He does not look even the slightest bit pissed.

I frantically grab the upper ridge of the roof and yank myself up. My tight shirt splits straight down the back. I scramble to the top of this unmanned train. The troll's hand reaches up and grapples for my soggy tocs. I kick feverishly.

"Hey!"

Both me and the giant hand freeze.

Yes, I heard it. The distinct sound of someone yelling *hey*.

"What the hell are you doing?"

The voice is muffled. It sounds like it's coming in stereo from both sides of the train, but that's just an illusion of wind and acoustics. It must be coming from beneath me.

"Get down here and put your hands on your head! Now!"

The hand sinks like Mighty Joe Young back into the light. I lie on my stomach in the darkness, the wind gushing up my shorts, and listen to Data kicking the piss out of about a hundred BART cops. Something actually strikes the ceiling directly beneath me. It knocks the wind out of me. Is somebody firing cannonballs straight up at me? Or did Data just bounce somebody's skull off the ceiling?

I slither further along the spine of the train, get to the back of the driver's car, and hit a two-foot-high wall. I can crawl no farther.

My eyes now adjusted to the light, I can glance up and watch the warped tunnel ceiling undulating like an upside-down ocean. The hurtling stone ceiling passes within one foot, then six inches, then two feet from the upper lip of this wall. I can't crawl over it without the ceiling giving me a millstone backrub.

The biff and bop sounds downstairs slowly diminish and become sporadic, like a microwave popcorn bag reaching the end of its cycle. Then silence. I exhale for the last time for the rest of this minute. I crane my neck to look over my shoulder and witness the dawn of Data's death mask. His bloody forehead gleams with the slightest sheen of sweat. He is staring straight at my balls. He is smiling.

I frantically look back at the four-inch space between the rippling ceiling and the top of this wall, then look back at Data's glistening unibrow. Data puts a knife in his teeth, pulls himself up, and begins crawling towards my favorite organs.

I look back at my crawlspace. The ceiling is two feet above now—no, a foot-and-a-half. Now it surges down to almost touch the top of the train, then shoots up to three feet.

I have to get over this wall. Maybe I can scramble over before the roof peels me like a shrimp. I quickly stick my head up to see how thick this wall is.

It goes on forever. This is not a wall, it's a permanent increase in the train's height.

There is no place to go.

Something brushes my toes. I pull up my knees and scrunch into my corner to give myself another split-second of life.

The train brakes. The top of the stainless steel BART is smooth, so smooth there is minimal friction, and nothing to hang on to. I slide back towards Data, who in turn slides away from me and off the front of the train. The train stops decelerating and snaps to a halt just as I pass over the upper lip of the train. I teeter, then fall directly down through the broken windshield, which is aerodynamically slanted backwards.

I'm sitting inside the train in a shimmering diamond pile of glass, surrounded by three BART cops taking a little nap. To my right, a confused BART worker is pulling the brake at the Civic Center BART stop.

Where's Data?

I scramble to my feet and search out the window. The BART headlight reveals a WWF wrestler in a wrinkled suit lying across the tracks twenty feet in front of us. He is stunned, rolling to his side, slowly trying to get up.

"Have you opened the passenger doors?"

"What?" asks the mesmerized BART worker.

"Have you opened the passenger doors?"

"Sure. Force of habit."

"Well, you see that crazed giant stumbling towards you in front of the train?"

"Yes."

I spread my arms around the carnage of the control room. "He did this."

The man thrusts the door lever. Along the steel centipede behind us, a hundred voices holler in protest. Engineer Bob here just snipped the mass of shuffling commuters in two.

Meanwhile, Data, bloody-faced, staggers like a drunken man towards the open window. He looks slightly peeved.

I inhale to scream at the man to gun the engine, but my voice is drowned out by him gunning the engine. The BART train surges forwards and strikes Data at ten feet. Data splats against the front, gets an arm inside the window, and hangs there for a moment. As the train accelerates, me and my new friend stare as Data pulls himself up over the lip of the window and lands on both feet directly in front of me.

He smiles at me.

I instinctively freeze like a rodent hypnotized under my snake's gaze. Then Engineer Bob hits the brake. The entire wailing biomass in the train slides forwards like a squeezed tube of toothpaste. Data, taller, careens backwards, the back of his knees hit the ledge of the open window, and he tumbles back out onto the train tracks. I, shorter, hit the ledge of the window with my nuts, jackknife against the edge, then slither to the floor and curl up like a porcupine.

Unable to breathe, I try to gasp to my friend to hit the accelerator again—just keep running him over and propelling him out the window until the Terminator robot is finally dead, but he doesn't need my instructions. He peels his face off the control panel and slams the accelerator. Everything soft and squishy on this train slides backwards as we jolt forward twenty feet. Something thuds the wall against which I am lying, leaving a face-shaped indentation.

Unable to walk, I lie there and wait for the ogre to climb in and squish me like a bug.

Long moments pass.

Clutching my gonads, I stand up as best I can, peer through the windy hole, and see . . .

. . . nothing.

I nod salutations to Engineer Bob, crunch across the broken glass, step over the snoring bodies, duckwalk back through the sliding doors, and sit down on an empty BART seat. Passengers gape at me. I try to smile and nod at them, but I'm too busy wincing.

I'm safe, right?

What would I do if I owned a network of thugs in this city? Hmmmm.

I lean over to a guy sitting kitty-corner from me.

"Hey, dude." He cringes like a doe when he realizes I'm speaking to him. "If somebody happened to be chasing me in a car, could they head me off at the next BART stop?"

The dude stares at me warily. He decides he'd better answer my question. He shakes his head.

"Why not?"

He swallows. "The traffic."

"Oh! The BART travels faster, because there's no traffic!"

"Correct."

"Thank you."

He gets up and walks to the next car. Slowly, a couple people follow him. The people nearest me change their seats.

"But then again," I say out loud, "a mafia boss might have

cars stationed all over this city, which suggests they could have killers with machine guns stationed at every BART stop from here to the bay."

I look around at my fellow passengers to see if this seems reasonable. They all silently nod.

My eyes fall on the BART map. "Waitaminute," I think aloud, the waves of blood in my head reaching a furious peak. "The next stop is Powell, right?"

Nobody answers. When I glare at them, they all frantically nod. I feel like I'm in a store full of those dolls with heads that bob on springs.

"And that's one block from Mission and Fifth, right?"

More smiles and nods. The world must look very affirming to the man who has dynamite strapped to his chest.

"My God! I'm headed back to where Chen lives! One block from where Spider was just murdered!"

Half the passengers get up and flee to the next car.

I achingly take my rollerblades out of my backpack and pull them on over my wet socks. I'll need serious speed juice in a moment. When I bend down to tie my laces, a mixture of brown rust and fried rice falls out of my hair.

I haven't had this many co-passengers staring at me since I was flying home from my Boy Scout trip to Mexico, heard about superdogs with bionic olfactory nerves, and ate my entire peyote stash. I think I've relied too much on my blader helmet to cushion the wanton blows I've been taking to my second favorite organ today.

When the doors open at the Powell Street station, I scrunch down in my seat, expecting fifty Chinese and Italian hitmen to storm the BART train looking for me. Instead, I get fifty policepersons. They bustle on like spilled blueberries and hie straight for the control room. After that game of tag with Data, these guys look like fat cub scouts. In the whirl of chattering passengers, it's easy to step through the doors and start rolling. Outside is a small ambulance crew, waiting to make sure their own asses are safe before they charge on to save any lives. Everybody is talking about the hijacked BART train. I just roll straight through everybody, head up the escalator, churn up speed, and leap the turnstile. All the real cops, fortunately, are downstairs on the train. I chop up the second escalator and out into the sunlight before the BART boys can marshal their forces to stop the toll jumper.

When I rip out on to the street, I smell smoke, see a sirening fire truck speed past. There are no gangsters.

Chen's place is thataway, near the roped-off homicide site. So I head thisaway.

I lose myself in a crowd of twenty rollerbladers.

I slam a quarter into a pay phone. Denny's number is easily memorized: *You and I ate pee. Oh gee.* UNI-8POG. 864-8764.

Denny's speakerphone clicks on.

"Denny the Menace speaking."

"Denny!!" I froth. "Get the fuck out of there!!"

"What? Why?"

"This guy I was training! Spider! They killed him! They shot him right on the fucking street!"

"Who?"

"I don't know! The Chinese mafia or something!"

"Chet, what are you on?"

"*Denny, shut up and listen to me!!* Mel works with these guys who killed Spider! Denny, I swear to fucking God, Mel just gave them my address! They have my social security number! They're organized crime! They're on their way there! Lock the doors in the bathroom and motor that chair the hell out of there! They'll kill you! I know they will!"

"Okay, okay." His voice is shaking. "You're totally scaring the shit out of me."

"Good! If anybody asks, tell them you hate me. You don't even know me. Just get out of there! Now!"

"Okay. I'm gonna do this. I'm just gonna go stroll around the city for a while. And think. Chet, so help me God, if you end up making a fool out of me—"

I'm choking. "This is real, Denny. They know who I am, and they're chasing me all through this city. They're going to kill me. They shot Spider right on the street, man. They'll kill you. I know it. Just get the fuck out of there. Get the fuck out of there now!"

He hangs up.

A half hour later, I'm at Ho's place, still quivering like a wet Chihuahua, when the local news finally comes on and buzzes through the "Market Street Murder!" The story mentions a second rollerblader who was also a target, and asks if anybody has seen this man, please call this number. They show a sketch: bowl haircut, white beard, bug eyes. Who the hell is that? And why is my name flashing across his chest? Luckily, to us hardcore bladers, cars are anathema, so I've never deigned to get a driver's license, so they don't have a decent picture of me. The woman eyewitness giving a hysterical report seems to think the central protagonist in this conflagration is her little dog, who pants into the camera quite cheerily. Poor lady was tied to the victim as he was being graphically dispatched. For effect, they get a shot of Spider's cracked open rollerblade helmet, caked with maroon blood and hair.

Ho appends, "This sort of thing going on in Oakland is one thing, but when it happens in the *Financial District*! Gasp! My God, this man was even white! *Bankers* heard the shots!"

"Ho, I'm not feeling particularly political right now."

"Sorry."

I'm sitting naked beneath a giant down comforter, thinking, *Rudiger Spinkleman?* Spider's real name was *Rudiger Spinkleman*? I haven't taken a shower yet. Wily, always attracted to skank, lays his face on the arm of my chair and licks the crust from my hand. Ho is pacing in circles, blue pigtails bobbing.

Ho is wearing striking kewpie doll clothes: a Little Red Riding Hood dress, a matching bow in her hair, a Band-Aid on her bare knee, knee socks rumpled at the ankles—complete with round red circles painted on her cheeks like two Japanese flags. Crucifix necklace.

I whimper, "How did they draw that trippy composite of me? They must have thought the foam coming out of my mouth was a white beard. That's the only explanation I can think of."

"How about this?"

Ho runs her finger across my cheek and holds it in front of my eyes. It's white with clown makeup. I stand up, clutching the blanket around me, and look in Ho's mirror. My face is entirely covered with a white flour, except for a sunglasses-shaped clean spot going around my eyes: the spurt of dust from the pulverized tile. That bullet was meant to atomize my skull, not Dr. Chen's tilework. I look like a photographic negative of Spider-Man.

Ho peels open another Band-Aid and sits me back down. She pushes the blanket up my leg and begins to apply the tiny compress to one of the many glass cuts on the back of my legs. It's not until she's this close that I spot the teeny-weeny skull earrings. Daisy perfume.

Ho licks her fingers and spreads the tape along the back of my knee. Then she sits across from me and mommy-stares at me for a while. She leans back in her chair and crosses her feet on the couch next to my hip. Her teeny toes are visible through her clear-plastic jellies, and each black toenail is painted with a little white skull and crossbones.

As a separate story, the news stiffs expound on the Chinese restaurant "and the entire empty building above it" being the victim of arson. There is no mention of Chen's huge operation, nor the construction that was going on. The newswoman concludes with a two-sentence editorial about the dangers of youngsters burning down abandoned buildings for kicks, "and the innocent people whose lives they destroy." Shot of the weeping restaurant couple, whose business Chen probably financed as a front for his criminal dealings.

I'm, like, hysterical. "It happened one fucking block and

two hours from Spider's murder, and they don't suggest a connection?!"

The next news story talks about the BART train being hijacked and vandalized by a large businessman. There is no artist's depiction. Nor is there any mention of his steaming mangled corpse being ground into hamburger beneath the wheels of the train. I think I would feel much better if I knew that monstrosity was pulverized to dust. I fear him more than I fear the whole Chinese mafia.

"Dammit!" I detonate. "What the bejesus was in that envelope? Why would they kill us over it?"

I can see the gears in Ho's mind crank into Dickette Tracy mode.

"Well, what do they normally put in your envelopes?"

I shrug. "Mel seals the packages. The Italian palookas tried to kill me because the seal on our package was missing."

"You *knew* the stuff you were delivering was illegal! Don't you check to make sure the seal is secure before you deliver the package?"

"I—well, no."

"Are you insane?"

"Ho, I left my sanity on the corner of Market and Fifth next to Spider's twitching tongue."

She shivers. "Don't remind me. I mean, it sounds like he was an asshole and everything, but nobody is that much of an asshole."

I try to hide my face behind the blanket. "He wasn't so bad."

Despite the seemingly superhuman means by which I continually averted disaster today—most of which I cannot even remember—I am having severe trouble with my self-esteem this afternoon. I've realized that my sanity, constructed block by block over my relatively privileged and nonmurderous life, has held up to this crisis tornado like a house built of toothpicks. I have entirely regressed. I'm practically sucking my thumb.

"I've changed my mind," I declare. "I don't want the ultimate rush. I want safety. I want peace. I want boredom. I want to get thrilled over herbal teas and cozy wool socks like Marin people. Dammit, I want my mommy."

"Chet, you can't just hide here forever."

I cuddle my blankie closer to my chin, sniffle.

"You have to go to the police," she says.

I put my face in my hands. I cannot deal with seeing another street right now. They're out there. They own the streets.

Ho scrunches down next to me and puts her arm around my shoulders. "C'mon, bud. We'll wait til tomorrow. You can crash here, we can rise and shine, scarf a big bowl of Corn Pops, and then head to the police station and give a long report. Maybe they'll send a bodyguard to your home. The worst is over."

I sigh. I repeat that in my mind. The worst is over.

Ho gives me a little squeeze and purses her lips. "Sweetie? How long has it been since you've had sugar?"

"Hours," I whimper.

"Awwwwww. I'll give you a sugar bag and a spoon. You can melt it down and mainline it if you want to. Okay, my little honey bun? With emphasis on the honey?"

I stick out my lower lip and nod.

Ho slaps my Emerson tattoo in the face and stands. "First you have to take a shower, Mr. Stinkoid. While you're doing that, I'm going to strain against every fiber of my militant feminist being and walk your stuff down to the laundromat. This shirt of yours is pretty shot. I didn't know you were a Metallica fan."

Ho lifts something with a stick.

"I'm just going to chuck your socks, okay? They smell like piss or something."

"Uuuuuuuuh . . . okay."

"And I swear your hair smells like egg foo yung."

Ho throws all my stuff into her laundry basket, then stands behind me and massages my crinked neck. "So explain to me again how he sat on your head?"

I prance out of the shower pink and clean, then call Denny's number, just to make sure he left.

"Home of the Motorized Stud."

"You're there?!"

"Hell yeah, I'm here."

"What the f—"

"Yo, check this out, man: The cops have yellow-taped your room off. They're claiming it as evidence."

"The cops? Evidence?"

"Judging from the line of their interrogation, they want you for murdering that Spider-Man dude."

"Me?! Murder?!"

"They're not exactly subtle. You should have seen this one flatfoot—"

"Wait! They interrogated you?"

"Elana was here. She pretended to be my caretaker, gave them the sob story about how I can't talk. They figured I was retarded and harmless. Gave everybody on the floor the lightbulb-in-the-face third degree except me. You should have seen their faces when they come barging through the bathroom and see me in my wheelchair! Thought they had a connection to someone they could question, and instead they just find little old me, poor drooling retard in a wheelchair who talks funny. I just moaned and let Elana do all the talking. She said she didn't know you."

"But wait! This is impossible! How could they think it was me? The news just said they were trying to kill me!"

"That was the five o'clock news. The seven o'clock news just said you went on a shooting spree in the Financial District."

I drop my towel and sink to the floor. "Oh, my God . . ."

"I don't know, maybe they got the networks paid off or something. But listen up, dude, you got to go in and explain everything to them. The longer you wait, the more it looks like you're a fugitive. If you just walk in and tell them the truth, they'll investigate. They might hold you for a while, but they'll figure everything out. You'll be safe with the cops. I'm sure that Chin guy—"

"Chen."

"Whatever. I'm sure they know who he is. He's the one who did it, right?"

"Right."

"He's a fucking drug dealer. He's got to be. Just don't let them give you that lie-detector test. Every good techie knows them things don't work. And we're both good techies."

"But Denny, man, I can't afford some lawyer."

"Just go in thinking witness, not suspect. Tell them you heard you were a suspect, and you came in of your own free will to explain things. They won't bust you."

"Okay. Me and Ho are going to see them tomorrow."

"Okay, blood. I'm looking forward to you getting back here so I can make fun of your pussylessness again."

I crack a smile. "All right, man. Catch you later."

"Peace."

I hang up, stand, and pull out Ho's foldout couch. Wily starts to get excited, and then I hear Ho unlocking the door. I quickly bury my naked body in the bed.

When she comes back in, carrying my folded clothes, I pretend I'm asleep.

My eyes pop like Pop-Tarts out of the toaster of my skull when I see my pretty mug on the *front page*! I get down on one knee and peer through the newspaper-machine glass.

BIKE MESSENGER KILLED

San Francisco—The man suspected of shooting and killing a bike messenger at Market and 5th at 9:15 yesterday morning is still at large, police said.

The San Francisco Coroner's Office identified the victim as Rudiger Spinkleman, 22, who suffered three gunshot wounds to the head. He lived in the Mission District with his common-law wife and their 2-year-old daughter.

Police say Spinkleman was in-line skating when another messenger on in-line skates allegedly shot him.

Police have identified the suspect as Chet Griffin, 22, who fled the scene.

Griffin has a previous criminal record for computer crimes. "Cybercrime leads to real crime, even murder," said Detective Dick Gambill, head of the Federal Computer Investigations Committee. "The digital underground is the only place where one frustrated young male can terrorize an entire corporation."

"Griffin is a weird person," said a neighbor. "He paints his apartment black and writes on the walls in his own blood. He's covered with scary
KILLING Page A11 Col. 1

That's all I can see. Fortunately, the picture is a blowup of a courier group shot taken by some journalism student a few months ago, so my face is all pixelated and fuzzy.

If I had a subscription, I'd cancel it. One thing that sucks about being broke, you can't boycott anything.

I put my bologna and molasses sandwich down next to my skates and reach into the small of my back to tangle up the loose threads of my shredded Metallica T-shirt. The rip in the back has gotten much bigger since Ho washed it. Looks kind of fresh, actually.

"C'mon, Barnacle!" Ho jumps on her skateboard, spurs it like a horse named something like Shadowhawk. "To the police station!"

She rips a full-blown gnarly grinder along the curb, verts a streetstyle handplant, and hits ground zero. Damn.

"Back off, suckers!" she shouts, copping an Elvis karate stance. "Megabitch is in an ass-kicking mood!"

Ho likes to pretend she's this superheroine named Megabitch. Megabitch is supposedly the ringleader of some feminist alternative to the Justice League—you know, all those superheros like Superman and Batman and the top-heavy bimbos who pass as superchicks. Well, Ho has this whole fantasy world of hairy superdykes named the Itty Bitty Titty Committee, who kick the testosterone out of Evil Sexist Oinkers. Ever since I informed her that this was an insult to the great and noble Justice League, she's been giving all her arch-villains names like: MiniChet and the Griffin and Chetsterino. Don't ask me. It's a Ho thing.

"Stand back, criminals! Megabitch is in your face! Come, sidekick! We must confer with Commissioner Gordon!"

She takes off.

I call after her, "I appreciate your enthusiasm, Megadork, but the cop stop is thisaway."

She does a totally cool triple roundabout that is, like all things totally cool, totally unnecessary. She zips straight at me, dodges me at the last second, and flattens my sandwich lying innocently on 'crete.

The Ho motif for today is: man. She's wearing guys' jeans with a wide black studded belt. Her jeans sport a worn white square on the back pocket where one would keep a wallet or a hip flask. She's wearing a black T-shirt with the sleeves rolled up her shoulders as if they are holding ciggie packs. Keys hanging on a chain. Her blue hair is microbraided straight back from her forehead all the way down between her shoulder blades, emphasizing the shaved sides. On her bare shoulder is a lick-on child's tattoo of a butterfly.

"How does a law-abiding citizen like you know where the five-oh station is? Are you a narc?"

"No. I make deliveries there all the time."

As we skate by my bank, I'm all, "Let me get some cash out of my ATM."

"Do you have to do it now?"

"I'm going to need all the money I can get. I might need to get a lawyer or something."

Ho pulls a G-turn, ollies the curb, mute-grabs her board, and stands with her hands on her hips. I rocker into a pivot roll and topspin at the ATM. There is no line. I stick my card in, punch out my code. It asks me for my code again. I punch it out.

Invalid account. Consult your branch manager.

"It ate my card."

Ho steps up, reads the message.

"I never closed my account," I say.

"Sounds like somebody else did," she says.

Ho tailspins a triple three-sixty with a one-eighty tagged on the end of it to face her the opposite direction. Wow, man. A twelve-sixty. I would go so far as to rate it of hyperfresh caliber.

Of course, I have to act like I see twelve-sixties all the time.

"Shouldn't we go check this out?" I go.

"Chet, right now you are a murder suspect. Let's talk to the cops, then you can settle your bank problems."

She starts to goofy-foot off. I stare at the message, which keeps blinking at me.

"This is getting too weird."

We leap into the bustle of the cop station—phones ringing, papers shuffling, hookers complaining, and a flurry of other activities generally useless to society. We all complain about cops, but, when the chips are down, *damn* if they ain't the first people we run to.

"Remember, Ho. No donut jokes."

"Do you think I'm stupid?"

"Ouch."

"What?"

"I just bit my tongue trying not to answer that."

Ho becomes possessed by a spasm of the willies.

"Whatsamatter?"

"Would you please not talk about bitten tongues?"

"Oh. Sorry."

She punches my arm. We are directed to a long desk where citizens make reports. The receiving cop with her top button buttoned looks at our attire, cops attitude, and snorts, "Can I help you?"

"Yes," says Ho, officiously snapping her plank into her armpit. "We'd like to see the chief please."

"Do you have an appointment?"

"No, we sure don't, ma'am," says Ho of the Blue Hair. "But this concerns yesterday's shooting and the Chinese mafia here in San Francisco, and we'd like to speak to somebody in charge."

This raises the cop's eyebrows. She leans forward and motions us closer. Me and Ho glance at each other, shrug, and lean across the desk. She murmurs, "Okay, I'm going to refer you to the Organized Crime Task Force. They work cross-jurisdiction and have especially assigned themselves to this case. Come with me."

A citizen sitting on the bench shouts, "Hey! I've been waiting to make this domestic violence report for an hour!"

The other benchwarmers look up with scowls of moral outrage worthy of Mario Savio.

"You'll just have to wait!" shouts the cop. She gestures to a nearby dude who looks like a homeless guy or a druggie or a Ho friend: a plain-clothes cop who seems to be doing nothing but waiting for us to arrive. Me and Ho are escorted across the station.

Ho grins as we march. "See what a little assertiveness can do?"

"Ho, tie down that take-charge personality for once! *I'm* the witness here! *I* get to do the talking! You weren't even shot at!"

"Oh, now you think you've out-badassed yourself just because you were stupid enough to get shot at?"

"You got to admit, it *is* something to boast about. Just think, for the rest of my life, I get to tell people I've been shot at. You can't get much more totally fly than that."

"Unless you've been to prison."

"Bite your tongue. I'm fly enou—"

"Ick! Dammit, Chet! Would you stop it?!"

"Oop! Sorry."

We arrive at a glassed-in office wherein blusters a huddle of detectives surrounding a desk. The grungy plain-clothes cop swings open the door and hustles us inside. I can hear the voice of an unseen woman firing orders. She must be seated at the desk.

A burly cop detaches himself from the powwow and steps forward. The plain-clothes cop announces, "More witnesses to the shooting in the Financial District, Sergeant," and quickly exits, making a point of shutting the door behind him.

"Terrific," says the Sergeant, folding his hairy arms. "Another one. Look, folks, we know it ain't the Chinese mafia, or the Italian mafia, or the Eskimo mafia! Okay? So if you've come here to talk mafia, we already got everything under control!"

The guy is putting on such an obvious performance, I get caught up in the act. "Well, officer," I say, putting my fists on my hips like Superman, "you may have heard the name . . . Chet Griffin!"

"Yeah, so?"

My shoulders slump. I expected him to at least gasp or something.

Ho steps forward. "Well, let's just say he's a close personal friend of ours. And *that*—" she detonates, pointing dramatically to a sketch on the wall of some alien with a bowl haircut, bug eyes, and white beard "—is definitely *not* him!"

I scowl at her. Ho is enjoying this just a bit too much.

The sergeant's hubristic smirk deflates, and he abruptly whistles to his colleagues. The council stops deliberating and looks his way. The sergeant circles his finger over his head and points out the door. Most of the standing cops obediently exit, leaving only the seated woman and two cops hovering against the wall like Buckingham Palace guards.

"Lieutenant?" the sergeant calls. "I think you'd like to talk to these folks here."

"I don't want to hear another mafia report, Sergeant," grumbles the lady cop, shuffling some ubiquitous paperwork. "You're in charge of that."

"They're personally acquainted with the suspect."

Her face gains gravity like a gargoyle who hates incense. "All right, Sergeant, you know the drill. Privacy please."

The sergeant waddles out the door and closes it behind him.

Me and Ho are left standing in silence, alone with the Great Pooh-bah High Grand Wizard Chief Bigums Lieutenant of the Organized Task Force or whatever. The two overhanging cops stare like the statues of Eastern gods.

The lieutenant studies us. She wears thick eyeliner and looks somehow familiar, as if she's dressed in drag.

"Come around here. You first."

She stands and motions me around the desk. I obey, feeling uncomfortable because it looks like noncops aren't normally allowed back here. The two hovering cops stand by the exit. The lieutenant turns her back to Ho and leans her bountiful hams against the desk. She has me stand opposite her. Over her shoulder, I can see Ho frantically gesturing to me. I ignore her.

"Don't I have to fill out a report or something?"

"Just tell me everything you know about Chet Griffin."

Behind her, Ho is having an epileptic fit: pointing, rolling her eyes, her hands fluttering mothlike about her face. It's quite distracting and annoying. Did I mention tongues again? When I glance at her, she is feverishly pointing above her left breast. The two hovering cops step closer to her.

"I'm glad you're taking such a personal interest in this, officer. I always thought that five-ohs—I mean, uh, officers of the law—get a lame rep when it comes to people my age. For instance, the Rodney King and O.J. debacles in no way typify—"

She waves my words away as if they're gnats at her face. "Where is Chet Griffin right now?"

I laugh. "Well, actually, ma'am—"

Finally, I see what Ho is spazzing about. The lieutenant's badge. I take a look.

Gina Corlini.

No . . . it's a coincidence.

But wait. When Mel gave me the promotion—the person he hung up on—wasn't her name Gina?

"I want to report a rash of flashers, ma'am."

"Flashers?"

"Yes! Many, many flashers! The kind with overcoats! I think there's a gang of them, officer, and they frequent the Castro!"

This does not exactly thaw the frozen tundra of her face.

"What does this have to do with the murder in the Financial District?" she demands.

"Well . . . well! That's because I think the flashers did it, ma'am. You see—"

"I notice you're wearing rollerblades." Her eyes bore into mine. They are the eyes of Mel Corlini. "Did you have any association with Chet Griffin?"

Without taking my eyes off hers, I begin circling around her desk. "Chet who? Oh! Did *he* have rollerblades? How interesting! A rollerblading flasher! It doesn't surprise me, considering rollerblades are so immensely popular in the city these days! Have you noticed?"

I complete my half-circle and my shoulder strikes Ho's. We both smile widely at Gina Corlini. She looks at us—a blue-haired nose-ringed chick and a tattoo punk with a ripped shirt—and I realize my tactic has worked. She has decided we are a pair of loons.

"Look, talk to Officer Benjamin," she sighs. "Cubicle four. He handles these kinds of reports. I don't have time for this kind of crap right now."

"Sorry to waste your time!"

I reach for Ho's arm, but she is already backing up and firing Ho-smiles. Gina Corlini actually gets up and follows us, her eyes never leaving mine. Me and Ho walk backwards across the room, smiling and bowing. We bump into the two zombie cops, apologize profusely, then keep backpedaling. We nearly sandwich ourselves in the doorway of the glass cubicle, then turn our backs and hurry across the cops-and-robbers ticker-tape party towards the front door.

Gina Corlini turns to the sergeant to scold him for not handling a pair of nitwits who've never seen flashers in the Castro before. As the sergeant starts to make excuses, Gina calls, "Hey, kids! Cubicle four is that way! Right next to—"

She never finishes her sentence. I look over my shoulder. Gina Corlini's eyes are focused on my back—on the hole in my ripped shirt. Her eyes narrow as her face hardens to Mount Rushmore status. Then she snatches up a police radio.

We turn and scramble out into the sunlight. Ho clatters on

her board. We both take the cement steps on one simultaneous leap, hit the 'vard, and totally aggro. We instinctively gun towards a crowd, skate through a duckling line of crosswalk children. We slice a tight corner and begin to plow. I'm trying to think up a reasonable course of action, then Ho psycho-berts to a stop and yells: "Here! Here! Here!" I look over my shoulder. She's feverishly waving me over. She's standing at the tail end of a three-person line to board a bus. I compress into a pivot roll turn and get behind her. She's shoveling me change.

"Ho! We haven't got far enough from the cop station yet!"

"We get on the bus, we're home free! Just duck down beneath the windows!"

Ho climbs on and inserts her change. I'm so busy looking over my shoulder, my toe wheel catches on the tall step. I fall forward and beefaroni my shin.

"Aaaargh!" I scream. Every passenger is ogling at me with concerned looks, except the bus driver, who rolls his eyes.

Looking down at my boo-boo, I see pizza. A good four-inch section of my skin has peeled upwards and bunched into a doughy ball beneath my knee.

"*Chet!*" shrieks Ho, registering nil on the empathyometer. "*Get on the fucking bus!*" Then she abruptly smiles at the passengers.

I climb on, still looking over my shoulder, and insert the change. The bus door folds shut at my heels and the bus begins to rumble along. I limp down the aisle. Ho grabs me and pulls me down beneath the windows.

"Jesus!" she harshes in my ear. "I thought couriers were fast!"

"But it really hurts! A lot! Look! Blood!"

"You and your damn tattoos! Why don't you just paint *I killed Spider* on your forehead?"

I peek over the lip of the window as the corner we just came from fades off.

Never saw a five-oh. Damn. In an emergency, gangstas sure are more efficient than lawmen.

* * *

Pacing back and forth, I'm wearing a path into Ho's peeling linoleum. Ho is following me with every step.

"See?" I shout. "You can't trust authority! They're in on it! I have to deal with this alone!"

"Why don't we just call some higher-ups on the cop totem pole?" Ho suggests. "The FBI or something."

"No! Didn't you see all those other cops hovering around? They're *all* in on it! We can't trust *any* of them!"

"Chet, just because one top cop is related to one of the criminals doesn't mean the whole police force is—"

"Forget it, Ho. I turn myself in, that Gina Corlini will have me whacked."

"I thought you said people trying to kill you is totally fly? Now the mafia *and* the cops are trying to kill you!"

"Ho, *having been* shot at is always fly! But *getting* shot at totally sucks! I don't want to be cool anymore! I want to be boring! Oh God, Ho, I don't even have insurance!"

She clamps her arms around my shoulders and squeezes, stopping my pacing. "Okay, honey, relax! We can figure this out!"

"What was in that package? What the hell was in it?"

Ho makes a steeple with her hands and rests her nose on the tippy-top. Ho is dealing about as well as a blackjack man in Vegas. "So now we can't employ the help of the law," she considers in a Walter Cronkite monotone. "We have to find a way out of this ourselves. Do we have any proof of anything?"

I am touched that Ho continually uses the pronoun *we*.

"She's related to Mel. I know she is. She's probably his sister."

"Being related to a stock criminal is not a crime. Besides, we have no proof of anything. We can't even prove that somebody else shot Spider. The media seems to be confirming that you did it."

I'm starting to panic. Everybody is against me. "If only I could get one of those packages in my hands, I could see what they were delivering. Then I would know why I'm hiding."

"Maybe you could contact one of your courier friends, get him to let you look inside one."

"*Friends?* My courier friends hate rollerfags, especially now that the TV is saying I killed Spider. Besides, Mel has these special seals he sticks over the opening of the envelope. If Chen sees a broken seal, he goes into *code red*, and we get more murder and arson." I sigh. "It's no use. I'm shut out from the circle. I can't get my hands on a package, and I can't open it anyway without setting off violence. They have a fool-proof system. There's no way . . . no way . . ." I look at Ho. "Unless—"

"Unless, what?"

"Never mind."

"C'mon. We should consider everything."

"It's insane."

"Really. Tell me."

I look at her. She is staring back at me eagerly, as if she half suspects what I am about to suggest.

"I have a plan."

I **walk** fourteen miles without ever leaving Ho's fifteen-by-twenty apartment. When Ho finally rolls in all sweaty, I pounce on her and grab her by her bare shoulders.

"Whoa!"

"What did they say? What did they say?"

"They said, 'Ooo. A chick. We don't get chicks around here much.' Then they scoped my butt."

"What did you say to Mel?"

"I said, 'I heard on the news somebody here got killed, so I figured you had an opening.' "

"Oh, my God!! You told him that?! You fool! What did he say? Did he try to kill you? I hope you didn't try to escape on a BART train—"

"He said, 'I like your attitude. You're hired. Deliver this to Mission and Seventh.' " She pulls out her water bottle and guzzles, dripping tiny clear snakes down her neck.

"He let you skip to the front of the line?!"

"Yeah. Like I said, they don't get chicks there very often."

"Okay, okay," I go, hyperventilating. "So now we have to figure out a way to get you my old special delivery job."

She yanks off her shades and helmet. Her damp hair cascades over her shoulders like a grape juice Niagara. "Don't waste that limited brainpower. I already got it."

"How?"

"I just told him about how skateboards are way faster than blades, and if it was me being chased by that bullet, the bullet would have lost."

"You—"

"So now, after one o'clock, he's got me training one of the other roids there how to surf a plank. Skateboards are the new technology now. He wants two of us."

I don't want to show how impressed I am with her espionage, so I just nod thoughtfully.

She slaps me on the shoulder. "Breathe into a paper bag or something, okay?" She yanks open the fridge and points her butt at me. "What's to eat?"

Before dawn the next morning, I wake up, jack myself off fantasizing about holding Ho's nipples to the open fridge, and meet Denny at Datavox before it opens.

A voice from the dark: "What's up, Unabomber?"

I pull off my hood and sunglasses as Denny flicks on the overhead and wheels out enough hardware to take over a small cybernetic nation. I gawk at the wiretaps, laptop, printer, code busters, phone phreaking equipment, and lots of other jury-rigged contraptions and punch-pads made from parts that must have once belonged to Pacific Bell.

Strings of slaver drip from my chin. For a hacker, this is equivalent to putting away your sword and shining armor and dudding yourself up with an AK-47 with a laser sight beam, infrared glasses, radar headphones, and a bulletproof grenade vest. As of now, I am the Terminator of the Underground. For a moment, I forget the threat of death and quiver and drool over all this illegal hacker booty.

This is not exactly doing wonders to help me kick my addiction.

"Hey, Denny, this isn't just legit programmer stuff. It's hacking stuff. Where'd you score it?"

"From some busted computer cracker. It just sits in a closet now."

"It just *sits* here?"

"Yup."

"Soooo," I snivel like Renfield, "if nobody wants it, why don't you just let me keep it?"

Denny sighs.

"C'mon, man!" I foam greedily. "You Datavox slugs can't use this secret-agent hardware!"

"Chet, I'm trying to help you hack into Mel's systems. I'm putting my ass on the line by aiding and abetting a murder suspect who happens to be my bud. If you don't want the stuff—"

"I want the stuff! I want the stuff!" I shout, hugging the pile and kissing it.

"I knew that would work."

"Denny, there's one more thing I need."

"I'm afraid to guess."

"Can I snark your old ham radio?"

"Chet!"

"C'mon, man! It's key!"

"Okay," he grumbles. "Let me see if we have one back here. If not, I guess we can pick mine up at my place."

Denny wheelies around and heads for the next room. To my shock, another figure emerges in front of him. The guy's head looks like a tarantula. I thought we were alone.

"Hey, Quentin," says Denny to the rasta man. "What are you doing here so early?"

"Wassup, Den. Doing a little private programming before we open up shop."

Denny leaves me alone with the dude, who starts shuffling through a pile of programming manuals. I feel uncomfortable, so I strike up an exchange.

"I can't believe you guys have this illegal shit laying around."

Tentacle Head looks at the cart of ill-gotten plunder and brushes a hanging cattail out of his face. "No biggie. Our boss is too dorkulated to know what it is."

"So you guys don't care if I borrow it?"

He shrugs. "No prob."

"Man, I'm so stoked! I should apply for a job here."

Quentin snorts. "Why? The pay sucks."

I snort back. "Yeah, right."

"I make a little less than a good poet."

Denny emerges. "Can't you buy one?" he asks.

"Den, I have eleven dollars and some change. That's it."

Denny uses my boasts against me. "What about that five hundred you made Monday? Plus that two hundred you made Tuesday? Plus the one-fifty you made Wednesday?"

"The first five hundred is still locked in my room, assuming the cops haven't found my secret hiding spot and confiscated it. I can't get access to the two hundred or so in my savings account. Jesus, it just hit me that for the first time in my life, I have broken the great one-thousand mark for total dollars possessed at any one moment. This is the most money I've ever had in my life, and I can't get any of it."

"What about that other three-fifty cash?"

"The other three-fifty I gave to Ho today."

"Why?"

Monday morning. Ho and I are standing at the toes of Watermelon Hill. The sun scrutinizes me like a cyclops. I secure my sunglasses, brown wig, and beard. Ho has lent me some of her friends' baggy skate clothes. I look at my reflection in the side-mirror of a parked car.

"Jesus. I look like I'm going out for Halloween as Rick Rubin."

"Relax, Rick," says Ho, looking way cute in her Cabbage Patch overalls. Her lollipop-blue hair is so poofy today, she looks like one of those sexless trolls you hang from your rearview mirror. "We had to cover up your tattoos. Even I don't recognize you."

"Everyone can tell this is a costume! Couldn't you have bought something more expensive?"

"We had to use that money for the rent on this place."

"Are you sure you rented the right place?"

"Is a bear catholic? Here comes the trolley."

The cable car I take every day stops in front of us. I find my sneakers are cemented to the street. Ho pushes me up on to the car, pays, and we sit. Behind my sunglasses, I scrutinize every face in the car, each of which has quite obviously recognized me and is now pretending to be casually reading a paper or looking at the passing view. The only part of my face exposed to the air is the tip of my nose. I have a very distinctive nose tip. There's a blackhead on it. I know somebody will recognize me because of it.

Ho, to steady me, reaches over and holds my hand. She pats my forearm.

Chink, chink, chink. The cable car carries me closer to Mel's building. We pass several bike messengers grinding up the hill. One of them actually hangs on the back, the driver shouts for him to let go, and he obeys. Even back in the days when I was maddened to get back to the top to make another delivery, this trolley ride never seemed so long.

"We're getting too close!" I whisper. "Let's get out here!"

"If we get out here, we just have to walk a block to the apartment. Let's get out right at the front door."

My world starts to spin as I see Mel's building loom ahead. Out front, a coterie of couriers are locking their bikes to the bike rack. The cable car stops at the building next door, and me and Ho climb out and hit sidewalk.

I stop dead in my tracks.

I am face-to-face with a sweating bike messenger named Vogue standing without his bicycle and gulping from his water bottle.

He pulls off his headphones and says to Ho, "Hey, what's going on, homegirl?"

"Hey, Vogie. Doing lunch?"

"Yeah. Want to come?"

"No thanks, bro. Just finished my lunch break. Catch you later."

"A'ight. Peace."

Vogue yanks off his sunglasses and stares directly into my face. From his headphones issue the sounds of a thousand gnats crashing cymbals. He turns to the cable car man.

"This takes me to the Gentle Delicatessen, right?"

"Yep. Climb aboard."

Vogue is gone. I'm standing still like a mummy. Ho grabs my arm and drags me up the sidewalk.

"See?" she whispers. "You might as well be invisible."

" 'Hey, girl'? 'Hey, Vogie'? How come they hate bladers, but they don't hate boarders?"

"They do hate boarders. With a passion. But I'm a chick."

"Oh."

Ho drags me up the steps of the building next to Mel's place.

"Is it month-to-month?"

"Yes!"

"Does it have a phone jack?"

"Yes!"

"Did you get a room on the north side?"

"Look, Chet. I took care of my shit. You just worry about this cockamamie plan of yours."

She unlocks the front door and leads me up four flights of rickety stairs. There is no elevator. This slum is held together with staples and paper clips. There is actually a warning sign about water damage where the floor might fall through. We emerge onto the third floor and walk down a crusty hallway where every apartment door is wide open and empty. Ho takes me to the only closed door at the end of the hall and inserts the key.

It opens. We step in and she shuts the door behind us. I quickly pull down the shoddy window blinds before I yank off my wig and beard.

There is water damage all over the walls and floor. I can hear the drip of a leaky pipe. A skankified couch, disemboweled lounge chair, and mildewy mattress stain an already scummy scene.

Ho's like, "It's only three-fifty month-to-month because this whole floor has been condemned. The landlord is renting this to us illegally. But we still get electricity."

I pull open a three-foot steel flap in the wall. "A laundry chute?"

"I guess this building must have had a laundry service at some time."

"Great. Now everybody in the building is going to hear what we say in here."

Ho fakes a smile and says, "I got to go to work now. The

PG&E and phone guys will be here late this afternoon. I should be back by then. Afterwards, I'll borrow the Spit van and move all your technoid stuff here. Then I'll drag my bed in here. Guess you'll just have to hang."

"Don't forget to open that safe-deposit box!"

"I already did," she smiles. She takes a step towards the door.

"And my comic books!" I shriek. "And some sugar!"

She comes back, wraps an arm around my shoulders, whispers in my ear, "It's going to be okay," and places an extra key in my hand. Before I can react, she's out the door. She locks me in.

Reaching new heights of paranoia, I stay in the closet when the PG&E and phone guys arrive and hook us up with electricity and a phone, both in Ho's name. After they leave, Ho taunts me for being a chickenshit and then calls her bandmates. Practice is canceled because Chugger, the drummer, has to work late at his day job knitting baby booties. (*Cutesy Boots* was cleaned out after the first lady gave a speech about barefooted orphans.) Me and Ho have nothing to do but wait until nightfall, when Chickenshit Chet plans to sneak over to Mel's to perform a commando operation.

"Chet, what's your most luscious sexual fantasy?"

"To go on a date."

Me and Ho are sitting by the back window, sipping sodas from crazy straws and scoping chicks. The roll-down blinds are only open a tiny bit. Nobody can see in. We are leaning on our forearms against the sill like Charlie Brown and Linus on their brick wall. We're playing the Meters on Ho's box. My kind of funk.

"C'mon, don't give me that self-deprecatory bullshit. It's very un-Chetish. If I was a guy, you'd have one on the tip of your tongue and spit it out with much relish."

"And mustard. And Tabasco sauce. And whipped cream,"

"And don't forget those long warty kosher pickles. C'mon, Chet. We're buds, ain't we? We both dig chicks. Let's hear it. Just pretend I'm a guy."

Great. Just what I want to do. I keep looking out the window.

"C'maaaaaaaaan, Chet! What's your wettest, juiciest, most flesh-slapping sexual fantasy?"

"To dry-fuck Catwoman while swinging from a chandelier over the president's desk."

"I mean a fantasy about somebody real. Somebody we both know."

My eyes fall lingeringly on Ho. She catches me looking, and I quickly look away.

"Funny," I murmur. "I can't think of one."

"Oo! Oo! Oo!" erupts Ho, poking my shoulder and pointing. "Check out that Eurotrash honey! Now *that's* fine!"

I sip my spritzer and shake my head. "Nope. Not my type. No vampire girls for me."

Ho twists open another bottle, flexing her forearms in a red plaid flannel shirt and worn jeans that a lumberjack in a Marlboro ad would have been proud to wear.

"How about that black goddess?"

I nod. "I like the way she carries herself. She has a sort of a—Oo! Oo! Oo!"

"What? What? What?"

"Check out the blonde walking the dog!"

"*Ernt!*" squirts Ho like a gameshow buzzer. "Negatory."

"Ultra-sex-kitten! She wants me so bad!"

"Ak! Ak!" Ho sticks her finger down her throat. "Bleach job!"

"You should talk. Wait! She's turning her back! C'mon, baby . . . come ooooon . . . yes! Look at her go!"

"Okay, I admit she's got good booty."

"She's got stellar booty. I could chew that like gum."

Ho looks at me. "You like firm butts, don't you?"

I shrug. Then nod.

"Like mine?" she asks.

I stare at her. She is smiling at me coquettishly. We both laugh, and she sips her soda.

"It's just that I've gotten a lot of comments on it," she says dismissively.

"From dudes or chicks?"

"Both. Well, you know, catcalls from pigs, but some women will get to know you well enough to point it out. Even straight women will."

I can't let the statement pass. She's fishing, so I bite. "Well, they should. 'Cause you do got a nice butt."

She doesn't look at me. I don't look at her. We both keep staring at the strangers.

After a long minute, Ho smiles to herself.

"What?" I say.

"You know, you're the only straight guy I'd let get away with saying that."

Irritation flares at the back of my neck. Her words touch off a long string of issue beads I didn't know I'd been connecting. "Ho, if you're bi, what's with all this lesbian lingo?"

"You call *that* lesbian lingo?"

"Which group are you identifying yourself with?"

"Jesus! Why do I have to politicize my sexuality?"

"But if you *call* yourself gay—"

"There's no such thing as being straight or gay. Sex is an act, not an identity. When I'm with Megan, I'm loving her. When I'm with a guy, I'm loving him. Right now, I'm talking to you, so I don't have a sexual identity. I'm just a person."

"So you're bi."

"Look, why do you have to put me in some box? I'm not gay. I'm not bi. I'm Ho."

"So when you're talking to me, you have no sexuality at all. I get it now."

"Hey, you've orchestrated your whole life to defy all these categories, so why do you have to put me in one?"

"So you're saying I'm limited because I'm straight?"

"I love masculine energy. I love feminine energy. I just love sexual energy, Chet. I like it best when a person has both."

Ouch. I didn't know I could get hurt in that spot. And as a straight white male, I haven't developed any calluses there. "*I* don't have both."

"Yes, you do. Or at least you could if you let up on the

macho trip. Just try and bring out some of that feminine energy in you."

"Sure. I'll get right on it."

"Wear a skirt. Switch that black nail polish to pink."

"But clothes aren't what you're talking about."

"Try nurturing. Get a pet or something. Start *somewhere,* for Christ's sake."

"I already got a snake."

"That's not a pet. That's an emblem."

"He needs *lots* of nurturing!"

"It only needs to be fed twice a month! You can go weeks without touching it, and it doesn't even care! Typical for you to find the most low-maintenance pet in creation!"

"Excuse me if I don't want some slobbering beast smearing his funk all over my shit."

"Okay, forget the pet idea. *You're* a teddy bear sometimes. Be that. Forget daddy's ghost." Then Ho flinches.

"Daddy's ghost?"

"Forget I said that."

"But he *hated* snakes!"

"I got to go."

"Go? Where?"

"We said Thai tonight, right? Well, Thaied Up closes in twenty minutes."

When Ho goes out to rustle us up some cheap pseudo-Thai food, I punch out Denny's number, UNI-8POG.

"You've reached the Den of Denny. How can I help you?"

"I don't believe this! I'm usually pretty aggressive with women, right? I mean, even a little assholish at times."

"I agree."

"So why can't I just seize Ho? Just *do it*! Why can't I?"

"Because you're a wuss?"

"I mean, sure, I don't want to jeopardize our friendship and all—"

"God forbid."

"But me and Ho are tight enough that we could survive

that. She'd just reject me, get pissed, get over it, and we'd be buds again."

"Of course. But, just for the record, Chet, *our* friendship definitely *would not* survive that, so if you're implying—"

"Of course, my timing would be pretty bad. I mean, 'Oh, like yeah, he waits until we're both on the run from atomic gangsters and mutant cops to throw a pass at me—' "

"Chet, I understand you're hard up and everything, but just make sure you wash your hands before you touch any of the computer gear I lent you."

"But I'm like constantly obsessing, 'What is she thinking? What are her intentions? Why is she risking her life for me?' She's so damn *mysterious*! It's driving me crazy!"

"You know what I think, Chet?"

"What?"

"You need to get laid."

"Yeah, the pope is Catholic, the sky is blue, you need a lobotomy—these are self-evident truths. I know it with Cartesian irrefutability: 'I am. Therefore I am horny.' "

"I notice there is no *I think* in this equation."

"You got to admit, she'd be great for me."

"Are you kidding? She's cute, intelligent, passionate, *com*-passionate, omnisexual, and she's got terrible taste in men. She's *perfect* for you!"

"But I'm not so sure I'd be much good for her."

"Sounds like that's your problem right there."

"What? Bad self-esteem?"

"No. An honest assessment of your own dweebhood."

"True, but Ho is not like any other woman. She's different."

"*That's* the understatement of the century."

"No, I mean she's different in a way I can't handle."

"Wow . . . I can't believe Chet Griffin is admitting this."

"I mean, not like how other guys can't handle her. I mean, this has more to do with handling *how I feel* about her than handling *her*. You know what I mean?"

"How you *feel* about her?"

"Well . . . yeah."

"Chet, does this have something to do with your mother?"

I watch one tiny dust mite skate down the thin golden sunbeam that eases through a hole in the window shades. I listen to water drip from the pipe leak.

"Chet?"

"I'm here."

"This is eerie. You've actually shut up for the first time in your life. Why aren't you talking?"

"You just made me realize something."

"What?"

"I can handle lust. I just can't handle love."

"Uh-oh."

When I step into our apartment and pull off my coat, wig, and beard, Ho throws her scissors down on a pile of pink ribbons and marches at me.

"Chet!" she yells. "The *point* of this plan is that you're not supposed to be seen outside this—What the *hell* is *that*?"

"What?"

"*That!*"

"What? You mean this?"

"No! Your muscle shirt!"

I cross my arms. "You're referring to my lipstick."

"Yes. The strawberry-flavored kind."

"Ho, there are many sides to my fashion sense that *you* are not aware of."

"Don't you think it clashes just a bit with your plaid boxer shorts sticking out of your saggy pants?"

"Excuse me if I challenge your preconceptions."

"Chet, that sugar lipstick is meant for grade-school girls who want to play grown-up."

"Oh, yeah, like how many grade-school kids shop at Safeway?"

Ho starts laughing.

"What? What's so funny? Oh, tell me your cross-dressing friends wouldn't sport a little rouge!"

"Well, they would. It's just that they have a sense of color."

"Oh, I understand! It's cool for your butch/femme androgeno-dykes, but it's not okay for narrow-minded Chet!

Okay. Fine." I start scrubbing it off with the front of my shirt.

Ho marches back to the table, grabs a package, and tosses it at me. I catch it.

"What's this?" My eyes light up. "A present?"

It's wrapped in black paper with a pink ribbon, à la Ho. Drooling, I rip it open, and find my present is wrapped in translucent spandex—no, it's a stretched-out non-lubricated condom.

"Cute," I say, and tear it open with my teeth. Whatever it is, it's pink. Oh no.

I hold it up. "A pink shirt," I go. "From El Salvador. With the woman symbol over the left tit. How thoughtful."

"Turn it around," she says.

" 'Soy Feminista'? What the hell is that? Some kind of tofu-eating brand of feminism?"

"No, brainiac. It says *I am a feminist, so don't fuck with me,* in Spanish. You are required to wear this shirt at least once a week—*and behave accordingly!* Just one day a week. That's all I'm asking you."

I smile. "Thanks."

When I hold it up to myself, Ho stifles a smile. "Who knows? If you start thinking chick, maybe you'll get all nurturing and shit."

"Girl, I nurture you plenty."

"I don't mean me. I mean yourself."

I huff and toss the shirt on my computer chair. "Why are you and Denny always implying that I need to be *improved* in some way? *I* don't analyze *you*! Why don't you keep your sexually enlightened nose out of my shit?"

"Oh, c'mon, Chet—"

"No! What did you mean by that daddy-ghost comment before?"

"Look, I'm just—"

"Hey, I don't need subtle messages, okay? Keep your psycho-femi-babble to yourself."

"Chet, I would never femi-rap with a straight man."

I gasp. "How dare you?"

"What?"

"You just called me straight!"

"You call yourself straight!"

"If you refuse to say whether you're bi or gay, calling me straight is heterophobic!"

"I don't want to be penned in by those labels! Why does who I love have to restrict who I am? Chet, you prefer cheese puffs, but nobody calls you a cheese puffist."

"At least I don't act like a lesbian yet sleep with men!"

"No, you act like a moron and sleep with yourself."

"That's an entirely separate issue! Ho, lesbians have labored for decades to carve out an identity!"

"So? Why should I confine my identity to their agenda?"

"Oh, sell out to the patriarchy, why don't you?"

"Chet, since when do you give a flying fart about women's issues?"

"You're selling out my sisters!"

"Feminazi!"

"Heterosexual!"

"Okay. Fine. Whatever. You want some vegi-duck, or what?"

"I mean, thanks for the shirt and everything—"

"Don't!"

"Don't what?"

"Don't reassure me! Please! You said what you said, so let's just eat. You can just keep chasing your little Debbies for all I care."

"Oh, I see! Debbie dumped me because I can't *nurrr-turrrre* my inner fucking child."

"Look, man, it's no sweat off my ass. There are all kinds of armpit-shaving girly-girls who put their hands over their mouths when they giggle for you to fuck."

"What does who I fuck have to do with jack?"

"It all comes down to one subject with you, doesn't it? We can never get away from you and your cock. Even at that last Spit show at the Padlock."

"Oh, *now* I see where all this is coming from—"

"You were so like trying to be intimate with me because I'd opened up to you before the show, and all you could come up with was, 'Duh, I'm horny, too.' I mean, get real. You're such a guy."

"Ho, if I remember correctly, being too horny for Megan was what you were primarily talking about."

"That was *not* what I was primarily talking about. It's just what your ears were primed for. If that's all you heard me say, I don't even know why I open up to you."

"Open up?! Excuse me, *Ms.* Mystery, you've opened up to me jack shit since we started this adventure."

"Can you blame me? Chet, I'm sharing this major sadness about my last relationship, and all you're hearing is how horny I am."

"Major sadness?" I laugh. "You said you were totally amped to be leaving Megan—"

"To *start my life,* Chet! Not leave Megan!"

"I'm just saying you weren't acting too emotionally connected to this person you shared an apartment with."

"Okay, well I guess you didn't hear a fucking thing I said. But that's fine. Now I know the kind of friendship we're going to have. Have some bok choy."

"Oh, I guess Chet is only good for witty banter and sexual innuendo, is that what you're saying? You think there's something wrong with the way I relate?"

Ho waves a carton at me. "Here. You want hot sauce on yours? How about some duck sauce? Soy?"

I snatch it. "Hot sauce. Gimme some chopsticks, because I'm sick of this lameass subject."

"So am I."

We eat in silence. Ho shovels food into herself like there's no tomorrow.

When the sun goes down, Ho says, "Well?" I wait. I wait until the sun is on the other side of the planet, and then I pull off my gray flannel shirt and squirm into a black turtleneck I usually reserve for industrial dancing night at the Trocadero. But tonight it is part of my ninja outfit. I pull on black sweatpants. The *Mission: Impossible* theme is tangoing through my head. At precisely one o'clock, I step out into the darkness.

The fog is thick. Which is good in a practical sense, I suppose, but in a psychological sense, it totally freaks me out. I ease through the wispy phantoms, my hands groping around my body to make sure I got everything: penlight, lock pick, some clips and digital testers some unlucky hacker stole from Pacific Bell, lists of access codes, Denny's ham radio, Ho's Walkman, and a tiny screwdriver.

The street is deserted. I listen to my feet clop along the sidewalk, take one last look up and down the street, and saunter down the alleyway between Mel's building and mine.

A window blind snaps up. I freeze. The unlidded window casts a square spotlight down through the refracting corpuscles of moisture and culminates in a faint rainbow beside me. I am the pot of gold being searched for. My temples pounding, I strain my eyeballs to follow back along the golden beam without moving my head.

It's Ho. She is peering out into the dark alleyway to see if she can see me.

I wave. She keeps peering up and down the alley.

Some guerrilla warrior she is. She doesn't even know you have to turn off your own light to see into darkness. I'm invisible to her. I walk deeper into the alley in search of Mel's phone box.

There it is, near the dank back of the alley. Scurrying sounds ripple through the trash as I approach and hit the penlight.

Phreaking powers, activate.

This is an easy one. Brings back memories. I can tell immediately which lines are Mel's. The lines are set up according to the floor plan of the building. I clip one of Denny's test sets to Mel's phone line. I can punch out a standard number I hacked from the phone maintenance droids to find out which number belongs to which "cable and pair," which is a specific set of wires assigned to Mel's office by the phone company switching office. When I enter the code, the phone number comes back. I write it down.

Then I clip Denny's handheld ham radio to Mel's phone line. Back at my digs, I can tune in to a little-used frequency on FM radio and listen to all of Mel's phone conversations. By rigging up a cheap tape recorder, courtesy of Denny, I can record everything said over that phone. To test it, I plug Ho's Walkman radio into my eardrums and flick the connection on and off. Through the headphones, I hear a distinct click. It works.

Hee hee hee.

But this is all easy, basic phone phreaking stuff. Now I have to do some hardcore gangsta shit, some real-life breaking and entering. It's not until this moment that I get butterflies. When an innocent bystander notices you diddling with a phone box, he either assumes you're a repairman, or he is overwhelmed by the technical explanation you throw at him before you walk away. But nobody stops to ask you a question when they see you climbing through a window.

I take a last look up at my apartment. Dopey Ho has not pulled the shade back down. She struts into view, wearing nothing but her spandex pants and a tank top. She is talking to herself. She's looking at my notebooks filled with secret computer codes. She opens my desk drawer and looks at my comic books.

Hey. She's going through my things.

Strangely, I do not feel violated. I feel warm.

She steps up to my hacking throne and picks up my gray flannel shirt. She slips her arms through it. She plops my hat on her head of cotton candy and struts around a bit, coming in and out of the window's view.

I laugh. It's a good imitation of me. Ho looks exquisitely cute in my clothes. I silently air-guitar a Spanish serenade.

She laughs to herself, pulls off my shirt and hat and carefully puts them back on the chair. She disappears from the window.

Hosing down the riot that started in the secret brothel of my heart, I walk around to the front door of Executive Towers and ring the night doorman. He approaches and peers through the glass.

I grin like a salesman. "Hey, bro. You recognize me?"

He squints at me, then his face changes to something like

shock. I start to get worried, but then he smiles.

"Yes! You're one of Mr. Corlini's couriers, right?"

I beam. "Yeah. Mel sent me over here to pick up some stuff."

"Well, come right in!" he says.

He opens the door for me. I step in and shake his hand. "Thanks, man. This will only take a sec."

To my relief, he does not escort me upstairs. I'm left to walk up by myself. He watches me as I walk up the first flight and turn the corner. Then he scurries off. I start up the second flight of stairs.

Then I go into hallucinogenic convulsions as the doorman's voice speaks from *inside* my skull. Of all the times for Yahweh to appear before me, it had to be now! I start praying fast before he smites me. Look, Jehovah, about all that unaccounted for seed I squirted—

Wait, it's not God. It's Ho's Walkman. The doorman's phone must be connected to Mel's line. Why would Mel connect his line to the doorman's?

Yes, hello, Lieutenant Corlini. This is Mike Brackman at Executive Towers. You gave me your number in case that murderer showed up here. Well, he's here. The answering voice is a female mumble I can't make out. *Yes. I just let him come inside and go up to Mr. Corlini's office. I can't imagine what he's up to, but if you come quick, you can catch him.*

I stand frozen at the top of the stairs.

Damn, that guy is cold as a razor.

I could just turn around and run right past Brackman. But then what the hell am I going to do? Listen to Mel's phone conversations for a month? If he made a habit of incriminating himself over the phone, he wouldn't use us couriers. I need to see inside those deliveries, and I need to see inside a bunch of them.

My eyes focus up the flight of stairs. I lick my lips. What I need is fifty feet away.

I break into a run up the stairs and down the dimly lit hallway carpet peppered with my old skid marks and get down on my knees in front of Mel's lock. I stick in the lock pick and fiddle with it for a while.

Waitaminute. What the hell am I hiding evidence for? The cops already know I'm breaking in here!

I stand up and kick the door. It splits open. I leap over Mel's desk, yank open his top drawer, and there they are, his seals. I snag half of them and shove them in my backpack. I'm just vaulting the desk when—

"Hey, what the fuck?"

Mel Corlini charges out from a side room in his robe and squints at the busted door for a moment. Then he spins and looks me square in the face.

"You *live* here?" I ask.

"Waitaminute," he says, as his squint turns to a gape. "Chet!"

I give him a head butt in the face. He cries out, clutches his nose, and stumbles backwards. I follow him as he back-pedals out the door, trips on some splintered wood, and lands against the opposite wall of the hallway.

I jump over his legs and jam down those stairs. Brackman wisely decides not to fuck with me. When I get out onto the street, I stop running, so as not to attract attention. I do my best to saunter. My breath quietens, and I hear—

Sirens.

I quicken my pace. I strain my ears, trying to discern whether this death keen is coming up the north or the south face of Nob Hill. It's getting closer. Wait, it's coming from the east! Now the wail is close and no longer singular. There are three of them, coming from three different directions.

I break into a sprint up the street as the far corners of the block strobe red white and blue. The sirens pierce. The fog flares up and glows like in a Spielberg flick. The ruby pulse of the electric artery throbs. Headlights whitewash my skin as I gun up the front stairs, stop to fumble with my keys, and push through my front door.

Did they see me? I sprint up to the third floor, thrust open my apartment door.

"Ho! The cops are—"

It's dark. Where the hell is she?

"Ho?"

I hear several people coming in through the front door downstairs. I shut the door behind me and lock it. I pull off my turtleneck and put on my gray flannel shirt, so I look different. I fumble with the shirt buttons. I turn on the light, then change my mind and turn it off.

I walk circles with my hands on my head. Fuck, oh fuck, oh fuck. What am I going to do?

Before I can finish thinking, something is inserted into the keyhole.

I spin around and stare at the door, which clicks and rattles.

My brain shoots off in a million directions at once, locking my body in one position. Will they kill me right here? Or will they take me down to the station, and then kill me? Should I jump out the window? What should I—

The door opens. Somebody leaps at me. I scream.

"Aaaaaagggghh!"

It's Ho. She grabs my woman's wig off the chair.

"Ho! What's going—"

"Shut up!" she rasps.

She throws the wig on over my head and tears open my flannel shirt. The buttons ricochet around the room. The shirt flutters to the floor. She shoves me backwards onto the bed, pulls her tank top up over her head, hurls it aside, and jumps on top of me, naked from the waist up.

"Ho, I'm flattered, but this is no time for—"

"Shut up!"

As she's pulling the covers over us, I hear a violent rap on the door. "Open up! Police!"

Ho shoves her warm torso against me and straightens my wig just as the door is opened. She spins on them, exposing her bare shoulders, and gasps, "Oh!"

I ad-lib in my highest soprano, "Heavens to Betsy!" and wave my hairy wrist.

Ho grits her teeth at me. I can't tell if she's pissed that I jeopardized my disguise or if my imitation offends her inexplicable feminist sensibility.

The first cop freezes and regards me with nausea. He yells, "There was a break-in at the building next door!"

"Well, try next door, Nancy Drew!" shouts Ho, not needing to fake how out of breath she is.

The cop shuts the door, saying, "We're sorry," but not looking particularly embarrassed.

Ho jumps out of bed, rushes the door, and locks it. She retrieves her shirt and pulls it back on. She flicks on the light.

I sit up in my wig. "What the hell is going on?"

Ho gasps, "They saw you come out of Mel's place and run into this building! Most of the cops figured you must have run through and gone out the back way, but some of them wanted to check up here! There must be eighty cops! They probably abandoned every crack bust and domestic incident in the city to come bag you. I ran down the other stairway to find you. I saw them coming up the steps, but they didn't see me. Sorry about your shirt, but they were right behind me. Think of it, Chet. There must be the whole damn legion out there looking for you. Check it out. They didn't even notice all this stuff."

She points to all my illegal ham radio and recording equipment. It takes me a long time to recognize the significance of what she's pointing out, because I'm thinking about skinned cats, old naked nuns smeared in axle grease, ice water spilled on my crotch, Cher, and anything else to make my ten-hut cock fall into an at-ease position so I can climb out from under these covers.

Ho puts her hands on her hips and smiles through a veil of blue hair. "I just saved your ass, Chetster. You owe me one. Am I a totally rad double-oh bitchcake commando, or what?"

The cops, with unprecedented dedication, wake up every person in every building on the block and assault them with questions. They drive up and down the streets all night, stopping passing cars, checking alleyways. They think it's impossible that I got away without being spotted—nobody could slip by that many cops—so they are certain I must be hiding in a dumpster somewhere. This sure is a big production for a measly breaking and entering call. When they come knock on our door, I put on my wig and cower in the closet while Ho strips naked, soaks her hair in the sink, and answers the door in a towel. No, she hasn't seen any suspicious-looking white male around here. She's the only one who lives on this floor; she never sees anybody. If she sees someone, she'll let them know.

We turn off the lights and light some candles. Ho sits in the corner trying to write a song. I lie across the mildewy couch and try to think. I hold one of Mel's seals against a candle. Specially designed. On the bottom is the address of the place where you can get them designed for you and only you. Expensive stuff.

I am banking on the probability that Mel reported no loss on his robbery. I only took half the seals in his drawer, and I bet he didn't notice. Anyway, he's tired of looking stupid. He doesn't want anyone to know it was me who gave him the black eyes. I bet Brackman is already fired.

Ho practices her bass until she gets bored. Then she starts to drink. She goes to pee about twenty times. She only weighs like a hundred pounds, so after five beers she's toasted. She struts around the room barefoot, wearing her ripped tank top and spandex pants, doing kung fu moves and giggling.

She pounces on her board, tries to do a very noisy wallie off our wall, and lands on her ass. The board shoots across our floor and clangs against the radiator, sending vibrations through the whole building. She rolls over onto her stomach, laughing, then props her chin on her elbows to look at me through her mess of hair, to see if I get the joke. I look away, trying to look stern. I have my dark hacker plot to contemplate, after all.

Ho won't be ignored. She jumps up, cavorts over to the couch, and gets me in a nelson.

"What the f—Let go! Ow! Are you crazy?"

She is giggling like a lunatic. I start laughing and do a reversal on her. I wrench her arm behind her back, pick her up under her knees, and throw her to the other end of the couch. Trying to be an expert stylist, Ho somersaults over the arm of the couch, lands on her ass, and disappears.

Silence.

Just when I start to think she is hurt, a fuzzy blue head pops up over the arm of the couch and peeks at me, snickering.

I'm trying not to laugh. "Ho, you are a dingbat," I say, lying with my back against the opposite arm of the couch.

She ducks back down and then crawls along the front of the couch on her belly like she's sneaking under barbed wire. I lie there and watch my imbecile friend wiggle along with about as much stealth as a freight train, her shoulders heaving with hysterics.

"Gee, I wonder where Ho is?"

She peeks her head up, yells, "Boo!" and leaps at me, cackling.

"Ho, what the—Would you get off! You are a fucking—! I'm gonna—augh! That does it!"

I weigh about 75 percent more than Ho does, so she's a dead man—or woman or whatever. I get my neck under her waist, wrap her around my shoulders like a Ho scarf and stand up.

"I apologize, Ho! Did I stop paying attention to you for five minutes? Here, let me make up for it!"

I spin round and round. She yodels. Good thing we have no neighbors on this floor.

"I'm gonna spew!" she yells.

"Bullshit!" I yell back.

She emits some very convincing retches and belches. I screech and hurl her onto the couch.

She hits hard and bounces up. "Agh!" she cries out, and rolls her face into the back of the couch. "Nnnnnnn," she moans.

I rush forward. "Oh, Jesus! I'm sorry! Are you okay?"

Fuck, if she broke her arm, we're screwed. We need each other. I put my hand on her back.

Her face slowly turns to me, contorted in extreme pain. A corkscrew of guilt twists straight through my heart. Then she suddenly bursts with laughter.

My eyebrows tilt back in the other direction.

"You bastard, Ho. You are fucking sick."

She rolls over onto her back and holds her stomach while she cackles and kicks her feet.

All right. She got me on that one.

"Ho, you are sloshed as a sloth."

"Can you say that tem tines fast?"

"Can you say it one time slow?"

I sit at the other end of the couch, and she curls her toes underneath my thigh. Still on her back, she props herself up on her elbows and eyeballs me. I finally smile and plop my hat on her head. Her blue hair poofs down over her eyebrows.

I slap her foot. "We really should get some sleep," I say.

Ho suddenly sits up and leans on my knee. She leans close to my face.

"What?" I ask.

Her face is inches from mine.

"Ho . . ."

Her heavy head falls forward and lands on my shoulder. She starts giggling again. The tension explodes, causing me to laugh and push her off me. Her head lolls like a coconut, and she falls backwards onto the couch. She lies stretched out with her arms over her head, silent, her eyes closed.

"Ho?"

She doesn't move.

"Ho." I wiggle her toe. She squirms and moans and rolls over and curls up in a ball.

"You're beautiful, Ho."

She is breathing slowly.

I sigh and genuflect beside her. I gently insert one hand under her knees, and the other behind her neck. I make sure I have a grip so I'm not pulling her hair, and I stand up. She feels like a fawn. I carry her over to the bed and lay her down, letting my nose gently brush against her soft ear—maybe it was an accident, maybe it wasn't. I pull the covers up over her, tuck them around her shoulders. She coos a Cindy-Lou-Who noise, but is otherwise out.

I go back over to the couch, put my hands behind my head, and try to think about my plan.

But now I can't concentrate.

My stiff cock peers at me mindlessly, asking, *Well?*

"Shut up, you. I've had enough of you for one evening. And wipe that pout off your face."

Little bastard wouldn't let me sleep that night until I vigorously appeased him.

In the same room with Ho.

Next morning is Tuesday. Ho's alarm clock screams at 5:00. Ho, suffering from no hangover, showers, dons her armor, scarfs a ham sandwich, and charges out the door. I, jittery as a ballerina on opening night, punch on my FM radio, jab the tape recorder on pause/record, flick my printer and computer into action, and stack the stolen seals next to my keyboard. Now, all I can do is wait. I try to expend some of my energy on hacking. Maybe I can find a way into Mel's hard drive.

I'm still floating through the outer clouds of the datasphere when a key twists in my lock. In pops pom-pom-head, already sweating.

"Wow!" I go. "What was that? Fifteen minutes?"

"This one's going to a sandwich shop in Western Addison," she breathes.

. I take the package, raise the razor. I can't help but hesitate. I look at Ho.

"Go for it," she says.

I cut the seal with a razor and peel it off. I pull out a computer disk, unsheath it, shove it in my disk drive, and call up the info. A block of text flashes on my screen. Ho leans over my shoulder. "What's that?" she asks.

"It's cryptography," I say. "Code."

"His messages are coded?"

"I guess so."

"Damn! This is some serious biz! It's like working against the KGB or something. Can you crack it?"

I run a scan, scroll up and down. "No," I say.

"Print it out anyways."

"It's not going to do any good, but okay."

I save the information on my hard drive, on disk, and then print it out. I put the disk in a shoebox, and the printout in an empty computer paper box. At the end of the workday, both will be squirreled away in Ho's safe-deposit box. I resheath Mel's disk and stick it back in the package. I pick up a fresh seal.

"Here goes nothing," I say.

Ho crosses her fingers.

"Do you want to do it?" I ask. "It's your ass."

Ho shakes her head. "No. You should be the one to do it. I can't be delicate when I'm in bionic mode."

I fold the package tight along its old fold lines and place the fresh seal exactly over where the glue from the original seal is. I rub it flat with my palm.

"Perfect," says Ho.

"Piece of cake," I say.

Ho snags the package, hops her board, and is out the door.

During the course of the day, Ho delivers six packages: that first one going to the sandwich shop, another garbled computer disk going to a hair salon, and three legit deliveries—one with photos, one roll of architect's blueprints, and some court documents that have to be signed by a judge—but her last delivery is the most interesting. Mel had her deliver an empty sealed package to Michael Levy, who opened the package, inserted a computer disk, and sealed the package with an identical seal. This was a package going *back* to Mel. When we called that information to the screen, we got more cryptography. But it was clear that this encryption was an entirely different form of code. Very interesting. I saved everything on hard drive, floppy, and paper, and sent Ho out with a new seal. She was given no big-paying last-minute deliveries, but she was given cash for six low-priority deliveries at fifteen dollars each, plus the fifty-dollar flat rate. She walks in the door with a hundred and forty dollars.

"Cool!" I shout when she tosses me the greens.

"Uncool," retorts Ho. "Mel says he's not paying me by the day any more. He'll keep track of my deliveries and pay me on Friday from now on."

"That asshole! He still owes me a paycheck, plus Thursday's cash money."

"Yeah, but you're dead."

"True enough. But this will do us for food and stuff till Friday. We can sit here and do this for weeks if we want."

Ho regards me with the sense of humor of Moses. "No. Let's get it done fast. I don't like how I have to sneak over here before every delivery. Mel never leaves his office, especially now that he has two black eyes, but one of the couriers might notice and squeal. I'm trying to flirt with all those shmegma-heads at once. But if I don't fuck one of them soon, they might start getting vindictive. My day has been most unfresh."

She flops into a chair. I stand behind her and massage her neck. "Relax, chickipoo. Our plan is going great so far."

Ho rolls her head around. "Sounds like it's backfiring to me. You can't even read the data."

"Temporary setback. When I was Mel's speed jockey, I never saw him insert any disks into his disk drive except the ones that came from Levy. He was always able to read the messages instantly, without using any encryption disk. So thus I deduce that he must keep his encryption program on his hard drive for the sake of speed. Give me a few hours, and I can find a way onto his hard drive and steal the code. Once I do that, I'm sure I can read the data."

I can feel Ho start to soften beneath my hands. I put my mouth close to her ear, whisper, "Feel good?"

She jumps up and whirls on me. She has not taken her sunglasses off yet.

I hold forward a printout of a map like it's a shield.

"Check this out. I hacked the underground sewer system. Here's a blowup of our area."

Ho snatches it and looks. "So what?"

"All the storm drains along the curbs of Nob Hill are wide enough for a person to crawl through. Mel's messengers fetch frisbees out of them all the time. If the bad guys ever come after us, we can escape through the sewers. Late tonight—or tomorrow night if you're too tired—you can go around and check sewer openings and mark their corresponding locations on this map."

Ho sighs and scratches the back of her neck. She is clearly exhausted.

Ho looks most attractive in her work armor. It is at these moments when she is most Ho, with those head-swivelling spandex pants she wears, the spandex halter top, the iridescent array of helmet, elbow pads, wrist guards, knee pads, hip guards, backpack, and her patented sheen of sweat. Her graffitied skateboard has a little license plate saying, simply, "HO."

Ho sees me leering at her, grabs her board, and heads for the door. "I'm sleeping at my place tonight."

"Why?" I say, following her. "You're going to leave me here all alone?"

"Wily is lonely," she says, and shuts the door in my face. I listen to her surf down the hall and ollie down the steps.

"So am I."

E-mail to Chet:
Did you know the cops haven't confiscated the stuff in your room? Don't you think that's weird?
Love and Kisses,
Denny

It's Thursday night. We've amassed quite a bit of disk info, all of it indecipherable. Not surprisingly, I don't get much evidence over the phone tap. All I get is an endless stream of courier delivery reports and Mel profanity. But between 12:30 and 1:00, greedy Mel is willing to take last-minute information over the phone. I taped quite a few conversations between Mel and Levy at these times, and one between Mel and my old friend Spock. Chen's men burned their old headquarters and set up shop two blocks away like a bunch of worker ants. Their audacity in the face of the law is truly awe-inspiring. They know exactly what they're doing.

I don't see my blue angel very much. I see her most when she's delivering packages. After one o'clock, she trains couriers how to shred on a skateboard. At night, she leaves to go practice with her band, skate Fort Farley, or walk Wily.

Ho takes frequent trips to the library and reads up about the stock market, insider trading, and the Securities and Exchange Commission. I find myself hurt that she is putting more effort into saving my life than attending to our budding relationship. I'm as blue as the clot in Ho's bathtub drain.

I am not just a hacker. I am also a blader. To be chained to this computer, caged in this room, while Ho is out surfing the streets, is torture for me.

To keep myself busy, I hack my way onto Mel's hard drive and steal his encryption keys. Dumb Mel sends e-mail messages from the same hard drive his encryption keys are stored on. Where did he go to criminal school? All I have to do is wait for him to open up a phone line, then slip in and steal the program. If he had recognized my worth as a cyberman a month ago, he could have hired me to protect him from this kind of intrusion.

There are two different encryption codes: one is for the bankers, and one is for the small-business owners. Mel is the only one with both types of code. Mel is the translator; the bankers and the small-businessmen can't communicate without him. I use the encryption keys to translate the messages we've stolen so far. Now I can trace the flow of information.

This is what happens:

Ho runs a coded disk from Levy and delivers it to Mel. Mel tells her to wait while he pops it in his computer and uses his first encryption key to translate the code. What he sees is this:

Invest $70,000 in Procter & Gamble

Mel changes it to *Invest $5,000 in Yeast Infection* and codes it under a second encryption program. Then he sends it out by courier to fourteen businesses that possess the second encryption key, which translates the message, and they generally try to contact their brokers before one o'clock. Fourteen businesses, investing $5,000 each, invest a total of $70,000 of what I assume is the banker's money.

But Mel is running a side operation behind Levy's back. Mel also sends his Extra-Special Skateboard Courier to Chen, with an encrypted message telling him, *Invest $50,000 in Yeast Infection*. Mel is probably talking about his own money here, which he has funneled to Chen. Chen will invest it for him, with the understanding that Chen will also invest in the same stock. So Mel is making a profit funneling the banker's money, and he's also making a profit funneling his own money through Chen.

This is pretty damn sly. Mel, of course, is forbidden by the bankers to trade stock in his own name. They want him to have no connection whatsoever to the stock market. He is supposed to make his profit by taking a percentage of the money he handles for the bankers. But Mel is a greedy man. He finds it intolerable to have access to so much information and not trade stock on it. So Mel finds someone else to invest through, which adds yet another element to the web. For some mysterious reason, Mel chose the Chinese mafia.

Ho comes back from making a paper-evidence deposit in her safe-deposit box. By the time she gets back, she has put a lot of thought and research into the whole nature of the SEC and stock crime, and I think I have figured out what is being transferred through these disks. It's time to put our heads together.

"All right," she says, slumping into a chair and throwing one leg over the armrest. "You first. What have you got?"

I turn my computer chair around and face her. "What we have here is an information trail. The bankers send illegal info to Mel, and Mel sends the info to the small-business guys, who must be investing on it."

"That's what I figured," says Ho, chugging her water bottle.

"What I can't figure out is why all this very incriminating secret information is being scattered throughout all these small-business owners. Why can't Levy just send his money to Mel in bulk so that Mel can invest it en masse, make ten million, keep a cut, and then send the rest back to Levy?"

"Because a ten-million-dollar profit made by anyone is going to attract the attention of the SEC," says Ho.

"Well, why doesn't the SEC get attracted to a ten-*thousand*-dollar profit?"

"Because there are always hundreds of those," says Ho, stripping off her wrist guards. "The SEC doesn't have the resources to pursue every single lucky buy."

"So the SEC concentrates on the big ones."

"Right." Ho wipes her lips on her wristband. "The SEC has a computer program that automatically flags any unusually large and lucky stock buys. If someone invests a hundred thousand dollars right before a corporate takeover and makes three hundred thousand, the SEC is going to be all over him, demanding that he explain how he made such a lucky buy. But if you can disperse that money among a hundred people, then scattered among, say, four thousand stock purchases are a hundred who spent one thousand dollars and got three thousand back immediately. Those purchases are not going to be flagged by the SEC computer program, and the SEC cops won't waste their time. They know middle-class wage slaves can't get access to insider information, because they have absolutely nothing to offer millionaire investment bankers."

"So by breaking it down in small increments, the bankers avoid suspicion."

"Exactly. The whole Levy and Wozniak scheme flows steadily right under the noses of the SEC, and blends in with the natural behavior of the market."

"Damn, they're totally flossin."

"I just can't imagine how Mel lures all these small-time stock players into his web," says Ho.

"I can. First he puts his name in the yellow pages as a lightning-fast delivery service. Business owners who need speedy delivery start to do regular courier business with Mel. Once Mel gets to know them and their financial situations, he hits them with a little stock proposition. Nothing big, just the opportunity to make an extra few thousand dollars a year. Depending on how dishonest or desperate these guys are, they say yes or no. If they say no, they don't report it, because nobody ever reports a measly old stock tip. If they say yes, they are unknowingly drawn into a huge conspiracy."

"Are there that many dishonest small-business owners?"

"There are that many desperate ones. The little guys are all straights with families, homeowners with kids who cannot invest more than what Mel gives them. Mel gives them, say, five thousand dollars, tells them to invest it in such-and-such a stock. It goes up to fifteen thousand, Mel tells them to sell, and they pass the money back to Mel, while getting to keep two thousand or so. It's easy money, and it's for little Jane's college education. But these small-timers have a lot to lose, and they don't understand the nature of the SEC, so it's easy to drop them. Each of them is used four or five times, and then Mel sends them the message: *The heat is on. Shut down your account and find another courier business.* Inexperienced and paranoid, they are quick to bail. The power of knowledge is kept from them, so they basically do what they're told."

"That's why Mel likes to work with you broke slobs," she says. "If somebody is always on the financial edge, Mel knows how to control them."

I lean forward in my chair. "The brilliance of this is that nobody knows who anybody else is. The investment bankers don't know who's investing their money, and the wage slaves don't know whose money they're investing. The only guy who knows everything is Mel. In fact, he's the only guy who knows both cryptology languages to translate the couried information."

"Sounds yummy."

"Mel is the locus who organizes everything, the spider at the center of the web. Since he doesn't invest in the stock market personally, there's no reason for the SEC to have even heard of him."

"But isn't that risky?" demands Ho. "I mean, if Mel is busted, he can rat on everyone and bring the whole conspiracy down."

"That's the beauty of the plan. Only one guy knows everything. Sure, if he's busted, everyone is busted. But if anyone else is busted, nobody can finger anybody else. It's perfect."

Quoth the maven, "No way."

"What?"

Ho shakes her head. "I don't know. I ain't down with this. It's still too risky for one guy to know everything. If a small-time guy is busted, he can finger Mel, who will finger everyone. If one of the bankers is busted, he can finger Mel, who will finger everyone. I think there's something with this Chen guy that helps it make more sense."

"Chen, Chen. Chen is always the wild card. I still have no idea how a Chinese mafia boss fits into all this. Introducing that violent element into this white-collar crime seems totally pointless."

"So who the hell is Chen?"

"Only one way to answer that. Follow the money. How do the investment bankers get their money spread out among the small businesses, and then get it back?"

"So all this work I've done is pointless."

"Not pointless, just not enough. We got the information trail. Now we need the money trail."

"So how do we get that?"

I sigh and look at my reflection in the computer screen. "The only thing I can think to do is hack into the banks."

Ho gives me a look. "We're just getting deeper and deeper, aren't we?"

"It's the only option we have."

"Chet, I don't know if I want you returning to your hacker skills. We've broken so many laws already! We're illegally bugging phone lines! We're using jury-rigged gizmos that were confiscated from hacker outlaws! Now you're going to become a computer thief again! We're becoming like our enemy."

I glare at her. "The mafia and the police are trying to kill me, Ho. If you can think of some legal way to save my life, I'm all ears."

She becomes angry and jumps to her feet. "This is crazy!" she shouts. "Why don't you just run to Mexico?"

What happened to *we*? I get up and follow her. "No way. That's not the way I'm doing it. They fucked with me for no reason. They killed my friend Spider—"

"You hated Spider."

"It doesn't matter. I'm not running. As long as I have the power to take them down, I'm going to use it!"

Ho whirls on me. *"Power?"* she yells. "Tell me, Chet, what *power* you have? You spent the last of your money on this rat hole! First you get the mafia after you, and then you intentionally commit every crime in the book to make *damn sure* the cops will be against you! And now you're going to put the FCIC on your trail, too! Every powerful entity in this city wants you dead, and the more you find out, the worse it gets! They have the guns, they have the laws, they have the manpower. What do *you* have, Chet?"

I punch my forehead. "This! I have the *knowledge*, Ho! You and me are the only ones who understand what these scumbags are doing! If we run, we let them get away with it!"

"Oh, what *complete* and utter bullshit, Chet! This has noth-

ing to do with some Boy Scout code you live by. It's all about
your problem with authority. It's all about your father! You
are one little guppy in a sea of corruption, Chet! And you
can't fight back! You can't! You and me are just two little
peons! We don't have any say in this world!"

"*You're* the peon, Ho! Not *me*!"

She puts her hands on her hips and gets in my face. We're
circling each other like hissing cats. "How are *you* not a peon?
You're more broke than I am!"

"Money is a fading currency, Ho. The new currency is information. Power is knowledge, not possession."

"Spare me the rhetoric, Chet! I know you! I know all about
your addiction! Once you plug in again, you won't be able to
plug out! Once you get a taste, I'll lose you!"

"To jail?"

"To yourself! I *forbid* you to do it!"

"Yes, Mommy."

Her face splits open with rage, and she whirls towards the
door and grabs the knob. Then she stops. She stands there
with her back to me, her arms folded.

I step up behind her. I knew when I said it Ho would hear
me comparing her to her ineffectual hippie moms. I start to
put my hand on her shoulder, then think better of it. I whisper,
"I'll only go in for a week or so. Just to collect the data to
turn it in to the SEC. Then I'm off. I promise."

"You can't promise when it comes to this." Her voice is
husky.

"I know what I'm doing, Ho. I swear."

"This has nothing to do with a logical course of action. It's
all about your craving. You're using this desperate situation
as an excuse to go back to hacking."

"Ho, you're blowing all this out of proportion."

"Am I?"

"I can control it."

She doesn't answer. I put my hand on her shoulder. She
spins around and wraps her arms around my neck and buries
her face in my neck.

"I just don't want you to hurt yourself," she says.

"Hurt myself?" I laugh.

She grabs me by my shoulders and shakes me. "This is suicide, Chet! Fucking suicide! You've rented a room next to your killer's place, you broke into his office, you keep getting yourself in chase situations like you're in some action hero flick! And now you want to shoot electrons into your optic nerve again! It's not an addiction for everyone, Chet. But it is for you. This is not about saving your life or vindicating you. This is all about finding the ultimate rush."

I find that I have nothing to say. My mouth, opened for a retort, hangs limp.

Ho steps away from me and leans her shoulder against the door. In the silence, I suddenly become aware of how much noise we were making. I stomp over and slam shut the laundry chute. I sit down at my computer.

Ho mumbles to the wall. "So I guess I should keep working."

I let my voice fall to her level. "I think we have enough info evidence already."

"Not for the evidence. For my cash payment. I get paid tomorrow."

"Oh. Good. We'll do one more day of collecting evidence to see if we can figure out where Chen fits in. I'll stay here and hack. Then I guess you can quit the job and go home, if you want."

This does not elicit the *Oh no! I want to stay with you!* response I was fishing for. Ho goes into the bathroom. I hear her shedding her skate armor. Then the sizzling hiss of the shower, spraying her shoulders with froth.

After futzing around in cyberspace for a minute, I stretch, trying to exorcise this unbearable tension. I don't know which is eating me up more: the city trying to kill me, or being trapped in a room with an unbearably desirable dyke. If I could just say "I love you" to Ho, I could handle a purely Platonic relationship with her—if it wasn't for this bratty creature between my legs who has never had any respect for my overall life plan—who, in fact, has gone out of his way to fuck it up quite a few times. My eye falls on Ho's open guitar case. She has a little socket where she keeps all her bass picks, which are as multicolored as the infinite recesses of her personality.

Hey. What's that?

I pull my chair over and pick out from the colored pile of plastic coins a pebble-sized nugget wrapped in aluminum foil.

It's half-peeled. Untasted. Dehydrated. Dirty.

My Hershey's Kiss.

The rush of water cuts off, and I hear the shower curtain rings scrape. I quickly replace the chocolate and pull my chair back to my computer, trying not to think about that flimsy door that separates me from Ho's glistening nakedness.

When she comes back out, I don't look at her. If I see her standing there in her towel, this "friendship" thing is over, one way or the other.

She saunters over and puts her damp hip against my shoulder.

I squint shut my eyes. *Girl, you are playing with fire.*

After a long moment, she says, "You've slept on the couch long enough. My bed is real comfy."

I spin on her, my heart thudding like a fist against the bars of my ribcage.

Her face is blank. "Let me sleep on the couch tonight."

I'm glad this is the last day. After hours of sleepy screen staring and radio listening, my brain is about ready to fitz out. All day, I've heard nothing but location coordinates, delivery times, orders, call-ins, and courier lingo. Doesn't Mel get tired of hearing all this spew? I guess it wouldn't matter if someone was reading him a dictionary; if it's making him money, Mel will listen to every phonetic and Latin root. Then, at 1:50, another random call comes in. It's Spock's voice.

"Send your best courier to us. We got something for her."

"Fine. I got something for you, too."

One minute later, Ho bursts in, breathing heavily.

"Last run of my last day," she gasps. "So I'm really busting it out."

"Okay," I say, taking the package. "But he says Chen is

sending something back. So that will be even more important to us than this."

Ho's face twists. "Why do you think Chen would send stock info back?"

"It's not stock info," I say, grabbing my sticky razor. "Chen has only got one reason to contact Mel, and that's to talk about their arrangement."

I go through my ritual of slicing, opening, inserting, key punching, re-enclosing, and resealing. I hand the package back to Ho.

"Haul ass," I say.

"You got it," she says, and turns her back.

I hop back on my keyboard and call up the second encryption key. I run it through, get *Invest all of it in Teen Spirit. All of it!*

I page through my list of code names to find out what *Teen Spirit* signifies. Let's see, *Litter Box* means Ralston-Purina, *Dead Arabs* means General Electric. *Radiation Cancer* I think is something like McDonnell Douglas. So *Teen Spirit* must be—

Some backseated part of my mind realizes I never heard the door slam.

I turn and find Ho staring at me. Our eyes meet. Neither of us moves.

Drip, drip, drip goes the leaky pipe.

Finally, she whispers, "What are you thinking about?"

"Sh."

I let my eyes leave hers and run along her torso. She does not move, and yet under the touch of my eyes her entire body slowly transforms. Athletic muscle becomes voluptuous flesh.

I bring my eyes back to hers. She does not blink.

Scratchy voices emit from my ham radio.

"Yeah?"

"Mel, it's me, Spock. Did you send the package?"

"Yeah. Ain't she there yet?"

"No, she ain't."

"Dammit! Call me when she arrives."

Ho smiles at me. Her downy hair flutters like a floating cotton seed. "I got to go."

I nod.

She slowly walks backwards until her shoulder strikes the door. She opens it and steps outside, smiling at me one more time.

The door shuts.

A full minute passes before I realize I am not looking at my screen. I'm staring past it at a blade of sunshine sneaking through a hole in the window shades. I'm awash in reverie, grinning like Goofy.

The ham radio kicks into action.

"Mel, it's me, Gina."

I jump to attention. I break out in an icy sweat.

"What's up?"

"I just got word from the boys on the investigation."

"Yeah?"

"They said his landlord says he hangs out with a punk rocker girl named Ho. Didn't you tell me the girl you hired to make the secret deliveries is named Ho?"

There is a long stunned pause that Mel and I share. Then:

"Hang on, I got a call on the other line—Yeah?"

"Yo Mel, man, it's me, Joshua Norlands."

"Dammit, I want bug names from you assholes!"

"Sorry. It's Vogue."

"What are your coordinates?"

"Yo Mel, I got some shit for you. You're gonna trip off this."

"What?"

"You know that skateboard chick you hired? Well, check this out, man: I noticed she always heads in the same direction when you assign her, so, just for the fuck of it, I put a tail on her, and it turns out she goes down that alley to the building right next to you, man. So I follow her upstairs, right? And get this: When she opened the door to go inside? I saw that rollerwimp dude who nixed Spider in there. It's third floor, apartment 3-D, man. I think they got some kind of conspiracy going. Is that some shit, or what?"

Mel hangs up.

I'm left with both hands gripping the sides of my desk. I can't move.

A slow bead of sweat meanders down my forehead and cuts through the forest of my eyebrow. It hangs suspended for a long moment. Then it abruptly skis into my eyeball and stings me like a hornet.

I leap to my feet, shove my rollerblades in my backpack, and race down the steps out onto the sidewalk. Bike and skateboard messengers are recognizing me and trying to decide how to react. I look up and down the street.

"*HOOOOOOO*!" I scream, and listen.

Nothing.

One of the bike messengers screams, "He's got a gun! He's come back to kill us, too!"

Suddenly, I am standing in East Pandemonium. Innocent bystanders instantly catch the virus and start stampeding, screaming about a gun. One motorist waiting at a red light abandons his car with the engine idling. Since I am the only one standing still, everybody instantly recognizes me as the gunman.

"I don't have a gun," I protest ineffectually, wishing I did.

In five seconds, the street is empty. I'm alone. I can't see Ho anywhere.

She's on her way to Chen's. *To Chen's!*

I jump in the abandoned car and bend the shift into drive. I scrunch my head down so I can barely see over the dashboard and just let it coast along. I've gone a half block when suddenly I am surrounded by Chinese legionaries armed with Uzis leaping out of cars and sprinting at me. I squint shut my eyes, say the name *Ho* to myself as I prepare to be punctured and crucified by a thousand flying nails.

But nothing happens. I open my eyes.

They are running right past me and heading towards my building. Some of them run straight past the driver's side of my car. Then a man brazenly brandishing his Uzi steps out in front of my stolen car and holds his hand out for me to stop. I instinctively hit the brake.

He turns and waves on a limousine with darkened windows. I duck below the dashboard. I know who is in that limo.

After it passes, I peek in the rearview mirror and see a petite woman with blue hair and a skateboard under her arm sprint up the front steps of the building I just escaped from. Chinese hellhounds dash in behind her. Data emerges from the limousine with no discernible weapon.

Whose slums these are I think I know.

The man who stopped me waves me on and joins the rush towards the building. I put the car in reverse, swing to the wrong side of the street to pass the motorists backed up behind me. I am following ten feet behind the running hit men. In a moment, I am back in front of my building.

I gape helplessly as Chen's highly paid shock forces take the building with terrible efficiency. They block the entrances, brandishing automatic weapons in open daylight. I watch through the stairwell windows as they ascend to the second and third floors and barricade both stairways. They don't move helter-skelter, like desperate killers. They position themselves like trained professionals. They stop and marshal their forces, wave one another up and down the hallways, rub the walls with their backs, nod to each other and then rush down a hallway.

They send word downstairs to make sure the traffic is cleared before they move on apartment 3-D.

A Chinese headhunter looks directly into my face and tells me to move on. I take my foot off the brake, drive twenty feet until he turns his head, and park in a red zone. I jump out of the car and make a desperate sprint for the alleyway between my building and Mel's.

The swarming apaches pay me no mind. People are running in different directions, some mercenaries, some confused pedestrians. Most of Chen's minutemen want to get this hit done fast and get back in their cars.

I trot down the alley. It is quiet in here. Around the corner, adrenalinized male voices are shouting people away, who see the Uzis and scamper to obey.

I climb up on a dumpster and leap for the fire escape ladder, barely catching the lowest rung. It rattles down and nearly guillotines me as I land on the driveway. I clamber up noisily to our room on the third floor. I can't see inside, because the shades are of course shut. The window is locked.

Rollerblade time.

I swing my blades by their shoelaces like a flail. The window splinters into cascading shards. I hear a woman scream inside.

A voice from below shouts, "Hey!"

I turn and look. An Asian man is standing at the mouth of the alleyway, pointing his machine gun up at me. "Who the fuck are you?"

I raise my hands. "Uh, Spock said for me to come up through the fire escape, and—uh—"

Another guy rounds the corner and looks up at me. "Hey! That's Griffin!"

I dive through the window as a gazillion bullets splatter and raise dust from the brick wall. I land on top of my computer as the whole desk tips and sends me headfirst to the floor. The computer screen smashes. My face French-kisses the floor wax.

Then something ferocious digs its teeth into my ear. They've got me!

"Eeeeeeeeee!!" I shriek.

Ho says with her mouth full, "Chet?"

"Ho! Let go of my ear!"

She releases me and we both roll away from each other. Ho grabs her board like it's her anchor to sanity. Her face is flaming with passion. "Chet! They're onto us! They even know who *I* am! They've come back here to kill you!"

"How did you know?" I shout, nursing my ear.

"I was heading down Watermelon Hill, and they came after me! I grabbed the rung of a passing cable car! Chet, they're surrounding this building right now!"

"Well, why the hell did you come back?!" I scream. "Didn't

you know you'd be trapped inside this building?!"

Her voice abruptly lowers. "I came back to save you. What were you doing on the fire escape?"

We can clearly hear the shuffling and whispering outside our wonderfully soundproof door. The fire escape is rattling with ascending jackboots. Ho looks at the door, then looks at me.

"Chet, we're about to die together. You're wondering why I've risked my life to help you. I just want to tell you—"

"No!" I shout. I grab her hand and yank her to the laundry chute. I judo trip her so her head goes down the hole and her ass is sticking out. I lift her legs and shove her down, and then dive in after her as the door cracks open.

It's not until the next second that it occurs to me that I might just have killed the both of us anyway. I didn't realize these things were vertical drops. I thought they were like playground slides. I am considering the irony of this when I land on top of Ho in a ten-foot pile of stinky Depression-era clothing.

Poof!

Ho pushes me off her and we both stand up, coughing in an unholy cloud of dust. Extremely pissed-off rats are scattering from their home and chattering at us.

"Now what?" yells Ho. "We're in the basement! We're still trapped! We're still going to die! Can I please have my sappy dramatic moment now?"

"Sh!" I say. I listen up the laundry chute. Straight up, I can see the faint light from our room, which shifts and breaks with the movement of many bodies. I hear voices, speaking in Chinese.

Then a very plain flat voice interrupts, "Enough with the chink talk. Where are they?"

"They not here!"

"Didn't you say the woman ran up here? Didn't you?"

Silence. I hear the slap of skin on skin. Then more silence. The light is momentarily blocked out.

Then Data's head sprouts from the side of the upgoing corridor. We meet eyes. His arm appears. I tackle Ho and send her flying to the grimy floor as bullets crack down and pelt into the soft laundry pile. The metal chute reverberates like the voice of vengeful God.

Beyond the ring of my ears, I can already hear a thousand feet thundering down the steps.

I stand up, recite a mantra: "Oh my god, oh my god, oh my god, oh my god."

Ho digs through the laundry for her plank. Then her eyes focus on a rectangle of light lying along the ceiling. She grabs my hand. "C'mon!"

She pulls me over to the basement window and tries to strike it with her fist.

"Ow! Dammit! I wish we had something to break it with!"

Rollerblades flail. Window shatters. Glass tinkles about our feet.

"Well," says Ho.

I yank off my shirt, lay it over the jagged glass, pick her up, and shove her ass through the window. She gets through, spins around, grabs my hand, and pulls me through.

We are squatting in a three-foot-deep cement drainage trench at the back of this building.

"Do you smell smoke?" I ask, pulling on my shirt.

Ho sniffs. "Yeah."

We have no time to consider this curious detail. I peek over the lip. A squad of mercenaries is standing by the back entrance. In the other direction, forty feet away, I see our salvation.

I duck back down.

"Ho!"

"What?"

"I see our salvation about forty feet away. Look!"

She peeks up. "Are you crazy?! There's about five mobsters with guns by the back door!"

"In the other direction!"

She peeks again. "Great. A street. Wonderful, Chet. Maybe we can hail a cab."

"Not the street! The storm drain!"

"The sewer?"

"Yes!" I cry eagerly. "Our escape plan! Remember?"

"Chet, if you want to run forty feet right in front of those guards and dive down into the city's sewage, you go ahead. I'm staying right here until we figure out—"

Suddenly the basement is alive with the sound of Sergeant Fury's brigade. Ho is up and out of the trench and sprinting like Jesse Owens for the sewer salvation. I'm right behind her.

I don't hear the guys on the stairs behind me react. Then, straight in front of me, a fat Asian man with a gun and a can of gasoline saunters around the back corner of Mel's place.

"Hey!" he shouts.

Ho dives head first through the one-foot hole in the curb and into the city's offal. I dive in after her.

After my faceplant in the swill, I get up on all fours and peer around the darkness. We are sitting in a faint shaft of daylight beaming down through the sewer opening. Ho is already slopping around on her feet, clutching her board. She disappears into shadow.

"Chet! Get over here before he shoots down!"

"Wait. I have to find my blades."

I finger through the sludge sculptures until Ho shouts, *"Chet!"*

I look up and see the fat man's face sticking through the sewer and leveling an automatic weapon at me. I grab the nozzle and push it to the side. My hands jolt with an intense shock of vibration as it sends a lightning spray through the splattering slop at my feet. He is strong, and he yanks his gun out of my grip and back up into the sunlight. Without hesitating, I leap up, grab his ears, and pull him down into the sewer.

But he's too fat. He gets caught at his stomach and blots out the sun. His gun is outside on the street. I hang from his shoulder lapels, using my weight to drag him down. He is hollering with red-faced colic. I yank until he can sink no further. Then I let go and clap the funk off my hands. That will make a nice project for the fire department. Just a few fingers of light sneak through the opening. I can barely make out his face in the darkness; it is fleshy and ugly and extremely bummed out.

Just for the fuck of it, I take his face in my hands and give him a big sloppy kiss on the lips.

Ho shouts, "C'mon, Chet!"

I find my blades, shove them in my backpack, and inch forward. Five feet from the fat man, I am blind. "Ho? Keep talking!"

"Keep going straight!" Ho shouts. She can apparently see my silhouette against the faint light surrounding chubs.

I keep walking slowly, my hands in front of me like a blind man. Voices from above, muffled by the sumo wrestler's blubber, are shouting. Slim-fast starts to wail with anguish. Down here in the echoing chamber, it is distorted into nightmarish proportions. The soulless thugs are pulling his legs.

I feel Ho's fingers. We clutch hands in the darkness.

"Chet! Quick! Where's the flashlight?"

"Flashlight?"

I don't need to see to know Ho is copping that hands-on-her-hips attitude. "You thought to hack the drainage system of the entire city and didn't think to bring a flashlight?"

"I didn't bring the map, either."

"Great."

"Hey! I didn't see you remembering to bring anything when I saved your ass with the laundry chute!"

"Chet, I was packing up the evidence! I had it all in boxes when you came flying through the window like SuperChet! And then you just hurl me down four floors to the basement!"

She hits me on the arm.

"Hey! That saved your life!" I say, and hit her back.

"And then land on top of me!" she says, and hits me again.

The two of us start a perfectly rational slap fight, blind and in a sewer with a fat man ululating and well-armed Chinese killers running around over our heads. After a while, we come to our senses and lean on our knees, gasping.

"Well," says Ho, "I guess we'll just have to hold on to each other and wander around until we find another sewer opening."

*   *   *

We shuffle through the bowels of darkness, clutching each other, unable to contain our *ewg*s as we occasionally brush against a slimy wall. We cover an unknowable amount of space.

When Ho speaks, her voice buzzes as if her sinuses are clogged. "Phew! I'll never complain about your B.O. again."

I'm pinching my nose, too. "Hey," I go. "Is this a second passage?"

"Where?"

"To my left. I can't feel a wall here, and I feel a draft."

To our unholy dread, we hear many echoing voices speaking in Chinese *directly in front of us.*

"My God," Ho whispers. "They climbed down here through other sewers."

"We better take this left."

We get accustomed to walking blind and quicken our pace. Warm liquid starts to seep into our shoes. Total grodis maximus. We try to get on Ho's board, but it doesn't roll well through the sludge. Sounds from the street make me feel like I'm in the belly of a whale. Who knows what vermin crawl around down here?

I figure we are traveling beneath the building behind ours and coming out to another street. We eventually spot another shaft of light and hurry towards it. We're forty feet away when a pair of legs sprout from the ceiling and hang like stalactites for a moment. We freeze.

Slowly, the ceiling strains and shits out a huge silhouette that is unmistakable. He lands in the mud, stays in a crouch, facing us.

Ho gasps, and I clap her over the mouth.

Data is staring straight at us.

He does not move.

I whisper in Ho's ear, "He can't see us. He's listening."

Voices begin to materialize behind us. When their flashlights come around the corner, Data will see us against the glare. I pull Ho closer and move towards the wall. My back strikes something straight and iron.

I feel it with my hand. It's a ladder.

I look up. Leading where? I see no light.

I pull Ho to the ladder so she feels it and knows it's there. The voices behind us are getting louder. In front of me, I hear Data speak up into his rectangle of light, "Get me a flashlight. Do any of you guys have a flashlight?"

I release Ho, who spits and wipes my slimy paw prints off her mouth. Swiftly, I scale the ladder, and find that it ends in a manhole welded shut. But when I grope around me, I see that the upper three feet is entirely surrounded by steel and stone. There is three feet of space between the sewer ceiling and the street.

I climb back down and find Ho clutching the ladder. The echoing sounds of sloshing are getting louder, and I can just barely discern a faint antishadow of white light appearing along the far wall where we just turned left. The effect creates a reality of distance and three dimensions I had almost forgotten.

I push Ho up the ladder and skitter up after her. We curl up into the three feet of space like a little egg roll and stay quiet.

Gunfire reverberates beneath us. We both flinch and shudder. When the gunfire dies down, I hear Data's voice, bellowing like the anus of Satan, "Stop! Stop! It's me!"

His voice is blank and passionless. I get the feeling he will punish the people who fired at his silhouette and caused him to dive down into the muck, but Data seems incapable of feeling or expressing emotion.

Slowly, Ho's skin becomes visible. Stark whiteness curls along the familiar contours of her face. I look down. I can see.

Wide triangles of light beams slowly narrow upon the apexes of flashlights and human bodies passing along beneath us. I can hear people crying desperate excuses at Data. I find, to my surprise, that I am terrified for them.

Several mercenaries pass beneath us. Most of the lights fade, but one guy, straggling along behind, probably more discerning in the corners he checks, stops at the ladder and thinks to point his flashlight straight up at us. The mouth of the hole below us fills with a supernova that shines up between our legs like a blazing tropical flower. The man's eyes meet mine; his face alights with triumph.

I let go of the ladder.

I plummet until my ass crunches a human face, which seems to detach itself from its neck and crack onto the sludged stone floor. His nose goes straight up my butthole. I am left sitting on a man's face, feeling rather intimately violated, watching five or six backs follow scintillating white torches through this endless licorice tube. They never look back. They turn the corner and disappear.

I stand, pulling my shorts out of my ass. The dude is out like a light.

Ho climbs down after me. "Good move. I think you broke his neck. You okay?"

"I'm fine. Which is more than I can say for Golden Retriever here."

"The last thing he saw was your ass growing and engulfing his face. That would make anyone unconscious."

"His skull hit the pavement pretty hard. Do you think he's dead?"

Ho shrugs. "I'm not going to feel his pulse. Fucking gangster."

I pick up something dark. An Uzi.

"Cool," I say.

"Don't *cool* me," says Ho. "This is no time for boy stuff. Don't even *think* about trying to fight these dudes."

"I'm not. I just think we better take it with us."

I pick up his flashlight and turn it off. "I also think we should follow those guys, with an eye towards knowing where they are. Then, after they climb out, we should wait until nightfall, and then climb out and make our getaway."

"You want to stay down here until nightfall?" Ho says, her voice shivering.

"Why not?" I challenge bravely. "We have a flashlight now. And a gun. I'm getting used to the smell."

"Aren't the cops going to come by sometime? Don't these guys have to climb out of here and bolt?"

"Ho, if the cops haven't come by now, they're not going

to come at all. The gangsters have more firepower than the cops anyway. The cops probably just sent a symbolic contingent to calm the natives. It's us and them."

I flick on the flashlight.

The batteries in the flashlight flicker out.

We get lost. Exhausted, we sit down in the muck and rest our heads on our knees. We lose track of time. This is the place I have been dreaming about since I was six.

We both jostle when we hear a gunshot, and a man screaming like a ghoul. Then another gunshot, then another. Silence. This dungeon echoes so loudly, I can't tell what direction the shots are coming from. But the screams sounded even louder than the gunshots. When the gunshots silence the wailing, I feel a strong sense of relief. Death is more bearable to witness than pain.

"I feel like we're already dead," I mumble.

"Stop it."

"We're already buried. We're buried alive."

"Chet."

"Maybe they already killed us, and we'll walk around in this underworld forever."

Ho whispers, "You know, I just realized, you were so scared riding that cable car, and you wouldn't leave our secret base, not even to help me move your stuff in. You were *so* careful. The only time you risked your life to go down the hill was for strawberry lipstick." She laughs: "To impress me."

I clench my ears. I feel like I am being swallowed down my snake's endless throat.

My voice quakes with desperation. "Ho, I have to get out of here. I need sky. I need air. I think I'm starting to have an anxiety attack."

"I thought I would be the first to crack."

"I can't . . . I can't . . ."

She takes my hand. "Okay, honey. We're getting out now."

We move through the house of horrors. The darkness is peopled with the freaks of my innermost terrors. The plastic footwear around my neck drags me deeper into the dead earth. We see no slanting shafts of particled light. Just as I begin to lose the thread that binds my fractured psyche together, starlight glitters overhead. I yank the warm hand.

"Ho! Look!"

"My God! It's nighttime!"

"Is it real? Can you see it?"

Ho breathes deep. "I can *smell* it! Give me a boost! Quick!"

As I'm pushing her up, a noise like thunder envelops us, and blackness moves in and takes the starlight. I drop Ho and we huddle like lemurs at the approach of a jet. Then the noise stops, and I hear the clop of footsteps above us.

"All right," says a voice. "Keep a car parked over every sewer. They'll start to panic sometime."

After a dark minute, Ho whispers, "Is the car empty? Or is somebody sitting in it?"

"This sewer is twice as wide as the wheel. I think we can squeeze through."

I interlock my fingers at my knee. Ho puts one slimy sneaker into my hands, climbs up, and stomps the other on my face.

"Yuck!" I whisper. "Dammit! Step on my shoulder, not my face!"

"Quit whining, Chet!" she whispers back. "C'mon! Heave Ho!"

I push her up onto my shoulders as a black goober in the shape of her sneaker treads falls into my ear. The skwish is magnified a thousand times against my eardrum. A wheel is blocking the hole, but Ho wriggles through with ease. I finger gunk out of my ear and hand up the Uzi. I jump up, grab the grating, and pull myself through.

I get up on my knees, muster my courage, and peek over the lip of the passenger window. The car is empty.

Crouching behind this luxury car, my ears are opened to frequencies of sound I had forgotten. Subtleties of distance and direction come crisp and clear. The echo effect is gone. For the first time in my life, I wonder at what a finely tuned instrument the human ear is. I am so caught up in sensory overload, it takes a moment to process and denominate what I would normally define instantly.

Sirens. Radios. Bells. The frothing rush of water. The primal crackle of fire.

As we stand, we see it over the lip of the hill. The upper edges of flames are wriggling above the crest of the buildings. Black smoke combines with the night fog to make reality a mere intrusion on the moist nightmare that has arisen like Cthulhu from the sewer. Night is palpable. The stars are being slowly eaten. Shadows have lost their anchors to nouns and float of their own volition through the pre-apocalypse war zone.

Which makes us relatively invisible.

Then through the floating shadows we espy silhouettes materializing. They shudder into our view, then fade away again, walking perpendicularly to our street. They hold firearms out in the open.

We duck back down.

Ho whispers, "What now, Sergeant Sewer?"

"Hey, this car is unlocked."

"So? You know how to hotwire a car?"

"No. C'mon, get in."

"Shotgun!"

Ho climbs in after me. We stay down below the windows so no one can see us.

Ho puts more attitude into her face than a customer service representative. "May I ask what we are doing, Chet?"

I test the steering wheel. It's not locked in any position. God bless these classic Lincolns. "We can sneak away quietly," I whisper.

I peek through the windshield. There is nothing in front of us for ten blocks. I release the brake, duck back down, and we begin to roll down Watermelon Hill.

"Turn the lights on!" Ho rasps.

"No! They'll see us!" I whisper back.

"They're going to see us anyway! With the lights on, they won't be able to see through the windshield, and they'll think we're more of them! Don't you think a car with no passengers gliding down a hill at night with no lights will look suspicious?"

"It's a stealth move! Just like on *Starsky and Hutch*! I know what I'm doing!"

Then we hear a voice shout, "Hey, Sulu! What's your car doing rolling down the hill with no lights?"

Footsteps are clacking after us.

I am horrified to realize that, once again, I am fucked because TV has lied to me.

I peek over the steering wheel. I'm veering to the left, about to collide with some parked cars. I have no choice but to turn the wheel. When the hirelings see that, they about-face and sprint back to their cars, shouting to their fellows.

No sense pretending we're not in the car now. I sit up, put the Uzi on my lap, and man the controls. Suddenly, silhouettes step out in front of us.

"Hit em with the high beams!" froths Ho.

The high beams act like a separating agent for fish at the bottom of the ocean. Innocent pedestrians jump aside. The gangsters stand tall and reach inside their coats. We will collide with them in five seconds.

"Uzi them, Chet!"

Letting go of the steering wheel, I lift my Uzi out the window and try to shoot it lefty. When the gangsters see that, they scatter. I pull the trigger. Nothing happens. I bang it on the side of the car.

"Dammit! It's broken!"

As the gangsters pass on either side, I throw the Uzi at the littlest one. Instead of clonking him in the forehead and laying him flat, it lands gently in his hands. A perfect pass. I just catch his face looking at me like I've got to be the stupidest enemy he's ever had the pleasure of annihilating when our car hits O'Farrell Street bump and the hill steepens to something close to a vertical drop.

I never thought the fear of death could play second fiddle to embarrassment in my psyche until that little guy pointed my Uzi at us and started splattering the back of the car with a rain of lead. All the car windows crumble to cornstarch. Sparks spatter on the street to my right and left. The guy is spraying the whole street.

Ho, beneath the glove compartment, shouts over the gunfire, "Did you pull the trigger?"

"Yes!"

"Well, did you flick off the safety?"

"What's a safety?"

"Jesus, Chet!"

"I thought you said you didn't know anything about this boy stuff!"

"Well, I know how to shoot a goddam Uzi, Chet!"

"You do?"

The gunfire stops as one of the Italians grabs the little dude and tells him to stop firing at his car. By now we have gained some serious momentum.

"I knew I should have carried that thing myself!"

"Well, how was I supposed to know you've shot an Uzi before?!"

"Chet! This is the nineties! Everybody's shot an Uzi!"

We descend into a smokeless region. The black nightmare rises above us. Now we can see. It's like skiing down through the mountains and emerging from a cloud.

This would drive even an accountant to get philosophical. I decide my last words had better be deep. I shrug and proclaim, "The Lord giveth, and the Lord taketh away."

"The Lord helpeth you out, and the Lord fucketh you up. Real swift move, Chet."

"Sorry, Rambette. You can wield our next Uzi."

The gangsters are running and driving down the hill after us.

We're screwed. I can't keep coasting down Watermelon Hill and hope all the lights stay green. Eventually, this car will stop, whether it collides with something or loses momentum at the bottom.

Then I notice a bus parked at a bus stop on a cross street. "Hey, check it out!"

"A bus," notes Ho. "So what?"

I wrench the wheel and turn the corner so we are temporarily out of the chasing hit men's view. I stomp the brake, grab Ho's hand, and leave the mutilated car with the high beams still on. We run across the street, get in line with the bus passengers, and climb aboard just as the gangster Lincolns are rounding the corner. We're the last to get on. Ho throws the ragged-looking driver a buck and some silver, gets a transfer, and ducks down in her seat. All the nearby passengers wince and hold their noses.

I reach in my pocket. Sawdust.

"Ho? Do you have another dollar?"

She looks at me wide-eyed. "No, I don't."

"Change?"

She shakes her head.

The bus driver is staring me down. His breath smells of Jack Daniel's. The bus is not budging.

I glance over his shoulder out the window and see the berserkers surrounding their bullet-raped Lincoln sitting like a big sponge. When they see nobody inside, all six immediately look across the street at this bus and make eye contact with me.

I turn to the passengers who are staring at the sewer slime hardening on my face. "Can anybody on this bus spare a dollar?"

The fine citizens of San Francisco avert their eyes.

The killers tearass across the street and come around the bus.

Ho jumps up, announces to the driver, "If you start driving now, you can feel my tits."

The driver stomps the accelerator without shutting the door and makes a grab for Ho. The gangsters holler.

"Wait!" Ho yells, dodging the grab. "I'll sit on your lap the whole goddamn way if you don't stop for those guys chasing us."

The driver nods towards me. "I'd rather *he* sat on my lap."

Ho and the driver look to me.

"Oh, Jesus fucking Christ," I moan.

Ho glares at me. "You want to get killed instead? Sit on his lap!" She grabs me and shoves me down on the guy. "God, you're such a homophobe!"

"Rub some more muck on him," says the bus driver.

Ho pulls gook out of her hair and smears it on me. I sit there whimpering, not exactly living out my precise Ho fantasy. Looking out the passenger windows, I can see the bobbing scalps of the gangsters slowly progressing towards the open door.

If this isn't enough to ruin the moment, the bus actually *takes a right turn.*

"What the hell are you doing?" I shout.

"This is my route," he slurs drunkenly.

The bus trudges uphill at fifteen miles an hour. A fist grips the silver bar outside the door, and I leap down the rubber steps and kick the face that pulls itself into the door frame.

I bend the lever to shut the door myself and get back to my lap dance. The guy's cock, to my surprise, has completely deflated.

"Waitaminute," he says. "Those guys look pretty well dressed. Are they mafia? Will they kill me?"

"No," I say, as a plate of glass behind me and the front windshield simultaneously shatter. Everybody on the bus, including the driver, throws themselves onto the aisle floor. With no foot pressing the accelerator, the bus falls to about one mph.

I push Casanova off me and jump up on the driver's seat, bending levers, stomping pedals. "How do you work this thing?"

Pissed-off murderers grab the silver bar and jump onto the ledge of the doorway. One of them kicks the middle of the door, and the high-tech contraption bends inward like a window shutter. I find the right pedal, bend the stick to R, and slam the gas.

Now I know what a windshield tastes like. I peel my tonsils off the cracked glass and try to control this monster hurling itself back down the knees of Watermelon Hill at thirty miles per hour. The passengers on the floor have all slid to the front of the bus like sacks of sand. Ho is entirely buried. A lone fancy shoe is wedged in the door. The foot soldiers are scattering left and right to the sound of the bus automatically sirening its reverse gear. Craning my neck to look over my shoulder and whimsically wielding the controls, I haven't the foggiest idea what I'm doing.

All the chasing footmen spread out to reveal a Lincoln grinding up the hill. Suddenly aware of my power, I jam the accelerator. He swerves up a driveway, revealing a second Lincoln right behind him. I see the eyes of the driver bug out of his head as he swerves. The back of the bus catches him right behind the back door. BOOSH! The back end crumples like tinfoil as the front end is spun around, ricochets off the side of the bus, and spins into quadruple three-sixties up the hill.

My neck vertebrae that were bent out of whack when Spock sat on my head in the garbage can are snapped right back into alignment. All the passengers have slid down the rubber walkway to the back of the bus.

"So much for sneaking away quietly," comments Ho from beneath the skirt of a blubbering grandmother.

As we hurtle back to Eddy Street, I'm going to try my first maneuver in this thing. I wrench the steering wheel and the bus goes up on two wheels as it swings back to the original bus stop. All the poor passengers get smushed beneath the seats in the left-hand corner of the bus. People have said, *Fuck panic! Now I'm pissed off!* But their shitty night is not over yet. My heart jumps straight into my sinuses as the cityscape blur hurtling laterally across the back window settles on the front end of a Winnebago most certainly filled with a healthy, white, Republican, *Leave It to Beaver* sort of family. I stomp the brake, and nothing happens. I stomp on what I thought was the clutch, and the bus slams into a skid and stops dead about a foot from the front of the behemoth camper waiting patiently at a light.

I just barely catch the faces of Ward and June staring at the back of this mangled bus before I start bending levers, slamming pedals, and pushing buttons. Windshield wipers flay, fluid squirts, lights blink, air conditioning roars like a lion with laryngitis.

Finally, I get this thing going forward. Now I can head perpendicularly across the base of Watermelon Hill. I can't see through the spiderweb of cracks in the windshield, so I close one eye to peer through the little bullet hole in the middle. I get about one block when I find a mutiny on my hands. Passengers scream for me to let them out.

"No offense, folks, but eat shit!"

The innocent bystanders grab me by the collar and beat my head. Ho is trying to pull them off. "Wait! He's a good guy! He's a good guy! *They* were the bad guys!"

Who is she kidding? They were wearing suits. I have tattoos. I'm dragged out onto the street. I get my ass kicked by the SF citizens who are luckily more concerned with getting the hell away from this shoot-out/bumper car race than stomping my head. Me and Ho find each other and start fleeing like every other biped within five hundred yards. To my amazement, Ho is still clutching her board. Talk about a dedicated street surfer.

She drops her plank to the street, pushes me on top of it.

"I can use my blades!" I shout.

"You don't have time to put them on," she goes, jumping up in front of me and goofy-footing us some momentum. "This is faster on downhills anyways." Of course she has to get in that last dig. "Double weight on the board gets us extra speed."

She places my hands on her waist and kicks us along, doing all the work. Her blue hair is in my face. I can hear her heavy breathing.

A breeze is icing my crotch. I feel with my hand.

"Oh, shit. Not again."

*   *   *

We burst into Ho's apartment, and Ho leaps on Wily in a desperate hug. I burn with envy. I can tell she was longing for him the whole time we were in the sewer. Guess I don't count as comfort.

"Come on over and partake in the hug," she says to me. "Wily chilled his nose for you."

"No thanks," I go.

Smushed against that mongrel's neck, Ho's flower-opening smile is about as arousing as a mohel's scalpel.

Speaking of trained emasculators, the unignorable Wily is ogling my genitalia, wagging his tail and licking his nose to moisten it for another game of parry-and-thrust, with a vacant but otherwise cheerful look in his eyes, which goggle like Cookie Monster's. Then I am horrified to realize why the Cookie Monster analogy jumps to mind.

"You had him *dyed blue*? Is that legal?"

"It don't hurt him."

"Shucks. I was hoping it at least burned a little."

Ho gives Wily a kiss, and Wily runs over to greet me. "Now we match," she smiles.

"Ho, you are in desperate need of psychological help."

I submit passively to Wily's snuffling inspection until he is suddenly grabbed by his collar. Poor Wily is dragged with nails flailing to the kitchen. Ho kicks his splashing dog dishes in after him and shuts the door. Wily whimpers like a new-born kitten.

"I'm sorry, honey!" Ho shouts through the door. "I can't have you molesting Chet!"

I look down and see a faint blue patch in the damp crotch of my shorts. I sigh. "I'll shower first, okay?"

I step into Ho's bathroom, hit the hot water, and lather up. Some of the grodius is so thick I have to scoop it out of Ho's drain when I'm finished. I towel off, pull my jeans and shirt out of my backpack, and put them on. I step back outside, toweling off my hair.

Ho yanks off her helmet. Her halter top is so soaked with sweat, it has changed from purple to dark blue. Even her hair is damp. Ho kicked some serious asphalt to get us here.

She leans to the side, shakes out her hair, and looks at me.

"They think I'm your girlfriend."

"They're such idiots," I proclaim.

"I know."

"Can't a man and woman be friends without them assuming there's something sexual going on?"

"They really have to open their minds."

She twists on the sink, fills her bottle with frothy water, and chugs. Clear snakes dance from the corners of her mouth down her collarbone.

I blink and shake myself out of my trance. "We have to get out of here before they figure out where you live."

"They'll probably be here to kill us in a few hours. They have connections, you know. They can do detective work."

"We better leave right now."

She shrugs noncommittally, peeling off her elbow pads. I feel a sudden flower of tenderness bloom in my chest. I want her to look at me. "Ho."

"What?" Her eyes flash green.

"They know we work together. Now they want to kill both of us."

Her torso is expanding and contracting with elated breath. She nods. "I know."

She seems suddenly so stupid. A wave of sadness moves through me. "I'm so sorry I brought you into all this, Ho."

"Don't. I did this for you, Chet. For you. I have no regrets. I'm glad I did it."

She smiles. Her energy infects me. I feel our breath rise together with undeniable elation. Now that she is here on the brink with me, I am no longer afraid. We don't speak of it, but there is something unspeakably titillating about our predicament. Tiny bubbles of sweat jewel her shoulders.

"Ho, when you thought we were going to die, what was it you wanted to tell me?"

She pulls a strap off her shoulder. "I'm going to take a shower," she says, and turns her back to me.

She pulls the spandex halter top down past her waist as she shuts the bathroom door behind her.

I'm staring at myself in the hallway mirror when I feel Ho's presence next to me. I turn to face her. We are standing two paces apart. We stand utterly still. She is wearing a pink bathrobe that only reaches her thighs. With her green eyes and damp blue hair, she looks like a sprite from another planet. The plunge of her T-shirt tells me she is naked underneath. But when she sees my eyes feasting her, anxiety passes over her face.

"I'm not just going to be one of your slam pieces, right?"

The quiver in her voice torpedoes through my insides. My emotions collapse to blubber. I stumble forward and take her in my arms. She buries her nose in the valley of my collarbone. Against my neck, her voice contains a perturbation I never knew she was capable of, like the warbling of a bird. "You can't just be like how you are with other women. Not with me. Dammit, I won't stand for it. I won't—" She swallows, squeezes me tighter. "I'm special," she chokes. "This is special."

Can't talk. Too hard to breathe. Something is kicking against the inner lining of my stomach.

"Please, Chet. I swore I'd never be with a man again. If this gets all fucked up, I won't be able to survive it. Not with you. You have to love me, Chet."

When it comes out, it's like an egg squeezing out of my psychic uterus, dripping with plasm: "I don't know how."

"Yes, you do. You already do."

"No. I can't risk it."

"Risk what? Say the word, Chet."

I swallow. "I can't risk loving you."

"Why not?"

"Because if it fucks up again, I'll kill myself."

"It's already too late, Chet."

"Ho, no—"

She roughly grips the scruff of my neck and looks into my face. "Chet, we already love each other. Just don't blow it when we start fucking. You can do that. Can't you?"

"I—" I take a deep breath, look down the deadly plummet, and step over the edge. "I think I can."

Ho steps back. The left half of her robe slowly falls open. Poking up beneath her T-shirt is her erect nipple.

Warmth washes up from my pelvis and out my arms, energizing me. My mouth is flowing water. I want to spring forward and seize, but it's too good. I have to hold myself back, savor it. My breath surges and increases so fitfully it gets out of sync. I feel a head rush and my vision blurs.

Ho is standing still, amazed at her power over me. I can see her muscles slackening, her head lolling back just the tiniest bit.

After an eternity of agony, I take one powerful step forward, and she cries out as if I had touched her. I freeze. We are a foot away from each other now. I cannot speak; I have forgotten language. My mouth is open and flowing, my eyes gorging on her. I don't know where to start. Her own subtle dance parallels mine, draws me onward: her small breasts rising and falling, her shoulders held back, her mess of hair lying across one eye.

Ever so slowly, I raise my index finger to her right clavicle and slowly drag the right side of her robe across her breast. Beneath her shirt, her nipple springs outward as the edge of the robe drags over it. She writhes tinily.

My eyes magnetize to hers. I inch forward, raising my hands. It is the suggestion of my touch that makes her breath rise. Will it be her breasts, her neck, her face? Her face. I cup her soft face in both hands. Slowly, achingly, I pull her mouth closer to mine. With every exhaled breath, she releases the sexiest sound I ever heard, small, labored moans, wanting me.

Our lips stay centimeters apart. We are covering each other with our hot breath. She is making louder noises now, almost whines. My lip just barely brushes hers. A shudder of need moves through me, and I hold myself back for one extra second—I want her to see me shudder for her—as a moan vibrates up from my chest, and every muscle in my body spasms.

I draw her face forward and taste.

GRATUITOUS FUCK

Twenty minutes later, Ho leans forward on the table and sticks her ass into me, screaming with macho impatience. "C'mon, you slut-fucker!! Do me like a straight girl!"

Fuck foreplay. With a sweep of my arm, I knock the stuff off the table so I can see her in the mirror. The ripped T-shirt trailing down her back makes an irresistible leash-and-collar. I tug it back. She growls like an animal.

I reach around her waist. My fingers find the hole, slick and quivering like a snail. With my other hand I shove my dick underneath her ass and—

She flexes away. "Wait! Wait!"

"'Wait'?" I froth. "What wait? There's no wait!"

"Yes, wait."

"What could you possibly want to wait for?!"

"Condom."

"Oh shit."

She spins on me. "You don't have one."

I shrug. "Oops?" I offer.

"Oops, my ass," she says, turning it away from me and shuffling through her desk.

My bottom lip starts to quiver. "But—but—but—"

"Can the whimpering. I have some."

A big question mark coils into existence over my head. "But you're a dyke."

"True."

The overhead question mark asexually reproduces into triplets. "You've been saving male condoms for *three years*?"

"Yup."

I scratch my chin. "Why would a woman in a lesbian re- lationship carry condoms?"

"Because she knows damn well her first straight man won't have any. Put this on."

I snatch it. "Extra large?" I whine.

"Hey, I think positively, what can I say?"

I squint at the wrapper. " 'Glow-in-the-dark. Made for the well-endowed male.' "

"You wanna read, or fuck?"

Now fellas, I don't care what kind of literati you are, no man is that friggin cultured. I don't care if it's the label on a condom or *War and Peace*. This query shuts down the frontal lobe and kicks back an answer like a knee hit with a hammer.

"Fuck."

"Fuck, then." She sticks her ass at me. "I think this is where we left off."

I peel the foil, whiff. Ah, nothing more erotically charged than that scent o' Vicks VapoRub. I extract the oyster, open the little elf's cap, and squinch it on.

My cock accordions backwards like a Slinky. *Yipe! Yipe! Yipe!* it whines like a slapped cur.

"Uuuuuuugh." I shudder, staring down at my wilting soft- off. "I hate these things."

Ho's breathing is already at baritone level. "C'mon, baby," she husks, oscillating her butt, looking over her shoulder at me. *"Now."*

Tennnn-*hut! Boy-yoy-yoing!* My cock salutes me. Private Willie reporting for duty, *sir*! The rubber nearly splits at the sides.

I step forward, seize, and stick the tip in. I pull out, tease her lips with my head, then shove it halfway in, hear her yelp, pull out and tease her again.

She almost gets angry. Her foot stamps and quivers her thigh. "Oh, c'mon, c'mon, *pleeeeeasse!*"

She tries to reach beneath her twat and grab it, but I'm too fast for her. Then I give her one sharp slap on the butt and stick it in. Hard.

To my amazement, we both howl like wolves.

She's gonzo now, slamming her ass against me. "You motherfucker! C'mon, you motherfucker, let's see you fuck me! You fuck! You fuck! You *fuck*!"

Banging her hips against me, I can see her spine arched, the wings of her shoulder blades splayed, her downy hair caressing the top of her back. And over her shoulder, I can see her dancing breasts, her nipples at full attention, her belly button, my hands pulling her hips, the delta of her pussy. So beautiful. I won't let her hold still. I grab a fistful of her hair, pull her ear to my mouth, and whisper dirty words.

Ho pushes my hand between her legs. "Rub my clit, you fuck."

"Here?"

"No. Here."

"Here?"

"No. Right there. Perfect."

"Like this?"

"Less circular. More up and down. Ooooo, yeaaaah—wait, where are you going? Right here."

"Here?"

"No. Exactly right here. Now cut me in half, ratfuck."

"Where is this damn thing? It's like the Loch Ness monster in there!"

"Chet, you had it. Right here."

"Here?"

"Okay, good enough."

"Am I doing it right?

"Sort of. Keep fucking."

"Ho, I can't fornicate like this."

"Try. Keep going."

"Oh, I got it now."

"No, you don't. Right here."

"Here?"

"Christ, you are hopeless!" She pushes my hand away and fingers herself.

The vixen is gyrating her hips in circles, then jamming the bumpers of our hips together. I'm working my shaft inside her, probing for her orgasm, both of us in an identical rhythm, old as the ocean.

She is reaching the height, arching her back and singing opera. Those sounds drive me insane. I want to take her all the way, bring her right out of herself.

"Cum for me, Ho. Yessss, my nasty girl, I love you so much."

It is the sight of her reaching the beginning of an orgasm that makes my own shuddering begin. I grab her elbows and pull them into the small of her back as Wily starts to howl in the kitchen. She shakes her hair like a wildcat. I reach around and pinch both her nipples.

The table falls over. We fall to the floor. On our sides, I continue to jam her through our orgasm, growling wordless sounds, caveman talk or baby babble as a lightning bolt shoots up my spine and explodes in my brain. I reach a shuddering height that makes me yodel.

Then I'm dead, breathing like a moose. I am suddenly aware that the places where this hellcat had scratched me during foreplay sting like thorn scrapes after a dash through the jungle. My fingers feel paralyzed. I think I sprained all eight of them pulling her hips into me.

I sigh and close my eyes, secure in the knowledge that neither of us will desecrate this sacred moment with words.

"Wow, that was cool," chitters Ho. "I forgot how much fun the penis is. It's awesome to do some old-fashioned straight-couple fucking for a change—oops! Aw, I'm sorry. It's all you'll ever know, isn't it? Poor baby."

Ho reaches her arm back over her shoulder and grabs a fistful of my hair, brings my mouth to hers and sucks. I'm a rag doll. I can't flex a muscle. She shakes my head around. She starts giggling.

"Look at you," she whispers.

I moan incoherently.

"Look what I did to you. You can't even move, can you?"

I moan again and hold the base of the condom. She closes her eyes as my soft cock worms out of her pussy. Then she rolls over, holds my face, and stares into my eyes, which I do not have the energy to keep completely open.

"Look at you. I could slap you silly right now, and you wouldn't even be able to stop me, would you?"

"Mm-mm," I manage.

Her moist eyes glow green. She grabs and hugs me. I'm a slug in her arms.

"Oh, Chet . . . I'm so happy."

My breathing quietens like an infant being patted to sleep.

A blue light suddenly flares in the darkness. It hurts my eyes. I raise my face from the pillow and gaze across the faint blue glow lighting my forearm running beneath Ho's breasts and gripping her upper arm. Ho is sitting up and holding what looks like a hand-sized model of the monolith from *2001: A Space Odyssey*.

I feel a tender spot inside me twinge and recoil. "Don't tell me you're one of those women who watches TV right after you make love."

"You've been asleep for an hour."

I feverishly sit up. "You let me sleep for a whole hour?! We have to get out of here!"

Ho caresses my hair. "Sh. I want to see what they say on the ten o'clock news."

"Good idea." I snuggle against her. God, it's so good to finally hold her like this. I rub my hand along her throat and clavicle, circle her nipple's halo with my finger.

She slaps my hand. "Stop."

Yeah, I'll get tired of this *real* quick.

The newscaster starts right off with: "The hunt is on for several suspects who killed two people and set fire to an up-scale office building on Nob Hill today. One-time San Francisco mayoral candidate Mel Corlini was killed and his office in Executive Towers burned, authorities said. Another unidentified man was killed outside the building. Mike Holland reports." Shot of flames and firefighters. Voiceover says, "Witnesses say about twenty men with automatic weapons raided Executive Towers, killing Mel Corlini and setting fire to his office. They also raided a low-income apartment house next door." Shot of Hispanic man. "I saw them pouring the gasoline and lighting the fire, and I thought the same thing was gonna happen here." Shot of cops and yellow police tape around telephone poles. "Another unidentified man was found shoved head-first into a sewer and shot to death. Police have identified one suspect, this woman, Ho Pixie. She is described as five feet tall and weighing a hundred pounds. Her hair is dyed blue, and she wears a nose ring. Police have offered a ten-thousand-dollar reward for information leading to the arrest of this murder susp—"

Ho points her magic wand. The blue square pops and sucks back into the TV's throat, leaving behind a faint dwindling buzz.

I get up on all fours and face her. "What are we going to do?" I ask.

"I don't know, Chet."

"The tapes, the disks, the money. It was all in the apartment, right?"

"Right."

In the middle of the screen is a dying dot of light, like the mouth of a tunnel fading away, like the last view of a rat as it is swallowed by my snake. I sigh, trim down my priorities, reach down into myself and get my essence.

"I need to hack. There's no choice. We're stone broke. Without my tools, I'm blind, groping in the dark. I need my computer." I grip her shoulders, in no mood for an argument. "Ho, we *have* to go back to my old apartment."

"I'm with you all the way, Chet."

I find myself starting to cry. "I'm so sorry, Ho. I don't want them to kill you."

"They might kill us together."

"No. I don't want to die with you. I want to live. I want to live with you."

I break down. She sits up and licks my tears, drinking them down. She looks down and sees my cyclops snake is stiff. She runs one aching finger along it.

She yanks the sheet off herself, rips open a condom wrapper, and lies back. "Fuck me, Chet." She wraps her legs around my hips and pulls me down to her. "Fuck me gentle."

I succumb and close my mouth around hers. "They're coming after us," I say.

"We could die," she says, and cries out as she yanks me inside her.

Ten minutes later, me and Ho are jogging beneath the slow wheeling of stars, our arms full of luggage, yelling at each other. Sure, death is a real turn-on when you're horny, but now that the sweat has dried, we're both certain that extra boink was the stupidest thing we've ever done, and we both blame each other.

"You were the one lying seductively on the bed!"

"I don't think it was *my* cock that got hard, Chet!"

"You *made* it hard! I was minding my own business, trying to have a cathartic moment, and you took advantage of my vulnerable state!"

"Meanwhile waving that thing in my face! What was I supposed to do? Ignore it?"

We barge into Denny's dark apartment at midnight. Denny's floating green face looks up from its counterpart in the computer screen, widens its eyes, and opens its mouth.

"Yaaaaaaaaaaaagh!"

Me and Ho pull off our beards. "Denny! It's us! Relax!"

Denny gasps with relief. "I have to learn to lock that damn thing! Shut the door, before somebody sees you! Couldn't you guys have called? I've been worried sick!"

I shut the door. The soles of my sneakers feel springy. I peer down though the darkness.

"Carpeting?"

"Yeah," says Denny. "Now I don't have to look at that skanky floor. I saw you on TV, Ho. I can't believe you got away. Now they want both of you. Did you have to come here?"

"Denny, all the computer equipment is gone."

The green faces twist with surprise. "*All* of it?"

"Even the hacker stuff you lent me. I'm sorry. I'll pay you back someday."

"Yeah, from jail."

"Can you lend me a thou or so? So I can get some more hardware?"

Denny's disembodied head looks embarrassed. "Well, you have to wait till Friday. I spent last week's check on—uh . . ."

"On *carpeting*?"

"Well . . . yeah."

I want to ask him how he is managing to cop this yuppie lifestyle, but my mind is intent upon my task.

"Well, then can I borrow your computer?"

"Chet, I'm using it," he says.

"There's no choice, then," I say. "I have to get into my apartment."

I open his bathroom door. Denny jams his armrest lever and zooms over to me.

"Wait," he says. "You can't break the seal on that door."

I flick on the bathroom light. "It's exactly like the one on my front door. I just pull the doorknob and it rips, right?"

"Chet, if they see the seal is broken, they're going to think I tampered with evidence."

I get down on one knee and look Denny in the eye. "Denny, I know I just keep dragging friend after friend into this, and I know you don't want to end up like Ho, but the whole power structure of the city is after us. We have no money, no place to live. I only have one strength against them, and that's my hacking skills. I want you to say you're okay with this."

He's not looking at me. He's looking at the floor. After a moment, he nods.

I yank open the bathroom door. The police seal snaps clean down the middle. Close the door, and you don't even notice.

I step in and look around. Everything is so pristine, I can't help getting suspicious. I have an eerie feeling that everything in the room has been stolen and replaced with an exact replica.

"Nothing's been touched," I say.

Denny says, "They didn't let the landlord take any action to chuck your stuff or rent the apartment. It's all evidence."

I twist the nipple on my desk lamp. A conical pyramid drags my desk out of nothing.

"The electricity is still on." I lift my phone, get a dial tone. "So's the phone."

Ho hefts in her suitcase containing her precious wardrobe and throws it on my bed.

"This is crazy!" I go. "Don't they usually confiscate everything and put it in storage right away? If I'm a murder suspect, how come they haven't touched a single thing?"

Ho gasps. "Maybe the cops are trying to trap you!"

Denny shakes his head. "They wouldn't think a murderer would come back to his own home. It's stupid."

"But they know he's a hacker!" says Ho. "Maybe they know he'll try to hack his way out of this!"

"But in a city full of computers, why would Chet need to come here?"

"Maybe they know I'm broke and can't get access to cyberspace any other way."

"Sure is a lame trap, then. Since that first interrogation, not a single cop has been here. You guys could have been in and out three times by now."

"So what the hell is going on?" I say.

Denny shrugs.

Ho pops open her suitcase and dumps onto my bed her whole array of outfits. Lollipops, lipstick, a stuffed bunny, leather whips. High heels, sneakers, black boots. Blue, red, and purple hair dyes. A thin barbed-wire bracelet, like a leprechaun's crown of thorns, which she always wears with her adorable Catholic schoolgirl's outfit.

When I walk over to inspect my snake cage, Denny shivers, reverses his chair, and returns to his computer. I press my nose against the glass like a kid outside a bakery.

"They just *left* him here?"

Now I'm really steamed. If he had been a cat or dog, they would have taken him home and fed him. But no. All because of that damn Genesis story, he's left here to starve.

I give him a stroke which he seems indifferent to, reach into the sand beneath him, and touch paper. It's my $500. I always hide my cash under the sand of my snake cage. It stays there for now.

I call out through the bathroom, "Denny? When you get a chance, can you pick me up a medium-sized rat at the pet store?"

"Now I'm going to be your errand boy."

He sounds pissed. He feels taken advantage of. I still have another major favor to ask him, so I better pick them according to their order of priority. Skip the rat. I saunter through the bathroom to Denny at his terminal while Ho continues to unpack.

I take a deep breath. "Denny, there's something I need."

Denny does not make a sound. He keeps staring at his computer and hitting the page-down button. Furtively, I tiptoe forward.

"I always promised I'd trade something righteous for this, but I don't have anything decent, and I need it now."

"What?" he snaps, with emphasis on the *T*.

I spit it out. "I need your access to Pac Bell's tracing systems."

Denny snatches up his Pac Bell notebook almost defensively, caresses it, and looks at me. "You're really going back hardcore?"

"I have no choice, Denny. I have to figure out what Mel and Chen were doing, so I can get the cops off my ass. Nobody will do it for me. I have to do it myself."

Denny rubs the spiral spine of the worn notebook like it's his teddy bear. He knows if he lends this to me, he implicates himself.

"Chet, I need you to tell me *why* you're doing this. You and Ho could just run to Canada and live happily ever after! How are you going to use this weapon?"

"Those rich nazis fucked with me. I'm taking them down."

Denny shakes his head. "That's not good enough."

"Denny, it's not about me and Ho any more. This is a cabal of drug dealers, stock criminals, and crooked cops that sucks the life out of people like us! Stock criminals destroyed my father. Drug dealers are killing my brother. These fat cats are leeches on the labor of the folks you represent. I can use the power you give me to break up this concentration of control. This is all about the democratization of power."

Denny feigns a cardiac arrest. "Well! Listen to Mr. Me-Myself-and-I! A couple measly chase scenes, and all of a sudden you're Nat Hentoff." He tosses the notebook to me.

I smile and exhale as a knot of tension slackens in my neck. "Denny, you're the best friend a man could have."

"Fuck you." He smiles.

I turn and march back into my bedroom and announce to Ho, "Surf's up! Time to join the consensual delusion that is cyberspace!"

Ho spins on me and puts her hands on her hips in that Ho way of her's. "Let's get down to business. We have eleven dollars, right?"

"Right."

"Give it to me."

I obey.

Ho grabs her coat and pulls on her long beard. "I'm going out to buy eleven dollars worth of ramen noodles."

"How come *you* get to risk your life?"

"I thought you said you had hacking to do!" she shouts back as she marches towards the bathroom.

"That's very ballsy of you . . . I mean, uh, ovariesy."

Bearded Ho shakes her head to herself and slams the bathroom door behind her.

"Pick me up some blueberry-flavored Pixie Sticks!" I call.

She calls back, "*I'm* your blueberry-flavored Pixie Stick!"

I sigh, clasp my hands under my chin, raise one leg, and flutter my eyelashes. Ah love!

I look at my silicon baby, seeming to buzz with need for me, and feel an addict's rush of anticipation surge through my veins. I blow a kiss at my computer.

I have returned to you, my sweet!

First thing I do is break into the maintenance sectors of Pac Bell and PG&E and cancel the orders to turn off my phone and electricity. Then I bust into their customer representative sections and inform their programs that my service has been deactivated. As far as that department knows, I am no longer with Pac Bell or PG&E, so there is no need to bill me. Meanwhile, I continue to get their service. Luckily, their bureaucracy is as compartmentalized as a beehive. It takes weeks for departments to cross-check with each other. They can't even make coffee without filling out the proper forms, and nobody likes paperwork. Besides, I understand their colossal and awkward computer system better than they do.

It's all so pitifully easy, I feel like a mosquito slurping the nose of a paralyzed giant. Breaking into phone companies is kindergarten for phone phreakers. Now it's time to move up to Phreaking 101.

I spend the next day prancing through the inner organs of Pac Bell, running my phone line through a zillion switching stations throughout the state. It will take a legal police tracer about six months to trace my calls through all that bureaucracy. It would take an illegal tracing agent about eight hours, and only if I stay on the phone that long. So I can feast on illegal infozones with relative impunity.

Ho, in the meantime, watches TV naked.

When the nightly news comes on, the opening story is about arson and machine-gun fire in San Francisco. The police have raided a major outpost of the Chinese heroin and crack trade. Chen has retaliated violently. A Chinese-owned supermarket was burned, and the police comforted its owners by arresting them for cooperating with drug dealers. A squad car was set afire in the police department parking lot—an obvious warning to back off. There are extended shots of businesses burning and families weeping.

"This city is going insane," says Ho. The hateful firelight kindles her nakedness to a raging red.

"Gina Corlini is getting revenge on Chen for killing her brother."

We watch the supermarket burn.

I shake my head. "Stupid Mel," I say. "He thought being the spider at the center of the web gave him power. But it also made him a target. The more knowledge you have, the more of your coconspirators you can implicate. Anyone who monopolizes all the knowledge instantly becomes the target."

"And Mel was the only brain in the universe with all the knowledge."

"Right. As long as the conspiracy is profitable, Mel remains alive. But when the law focuses on him, he dies. When he dies, the conspiracy dies. All the strands hang loose and unconnected. So now we know where Dr. Chen comes in."

"How do you mean?"

"The bankers forbid Mel to trade directly with the stock market. He makes his money only through them. But the bankers are smart. They know Mel has lots of cash, and investment bankers know the temptations of greed. Without identifying themselves, they secretly contact somebody violent, a drug dealer perhaps, to approach Mel and offer to invest Mel's money for him. Mel thinks he is investing his own money through Chen behind the banker's backs. But Chen is actually working for the bankers, though they have no connection besides instructions and payoff. Maybe Mel doesn't even find out Chen is mafia until he's already suckered in. Meanwhile, Chen is also investing his own money in this stock info."

"So?"

"So Chen's role is to kill Mel if things go sour. The bankers don't even have to give Chen an order. He's a professional killer. The bankers know damn well that if things crack open, Chen will kill Mel and burn the evidence on his own initiative.

The conspiracy disappears at that moment, and nobody is culpable. Chen can't identify who was paying him. The transfer of money freezes wherever it is, the bankers take a small loss, and it's over. The bankers chalk it up as a worthwhile investment that is no longer viable, and move on. The only loser is Mel."

"So Mel is the dupe in all this."

"Mel figured it out before we did. But it was too late to get out. He knew he was in over his head, but he couldn't stop. He had no choice but to keep going and not make any mistakes. You, Ho, were the mistake he paid for."

"Now you and me are the only brains in the universe who know everything."

"Not everything. We still have to trace the money trail. But we couldn't do that without the knowledge we already have. We're the only people left alive who've looked inside all the packages going to all the coconspirators."

"That's why we have to die," says Ho.

"That's why every cop and mafioso in this city is looking for us. And they have big money interests behind them."

Ho switches channels. All the local news programs have started off with the same arson story.

"The spotlight is on," I say.

Something beeps. It startles me, because I've never heard that sound in my room before. I'm used to hearing it out on the 'yards. I pick my beeper up off my dresser, read it.

Ho's burning face gapes at me. "Do you recognize the number?"

"No."

"Who has your beeper number?"

"Nobody but Mel."

I toss it on my bed. It beeps a second time.

"What does it mean, Chet?"

"Somebody wants to talk to me."

Denny knocks on the door. Ho pulls on my long shirt and opens it.

"Here's your rat," says Denny, extending a brown paper bag and turning tail.

"Ewg!" says Ho, taking the bag with the tips of her fingers. "You're not going to feed him now, are you?"

"He's due for his biweekly meal in two days," I say.

"Ugh! It's moving! It's *alive*! Quick! Take him!"

"My snake won't eat him if he's dead," I say, taking the bag.

"That's *so* disgusting. You're way lucky you only have to feed him once every—Oh my god!!"

"What?"

"*Wily!*"

"Oh, Jesus."

"I left him in my kitchen!"

Ho hurls herself into an unholy delirium, sprinting circles around the room, foaming at the mouth, knocking things over, and firing contradictory courses of action. You'd think she'd left her baby in a burning building. I sit in my computer chair and gape for a half-minute until she calms down and snatches my phone.

Ho paces back and forth with the phone, and she clotheslines me repeatedly with the cord. She stomps her foot while it rings. "C'mon! C'mon! Pick up!"

I say as gently as I can, "Ho, honey, I don't think Wily can answer a—"

"Sh!" she harshes at me.

Then: "Hello, Mrs. Merryweather, this is Ho Pixie. I'm sorry to wake you. Have you seen the news tonight? Good. No reason. Just asking. Say, Mrs. Merryweather, you still have the key to my apartment, right? Could you do me a *huge* favor? Could you go over to my apartment and let Wily out? He's in the kitchen. Yeah, just let him out the front door to the street. He can take care of himself. Thank you."

She hangs up and breathes a sigh of relief.

"Ho," I say delicately, trying not to set off any more time bombs. "What if she bursts into your apartment while the gangsters are there?"

Kaboom. Ho's eyes widen. "Oh my god!!" she runs back to the phone and hits redial. No answer.

"They're going to kill Mrs. Merryweather!" she shouts.

"Wait! Won't it seem suspicious if you call her right back and contradict yourself?"

"Here, you take the phone and let it ring until somebody picks it up."

I take the phone. "What am *I* going to say to her?"

"Just tell her—um—just tell her—" Ho grabs her hair and stalks in circles, saying "Oh my god oh my god oh my god" for a good two minutes until the phone picks up.

"Hello?"

"Mrs. Merryweather?"

"Who is this?"

"Uuuuuuuh," I say in a reflexive Butt-head imitation.

Ho snatches the phone from me. "Mrs. Merryweather! Thank God! Are you okay? Yes, of course you're okay! Nothing to worry about! Did you let Wily out? You *did*?! That's wonderful! Oh, Mrs. Merryweather, I love you!"

Ho slops a big kiss on my phone and hangs up.

"I'm sure that did wonders for your reputation around there."

"Thank god!" shouts Ho, and flops down on my recliner. Then her face inverts and becomes sad. "Now Wily is out there all alone, crying, wondering why I have forsaken him. I can't believe I forgot him. I'm such a bitch."

I sit in awe. I have never seen such a spasm of desperate love in my life.

Ho reaches down the side of the old-fashioned recliner, manfully pulls the stick shift, and leans all the way back and closes her eyes. Then, infinitely ladylike, she crosses her feet, lets her Hush Puppy slide off her heel and dangle on the end of her toe.

Ever so tenderly, I reach forward, take her tiny foot in my hand, and remove the shoe. Five little pearls. Slowly, I bring my lips to her tiniest toe and kiss it as lightly as I can.

I feel her inhale with surprise and shift her weight on the chair. Her eyes are still closed. I bring my mouth down again and kiss her underneath her toes. Her breath rises. I get down on one knee and mouth her precious foot, worshiping its contours, dampening her five little shrimp, licking along the arch. I am spellbound to see her put her arms up over her head and arch her body. I lick between her toes. She grips her hair, which streams from between her fingers as if she's squeezing fistfuls of blueberries. At the uppermost tip of the most acute frequency, I can hear the siren-call that drowns out the throb of blood in my ears: It is the cicada-chirp of her clitoris. Never letting go of the mini-torso of her foot, I increase the intensity of my mouth as she writhes in the recliner, her eyes squinting tight now as she grips the armrests and arches her hips up off the seat and reaches an awe-inspiring orgasm, then collapses.

I house her foot back in her shoe, and place her ankle back on the footrest. I listen to her falling asleep. I lay a blanket over her, tuck it around her shoulders, and get back on my computer.

Next time, I'll do the soft back of her knee.

Sleep, my blue angel, punk tinkerbell dancing through the wasteland. You taught me that the ultimate rush is just a substitute for . . .

Oh, Ho. Ho, love is not a big enough word.

When the phone rings, I have Ho tied by her wrists to the chain lights hanging from my ceiling. We groan in a whining harmony of grief. We both know I have to answer it. It might be Denny.

I hold her hips and bend my knees to yank my Excalibur from her marble peach, march—*goy-yoing! goy-yoing! goy-yoing!*—over to the phone, and snatch it up.

"This better be you!" I shout.

"It is."

"Good. What's the scoop?"

"I can't find him anywhere. Though I have been following a steady trail of overturned garbage cans."

I yank the rubber. It stretches, peels slowly like sausage skin until it snaps into my fist. Ouch. Never remove a condom until after shrinkage.

"What about her place?"

"Ho's place has been sealed off, and cops are filling out their notepads. Every single one of her neighbors is describing the stereotypical punk rock chick: drug addict, no-job deadbeat, whore, does not take care of her dog. When they heard about drugs and murder, they weren't surprised."

I feel a pinprick icicle touch next to my big toenail, like a tiny arctic ladybug. My pendulous shlong trails a long silver dribble to my foot.

I look over at Ho, who is still tied up. I stretch the phone cord over to release her blindfold.

Denny continues, "Everything ever stolen from her apartment complex over the past decade is now being blamed on Ho. People even claim she's responsible for the graffiti. Ho should know that all her neighbors secretly resent her—except for that Mrs. Merryweather woman, who never said a word about Ho's phone call."

Ho feels my touch at the back of her skull and shakes her head away. "No."

"What?"

"Leave me this way."

I step away and sit my sweaty ass down on the recliner and watch my prize. Blind and bound. Hypnotically oscillating her hips ever so slightly, like a palm swaying in a breeze you can't perceive otherwise. Her arms up over her head, her spine arched, I can see each little vertebra nodule, like hard cherries under a dough pie covering. On her inner thigh is a raspberry birthmark possessing an irony we have yet to joke about: It's shaped like a stop sign.

"I stopped by Chugger's, and he said all Ho's bandmates have been questioned. They're analyzing her cartoons. One of the cops actually asked for copies of the lyrics to songs she has written. Can you believe it? I pretended I was a disabled police inspector—you know, like a drooling Ironside sort of guy—and the ignoramus lady on the floor below her went into great detail about the noises she and Megan used to make. Lesbian equals pervert, you know."

Ho spins once, slowly, twisting the chains around like you

do for a kid who wants to spin on a swing set. I receive rotating visions of her front and hind faces.

To my amazement, I feel my wily cock stiffen.

"So you know what we have to do? . . . Chet?"

"Uh-huh."

"Is Ho there?"

". . . yeah."

"What's she doing?"

Responding telepathically to some truth gleaned from my voice, Ho turns her sacred hind face to me, stands on her toes and stretches forward, sticking her apricot butt in the air. Rosy cheeks, winking butthole, pink labia, and blue muff (yes, she bothered): It looks like a cyclops Strawberry Shortcake grew the goatee of a Smurf.

I let the phone clatter and then drag across the floor as the coiled wire seizes back its springiness. I return to my Ho. New condom applied, and I drive my submarine into the creamy shrine of her snatch. We will ascend to the apex as the phone wails in protest, a single colorless computer note like an air-raid siren. My hand goes across her lips and teeth, begging for the pain, and she will draw blood from my finger at the end of the world.

"Chet, I have to leave you for a while."

Panic seizes me. "Why? I thought you said Wily could take care of himself!"

"Chet, they'll find out where my parents are."

"Oh, Jesus . . . I—"

"Mom is in Haight, and Dad is across the Bay in Berserkly. I have to put them on a plane somewhere. I got to take care of that shit, Chet. They could die."

"So just give them a ring!"

Anxiety pillages her face. She turns her back, puts her hands on her hips, and starts walking in circles.

"What?" I ask.

She stops and looks at me. "Who do you think I've been calling the last twenty minutes, Chet? My parents. And their lines are no longer in service."

"Wait. *Both* their lines are dead?"

She nods.

My head is spinning. More and more people are becoming implicated in my scam.

"This is insane," I say. "They go after people's families?"

"What about your brother Bobby?" she asks.

I shake my head. "He's invisible. He's never paid taxes, he has no driver's license, no steady address, and he's never been busted. Even I don't know where he is. He's about as easy to find in this city as a homeless guy."

"Okay, Chet. So I guess I'll see you in a couple hours."

She tries to hug me, but I push her away. "Nah, fuck this. I'm going with you."

I grab for my skates, but she grabs the laces and won't let go.

"No, Chet!"

"Fuck if I'm letting you go alone! Leggo!"

I yank, and she yanks back. "Chet! We came here so you can hack!"

"I'm going!"

"We don't have time! You have to stay at your computer! I'll be back here before nightfall!"

"Forget it, Ho! What's a couple more hours? I'm—dammit! Let go!"

I yank hard, somersault backwards over my bed and hit plaster. Ho's back thuds the wall next to my computer. Leaning against opposite walls, we stare at each other, gasping, each holding one of my rollerblades.

"Chet, I know this is hard for you." She puts her hand on my terminal. "But this is where your talent is, and this is what's going to save our asses."

"But the gangsters will—"

"It's probably just a coincidence! This is just reminding me to get my parents on a plane just to be safe."

"How do you know it's a coincidence?" I demand.

She shrugs. "The mob doesn't have the power to make the phone company disconnect lines, do they? I don't know. You tell me."

"Ho, the cops definitely can disconnect phones."

She shakes her head, hell-bent on denial. "But they wouldn't. They can't take phone service away from the relatives of arson suspects."

I throw up my hands. "They can't fabricate murder stories and feed them to the media! They can't accuse innocent skate punks of something they didn't do! They can't cover up for the mob! But they're doing it! They can do whatever they want!"

"I just can't believe it. Who would mess with the phone company like that?"

I walk over to the window and look out, but all I can see is my own reflection, just like when I stare into my sleeping computer screen. "MP Phred."

"Who?"

"Hackers. Hackers can definitely dick with the phone company."

"But you said none of them knows who you are. And even if they did, why would they be messing with me or my parents? I've never been on-line."

I sigh and toss my blade on the bed between us. She reciprocates. They bounce, clack together, and still.

I scratch the back of my neck. "You're right," I say.

Ho crosses the bed on her knees, gets close to me. "Chet, I have to go. Alone."

I nod sadly.

She hugs me and doesn't let go. I can feel her getting choked up. When she finally pulls back, she looks like she wants to say something, but changes her mind. She sniffles, clears her throat. Then she grabs her board.

"What's the number here again?"

"Just remember: *Hey you! I want to be you!* AUI-12BU. 284-1228."

"How did you scheme that?"

"Hackers can choose their own numbers and give them out to their friends. My beeper number is: *I am you. Gee, you are, too.* IMU-GUR2. 468-4872. You and Mel are the only people I've ever given that number to."

"Memorized. How come you didn't get me one of those?"

"I'll give you 418-4882."

"What's that?"

"I1U-I8U2. *I won you. I ate you, too.*"

"How *sweet!*" she beams, bouncing on her toes. "Your first present to me!"

I blush. "I been saving it for that special someone."

"You're soooo romantic." She saddles up and kisses me. "It's nine A.M. now. I'll call you at exactly five o'clock."

"And you'll be back before nightfall?"

"I promise."

I smile. Ho smiles and whispers, "Take care of yourself, okay, bud?"

"No, *you* take care of *your* self. I'm going to be holed up in here. You know where to find me."

"Right on," she says, and turns her back.

"Hey, kid," I call.

She turns.

"Catch."

In my best imitation of the famous Coke commercial, I toss her my brown wig. She catches it, smiles, and walks off through the bathroom. She's gone.

I pop in the Red Hot Chili Peppers' *Blood Sugar Sex Magik* and punch ahead to the perpetual orgasm that is the title song. Cobwebby strands of slaver hang between my neurons. My snake nuzzles around my shoulders, his tongue flicking at my ear.

I am an android. Only when attached to this machine, this tiny nerve ending wired to the vast matrix of transported humanity, am I complete. I live not in the universe, but in the duoverse. Even when I'm out in the sun on my rollerblades, I always have one foot in this world.

And now I am stepping out of reality.

The electronic full moon is out in cyberspace. I am reaching the deepest stage of the cyberwolf transformation, where I might forgo sleep, hygiene, exercise, and food, and sit at my terminal punching in rapt fascination for fifty hours at a stretch. I'm home.

Six hours pass like six fireflies in the night. I have traded enough secrets with other hackers to fiddle through some of the outer reaches of the overseas banking systems. I eventually find a loophole and send a Trojan horse through it. A Trojan horse is a section of code I hide inside an application program. When a legitimate user mistakes my gift for his own program, my little sliver of code graffiti gives me user access.

While this blind "luser" runs my Trojan horse, I need something to be happening on his screen to divert his attention from the hard drive light that flashes while I covertly suck his secrets. With hackers, most of whom are nose-picking teenagers who stop hacking only long enough to masturbate, I usually just throw on some pornography graphics, accompanied by digitized sound effects like "Oooh baby, yes! Yumeeee!" But this user is a banker, so I flash his screen with shit like:

```
AUTOCHECK VIRUS DETECTION PROGRAM V1.3
(C)OPYRIGHT 1998 BEN DOVER.
SCANNING FILENAME.1 FOR VIRUSES . . .
SCANNING FILENAME.2 FOR VIRUSES . . .
```

To make things look authentic, I play with the ellipses, which dribble across the screen after the word "viruses." I have the periods begin one at a time between disk accesses, to make it appear that the illicit program really is scanning the files for viruses. The luser-user won't even blink at the flashing green light. Meanwhile, my Trojan horse is scanning him for free passwords.

Surprisingly, I find the actual banking system fairly easy to hack. Old piggybacking tricks pass me straight through their fire wall. I even locate the records and listings for Wozniak and Levy with comparative ease. Things don't get complicated until I have to actually manipulate the data. That requires giving myself Super-User status without being detected. The only way to do that is to stairstep to root access, which is at the top node of the hierarchical directory tree. And this aspect of the system is as baffling as any I've encountered. Once I have to trace electrons overseas, it will get even more complicated. I can't do it all by myself. A hacker is powerless without his community. I must visit the black markets of information MP Phred hunts down and destroys.

I've been doing some detective work, dumpster trashing, shoulder surfing, and social engineering over the years, and I eventually made contact with the Grim Ferryman, an Underground sysop who specializes in banking systems. He's the leader of a proud hacking group who call themselves "One Nation Underground." I have no way of breaking onto such an elite bulletin board, so I can't steal their goodies. Instead I come on my knees bearing gifts, hoping to win the favor of the net.god. All day, I've been offering sacrifices, leaving some of my most precious knowledge artifacts on their outskirts, signing my name, and calling for the Grim Ferryman to graciously receive them.

Finally, the invitation is volleyed across the Styx: "Snake-byte, you are stellar. Come on in. Here's the code."

Yes! Access! If anybody can help me out with Wozniak and Levy, these guys can. I type chiclets, open up the treasure chest.

And get a blank screen.

My feeper begins to beep out: *Dum-dum . . . dum-dum . . .* with steadily increasing volume and tempo. It's the theme from *Jaws*.

Now I'm getting a graphic. Squiggly lines signifying water appear on my screen. As the crescendo rises, a triangle slowly rises from the water. It's a shark fin, with the letters "MP" written on it.

Dum-Dum! Dum-Dum! *Dum-Dum! DUM-DUM!*

The water squiggles. The fin bends and cheerfully waves at me.

Very funny.

A booby trap has just gone off in my face, but all it does is flash a novelty flag saying "BLAM!"

And I am standing in a graveyard of slain hackers.

I try to act nonchalant, but I can't shake off the nagging terror that quakes within me. MP Phred has chernobyled the elite bulletin board that only moments ago I was delivering illegal secrets to.

These are guys even I admire. How could he have outwitted them? And so fast?

. . . is he after *me*?

Humph! No way. Nobody is as good as me. I ain't scared of some self-appointed vigilante.

But when I attempt to log off, I find that my hands are shaking too much to type.

I am about to betray Denny.

I type Denny's phone tracing instructions into my hard drive, programming them to erase in one hour.

Then I go to the Underground BBS called "Grrrl Scouts of

Death" where I was last searching for information. I type out all my precious access codes to burrow beneath the legit facade and get into the Underworld. I hang-drop into the dungeon and experience a rush of warmth to see zillions of hacker kids jostling each other with boasts and arguments, addressing their cohorts as "d00dz."

Peering around the chats and graffiti walls, I find that the Adjudicator himself is already on. He's bartering in the marketplace, waving squawking chickens and gesticulating like a trader on the stock market floor. I break into his conversation.

"Shwing!"

"Snakebyte! Long time no!"

"Hey, dude. How would you like to *trace calls* any time you want?"

"Whoa! Feetch, feetch!" he types, short for "feature," standard exclamation on discovering a righteous new program.

He shuts all other d00dz out. We are suddenly in a plastic bubble. People can see we're here, but they can't eavesdrop on our conversation. It's a breach of netiquette, but when one of the Hallowed Lords shows up without an appointment, sometimes you just have to dis the fawning geekazoids.

"I'm totally @mped!" he types. "What have you got?"

I take a deep breath. Sorry, Denny, but it's also about the democratization of *knowledge*.

"I got the access codes and techniques to get into the section of the Pac Bell system where the Feds trace our calls. I even got curvaceous instructions of what to do once you're in. You can figure out what the Feds do to track us, not to mention defenestrate those little pain-in-the-ass mosquito hackoids who keep harassing you."

"K001 featurectomy, man! Utter primo! What do you want for swap?"

"I want every banking code you got, specifically those that get me overseas."

"I got what you need, SB. Are you tracing some kind of illegal money trail to Switzerland?"

God, he is so fucking hip. "Yes asshole, and erase these messages immediately."

"Right away. Just get me those ><cellent instructions ASAP."

"Hope that doesn't use up my zorch quota round these parts."

"Snakebyte, my man, you got infinite zorchitude with this net.god. Put it on the tab."

"Keep it under the lid, okay? Too many warez d00dz start breaking on and tracing calls, they'll get sloppy, bits will get barfulous, and some stiff at Pac Bell will clue in and change the protocol."

"Done. I'm sending it through. Copy it and do an immediate erase."

"No prob. Here's the phone phreaking gems. Happy hacking."

I slurp the info into my hard drive, erase the Chet-chat, sign off, and land myself in the outer menu. I dance back through the menus, slip through some trapdoors, and scale through the directory tree craving the company of other hackers. I can afford to be in a lurking mood. I got my treasures and weapons now. After that scare with MP Phred, I desperately need that psychological buttressing I feel when I watch through the shop window as my fellow hackers barter, brag, and haggle.

Suddenly, the cybernetic equivalent of a mushroom cloud appears on my screen. "Grrrl Scouts of Death" blinks out. The mega-warehouse of illicit info is gone. Users are left floating in a void.

The bragging, boasting, and strutting comes to an abrupt halt.

Twenty long seconds of silence.

Then—pandemonium.

On comes the usual tidal wave of fretting and fuming, billingsgate and bellyache, bitchings and moanings. The Internet is alive with bewailing. Imagine a stadium full of livid Buttheads and Beavi spitting and casting hexes and excommunicating each other. Hair is pulled from heads, teeth grind down to stumps, oaths of revenge are signed in blood. Manifestos are spontaneously composed. Old wizened hackers of twenty-one and twenty-two mourn the loss of the good old days of unpoliced computer crime. A hundred voices are raised to the cybernetic heavens, asking, What is this world coming to when a teenager can't crash the phone system of the New York metropolitan area anymore? Woe is us!

I can picture MP Phred at his terminal, laughing his federal ass off.

I feel like I just stepped out of a Salvadoran village an instant before it was napalmed.

What is more frightening than the devastation is the *speed* with which MP Phred gained access to this secret board. Every Underground BBS is surrounded by a gnat cloud of wannabes who spend their lives trying to squirrel together enough hacker kudos to be included on the board, and they rarely succeed. MP Phred takes one look at where the best Underground board is (this discovery alone is staggering), hops on, sets a logic bomb, and *kablam*—all in half a day. I feel like a blind fighter pilot with the Red Baron on my tail. Time to take some serious evasive action.

But, just like a skunk, MP Phred always leaves a trace of himself behind.

Immediately after he crashed and burned a whole slew of low-skill hackers, he sent a message through the Net that contained his weirdest gaffe of all: "And hacker heads whole stop delete word go roll."

I was like, *What?* Then I recognized that words like "stop," "delete," and "go" sound like commands you type outside the message. Sounds like MP Pig meant to say, "And hacker heads roll," but instead, it came out, "And hacker heads whole." Somehow, MP Phred forgot to step out of the message by hitting his Alt key, or his Ctrl key, to correct his mistake. This is stupid enough for a hockey jock on his first day in Computer 101. But for a computer whiz like MP Phred? The man eats, drinks, and shits computers! It's *unheard of!*

Besides, you never have to *type out* commands like "stop," "delete," or "go." You usually hit Shift-F8 or something, get a list of number commands, and then type the single letter or number of your choice. But even this isn't necessary. When you make a typing mistake, you just tap the Backspace key, or the Delete key. Whatever his mistake, there is just no reason for him to actually type out his commands while he is conveying his message.

Hmmmm . . . very weird. Very weird indeed.

I look at my watch. Oo! It's time! I unplug my modem and jack in my phone. The phone instantly rings. I snap it up.

"Yo."

"—Ho Ho and a bottle of rum."

"Ho! What's up, Sugar Tits?"

"How's my human scratching post?"

"Scarred, scabby, and happy."

"Bitchin. Listen, Dad's gone. Went to the Grand Canyon for the month."

"Where are you?"

"I'm at my Mom's flat. We can't get a flight until tonight, so you have to give me until midnight to get back. She's going to visit her old commune buds in Iowa."

"Did she know about her phone being cut?"

"No."

"Fuckin A through Z. Get her out of there."

"I'm on it. Look, she agreed to lend me two thousand dollars. When I come back, we can quit your pad and hole up someplace with your gadgets and make love and you can save the world. I know you won't get addicted, because my pussy will be there to distract you. I'll watch over you, and all will be tubular. Does that sound good?"

"That sounds great."

Silence. I feel like something more should be said.

"Hurry up and get back here, Ho. I miss you."

An affluxion rises in Ho's voice. "You know, I really want to tell you this. I never let a man treat me like that before. Not like you. It feels so wonderful to trust you that much. To let myself go and really feel safe. It means a lot to me, Chet." She's crying. "Just don't forget that, okay?"

"Never."

"You're a wonderful man, you know that? And you try

soooo hard, it just breaks my heart. I'm sorry I give you so much shit. You're great, Chet. Okay?"

"Okay."

"No, I mean really. I mean really, really—"

Her voice breaks off. Ho—my friend Ho—is crying.

"Wow," I say. "This is about the luckiest night of my life."

"You mean last night," she sniffs.

"No. Tonight."

She snorts a laugh. "The confirmation."

"This conversation."

"You're so sweet."

"Ho?"

"Yes?"

"It won't go bad. It's not like in the movies. I will never abuse you. I want you to feel good when I do those things."

I can feel her smile. "I know you do," she goes, and hangs up.

It's stuffy in here, because the shades are always pulled. Set against the liquid darkness is the white pyramid hanging from my desk lamp and the reptilian green glow of my computer screen. All I can hear is the buzz of my snake's sunlamp and the drone of the TV.

My beeper beeps. I ignore it. Since I talked to Ho, it's been beeping every ten minutes. It's always the same number.

Right now, I'm back in the U.S. banking systems, using my ill-gotten codes to get ever deeper. I'm looking over my cybernetic shoulder every thirty seconds, but it's relatively smooth sailing. The "Grrrl Scout" guys (may they rest in peace) have certainly done their homework. Everything clicks just the way it's supposed to, and I'm progressing steadily to the heart.

The only problem is, I'm scared shitless. MP Phred has me totally paranoid. Every time I hear a noise in the hallway, I set my fingers over my self-destruct code and listen. Every good hacker has a logic bomb written into his hardware so he can blow up all the evidence at any moment. If I press Shift-

Ctrl-Alt-@, my hard drive starts an endless loop message that writes over everything incriminating.

An hour ago, I was enraged to find my loophole sealed up. But now, mysteriously, another one appears. I'm certain it wasn't there before. I spend an hour writing a cuckoo's egg.

A cuckoo bird doesn't have the power to make a nest of its own. So it secretly lays its eggs in other birds' nests, who hatch the cuckoo's eggs for her. The cuckoo has the smarts, the dumb bird has the hardware. The cuckoo relies on the ignorance of other birds.

When I plant my cuckoo's egg, I am simply replacing the legitimate banking program with a program of my own. The system treats my program as its own baby, runs it, and unknowingly hatches my scheme inside itself. It opens up a hole for me. I'm in.

Then I mouse through the various directories and find—

I cannot believe my luck. A file called "PSSWRDS." Some dumb banker must have placed the codes on a computer file. I send my prompt over to it and call up the info. A message flashes across my screen:

DEAR SNAKEBYTE: I KNOW WHO YOU ARE. DON'T TREAD ANY FURTHER. I DON'T WANT TO WASTE TIME ON SOMEBODY OF YOUR SKILL. I LOVE CHALLENGES, BUT YOU ARE NOT A DARK-SIDE HACKER. WE ARE TWO INVISIBLES, BUT I'VE ALWAYS KNOWN YOU WERE OUT THERE. I KNOW YOU'RE BREAKING THE LAW, BUT SO FAR, YOU ARE NOT WORTH THE EFFORT. THERE ARE OTHER RODENTS I WANT. YOU STAY IN YOUR FIELD; I'LL STAY IN MINE. BUT IF YOU CROSS THE LINE INTO THIS SYSTEM, I WILL TAKE YOU DOWN, AND TAKE YOU DOWN HARD. DON'T FUCK WITH ME. LOVE, MP PHRED.

He tricked me. He disguised this file as a piece of juicy info, and I fell right into it. The actual words in his message are less terrifying than his implicit message, which is: *If I can trick you this easily, I can put you in jail.*

So MP Phred knows who I am. And he's been following me.

How could he have known? How could he pick this particular bank account in this particular bank and plant a disguised message here, one addressed directly to me?

MP Phred must be specifically protecting the banks. But he didn't stop me when I broke into the general banking system. No traps snapped in my face until I jiggled the locks of one particular bank account. A sheepdog in a flock of sheep, MP Phred is focusing his magnifying glass on one special lamb, the account of Wozniak and Levy.

MP Phred is working for Wozniak and Levy.

And he's showing me mercy. Why?

Why wouldn't he want me? I'm the one directly trying to break into the banking system he is hired to protect. Why let me off with a warning? Wouldn't a Fed let me wander in, allow me to dig deeper into the trap, and then snap it on me?

Could it be that MP Phred *admires* me?

Arch-enemies, we are more alike than the people we defend. You can dress a hacker like a Fed, but, at his core, he will always be a hacker.

I suppose I could play this cat-and-mouse game for months, but I don't have the time. My beeper keeps going off, I miss Ho, and the city is trying to kill me. MP Phred is the main barrier to saving my life. In order to take down Wozniak and Levy, I have to take out MP Phred.

To hell with sneaking past the cyber watchman, I'm going to bulldoze right through him.

I go search around the public bulletin boards for debates about computer security, looking for names, connections, lists of organizations. Forget Wozniak and Levy for a while, and concentrate on their pit bull. Find out who MP Phred is, where he is, what his weaknesses are, and crush him.

This showdown was bound to happen someday. I wanted to hone my skills for another year until I was ready, but now I have no choice but to face him one-on-one.

Gulp.

*   *   *

I was lurking on a renegade BBS when I happened to notice a listing for a legit and public bulletin board called "Clip Chip." The Clipper Chip is a thumbnail-sized device that the FBI wants to hook up to everybody's encryption codes so they can spy on us. This is the sort of BBS where I will meet lots of cyber lawmen who might accidentally give me clues pertaining to their patron saint, MP Phred. I take a peek and find the anarchists and stiffs are really going at it. I decide to jump into the fray and log on to their system, and we type out a passionate but good-natured debate. I'm not trying to convince anybody of anything; I'm really fishing for Phred footprints. So far inland from the deep seas of the hacker Underground, I feel safe, so I call myself Snakebyte. It's akin to brandishing your peg-leg in Kansas while Moby Dick is searching for the rest of you somewhere in the Irish Sea.

Somebody is lurking on the board, following our argument, and he notices my handle. He breaks on. "Is this *the* Snakebyte? Of hallowed hacker fame?"

My hands freeze in midtype.

Uh-oh.

I snort. Naw, it couldn't be.

I type, "Identify yourself."

The words jigger across the screen. "Sorry. Didn't mean to intrude. I'm Jim Pederson, from the Law Phreaks board."

Jesus. This guy doesn't even have a handle. A square. I type back, "Well, being a stealth bomber, I don't know about how famous I am."

He types back excitedly, "MP Phred told me about your duel. Sounds exciting. I wish I understood those games."

I push my eyeballs back in my sockets and type casually, "How do you know MP Phred?"

"I'm a property lawyer. He talked to me about property rights and issues of jurisdiction and the concept of boundaries in cyberspace."

"What did you tell him?"

"I told him they didn't apply."

"Thank God."

"I told him we need new concepts for possession/ownership for a new universe."

"I forgive you. Do you know his real name?"

What the hell. It's worth the chance.

"No. But he gave me his nickname and described his occupation right off the bat."

I can't believe this. Nobody is this stupid. No Hacker Tracker would bandy his name around the tame cyberburb regions.

"Why would he give you his secret handle?"

"I didn't want to talk to him when he tried to get on our board. Lawyers and law scholars only, you know. So he broke on. I still wouldn't talk to him. So he gave me his handle to legitimize himself. My curiosity was piqued, so I did some research, and, sure enough, he's legit. A real lawman."

"What sort of research?" I ask hopefully.

"Nothing really. I just asked my FCIC friends about some of the things he said, which they confirmed. He knows too much not to be a lawman. He mentioned you briefly, but he was more interested in acquiring information than giving it. I chewed his ear a good bit, didn't bill him, and that was that."

My debate partner breaks back on. "Am I to assume our national security discussion is over?"

"Kaput," I type back. "Anyway, where does he hang out nowadays?"

To my infinite amazement, this cyberstraight gives me the access code to "Tekno-Repair." I leave a juicy piece of porno access behind, steal his address so I can mail him some free law magazine subscriptions, and log off to go search Tekno-Repair for some cop clues. I'm on *your* ass now, Phred.

"Tekno-Repair" is the corny title for a place that debugs software—kind of like a place that specializes in changing tires or oil. You can do it yourself, but why not pay a little extra to make sure it's done right?

After going through their order forms, I pick out an order from an individual who describes himself as a "law enforcer on the electronic highway" for an *interface repair*.

Bingo!

MP Phred, it seems, detected a glitch in the software of his interface and sent a copy of it to these technoid dudes.

Scrolling through his order form, I learn that he paid for this repair work *privately*. Which is interesting. You'd figure if the Feds or Wozniak and Levy were hiring him, they'd pay for any job-related expenses. Maybe he saves receipts. I scroll down to its payment status, hoping to get an address or credit card or check number.

Hm. MP Phred, it seems, paid for it in advance, through untraceable wire transfer. So he left no address, no way to be contacted. He's making damn sure no hackers dig up the payment info and trace him. I am left to assume that he plans to do a *Mission: Impossible* stunt: wait till these guys reprogram his software, jump on, make a copy, steal it, and disappear. The tech dudes are probably not advanced or hip enough to detect that anyone ever got access to their software and copied it. They would assume they were paid for nothing. Meanwhile, MP Phred, in his own little mayo and margarine conscience, rationalizes his break-in by telling himself that he paid for the software repair ahead of time, so nobody got hurt.

Ha ha. Once a hacker, always a hacker, no matter what

kind of Boy Scout conscience you graft on to him with the stitching of a fat government paycheck. The Feds are after an improbable hybrid: an entity with the skills of a dark-side hacker and the dumb, aw-shucks, unshakable, boyishly American virtues of Jimmy Stewart. And they haven't found him in MP Phred.

But I didn't expect his address or telephone number. Phred is not that dumb. He would allow even for the off chance that somebody would follow him here. But scrounging through this treasure chest full of dust, I find one jewel buried at the bottom:

A copy of MP Phred's interface program!

Yippeeeeeee!

God, I am so cool.

The interface is the set of codes that translates computer language into human language, so that computers and human beings can interact. Everybody's interface is similar. Finding Phred's would not be such a big deal, were it not for the fact that, on initial perusal, it is utterly foreign to any interface program I have encountered.

Who knows what good it will do? Probably none. But it will buy me an immense amount of information power on the Underground boards. Imagine! "I have here a program heisted off MP Phred. What do you want to trade?" But I can't share it with my hysterical brethren right away. For now, this is mine, all mine. In these strings of code I will find clues to how the Terror of the Underground operates.

After a long evening of sleepless tinkering, I settle upon the indisputable fact: MP Phred's interface is alien. But this is not what worries me.

What worries me profoundly—what, in fact, makes me quiver in my boots—is that there appears to be *no human interface*! I am looking at the codes here, and I detect no proper human translation. Who is this guy?

Now I'm thinking about perfect grammar, perfect spelling, the fact that his word mistakes seem more electronic than human, and I am really starting to freak out. When I study the software, all I see is a machine interacting with another machine. It's a closed two-way operation. There is no human soul to complete the trinity. After a long search for the ghost in the machine, I find that the ghost *is* a machine.

It is within the laws of the possible that MP Phred built a second machine to communicate with his computer. But why? It might be fun, but it would impede speed and efficiency. And, if there is anything hackers worship, it is speed and efficiency. It doesn't make sense.

Unless MP Phred is a machine.

Obviously, a machine is not tracking us down, making Sherlock Holmes intuitive leaps, composing all those rhetorical flourishes. There is not the automaton built yet that can beat a hacker. There has to be a human element there.

But I can't get around the conclusion. What I have basically discovered here is a robot sitting at a computer hacking away.

Where the *fuck is Ho?!* It's three A.M., and I'd say that's just a tad bit past midnight! Why hasn't she called?

Two voices in the hallway outside my door:

"Okay, you have to save this seal, right?"

"Yeah. We peel it off and put it inside this baggy."

"Which key is it?"

"I don't know. Try all three."

Something jimmies into my keyhole.

I flick off my computer, twist off my desk lamp. Ho's skirts are piled on the floor! There are opened ramen-noodle packets scattered around! I don't have time to put my snake back in his—!

The door handle unlocks, turns, and jams.

"The top lock is locked."

"Try one of the other keys."

I frantically scoop up Ho's clothes and dash into the closet with my snake. I close it behind me as I hear the front door unlatch and open.

"Don't turn on the lights! Don't touch anything. Here's a flashlight."

A white blade materializes along the floor at my toes. I push myself behind the hanging shirts.

"What are we looking for?"

"*You* don't look for anything. Your job is to oversee me as I do the looking. I'm here to pick up a certain computer disk. We have to do this right. I'm tired of people screwing up these investigations. So let's be professional for once."

"So how long is this gonna take?"

"Hours, maybe. I'll have to search the whole place. I have to wear gloves and make a note of everything I touch or move. I'll work through his desk, check his night table, then go in his closet."

I hug Ho's wardrobe close and swallow.

"This is ridiculous," says the second cop. "I've never seen a murder investigation run like this. Corlini should have no power to stall Homicide before they put evidence in storage. This crap has been sitting here for a week. And she's got no business sending someone like me here. I don't know shit about homicide."

"Well, let's just find her disk and get out of here."

"I'm just gonna use the can."

"Wait! Shit! You broke the seal! And you touched the doorknob, you idiot!"

"What?"

"The seal! You broke it! We were authorized to break one seal! Not two! Now *you* do the paperwork when we get back!"

"I didn't break any seal. There's no seal on this door."

"What do you call this?"

"That was already like that."

A pause. I hold my breath.

"It was?"

"Did you hear anything snap?"

There is a long moment of breathless silence. Then I hear the opposite bathroom door kick open.

The first voice snaps into cop voice. *"Did you break that fucking seal?"*

I hear Denny moaning incoherently. Then a woman's voice. It's his girlfriend. Elana.

"He doesn't understand! Why don't you leave him alone?"

"Well, why did he break the fucking seal? Do you see that? It's a police seal! Major fine!"

"He's retarded," Elana extemporizes. "He didn't know. I've explained it to him since. It won't happen again. Can't you see he's sorry?"

I almost snicker to imagine the sweet puppy-dog eyes Denny is giving them right now. I hear him moan endearingly like Chewbacca. Wouldn't win him an Oscar, but the cops won't know the difference.

"He needed to go in there," she riffs. "The man next door borrowed something of his, and Denny wanted it back."

"And what was that?" the cop demands. "What kind of evidence did you steal?"

A pause. Much too long. I'm wincing and writhing in my closet. C'mon, Elana! Think! A razor! A bus schedule! A paperclip! Anything! Just don't say computer disk!

"A condom."

Hm. Pretty good.

I can almost hear the lawmen meeting eyes. Then: "All right. We're going to come by with some papers for you to sign. And then we have to go."

"Don't we need to get the computer disk?" queries the second cop.

"Not now that evidence has been tampered with. We have to reseal this room until the Homicide boys can get back and redust. Hand me the second seal."

Fingertips squeak along the metal surrounding the bathroom door handle.

My god. They're taping me in.

"There! That should do it. Write down the security code, date, and time. I guess we take this backing paper with us." He directs his voice at Elana and Denny. "If this seal gets broken again, I'm taking you both in for tampering with evidence, and then you'll both be suspects. You understand?"

"Yes, sir," says Elana.

Denny moans endearingly.

My beeper goes off. It's on my waistband.

I slam it with my hand to retroactively stifle the sound.

From the bathroom, the second cop says, "Hey! His computer just beeped."

My heart hiccups.

"So?"

"So how can it do that when it's turned off?"

My legs become two boneless penises.

"His computer *is* turned off. It sounded more like it came from across the room . . . in his closet."

My larynx chokes with a bubble of air.

"Well, let's check it out."

Semidigested ramen noodles begin their squirming ascent to the back of my throat.

"Jimmy, every seal we break, soil, or lose has to be accounted for with miles of paperwork. There's no need to break this seal on account of some wristwatch alarm. Let's go bring these broken seals back to the station and get this written up. So much for dinner at home tonight."

I wait long into the silence. They're gone.

I step out into my room, dump Ho's stuff back on the floor.

I'm taped in. I'm trapped.

I stare down my sleeping computer.

Time is running out. I'll use the notebook Denny lent me to trace MP Phred's line. Then, I'll send his phone number over the Internet. The hackers will do a "finger" on him, find out who he is, and fuck him straight up the ass for the rest of his life.

It can't be helped.

Sorry, MP, but you're standing in the way. You're protecting criminals who want to kill me and my beloved.

My snake wrapped around my neck and shoulders, Rage Against the Machine spitting spleen on the stereo, my mind on hyper-focus, I break into the phone company and follow Denny's instructions to the department that executes FBI requests for phone traces and taps. My modem handshakes with their modem to synchronize responses, and—shazam!—I'm in. When I peruse the record of recent phone traces, I see a

trace made from the connection at the bank of Wozniak and
Levy.

Holiest of holy shits.

MP Phred was using the same knowledge I have comman-
deered to illegally manipulate the same tracing functions. He
knows as much as I do. When I was jacking in to the bank
number, he detected me, hacked into this phone company, and
put a trace on my call. Rerouting my line through so many
switching stations certainly slowed him down. Instead of tracing me in four minutes, he squiggled helter-skelter through a
knotted bundle of crisscrossing lines for three hours until I
hung up. But he progressed steadily towards my location.

A real FCIC agent, following legal channels, could not have
done it that fast. Working your way legally through all that
bureaucracy, getting permission from different jurisdictions,
and doing it trace by trace, would take your average committee
of Feds about three months. Imagine a hundred cooks trying
to make a piece of toast. But MP Phred, by bypassing all the
legal mumbo jumbo, got more than two-thirds of the way to
my line in three hours. He's got my general location narrowed
down. He knows I live in the Bay Area, for certain.

But when he went through the Alameda switching station,
he got cut off by an automatic message: "This line is no longer
in service. Please check the number and dial again." Discon-
nected. As of yesterday, the Alameda phone computer treats
incoming traces as if they were wrong numbers.

MP certainly guessed that this was the product of my phone
phreaking. It would take him forever to figure out where in
all the miles of code I hid my microscopic bug, so he went in
and disabled the whole message, just uprooted it at the base,
which is worse vandalism than I've ever committed. Now
everyone in our neighborhood that calls a number no longer
in service will get loud screech over their line, but no recorded
message. But the next time I log on, he can trace me without
hindrance.

No Fed would fuck with established systems like that. MP
has bypassed all my intricate rerouting meant to befuddle peo-

ple who work through the law. Next time he traces me, it will go straight back to here.

But when he logs on the phone company's computer to play with tracing programs—or when he logs on to the same program at the bank that I log on to—I can trace *him*.

MP doesn't realize it, but we are both poised to destroy each other. This should cause deterrence through fear of mutual annihilation.

To my chagrin, I find myself chickening out.

I'm struggling with a software bug I can't locate. I'm irritated as hell from lack of sleep, fear, and malnutrition. This is not the best physiological mode for solving tedious problems.

I know a skater chick who is in deep shit with her new boyfriend when she gets back to his pad. She is definitely starting off our relationship on the wrong foot. I mean, hey, I hate it when a chick calls you every hour after coitus, too. But when there are all sorts of slathering rapists after her, I expect a call. Is that so much to ask?

Even worse, since she's taped out of this room, we won't be able to fuck until I get us out of this. I'll tell you, if it's not one thing with women, it's another. First they make you wait. Then they make you hold their purse while you're waiting. Then they bring fourteen of their friends to the bathroom with them. They complain that you never call, but then, the first chance there's a life-threatening conspiracy of mobsters and cops, they go and—

My beeper bleats.

Dammit!! I can't concentrate with all this beeper beeping and cops snooping and girlfriends not calling!

It's always that same damn number. I ignore it, but it's driving me insane.

Fuck it. I have to shut it all out and *concentrate*!

My beeper goes off again.

A lightning spasm of anger jerks me to my feet. I snatch up my beeper and march over to my phone. I stab out the number.

It picks up immediately.

"What do you want, Chen?"

"Ah, Mr. Griffin! I'm so glad you decided to call! The stakes have changed for us, have they not?"

"Cut the shit, Chen. You can't trace this. So stop wasting time and give me the lowdown. *Why the fuck do you want to talk to me?*"

"We got your girlfriend."

A hole opens up inside me. It's like a cigarette touching a spiderweb.

"You're full of shit," I say, my voice aquiver.

"Her hair is very strange color. Ring in her nose. Another in her navel. She about five foot, hundred pound or so. She have two thousand dollar on her. Nice bonus for us."

My lungs go into rapid-fire convulsions. They just keep trying to inhale without letting me exhale. I take the phone away from my mouth and repeatedly gasp. I get my breath back and shout into the phone, "You are so fucking full of shit, Chen, you goat! How fucking stupid do you think I am?"

"Got a dog name Wily. Got a birthmark on inside of her thigh. Shape like a stop sign. She very pretty girl."

"None of that means shit, Chen!" I sob.

"What makes you so sure, eh?"

"Because you'd let me talk to her if you had her!"

"That not possible."

"Right! That means you either don't have her, or you already . . ."

"Already what, Chet?"

I hang up.

I'm down on my knees ripping at my hair and banging my head on the floor.

It's time to use my power. I will become the Dark Angel of Death, destroyer of worlds. I will terrorize. I will sabotage. I will crash Chen, crash the investment bankers, crash the cops. I will shut down their bank accounts, swallow their wealth. I will leave a Godzilla trail of destruction through the electronic world all those people rely on. I will thrash and burn, binge and purge in an endless Sherman's March until they come and exterminate me in my den.

This is for you, Ho.

I polish my armor, sharpen my weapons, compose abbreviated macros, take the kinks out of my offensive and defensive software. In I go, my slit eyes aglow with the humming green light of my computer.

I reject the tender, the loyal, the needy. Unconditional love is a lie. Innocence is weakness.

Behind me, the TV airs some information significant to my plot.

"Sewer workers today spotted a man washing out of a drainage pipe into the bay. Gary Tsao says he fell into a storm drain on Nob Hill sometime last Friday and broke his neck. He remained there for two days until a routine sewer cleaning washed him to the bay all the way from Nob Hill, a distance of one mile. He somehow survived. We spoke to rescue workers." Another voice. "We had to get the neck brace on him while he was still in the water." Newscaster's voice. "A group of concerned citizens gathered outside his hospital window today."

Cheering sounds. "Yea, Miracle Man!" Then a nervous voice: swollen lips, slight Chinese accent. "Well, I climbed down to get my dog, and I guess I fell on my head."

"Tsao is listed in critical condition. A collection has been taken to pay the medical bills of this remarkable man. Donations should be sent to Grace Cathedral at Jones Street in San Francisco."

My mind swallows the data computerlike, stores it for later processing, and continues working.

I let her go alone. My fault, my fault, my fault.

Everyone I have ever loved has died. Bobby is a walking corpse. I love something, it dies. Chet Griffin's love is a curse.

A second piece of data slides under the sealed door adjoining the bathroom. It sits there for hours while I prepare my proglets. When I stop to crunch down some raw ramen, I go over and pick it up.

Denny already opened the envelope. It was addressed to him, but inside is a smaller envelope addressed to me. I open it.

It's a card from Ho, mailed yesterday. From a sex novelty shop, of course. It sports a picture of the Wizard of Oz male triumvirate. Dorothy is bent over taking it doggy style from the Tin Man. Scarecrow and Lion are squirting oilcans on the point of contact. The caption reads, "Don't Let It Get Rusty."

A reflex whispering begins on my lips. It takes me a while to recognize it, because it has been so long since I've done this. I am praying. I am praying that they have already killed her.

I realize now I have no hope.

I want nothing more than to hurt as many of my enemies as I can. By the time they kill me, I will have emblazoned Ho's name across their voided bank accounts and Quotron screens. I will assemble the evidence, mail it around the country, and take them down with me.

I toss away my ramen. Food is pointless. Sleep is pointless. I am a corpse, already entombed. I have one function, and that is to destroy.

When I sit down at my terminal, something scratches at my hallway door. I leap to my feet, smash my mirror, and grab a shard of glass sharp enough to cut a throat. No hiding this time. The reptile possesses me.

Someone warm-blooded sniffles along the base of my door, whimpers.

I approach and get down on my knees. I find that I have tears in my eyes.

"Wily?"

He barks.

I hug the door. "Oh, Wily, Wily! You're okay! You're okay!"

He yelps and whimpers, snorting and licking at the air coming underneath the door. I see his hot tongue dart through, giving itself rug burns to reach me. I give him my fingers, and he slops up my salty oils.

"They took her from us, Wily. They took her from us."

I lean my forehead against the door and weep for all the good things lost. Lost forever.

The beeper next to my keyboard beeps. I stab off my modem and snatch it up. Different number. New York area code.

I claw after my phone and dial the number. Somebody picks up.

"You know who I am! So who the fuck is this?"

"Chet, my name is Michael Leone. I work for Rocky Rachino, a businessman here in New York City. I believe you can help us."

"This I gotta hear."

"We want Chen. He is stealing our money, and, worse, he is showing us grave disrespect. I'll explain: Mr. Rachino made a business transition to stock investment four years ago. The venture was so successful, Mr. Rachino has specialized in it, offering his services to other businessmen who were interested in exploiting this unique market. John Chen enlisted our services. We flew some of our operatives out there to train him in the process."

"Spock and Data are *operatives*? Silly me, I thought they were just goons."

"These are Chen's pet names for those in his employ, and

we are frankly insulted that he would apply them to our specialists—but yes, you get the picture. Those two were to protect the man who worked the computers. We sent a number of our people out to aid Chen in the transition. But he reneged on our contract."

"From the perspective of the pawn in your arrangement, it looked to me like Chen was running things perfectly."

"Not exactly. The men you know as Spock and Data were assigned to accompany our *trainer,* the computer expert who was supposed to teach Chen and his men the operation. Our computer expert was not supposed to *run the business for him.* Naturally, when our operatives found themselves executing every level of the scheme, without any participation from Chen or his men except demands that a certain amount of money be made, bad blood was bound to arise. We feel that we are entitled to a cut of the profits—something of a broker's percentage, if you will—rather than just a flat payment. But Chen has refused. He has tried to make Mr. Rachino look like a chump. We thought he was taking this option to go legit, but instead he has used us, all the while remaining in the drug business. This makes Mr. Rachino look very bad."

"Switching from violent to white-collar crime is not exactly going legit."

The man laughs. "You are making assumptions about us that do not apply, my friend. New York Italian businessmen often suffer from stereotypes perpetuated by those ignoramuses Coppola and Puzo. But, be that as it may, our concern is that Chen continues to deal with drugs, which is something Mr. Rachino takes great pains to disassociate himself from. And now how does it look, with Mr. Rachino's operatives working alongside these drug dealers?"

"And chasing innocent bike couriers through the city and gunning them down?"

"I beg your pardon?"

"Look, Mr. Leone, I appreciate this calm articulation of your dire problems, but I'm looking for the actual point in all this."

"The point is justice, Mr. Griffin. Now, we could condemn

and punish Chen ourselves, but you understand that would be troublesome. We have learned through your friends Spock and Data that you and your girlfriend set up quite an admirable scheme to collect damning evidence against Chen. Your evidence is the weapon we need to prosecute Chen in open court. Now, we understand that you are in hiding because you have been accused of that accident with your friend Rudiger Spinkleman. My condolences."

"Deeply appreciated."

"You're welcome. Your evidence is very valuable to us. And naturally this valuable information should be bought with a hefty price."

"I get a cut of your bloody drug money? Cool! What's the going rate for stool pigeons?"

"We believe there are two things you need: One, you want to be exonerated so you can stop hiding. Two, you want Ho Pixie back."

Against my better judgment, a pilot light of hope glimmers in me. I doubt they will ever deliver Ho to me. But this does suggest that she might be alive.

Assuming this is not a trick.

"And in return?"

"In return, you deliver us the evidence against Chen."

"Can't he finger you?"

"No."

"Why not?"

"We know things about the legal system that you do not, my friend."

"Why can't I deliver them straight to the cops?"

He chuckles again. "Mr. Griffin, a man in my position spends a great deal of time acting in concert with law enforcement, and I can assure you that their organizing skills cannot be trusted. They investigate hundreds of cases at once, and they are not personally invested in any one case. They lose evidence, botch trails, and they are easily corruptible, as all poor men are. Mr. Rachino, however, is a rich man, and he has a personal interest in pushing this prosecution through. He will spare no expense for lawyers and judges to put this Chen where he belongs: behind bars."

"What do you know about Wozniak and Levy?"

He laughs again. "Mr. Griffin, I've provided a generous amount of information already. The question that remains for us now is: Will you deliver the evidence to us in exchange for your girlfriend?"

"How do we make this transaction?"

"You know the city better than we do. You arrange the drop spot. You give us the evidence, we give you Ho—that is her name, isn't it? Ho? I mean no disrespect—and we wash our hands of this whole incident. No one need know of our arrangement."

"All the evidence is deposited in a bank deposit box."

"Perfect. You deliver the key to us, we will give you Ho and convict Chen of the Spinkleman and Corlini murders."

"And then I walk away from this whole deal, and me and Ho live happily ever after, right?"

"Right."

"So I guess I'm just a moron, then."

"Excuse me?"

"How do you know I won't deliver a phony key? How do you know I won't keep copies of the evidence?"

He pauses. I continue. "You know damn well you can never get all the evidence, because I can always make another copy. You don't want the evidence. You want me."

"We don't, Chet, I promise you. We want Chen. The law cannot implicate us in Chen's crimes."

"Not even if I am recording this conversation?"

He pauses. "Are you?"

I let the suspense linger, and then laugh. "I've arranged that the moment I'm killed, copies of the evidence will be mailed around the country."

"And what result would that bring? An inconvenience to Mr. Rachino and Chen; death to you and Ho. Why don't we work together? We are both enemies of Chen."

"Then how did you get my beeper number?"

"From elements who have infiltrated Chen's operation."

"You're full of it."

He sighs. "Don't you want your girlfriend back, Chet?"

"I'm not into necrophilia, Leone."

"You're overreacting, my friend. Chen would never harm Ho so long as she represents a bargaining chip. And Mr. Rachino never forgets a favor. A very powerful man would be deeply indebted to you. We are the answer to your prayers. Deliver us the key."

"I'll think about it," I say, and I hang up.

I don't have the bank deposit key. Ho does.

Last week, as I was getting off the elevator in Chen's building, the man I saw carrying the crate embossed with a Spider logo was not Asian. He wore a green, white, and red flag of Italy tie.

The sun rises. As I'm emptying my chamberpot out the window, I hear voices in Denny's room. I freeze and listen.

"We talked to your landlord. Hell of a retard act you put up. We know you're buddies with Chet Griffin. We want to know why you went in his room."

No answer.

"All right. You're coming with us. Put the cuffs on him."

"Hey, chuckleheads," Denny says, "as much as I appreciate the kinkiness, you can't operate my chair if I have handcuffs on."

But, of course, they don't understand him.

"What the hell is wrong with this chair? Do you have a lock on it?"

Denny says, speaking as clearly as he can, "You can't push it! I'm the only one who can operate this chair! I need you to take these cuffs off me!"

A cop says, "Call those guys in the handicap wagon up here. Maybe they know how to operate this chair."

Denny continues to explain that only he can operate his chair until the cripple-wagon driver comes up and informs them that only Denny can operate his chair. I hear Denny's door shut and lock. Then silence.

Another friend dragged into my scheme. Now Chen will kill Denny too.

Trick or no trick, I have no choice but to take Leone's offer.

I am staring at Leone's beeper number when the ever-droning TV catches my attention.

"Gary Tsao, known as the Miracle Man since he was propelled a full mile through the city's storm drain system with a broken neck yesterday, has claimed he works for John Chen, alleged mafia boss. Police have posted guards around Tsao's hospital room, he has asked for no lawyer, and he is recording hours of testimony. We spoke to Chief Daniel Thornston." Another voice. "This individual claims his boss is responsible for multiple counts of arson and murder. He also claims he was involved in a gun battle inside the city's storm drain system." Newsman's voice says, "Authorities are investigating his claims."

"Wow," adds the anchorman.

Before I can consider this, my beeper beeps. I read the number. It's Chen.

I call back immediately.

"Hey Chen, my man, what's up?"

I'm listening for a tremble in his voice. I detect none. "We have the key. We find it within your girlfriend's shoe. Inside her bank deposit box, we locate the evidence. Paper and computer disks, just like the ones we find within your apartment." Chen ejaculates his patented avuncular chuckle. "Radios, computers, printers, phone equipment, stolen seals, peeled seals. Been looking inside our private transactions, eh, Mr. Griffin? You are a very enterprising and courageous young man! Under different circumstances, I offer you job! Call you Wesley Crusher! It a pity we have to meet under such a noncheerful circumstance."

"Okay, so the evidence is destroyed. I got no way to prove anything. No need to kill us. Let Ho go."

Chen chuckles. "Oh no, Mr. Griffin. This has merely changed the stakes."

"How is that?"

"I appreciate your interest in Ho. Very pretty. We will consummate our relationship tonight."

"What?"

"Good-bye, Chet."

He hangs up.

I am banging my fists on my desk when my beeper beeps again. A third and yet unknown number. I call it back, looking for a thread to pull myself out of this abyss.

"Chet, this is Gina. You know my last name."

"Jesus. My beeper number is being bandied around the criminal community like a squash ball."

"I am not a criminal."

"Then what prompted your arrangement with your brother? Sisterly love?"

"You shut up about my murdered brother! He gave you a job!" She suddenly swallows.

"Okay, Gina. Take a deep breath, count to ten, and start brown-nosing. You called to bullshit me, right? I have something you want?"

"The New York mafia and Chen are about to start a war. And my city will be the battlefield. I want to get Chen before it starts."

"And you want my evidence. Which you know I have because your business partner Chen told you."

"Look at the TV, Chet! Does it look like I'm dancing a waltz with Chen? You think I'd conspire to murder my own brother?"

"All I know is that Mel Corlini was the only man who had my number, and now everybody who should want to kill me has it."

"Right now I have someone informing on Chen, and you can corroborate his testimony. If you turn yourself in right now, we'll make a raid and rescue Ho."

"Then what? Jail?"

"You'll go on the witness protection program."

"Wonderful."

"Testify against Chen, and you'll never have to worry about employment again. You'll be given a modest house with a new identity. Your student debt will disappear, and police officers will be your waiters for the rest of your life. You and Ho can spend the rest of your lives together."

"And I say good-bye forever to everyone I know."

"I know your financial problems, Chet. And I know you have no parents to keep in touch with. You are an ideal candidate for this program. This will be like winning the lottery for you."

"Bullshit. You want me to turn myself in so you can kill me. The prosecution of Chen implicates you. You don't want Chen behind bars. You want Chen dead. You want me dead, Ho dead, and Chen dead. Only then will you be vindicated."

She explodes, "So what are you going to do with the evidence then? Prosecute Chen yourself? Alone, you're powerless, Chet! The only people who can rescue your girlfriend, imprison Chen, and protect you forever is law enforcement. You think I don't know you've returned to your criminal computer behavior? Don't you know your old friends the FCIC are after you again? Who is going to protect you from them? Me! You have to trust me, because you don't have any other choice!"

"I have plenty of choices, Gina. I think I'm going to go with the Italians' offer."

"Who? Wha? They called you?"

Damn. I can't tell if her surprise is genuine or faked. I hoped to determine whether Chen, Leone, and Gina are all acting in tandem in a psychological assault on me, or if they are all just reacting to the news reports, but Gina's reaction is flat.

"This is not about you, Chet. This is about all the innocent people who will die in Chen's war. You and your girlfriend are the only witnesses alive."

"And you want me squealing about how your brother ran this stock market ring? About your lucky stock purchases?"

Long pause, seething. "What choice do you have, Chet?"

"Spare me, Gina. I know what I represent to you. The fact is, nobody—not Chen, not the Italians, not you—can feel secure until the knowledge is annihilated. If I were you, I would have one goal in mind: kill Ho Pixie and Chet Griffin."

"I'm the only one who can save your girlfriend, Chet. Think about that."

"I want proof that Ho is alive. Then we can talk."

I hang up and turn off Denny's tape recorder.

I am inching through the banking system. MP Phred has not shown his face. I know he's leading me into a trap. In any other circumstances, I would bail. But I have no choice but to forge ahead. Soon, by my hand, the fortune of Wozniak and Levy will vanish off the face of the earth.

My damn beeper interrupts me. Damn it! Again? I pick it up. Chen.

Pissed off, I call it up, because I can't afford not to.

"What do you want, Chen?"

"Your brother Bobby, he cut a mean tattoo. My man Data go to him and get a nice spider on his chest. Very talented."

"Oh, no . . ."

"Are you going to come out, Chet?"

I don't answer. Our ears mash together across the wires of the telephone. I'm staring directly into the hot albino blankness of my lightbulb. Then my eyes fall on my snake.

"Okay, I take your girlfriend then."

My snake's eyes flash red.

"Look at you, Chet. A grown man, and you act like a big baby. Bobby more man than you. You hide and leave your little brother out in the cold, not protect him. Won't finish the ride we started together, you and me. You let your woman ride for you. You chicken."

I try to choke an answer. "Please, Chen . . . my brother Bobby . . . he's got nothing to do with this . . . he never hurt anybody in his life . . ."

"Yeah, he have trouble with that crack, though. He one of our best customers. Hate to have to eliminate him. He a nice boy. But if his brother turn himself in to police by tomorrow, no need to harm him. The police will protect you, Chet. Me and you friends! Chen and Chet! Same name almost! You go

to jail and you never hear from us again! We wash our hands
of—"

I hang up.

Voices reach me through the ghostly technology of the telephone. I can't see their faces. I'm fighting with phantoms,
clawing at screaming sirens flapping about my ears.

I hear Denny coming back from jail. His computer flicks
on. Then his stereo blasts Bikini Kill's album *Pussy Whipped*.
Their shrieking, banshee vocals caress my skin like bullwhips.

He was out on those streets. Those streets they control, the
realm I once sailed on.

Word is being sent through the cops to Chen that Denny is
my friend. Then they will come for him. One by one, they
will kill the people I love until they find me.

My eyes go to the broken mirror shard.

Is it my enemy's arteries I contemplate? Or mine?

If Ho was alive, they would have let me talk to her by now.
I have nothing to rescue.

I am only putting off my sure death. And I am putting it
off so I can remain alive long enough to electronically destroy
the institutions of my killers. But the stakes have risen. Their
command of reality is more powerful than my command of
cyberspace.

I have a choice: Destroy my enemies while they kill Bobby
and Denny. Or save Bobby and Denny by letting my enemies
go free.

Love is more important to me than revenge.

Could this jagged piece of glass do it? With robotic cold-
ness, I scratch the blade lightly along my wrist.

I bleed. I sting.

It hurts. Oh, it hurts. The hurt reminds me I am alive.

I smack the flat of the glass against my forehead. I can't
do it! I'm sorry, Bobby. I'm sorry, Denny. I can't do it this
way.

I slap my palms against my face. I hurt myself to know I
feel. I can't let this go. This throbbing flesh, this quivering

gristle, this decaying shit factory, is all I have. I can't give up this life.

I stare at my small habitrail. My mouth foams vampirelike. For the first time in my life, I consider devouring a rat.

But I need, now of all times, to express tenderness for another creature.

I remove the lid on my snake's cage. We speak in nonlanguage. I drop in the fat rat.

The irony of my impulse seizes me a second too late. I show kindness to my reptile by offering the mammal to death.

The trapped rat scurries from corner to corner, helplessly. Then she is frozen under the snake's gaze. She stares deep into the eyes of death, quivering. I'm just about to reach my hand in and snatch her away when my python snaps around her with deadly speed. Green muscles squeeze the innocent creature like a fist. I watch the mammal's face as she is suffocated. I know her now; I know she knows she is about to die. I can sense in her eyes that she is resigned to her fate. She just wants it to end quickly. I find myself asking, Does she have children? Did she breed, live, love? Then her eyes glaze over. Her little paws slowly stop flaying. Her mouth stays open, frozen like a statue crying to the sky. The snake releases. The rat falls limp. The snake unhinges its jaw.

I turn my eyes away. Always before, I had seen this ritual from the perspective of the hunter. Not now.

I need a new pet. A herbivore.

A nasal buzz moves in and out of my skull. I wave my hand across my ear.

A red-eyed fly lands on my toe, closes her front paws prayerfully, then rubs them together like sniveling Iago. I wiggle my foot. The bulbous black sack, a winged pimple, zips a figure eight quicker than Dorothy Hamill and touches down on the same spot with an elegant six-point landing, achieving the perfect robotic ten. Before the week is out, she'll lay her squirming brood in my eyeballs. Black as after the apocalypse, the size of snot, shit-sucker and -gestater, she jumps the moment my mind sends the message to swat. Her antennae intercept my brain's impulse; her pinhead mind is closer to my nerves than I am. Her black vulture buzz is the song of madness.

My pillow smells like Ho, who lies stinking in some maggot pit.

My mind becomes a three-hundred-sixty-degree eye, floating above me like an orb, ascending to the heavens. From the air, San Francisco looks like a cemetery of competing tombstones.

HACKER BATTLE

I'm a cornered animal, caged in the room with my finger on the Red Button. They've taken what I love and trapped me alone with my most powerful weapon. The fools.

My being morphs. My heart fades, my body rots, and my naked mind rises pure from the muck. I am Snakebyte, Shiva of the cyberworld.

My first victim: MP Phred, guardian angel of the powerful. Then megadeath.

The Adjudicator's keys and codes are moving me right through the bank accounts of Wozniak and Levy. I discover a shitogram:

DON'T DO IT, SNAKEBYTE. I GOT ACCESS TO
MORE FEDERAL TRACKING TECHNOLOGY THAN
YOU COULD DREAM OF. AND IF YOU'VE NEVER
HEARD OF IT, YOU CAN'T BLOCK IT. GIVE ME SIX
HOURS, AND I CAN TRACK YOU DOWN, AND THE
SECRET SERVICE WILL COME KNOCK-KNOCK-
KNOCKING DOWN YOUR DOOR. DON'T DISTRACT
ME FROM THE OTHER BUSTS I'M WORKING ON.

Yeah, right. Don't leave me messages, Phred. Talk to me directly. Predictably, rappin MC Phred has set up an open chat duplex, designed specifically for me, so we can converse while we duke it out. All right. He wants to play? I call up his duplex, and set it up as a permanent box on the upper left-hand corner of my screen.

So far, no messages. I'm going in blunt force, steamrolling, letting my presence be known and to hell with subterfuge. I punch out the last series of codes that should get me into the bank accounts of Wozniak and Levy. First blood is drawn.

The screen blinks out, bytes accumulate, available meg shrinks, the green light on my computer blinks rapidly.

Info flashes before me.

I'm in.

Words jigger across the box in the upper left-hand corner. I can watch as Phred types. "That does it! Looks like you're just like all the rest. Welcome to Phredland, you cunt."

How could he react so fast? There's only one explanation. He's passive computing, otherwise known as lounging. Somewhere at the bank, MP Phred has a personal computer wired to the modem lines. It collects the electronic impulses of my typing and sends it to MP Phred's printer, which gives him a real-time printout of every keystroke I type. Somewhere, a Fed is following along with every command and typing mistake I make. MP is preserving everything I type on printouts: every command, every misspelling, everything the computer says back. Evidence is being compounded against me.

Other hackers would run. But I got nothing to lose.

I type my very first message to MP Phred. "Come and get me, MP."

On he comes. MP Phred has gone into predator mode. I'm ready for him. My blood is pumping to the intoxicating beat of machine-gun fire on Ice-T's "It's On" playing on the stereo. I once rented an Ice-T concert video, popped it in the VCR, and the first thing I saw was, "Warning: This production protected by the FBI." Some gangsta. Ice-T, the Time Warner ho.

Time to set my death laser on the ultimate ho.

I go offensive. I try everything. Asynchronous attacks, superzaps, bait-and-switches, distracting nastygrams—I even try to induce buffer overflow, in hopes that I wash straight into open light, like a cyber version of the Miracle Man. MP Phred is backpedaling and swinging wildly, but my question-mark sperms are scurrying past the Human Diaphragm inward toward the Egg. I'm tripping up daemons that stymie me, but once you throw off the rituals of covert sneakery, it's amazing how quickly you can backspin off a tackle and progress downfield when all your offensive programs are written and ready to roll. MP Phred has got Iron Boxes set up all over the place, but he's got to be stupid if he thinks Snakebyte is going to waltz into one.

We each try to keep the other typing. We want to keep each other logged on, so we can complete our long-ass illegal traces through our mutual rerouting systems. I dial into the Pac Bell system. Lucifer is moving through the same nexus of Pac Bell switching terminals as me, both of us careful not to cross state lines and invite the jurisdiction of the FBI. So he's local.

We don't detract from our hacking to cast castigations at each other, but while we wait for our computers to process data, we invariably jump to the message screen.

"MP stands for Major Phony. You were a hacker once, and you got busted, and you sold out your peers. You're worse than busted; you're on the Fed leash. What a disgrace. You're jealous of our freedom. When your SS# goes through the Underground, the vultures will feast."

"And I know you, Snakebyte. Hyper-obsessive, self-taught, unemployed. Your modem runs on a low-baud number, a total limp-dick PPS, so you're flat broke. You're west of the bay. You think you're the only Sherlock on the Net?"

MP Phred's sentences seem to jump a word at a time, while my messages progress one letter at a time as I type. It's as if a machine is processing my taunts, and then replying with the proper simulated response. Who is this guy? Am I talking to a computer?

I access the classified file at Pac Bell that sends traces. MP Phred will probably access the same file, and we will both have the power to start a trace on each other. When I log on and look around I realize—

Somebody else is here.

It's the middle of the night. No FBI guys are tracing criminals.

MP Phred is already here.

But that's impossible . . .

How can he do this so fast? It's like his brain is plugged into the Pac Bell system.

Maybe MP Phred doesn't possess the new technology. Maybe MP Phred *is* the new technology.

A message: "C'mon, Snakebyte! You ready to play?"

I jump in headfirst, hammering out commands. MP Phred is watching every move I make. Everything on my screen is visible to him. Every key I punch jumps before his eyes. He can see me, but I can't see him. Faking left and right, I burrow head-on into the tracing system.

"Atta boy, Snakefuck! Come to papa!"

Frantically turning pages in Denny's notebook, I burst through the fire-wall bubble. My modem handshakes with their system. As I prepare to call into Wozniak and Levy's system and trace Phred's line, something catches my attention. To my amazement, I find a "trace request" already being processed. Listed is a record of a judge's warrant ordering a phone trace. The judge's name is "Shebit Yapeckerov."

MP Phred is manipulating the system to save it, raping it in order to protect it. Like so many impassioned warriors, he is becoming like his enemy, renouncing his principles to defend his principles. The reasons we join the war get forgotten as the war takes on a momentum of its own.

The last few bytes of info for the final trace come back. I've already passed through every Pac Bell switching station in our area code, so I know this last one will get me Phred's location. He's probably just as close to nailing me. But I'm not hanging up, and neither is he. I want to distract him. So, while I wait for my computer to process the last of the Pac Bell tracing systems info, I go for MP's jugular—in a psychological sense.

"And what's all this shit with wrong word choice? You got some weird kind of dyslexia? How come you never misspell? Are you autistic, or what?"

Before my prompt even types all the way to the question mark, he fires back, "This is between you and me! Don't go dragging the less fortunate into it!"

"Pretty politically correct for a guy who just called me *'cunt'*. Why so defensive?"

The data comes back. I click out of the duplex, suck the info for the last trace, and hit return. Somewhere in the Bay Area, a high-tech Pacific Bell machine is revving itself up for action.

I pull my ace. "Why is your interface all jury-rigged up? Are you an android or something?"

I sit back and wait for the prompt to move. It doesn't. It just sits there blinking while my hard drive slurps data and MP Phred's jaw hangs loose. I smile. He is thinking, *How the fuck does he know about my interface?*

A computer can't get its feelings hurt.

Fuck him, I'll keep needling. I type, "Can't you talk? Why do you always choose the wrong words when you type, like some fucking retard? What's wrong with the verbal section of your brain?"

A long pause. Then I get, "Ha! Gotcha! Got a final direct trace going on you! I'm gonna love putting your ass in jail, Snakebyte. Stop. Oh shit, wait! Delete previous."

"What the hell was that? Admit it, MP. You have wires sticking out of your skull and computer chips in your brain. You're not even a human being."

My data comes back. I'm a step ahead of him, but he doesn't know it. In sixty seconds, I will publish Phred's vital stats to the Underground hacker community, who will make his life a living hell.

"Open the pod-bay doors, Hal."

I set up the last kill command and pause before I hit the Return key. I am seized by a renegade spasm of mercy.

I step out and send a message.

"I got your line, MP! You put a trace on me, I'm sending a trace on you, and publishing your number to the whole hacker kingdom!"

"Let's see you do it before the Feds get there, asshole."

Shit. He's moving on me. I don't have time to explain why I can do it in a minute.

Fuck him. I send out the trace.

I frantically punch out the keys. All our painstakingly acquired skills and techniques have come down to a typing race. Right now, he's got my phone number. Now, he's got my location. I'll be in jail in ten minutes. Well, I'm taking you down with me, MP Phred.

A message comes through. "Congratulations! You'll be the first to learn my secret identity. Now let's see you send it through the Net before the Feds come crashing down your door."

I punch out the last commands, hold my finger above the button.

Sayonara MP Phred.

I hit Return, wait a moment, and the number comes back almost instantly.

864-8764.

Shit. It must have backfired. That's here. I'll try it through a different switch—

Waitaminute.

I look at the number again. That's not here. That's—

I jump up and sprint through the bathroom, burst the tape as I throw open Denny's door. Denny's back is to me. He has his headset on, and is talking out loud.

"Yeah, Jimbo? I got another maggot for you. I've already triangulated his position. His phone number is—"

He stops when his eyes fall on the number at the bottom of the screen. He spins his chair and looks at me standing naked with my snake wrapped around my shoulders.

Denny looks at me like he's meeting me for the first time.

"Snakebyte?" he asks.

"**You used** my own fucking tracer to trace me?"

"Well, I didn't know you were Mother Phucking Phred!"

"Well, I didn't know you were Snakebyte!"

"You would have turned me in to the FCIC!"

"You were going to turn me in to that teenage compu-mob! They would have strung me up! And now you broke the seal on that door, so we're *both* fucked!"

"What the fuck are you doing working for investors?"

"What the fuck are *you* doing breaking into their systems?"

"I asked you first!"

"Chet, do you really think I make my money through a part-time job with Datavox?"

"Have you ever been busted for hacking?"

"Fuck you! You answer *my* question now!"

"Have you ever been busted for hacking!"

"Yes! What the fuck are you doing on stock market systems?!"

I sigh, exasperated, and fall back on Denny's couch. Denny jams the lever on his chair and speeds up to me, suddenly unafraid of my snake, and leans into my face.

"I'm not gonna be interrogated by you without an exchange of information! You're a hacker! You should understand that! Now, tell me what the fuck you're doing stealing confidential information from private investment firms!"

"I'm tracking Chen, Denny."

"Through Wozniak and Levy?"

"Yes. The whole thing is their scheme."

Denny's furious face deflates. A few old pieces of evidence click in his mind. He puts his hand on his head. His shout falls to a whisper. "Holy shit."

"This is big, Denny. Real fucking big. So big I want to run to Siberia. They got everybody in on this. It's not just big billionaires. Little tiny twenty-thousand-dollar-a-year guys. Deli owners, middle-class families, the cops, the New York mafia—everybody is in on it. And the diagram isn't even complete. There are various third parties I don't even know about yet. And Mel was the switching station. None of the strands could talk to each other except through him. Me and Ho were the last people alive who knew about it. I'm the only one on God's earth who can do something about it."

"By crashing the bank system? Are you crazy?"

"You got to help me, Denny. I don't have time to do it myself. They're scheduled to kill my brother tomorrow. We need two guys."

"Chet, you're asking me to become a dark-side hacker."

I jump up and grab his shirt. "Denny! You can't just choose

the legal side of cyberspace and be assured you're doing the right thing all the time! You work as a political activist for labor, for Christ's sake! Cyberspace is no more pure than reality! The ideologies of your two occupations are totally contradictory! I know this isn't an act of charity by you! You were hired directly by Wozniak and Levy to protect their systems! You would never work for them in reality!"

"But terrorism?"

"Cyberspace is the frontier, Denny! And we're cowboys roaming through, looking for justice! You can't just join the Indians or the lawmen and expect no corruption on your side!"

"Spare me."

"Will you do it?"

"What?"

"Crash their fucking systems."

"That's—"

"Terrorism, I know. It goes against your oath as a Fed."

"I'm not a Fed."

"You might as well be. Look, Denny, they got the lawmen in their pocket. Mel is related to a police lieutenant! The boys who pay your salary are the bad guys! There's nobody to go to! We've got to do it ourselves!"

"I just wish you weren't so excited about it. You're like these young punks I bust. Cowboys."

"I'll do anything you want in return. Name it."

"Chet, just do me one favor?"

"Anything."

He suddenly raises his voice to a scream. "Get some fucking pants on, and get that slimy reptile off my fucking couch!"

Man, am I stupid. It takes no great mental leap to figure out it was Denny. By trying to take quantum leaps of thought, I completely overlooked what was staring me in the face.

Of course MP Phred isn't half machine. He's just disabled. You don't attach complicated electromechanical systems to your computer system for fun, you do it for necessity. Denny can't work a keyboard. That's why he uses his headset. I thought I was looking at a robot. I was really looking at Denny's voice machine.

Denny never made spelling mistakes because his voice machine automatically spells correctly. He sometimes wrote "sigh bare space" for "cyberspace" because his voice machine misheard what he said, and Denny didn't catch it. Commands like "stop" "delete" "go" could be inserted accidentally into his text, because Denny couldn't punch two keys simultaneously, like Alt-F3, to get out of his message. Denny communicated entirely by voice and a button or two. Different interface.

Doooiiii. Never mind.

CFED. "See-fed." I should have seen the Fed.

"Denny, I honestly don't know how I feel about you at this moment. You're half humanist, half machine. You seem schizoid. Or worse, a hypocrite. In this universe, you're a free political radical fighting in the name of labor. In the Infoverse, you're a nazi protecting billionaire investment bankers from gifted teenagers who are hungry for knowledge. Labor and stock investors live in a perpetual one-sided war over who gets company profits. How can you reconcile that? How can you even live with yourself?"

He turns to me, his crippled face puckered with pain. "You think you're the only computer hacker in this building, Chet? What do you think I am?" He shakes his head. "I'm just like you."

"Wrong!" I shout, realizing how deeply betrayed I feel. "You're a Fed!"

His hand snaps on my wrist like a bear trap. "No! I am *not* a Fed. I *sold out* to the Feds! There's a difference!"

I pull my arm away. "Big fucking difference."

I lean on my knees and bury my hands in my face. Denny snaps the lever on his wheelchair and comes close to me.

"Chet, they busted me. These privately hired hackers opened up my door and waltzed in here."

"Where was I during all this?"

"You were playing fetch somewhere. My door wasn't even locked. Assholes just walked straight in. Michael Levy personally contacted me and made a deal."

"So wait—the FCIC didn't bust you? Some privately hired hacker trackers did?"

"Wozniak and Levy hired a whole cyberbattalion to take me down. I was so fascinated with their banking system, I wasn't even aware I was being tailed until they barged in here. If only I wasn't so damn mesmerized by what I found, I would have detected them, and then I could have pulled some evasive action, and they wouldn't have tracked me down in a million—"

"So what were you doing in their systems in the first place?"

"Do I really need to tell you, Chet? The international banks are the hottest things around. Every hacker knows that. The best MIT graduates in the world design those systems, Chet. A door into their systems is the Gate of Heaven for hackers. Well, I got in, Chet. I surfed through the money pile of the richest people in the world. Sure, on a political level, I wanted to spit with disgust, but the *designs,* Chet! The designs! Some of those programs encapsulated endless complexities in a few lines of code, each folding in on each other in ultra-perfect self-contained helixes. It was like looking at strands of DNA!"

"But they busted you."

Denny's face falls as I bring him out of his hacker reverie. He *is* like me. "Right. They busted me. My handle was 'Wheels,' and Levy himself had heard of me. Hacker after hacker was besieging the bankers' systems, and Wheels was the one getting the closest. Nobody was crashing their systems, stealing money, or even permanently changing code. If W and L weren't so paranoid about it, they wouldn't even have known we were there. But they were paying a lot of money to the straight Dagwood Bumstead techies, some of them working for the FCIC, to search for traces of intrusion. They detected me, put a bead on me without my knowing, and came after me. I stayed on-line for two days without hanging up. They traced me back here and busted me."

"Now you know why they're paying you top dollar to protect their banking systems," I go. "They know the few stellar hackers who are capable of peeking inside their programs will not steal electronic money or crash their systems. They're not afraid of thieves, they're afraid of witnesses!"

"So they busted me. And you don't understand what that's like. You were busted when you were a minor, Chet. I was looking at prison."

"So they paid you to be a hacker tracker. Not the FCIC. Wozniak and Levy paid you."

"Right. They said they wouldn't press charges if I agreed to protect them from my fellow hackers. They knew I was the best. They paid me to bust Underground systems that specialize in banks, and to protect them specifically. So I did. It was either accept a straight job, or go to jail. And if I'm going to take a straight job, then I might as well take the money to soothe the ache to my conscience. You would have done the same thing, Chet."

I shake my head. "Between going to jail and ratting on my friends, hell no. I'd be in jail." I sneer at him. "I can't believe you would sell out, Denny. Not you. How could you betray me like this?"

"Chet, you don't understand how politics works!"

"I do now!"

"No, Chet, you don't! It was a means to an end!"

"A means to an end! Of course!"

"Chet, listen to me. Access to Wozniak and Levy gives me access to information to aid the workers' cause!"

"How the hell does busting talented hackers help you and your damn oppressed workers?"

"I didn't hire on with them just to keep my crippled ass out of jail, Chet! It was also to acquire power! Power to do good! Nothing can serve CFED better than someone who has access to the flow of corporate money! If I can predict corporate movements, then CFED can decide where to focus our limited resources!"

"But you pinkos never needed to see inside their bank accounts before!"

"Think of it, Chet! Access to the private flow of corporate money! What a golden key to put in my hands! And all I have to do is protect Wozniak and Levy from intrusion by teenage hackers! Is that such a Faustian bargain?"

"But, Denny, you got your whole heart and soul into this anti-freedom fight. I've been studying MP Phred for months. He was a fucking fanatic. You didn't just sit back and protect the castle, you went out and burned the surrounding battle camps. You were a marauder. You got your *jollies* off it, Denny!"

Denny's face is pillaged by pain. "Chet," he moans, "you can't know what it's like to be disabled."

"*What?!* What's that got to do with *anything*? You yourself always say—"

"It's an act, Chet. My whole ego trip is an act, a cover-up. I can do anything you can do, and do it better, but I can't change people's attitudes towards me. Even those cops, assuming I'm retarded—I've come to rely on their prejudices instead of fighting against them. But, in cyberspace, nobody knows I'm disabled. Everybody treats me like a normal person. In cyberspace, I am freed from this broken body and I can fly like an eagle. There's no glass ceiling holding me down. In cyberspace, I'm a king."

"King, my ass. You're not a king. You're a whore. A Wozniak and Levy whore. You're their damn slave. Worse, you're their hired fink putting your old comrades in jail."

"What makes you think I was putting hackers in jail?"

"You think I'm stupid? That's what MP Phred does! He puts hackers in jail."

"Chet, I only *said* I was putting hackers in jail. It's just terror propaganda."

"What about the Gibbon?"

"Gibbon!" he snorts. "I put a serious scare into him! Flushed him out, called his home phone and announced that the FCIC was coming to his house, so he better get back to his algebra homework. Burned his equipment in a panic, I assume, then wondered why no Feds came knock-knock-knocking at the door. If he gets back into Underground cyberspace someday, he'll do it under a different handle."

"All this for Wozniak and Levy!"

"Fuck Wozniak and Levy! Chet, I'm doing it for hackers!"

"You're harassing hackers to protect hackers?"

"Chet, I'm trying to scare them off! They don't understand how computer intrusion can destroy their future. The FCIC are fanatics! They treat teenage hackers like threats to national security! Unlike you and me, most Underground hackers grow out of their mischief making by the time they reach drinking age, which is about the time they start getting jobs with the companies they used to hack. If I can scare them away from the road you and I went down, eventually they will apply their skills to a well-paying career. But once a young hacker is busted, he's on record for computer terrorism, and nobody will hire him. So where is his talent going to go? The Underground. And he'll end up like you. A talent everybody fears."

"A talent you were going to put in jail."

"The *real* terrorists, the crackers who crash systems and make the true hackers look bad, those fuckers I'm proud to bust. I watched where Snakebyte was trying to go. Straight into the money flow. I was not about to let this punk steal money, much less crash those gorgeous banking systems. Your route wasn't towards the interesting programs, it was straight for the vulnerable heart of the system, their Big Red Button. When a hacker behaves like that, you know what he is after. You were behaving exactly like a terrorist."

"With my back against the wall, I was. Thanks to you coming between me and the Achilles' heel of the people trying to kill me. So you consider yourself a self-policed vigilante?"

"That's what I'm hired to be, yeah."

I rub my face in my hands. "God. Oh, god. All my illusions are falling down. Both of us are luminary hackers. We think we're kings. But we're really pawns. How can we be best friends in reality, but worst enemies in cyberspace? What drives us is the same demented lust for power that drives our wealthy enemies. We think we're free-riding warriors on the open plains, and then we look around and realize we're gladiators in a cage, with our enemies profiting off our battles. It's all a big lie. Cyber power itself is a lie."

"So where does that leave us, then?" asks Denny.

"With one of us about to be killed by Wozniak and Levy, and the other enslaved to Wozniak and Levy."

Me and Denny meet eyes. "What are you saying?" he asks.

"Bring down Wozniak and Levy, and we're both free."

Denny's room is alive with a sudden flurry of activity. We're clustergeeking big time: paging through technical guides, brainstorming, arguing, typing—sometimes at separate terminals, sometimes both of us at Denny's. The information I nearly killed myself getting access to flashes before my eyes on Denny's screen. We're not just dealing with phone wires now; we're dealing with satellites. We follow the thread overseas. To Switzerland.

"Run an account search under Mel Corlini's social security number."

"You got it."

Denny has the FCIC. I have the digital Underground. Together, we are unstoppable. We are the first hybrid of the New Age, when the computer subcultures of law enforcement and hacking will blend. Wondertwin powers, activate!

"It's not coming up," says Denny.

"Try this." I hand him an ancient napkin scribbled with secret codes. "It's something I picked up shoulder surfing."

"God damn!" says Denny. "I can't believe what you crooks pick up lurking behind a security systems analyst! How do you get away with it?"

"These are the skills you need to develop if you don't live the cushy life of a Fed. Damn! How could I *not* know you were MP Phred? It's like *Scooby Doo*. The guy you meet at the beginning of the story is always the guy who's unmasked at the end."

"And I would have gotten away with it too, if it wasn't for you meddling kids."

Denny uses his privileged avatar status to sashay around

the most tender sections of top-secret banking systems. Anybody checking would find MP Phred swinging his nightstick and tipping his hat, and get a warm feeling of burgher's comfort.

Ha! Snakebyte the cyberdemon has taken possession of MP Phred's soul, and no exorcism will save him.

I go out into the hall, walk around my apartment house till I find Wily snorting through the trash he has spread all over the hallway. Reacting as if I am Ho, he tackles me like Dino. We wrestle around in the hall for a while until Mrs. Crepbopple and Fifi step outside and see me rolling in filth with their old nemesis. I look up and force a smile. Wily ogles little Fifi. Mrs. Crepbopple crinkles her nose, yanks Fifi inside, and slams the door. I take Wily into Denny's apartment and feed him a can of Denny's peas.

Denny ignores the mongrel. "Chet, we can't crash their systems like terrorists."

"Why not?" I say, spooning the contents onto the linoleum and scratching Wily's ears. "What else can we do?"

"We want to document the money flow. So we got to let the operation run while we collect all the evidence to turn it in to the authorities."

"What's the point? The cops are on their side!"

"Not *all* cops! Let's just collect the evidence! We can always turn it in to some cop higher up in the hierarchy. Don't even tell me you think the whole national goddamn police force is in on it, just because you know one girl plays."

"Pete Rose framed O.J."

"Yeah, right after his affair with Tim McVeigh."

"You're still thinking like a cop, Denny. We don't need to collect evidence. We know what's right! Let's just nuke them!"

"And what will that do? Incapacitate them for a month or so! The bad guys will go back to business, and we'll be in jail. We should print out hard copies of the evidence. Tomorrow morning, I'll take a stroll over to my bank deposit box and enclose the paper evidence."

I realize, upon hearing Denny's reasoned plan, that I had

gone into self-destruct mode. I was sending myself in like a kamikaze pilot to take down the whole power structure with one final and catastrophic act of self-annihilation.

"What's wrong?" asks Denny.

"They killed her."

"Who? Ho?"

"Yes."

"How do you know?"

A hard-boiled egg materializes in my throat. The room starts to vibrate like gelatin. "I finally called back the beeper number. It was Chen. He said he knew she was my girlfriend. I haven't told anybody but you. I—"

Denny puts his half-paralyzed arm around my shoulders. I feel his strength move through me. "Chet, you were on TV, you know. Everybody is assuming you guys are a couple. It makes sense. You lived together, you James Bonded together, you've been arguing like a damn couple for a week now."

"But—but—" I'm sobbing, can't talk. Denny reaches into his holster and hands me his drool towel. I wipe my nose. I've never cried in front of Denny before. "But they know what she looked like."

"*Looks* like. And, anyway, so does everybody who watched the news."

"But they know all about this birthmark she has. It's in this secret place—"

"Don't cops usually issue descriptions of a fugitive's birthmarks?"

I pause, think that over.

"It sounds to me like he's messing with your mind, Chet."

"But where is she? Why has she disappeared? Why hasn't she called?"

I realize now that even he is stumped. His intent is to argue me down from certitude, past probability, to somewhere in the range of possibility. That's as far as he can go, because that's where even he resides.

Denny says, "The sooner we accumulate the evidence and turn it in to the authorities, the sooner we can save Ho."

I wipe my eyes, sniffle. Denny guns his joystick and wheels

past Wily. Wily the saber-toothed rottweiler cringes and cowers in the corner. Denny gestures at the broken seal on the bathroom door.

"When they see that, we're both screwed."

I sit at Denny's keyboard, storming through the Swiss accounts of Wozniak and Levy and Mel Corlini in the guise of MP Phred, sniffing along the money trail to Mel's second bank account in the Cayman Islands. All the payments from that Cayman Islands account go to a plethora of other Cayman Island accounts. I recognize the name Reginald Andrecht. I used to make speedy deliveries to Andrecht's Futons. So far, I detect no money coming back.

I am no longer trapped here. Right now, Denny is my eyes and legs. Through him, I collect information. On the walkie-talkie, his name is "Infospore." He can leave my cybercage any time he wants to, do speedy reconnaissance through reality like a pod exploring the moon. He runs errands, stops by Datavox for computer hardware. Denny has covered miles, and he never gets tired. Cops and strange cars frequently follow him, but Denny can weave through traffic and cut down alleys, so the tails never last longer than he wants them to.

Denny swings by Ho's mom's apartment. Nobody home.

For the last hour, my walkie-talkie has been filled with static. The last I heard of Denny, he was calling from the airport. Nobody had heard anything about Ho. We don't even know if she got there. The airlines are not offering information. If we want to know if Ho's moms has flown out from there, we have to hack their airline systems—or do some phone phaking, which is where my skills come in. (Denny calls it "phraud." What a fucking crass word.) He said he was checking the airport lost-and-found for clues, and then he was coming home. He signed off.

I can't wait until he comes back, because I want to tell him I already traced one arm of the money circle.

Denny buzzes through his door. Before I can speak, he throws something to the floor. It clatters, stills. It's covered with tasty but worn graphics. It's scuffed up bad. The little license plate is gone.

Ho's board.

Denny is doing all the hacking by himself. I'm sitting on the couch with Wily, unable to move. Denny has nothing to say, so he wisely says nothing.

I found a thread of pain on my pillow. I am holding in my hand a single long strand of hair, blue as Vishnu, blue as the kiss of a dying Eskimo on her great-granddaughter's neck, blue as the aftermath of a mastectomy, blue as the reflection of the earth in the face masks of the Apollo astronauts, pure blue as a flag will never be.

The TV breaks into a story about the Miracle Man Informer. He was directly responsible for eleven arrests today, the highest-ranking arrests in the Chinese mafia so far, and many are offering to identify their superiors in exchange for witness protection. Authorities are having trouble promising protection for so many stoolies. Chen will have just as much trouble offing all twelve of them.

Denny is on the phone with Elana, explaining why he might be busy for a good while. Abruptly, he says, "Up! I got a call on the other line. Can you hang on? Thanks, hon."

Denny glares at me with such significance that he pulls me out of my catatonic stupor. "Oh hi, Mr. Michael Levy!" he cries. "How are you?"

I'm up out of my seat and perched on the arm of Denny's wheelchair. Me and Den sit cheek-to-cheek with Levy's panicky vocal cords sandwiched between our ears.

That old frosty voice is unforgettable. "I'm extremely concerned about this Snakebyte fellow. You said you would have caught him by now. So far, nothing has been accomplished, and our FCIC friend Jim is complaining that you hung up on him."

"Don't you worry, Mr. Levy. I got that Snake backpedaling and trapped outside your system. He is momentarily shut out. I'm just waiting for him to break in again, so I can trap him."

"Can't you go out and find him?"

"Well no, not exactly, Mr. Levy. You can't exactly go out and find anonymous people in cyberspace—not if they're not connected to illegal bulletin boards. They have to leave traces of themselves in the programs where they intrude—mouse footprints, so to speak. What I do is basically analyze fingerprints. That's how I brought down all those other hacker criminals, and that's how I'll bring down Snakebyte."

I write down on the piece of paper: *Access codes to Switz.*

"Forget the other criminals," Levy intones. "Snakebyte is the one we want. How close are you?"

Denny, the consummate actor, clears his throat. "Well, Mr. Levy, if you really want us to protect your system from Snakebyte properly, we need the access code overseas."

I bulge my eyes at Denny, mouthing *We? Us?*

Levy is just as quick. "Who else are we talking about here?"

Ack! You idiot! You blew it! How are you going to explain a plural MP Phred?

Denny stumbles, looks at his computer screen as if it is displaying a lie.file. Then he comes up with, "Well, me and my computer, sir! We computer geekazoids sometimes speak of our computers as friends. Mine's name is Priscilla! After Elvis's wife!"

I mouth *Priscilla*? Denny shrugs. I swat him in the back of the head. He pinches my nipple.

"Is this really necessary?"

"I need it to track this hacker. It's a complicated technical issue. It's the only way I can set a trap for him. Don't worry. By tomorrow, he'll be in jail."

Levy recites his personal codes for us. Denny can instantly memorize any numeral or letter sequence, but I scribble them on the paper anyway.

Denny concludes with some confident and reassuring remarks about my certain demise, and the pleasure he will take in bringing it on, and turns off his headset.

"Nice social engineering, Moe," I go. "You should join the FBI."

"Hey, I made *one* mistake! But did you see the way I

picked up that fumble? God, I am slick!" Denny jerks his thumb into his chest. "Damn, *nobody* manipulates phone technology with my expertise!"

The phone instantly rings. Denny hits his headset button.

"Oop! I'm sorry, sweetikins!"

I laugh—for what seems like the first time in centuries. If I didn't have Denny here, I think I would go insane. He doesn't know it, but he's already saved my life.

"Of course not, honey-cakes! I would *never* hang up on you on purpose! Oh, but bunny—"

Their flirting sends me back into my wallowing depression. I flop on the couch, rub my face in my hands, and moan, "Ho is dead. I know she is. I can feel it. They killed her."

Wily lays his chin on my knee and licks my hand.

MP Phred and Snakebyte creep through the DigiBucks encryption programs, and we find to our surprise there is yet another element in this conspiracy: William Heitfreund, the president of a successful New York investment firm, who conspired with Rocky Rachino to form the prototype stock market scam. They are the template from which the San Francisco conspiracy is a mere copy.

"Judging from the flow of money," says Denny, "and then the sudden abortion, the scheme ran smoothly for years until some taxi service was gutted and turned into a basketball gymnasium."

"So in New York, the delivery system was a taxi service."

Denny points to a column on the screen. "Look at these numbers. Heitfreund and Rachino made tens of millions on this venture. When the conspiracy went sour, I assume the taxi service owner was murdered."

"Just like Mel."

"But this was three years before Mel even opened up business. Then suddenly there's this covert payment to Heitfreund. How did this scheme jump across the continent to Wozniak and Levy?"

"It's not like it's a quantum leap or anything," I say. "You can imagine that, once the New York conspiracy was over,

Rachino and Heitfreund's reputation for sneakery would spread through two very closed secret circles: the elite investment bankers of the world, and the American mafia underground."

"And Wozniak and Levy were inside one of these circles."

"Right. They must have known Heitfreund. When they wanted to start a conspiracy of their own, Heitfreund agreed to consult them. He told them they needed two things: one, a delivery service; two, a professional killer."

"This is what you and Ho figured out."

"The delivery service was easy. Mel Corlini's Speedy Delivery was perfect, especially since Mel was the brother of a police lieutenant. The packages are sealed and under strict taboo not to be opened. And the information is conveyed through the most unlikely of conduits: bike messengers."

"So Wozniak and Levy contacted Mel, made an offer. Mel accepted."

"But finding a professional killer was difficult. Wozniak and Levy probably had no contacts to organized crime. So Heitfreund talks to Rachino. Rachino contacts Chen. Chen is instructed to seduce Mel into a scheme to invest Mel's money behind Wozniak and Levy's back."

"But actually, Wozniak and Levy are paying Chen."

"Mel is unwittingly trapped. He also voluntarily runs the whole business, controls all the knowledge. His sister, police lieutenant Gina Corlini, is brought into the scheme, which keeps the heat off Chen. But how do Woz and Lev filter such large sums of money to the unseen legions of corrupted business owners—right under the noses of the SEC?"

Denny speaks into his headset and a new set of illicit records flashes before us. "Wozniak and Levy open one account in snowy Switzerland. The small businesses open accounts in the tropical Cayman Islands. Only Mel Corlini has accounts in both."

I type out our macro that matches social security numbers to names. I point to a Cayman Islands account. "This guy Pete Perata is the owner of the Gentle Delicatessen. Mel can look out his window and see the Gentle Delicatessen, which feeds his couriers. But the illegal money makes a trip around the world to get there. In the electronic world, sometimes the fastest way between two points is not a straight line."

"But in San Francisco," says Denny, wrapping his arm around my shoulders, "the fastest way between two points is badasses such as thee. The money may flow electronically, but the information flows on ball bearings. By the time the money returns, Wozniak and Levy get a sixty percent return on the profits of their illegal investment. Meanwhile, guys like you are throwing themselves off Watermelon Hill for five hundred bucks."

"Grrrrrr. Gets me Dennyized."

Denny feels my forehead. "Good god, Chet, what's happening to you?"

I grip my ears. "Must . . . fight . . . moral outrage! Must . . . cling to . . . apathy! *Nnnrgh!*"

"Very poor imitation of David Banner hulking out."

"That was Captain Kirk being mind-melded."

"Don't give up your day jo—oh, you already did."

The beeper on my hip beeps. I grab it. It's Chen.

"Use my phone," says Denny. "Hackers should never repeatedly call from the same line. Even if it *is* scrambled."

"No," I say. "Don't unplug your modem yet. Your tape recorder is in my room."

I march in, flick on the tape, and call Chen's line.

A female voice answers. "Hello? Chet?"

"Ho?"

"Chet!"

"Ho! Ho! Ho Ho Ho Ho!" I'm doing a Snoopy dance around my living room, ho-hoing like Santa Claus.

"How are things?"

"Ho! You're alive! You're alive! You're alive! Oh, Ho!"

I'm weeping. Damn, I've cried more in the last week than I have in ten years.

"Alive and kicking. How are you?"

"Hoooo! Ho, Ho, I'm so happy! I'm so, so—"

"My period's late."

"—so, so hap—*What?* But that's impossible! We used—"

"Just kidding."

"Aaaaaagh!"

"Got ya. Listen, say hello to Denny for me, okay?"

"Denny, shmenny. What's he ever done for me?"

"I'm sure he's compiled a list."

"Oh, Ho! I just—I just—"

Ho's voice suddenly becomes tender. "What's the matter, honey?"

I sniffle and wipe my nose on my sleeve. "I know I'm being total fem boy with the boo-hooing and everything, but—but—"

"But what?"

"I just—I just never had a woman risk herself to protect me before."

I can feel her smile. "C'mon. Not even your mother?"

I wince with pain, but then realize it's the dying whimper of a wound that has just healed. I feel certain that secret tender spot will never hurt me again.

"No. Not even her."

"I'll do it again if you want me to, Chet. Right now if you want."

"Well, that means so much to—Oh, my god!" I suddenly explode. "Ho!"

"What?"

"Have they . . . have they . . . ?"

"Not yet. Chen wants me for himself. So nobody else can touch me."

"Are they torturing you or anything?"

"Nope. My guard was giving me shit, so I lied and told Chen he felt me up. So Chen had him killed."

"Jesus Christ."

"So now everyone's afraid to fuck with me."

I hear somebody yell "You bitch!" and another curse her in Chinese.

"But you wanna hear the funny part?"

"There's a *funny* part?"

"Chen is impotent! Some rapist, huh?"

There is outright yowling in the background. It sounds like

a Jackie Chan movie just went into fight scene. In the distance, Chen's voice shouts, "Don't you hurt her!" A voice I vaguely recognize is growling near the phone, "Tell him what we told you to tell him!"

"Chill, Fredo!" Ho yells to him. "I'll get to it!" Then she puts her mouth back to the phone. "You know what I want, Chet?" she says. "Just once?"

"What?"

"I want to feel your hands on me as I'm waking up."

"Ooo."

The background voice growls, "You fucking bitch."

"I want to be caressed awake. Really gently. You know how you do it."

"Yes, Ho, I remember, but let's not get distracted from the business at hand."

"Ooo, baby, I can't stop gyrating on my chair. You make my clitoris buzz like the hips of a honeybee doing the nectar dance."

"Ho, don't get me started, okay? The last thing I need right now is a hard-on . . . Dammit, it's too late."

The familiar voice speaks again. "You better tell him what we told you to tell him, you filthy whore."

Ho says, "You know, Chet, hanging around with these minishrimp nimrods, I've really come to appreciate the size of your massive shlong. I mean, I have nothing to do around here, so I've been scrutinizing quite closely, and gangsters do tend to have almost no trouser bulge whatsoever. For instance, this Spock hemorrhoid holding this gun to my head looks about inchworm si—"

There is a tumble on the other end of the line. I hear the phone bouncing on the floor, then Chen's voice harshes into my ear. "Griffin, next time you get call from me, you hear sounds of your girlfriend getting her fingernails peeled back!"

"Okay! You want to meet me, *I* pick the spot! Got that?"

"We got the girl, Griffin! You got jack! *We* pick the spot!"

"Fuck you! I got paper evidence that brings down you and your whole operation! Meet me at Fort Farley tomorrow morning at nine o'clock!"

"Your brother dies tomorrow! Meet us tonight!"

"No can do."

"Then we start gang-raping your girlfriend."

"You got nothing to rape her *with,* Chen!"

"You got two choices, Griffin: Come finish what you started with me, or stay hiding and let Bobby and Ho die."

A screw pops loose in my brain. "Well, that's just dandy! Just hunky-fucking-dory! Another lose/lose choice handed down to Chet from the patriarchs! First Mel, then Spock, and now you. Well, fuck all of ya. *I'm* making the rules for this race. *I'm* steering! And I'm stopping this toboggan right now."

"Griffin, don't go crazy on me, okay?"

"Oh, I'm fucking loco, Chen! Cuckoo! Cuckoo! Cock-a-doodle-dooooo!"

"You taking drugs, Griffin."

"Working-class punks like me don't need drugs. We got rich pigs like you to fuck our heads. Now you listen to me, Chen, you old raisin-ass shrivel-dick impotent fart, and you listen good. I'm not doing this your way. I'm doing this *my* way. Meet me tomorrow at Fort Farley at nine o'clock. Abandoned military base, out in the open, so no cops can sneak up on us."

"You bring the printouts and disks, and I bring the girl. We trade."

"See you tomorrow, Chen."

This time, *he* hangs up on *me*.

I hang up, elated.

My downward plummet hits a ramp. I soar. I fly. But this time I don't come down. I find myself skating through a new dimension I'd never believed was real.

Denny is in the bathroom, wearing the quirkiest expression he's ever leveled at me.

"What?!" I demand.

"Nothing," he mutters. "I'm just wondering if my taste in friends is evidence of anything psychotically self-destructive about me."

*　　*　　*

MP Phred is using his exalted avatar status to creep invisibly towards some particularly tender secrets. I have nothing to do until he finishes jiggling the code.

I take my first shower in days, singing a spontaneously composed "I Love Ho and Ho Loves Me" song, which eventually evolves into a version of the *Barney* tune.

Then I'm stalking the furniture, walking miles around Denny's room. She's alive. I feel empowered.

Denny looks up from his computer. "Chet, will you sit the fuck down? You're making me nervous."

I flop down on Denny's oatmeal-colored couch, pop open some Gak, this harmless blob of fluorescent green goo, and get off molesting it. A beautiful invention. Makes Silly Putty look like snot.

"Chet, stop fiddling around! And put some pants on, for Christ's sakes! I'm trying to concentrate!"

The Bee Gees are playing on the stereo. I raise Wily by his front paws and the two of us dance some disco. I screech "Stayin' Alive" at the top of my voice, and Wily howls a disharmony.

Denny remotes off the stereo. I drop Wily.

"What's up, Eeyore?"

"The FCIC are after us."

"What? Who put them on our trail?"

"I did."

"Oh, God."

"I told them you were in W and L's system yesterday, and they expected me to bust you immediately. It hasn't happened. Days are passing, and some terrorist hacker is mealing around in the electronic money pile of the wealthiest banking systems in the world. I think they're panicking. Since I haven't accomplished anything, Wozniak and Levy have needled the FCIC itself into action, who have made busting Snakebyte their pet project. The banks are hiring private hacker trackers. Every rent-a-cop in cyberspace is perusing the outer edges of Woz and Lev files, looking for traces of an intruder. When they find out you brainwashed me into switching to your side, we'll both be cybermeat. As of now, the cops and crooks are chasing you through reality, and the entire FCIC is chasing both of us through cyberspace. Luckily we're doing this under my handle. But that will only fool them for a day. When they see the places MP Phred has roamed tonight, they'll come smashing down this door tomorrow morning. We've started the avalanche, and there's no stopping it from landing on us."

"So what's your point?"

"What I'm basically trying to say is that we have about six hours to prove our innocence, rescue Ho, and bring the cops, the mafia, and the stock criminals to justice."

"So I guess I better get dressed."

"That would be my suggestion, yes. And then get over here and help me. You'll have lots of time to play with Gak in jail."

My eyes fall on Ho's shaggy board, and I am reminded of the community that emblem represents. Ideas start to sprout. I just remembered I have $500 hidden beneath my snake.

"Denny, I've lost track of time. What day is it?"

"It's night, and it's Friday."

Something clicks in my brain. The furnace behind my eyes flares in that visionary way that always makes Denny nervous.

"So you got paid today!"

"Shit. I knew it."

"C'mon, Denny! When have I ever asked you for anything?!"

"Hello?"

"Leone!"

"Chet?"

"Have your boys meet me at Fort Farley tomorrow morning at nine o'clock! You deliver me Ho, and I deliver you the safe-deposit key! Got it? Good."

Click.

"Lieutenant Corlini here. How can I help you?"

"Gina! It's Chet Griffin. Chen *and* a division of Rocky Rachino's men will be at Fort Farley tomorrow. You want to duck-shoot some goons? Bring a SWAT team. You want me? Bring those iron ovaries of yours. Ho will be there, so rescue her."

"Chet, why don't you come down to the station and—"

Click.

"Mouth's Morgue! You kill em, we chill em! What can I do you for?"

"Hoofin Mouth! I figured you'd be up, man! It's Chet!"

"Yo, C-man! What up, cuz! You still riding them faggy blades or what? You got to make the convert, homes."

"When pigs freeze over, bud. Yo Hoof, check this out, man: You know how I'm wanted for murder?"

"Sure thing, dude."

"Well, the dudes who really did the deed? Kidnapped Ho! Trying to get me to fess up, dude."

"No way!"

"Way."

"That's bogus, man. They're fucking with our best Board Betty. What do you want me to do?"

"Hook up with your boys, and be at Fort Farley tomorrow at nine A.M. sharp. They're supposed to deliver Ho to me for swap, so she'll be there. I'll need her skate family present and accounted for."

"Fuck, dude, we'll probably be kickin out sessions there anyways. Grindable turf to the *extreme,* blood! But I'll send the word through the posse. I'll make sure *every* skate rat is there, dude!"

"I'm so stoked."

"Fuckin A, man. I'd love to stay on and shoot the shit with you for a while, Chetster, but I gots to get my ass in gear and be on this like a fly on rice. Catch you later, brother."

"You know it, homeboy!"

Groggy voice. "Hello?"

"Sergeant Halcott?"

"Yeah?"

"My name is Chet Griffin. Sorry to wake you."

"Chet Griffin?! How did you get my home number?"

"Sergeant, you were following the lead of arsonists who burned the building where Spinkleman was killed, correct?"

"Who is this, really?"

"And Gina Corlini swiveled the investigation to a wild goose chase, right?"

No answer. I continue. "And Gina's brother was murdered the same day."

"He was?"

"The same day Gina about-faced and put the pressure on a drug kingpin named Dr. Chen."

"Wait, let me get a pen. Her brother?"

"Mel Corlini, owner of Extra-Speedy Delivery Service, which was stationed in Executive Towers at the top of Nob Hill. Investigate. More arson."

"Waitaminute. That's Gina's brother?"

"Yep."

"So you're saying this Dr. Chen killed both of them? This Spinkleman guy and Gina's brother?"

"That's right."

"And the arson. It's all connected?"

"You got it."

"How can I corroborate this?"

"Check around the Chinese drug underworld. Ask about Chen. I'm sure your narcotics boys know him. He killed Spinkleman, he killed Lieutenant Corlini's brother, and he burned both buildings. And he has connections with your boss. All the guilty parties will be present at Fort Farley at nine A.M. tomorrow. You are cordially invited."

"But why—"

"Goodbye, sir."

"Hello?"

"Ms. Cadigan, this is Chet Griffin."

"*The* Chet Griffin?"

A true newsperson. Get her out of bed and she's sharp as a tack.

"Yes, ma'am."

"Why should I believe this is the real Chet Griffin?"

I give her my social security number. "My parents died in a toboggan accident when I was seventeen. I have a birthmark above my belly button. My guidance counselor in high school was an asshole named Mike Eily. Do some research, check it out."

"Notes taken. What is it you want to tell me, Mr. Griffin?"

"There's going to be a shoot-out tomorrow morning between the police, the Italian mafia, and the Chinese mafia at nine o'clock at Fort Farley. Ho Pixie will be there. I'll be there. Bring a camera crew. I promise I won't tell any of the other networks."

I hang up and dial reporters from all the other networks.

"Speak to me."

"Yo! Chugger! What's up?"

"Yo, Clyde, I hope you ain't going to kill me, man. I'm best buds with Bonnie."

"Relax, blood. I'm doing Bonnie."

"No shit?"

"Yeah. We're on interface now. We'll be holding hands and all that bletcherous shit."

"I was wondering when you guys were going to hit it. The rest of the band thought she was pure dyke, but I always knew better. So what's up?"

"I need a favor, Chug-man."

"Hit me."

"I need you to bring the Spitmobile to Fort Farley at nine A.M. tomorrow."

"The purpose being?"

"Have you been wondering why Ho hasn't come to band practice?"

"You boink better than we rock?"

"Well, yeah—that and the fact that she's shanghaied by the people who are really doing all the killing."

"Barnacle, whatever you're on, mail me some."

"You don't believe me? Just bring the Spitmobile to Fort Farley at oh-nine-hundred hours tomorrow. The place will be packed with cameras from every network, bro. You looking for exposure? I'm getting you some free, first thing tomorrow. Bring the Spitsters, bring the battery-operated axes, and put on a show."

"Sounds killer, dude! Will Ho be there?"

"You'll see her. And one more thing."

"What?"

"There might be a shoot-out at some point. So have an escape route handy. And don't park on the open skate scurb. Too much ricochet action there."

"Whoa, rewind, my man. Why the shoot-out?"

"You think Geraldo would come just to see *you guys* play? I had to provide a shoot-out!"

"Hey, homes, I don't think I want to be anywhere near one of your shoot-outs."

"Cameras, Chugger! Cameras!"

I hear the poor sap drooling over the phone. Each Spit member has the same weak spot. After agonizing for a nanosecond, he breaks.

"I'm there, dude!"

On the Internet, I hack up hundreds of police home addresses. Denny heads to an all-night copy place. Then me, Denster, and Elana spend the hours before dawn filling mail packages with audiocassettes, paper printouts, disks, and Mel seals. We hit FedEx and do a mass overnight mailing to every cop's home address, every police station, every TV station and newspaper and radio station we can think of. Each one gets a photocopy of directions to Chen's new center of operations.

The most detailed copies go to the SEC and the FBI.

Denny drops the tape recordings in a safe deposit box at "Bank of Apartheid," as he calls it, and we're ready to roll.

Here I am. It's broad daylight, and I'm out in the sun in my gleaming new red, white, and blue skate pads, waterskiing off the back of Denny's hurtling chair, with Wily flapping his tongue and galloping in loyal attendance. Wily knows something is up; he feels it in the air. He doesn't even check out some primo pink poodles we pass. I think he expects to see Ho. The wind blowing through our facial scruff, we glance at each other and share a big stupid manly grin.

My commando backpack is stocked with bottle rockets, my music box, Denny's police scanner, and a walkie-talkie. Denny is wearing his headset geared up to his walkie-talkie.

"No, Denny, *I'm* Dorothy, you're the Tin Man, Wily is Toto—except he needs a brain . . ."

"No, Chet, you're the wussy crybaby Lion, Ho is Dorothy, and this is the rescue part where we sing, Oh-wee-oh! Ye-ooooh-oh oh!—"

"Wait, Denny, listen! You're Glinda the Good Witch, who grants me my cyberslippers, Chen is—aw, fuck it. Here comes the fork in the road."

I swing off Denny's handlebars and slingshot down the 'vard veering away from Fort Farley. Denny does not react to my disengagement. Wily, without hesitation, follows me.

Denny, moving faster and taking a more direct route, will arrive at Fort Farley way ahead of me. But we stealthy *America's Most Wanted* desperadoes have to take more circuitous routes.

I pummel to the fullest along the straightaway that leans away from Fort Farley as the momentum snatched from Denny's battery slowly peters out. I am forced to grind as best

I can towards the far end of a nexus of abandoned warehouses that adjoins the fort. A view from an airplane would show me veering way off course, then abruptly fishhooking into the shadow of a small hill and vanishing.

I carve down the sloped side of a sunken drainage trench, then cut a hard left and careen into the open maw of a perfectly cylindrical tunnel, yawning like the mouth of a *Dune* worm. I am swallowed whole by the underground tunnels of the skateboard rats.

Stretching from the drainage ditch to Fort Farley is a mile-long cement pipe with a ten-foot diameter. The pipe angles downward at less than one degree, so the first half-mile or so runs aboveground until the pipe slowly disappears into the earth as cleanly as a scalpel into flesh. With perfect straightness, it burrows beneath the cluster of abandoned warehouses that adjoins Fort Farley. Decades of earthquakes have left the shell cracked in places, so the dungeon is graced by periodic sheets of sunlight. Churning through the thick syrupy darkness, I pass beneath a jagged vein of sky blue every hundred feet or so, so the stretches of darkness never quite envelop me before I approach another hanging drape of light. At some places, the fissures in the ceiling are so myriad that light and shadow strobe across my face as I plow.

Occasional puddle mirrors flash before me, and my wheels slice them open in twin fans: sudden sparkling refractions with a sound like shredding silk. The fissures in the floor are always directly beneath the overhead cracks, so every underfoot hazard is lit up by a convenient natural spotlight. Me and Wily always know when to leap.

Then my eyes sting with sudden sunlight. Spraypaint words flash across my optic nerve and still radiate long after I pass back into darkness. In the pitch-black, a beer bottle coinks off my toe and skids up the side of the pipe, then slides back down in front of me again and crishes against an abandoned skate axle. Without the visual world to offset them, the demonic artistry and skate slogans burn in my retina with neon fierceness.

But wait, chicks and gentledudes, it gets gnarlier. Closer to

Fort Farley, where the pipe sinks beneath the earth entirely,
the natural streetlights are digested and I am swallowed whole
by the inky throat of night. I must skate blind, my urethane
wheels feeling for the bowl-shaped bottom to stay on a steady
course through this hollow dragon spine, praying some nimrod
didn't throw a broken skateboard across the floor to send my
face plowing into the verminous darkness at my feet. I am
Jonah swallowed by the whale. Got to keep the fire in my
heart well-tended.

Fort Farley is a democratic skate mecca, harboring skaters
intermediate to advanced. But this pipe is only for the elite.
After a good morning's warm-up at Fort Farley, the best skaters hike into the apocalyptic row of abandoned warehouses
nearby. Inside one of the warehouses, a gaping cavity in the
floor leads straight down into the utter darkness of a dry, perfectly cylindrical tunnel. Some courageous skank planker on
'roids traveled nine hundred yards through the darkness and
found places where the pipe breaks open to sunlight. And
nothing makes a vert planker squeal with glee like a stretch
of cement pipe. Bring your spraypaint cans.

This is the dungeon I grind through, Wily's toenails clicking along behind me. Our breathing is answered by a thousand
ghosts. In this echo chamber, each sound hears its mimic. I
wrestle with the vagaries of my imagination and take comfort
in the pant of Wily behind me until I discern a glow. I canter
up speed, eager to embrace the faint light where the cement
ceiling is crunched open by a Godzilla stomp.

We stop beneath the cavity. Breathing heavily, I put my
hands on my hips and look up as Wily moils around my
thighs. Above us is an abandoned airplane bunker. Its tin walls
are rifled with ten-foot bazooka holes. Anyone peering down
into this gaping cavity would see a dank cement drainage pipe
and never dream it leads thousands of feet to the open cave
where I entered.

I climb up on top of a pile of five stacked mattresses. These
were hurled down here so skate kids can leap blind if they
want to. The ladder is usually left somewhere up in the building, but luckily I am just tall enough to dunk a basketball,

which means I can leap up ten feet, grab the sandy edge of the broken pipe, and pull myself out. It's hard with the weight of the rollerblades anchoring me to the underworld—but, hey, we're talking about one fucking pull-up.

I leap up into the abandoned warehouse and cop an appropriate *Power Rangers* pose. Nothing. I do some pointless somersaults and SWAT-team elbow crawls to one of the many gaping holes in the wall and peer out into the sunlight. Nothing but more abandoned buildings. There are a couple more rows of storage houses between me and the open spaces of Fort Farley where skaters pummel and criminals await.

I hear a whimper. I skate back to its origin and whisper down, "Chill! I was just covering for you!"

I find the ladder, stick it down into the pit, and set my wheel truck on the top rung, wondering how I'm going to carry that smelly cretin up a ladder. To my amazement, I find that Cerberus actually *climbs the ladder* to me!

As he pounces on me and slobbers, I can't help marveling at what amazing animals rottweilers are. I'm not saying they shouldn't be exterminated off the face of the earth as genetic abominations or anything, but I think I finally understand why some people are seduced by the mangy beasts.

Out in the open sunlight, we creep through the mute ruins, which are stark as the dried ribs of a dinosaur. I might be sneaking up behind one of the many groups of trigger-happy gearheads I had the courtesy to call last night. Wily, predator to the end, does not make a sound, but just tiptoes along behind me, following my lead like a true pack animal. His eyes zippered to slits, he is carefully sniffing the air like a professional.

We come to the last building before the open spaces of grindable scurb, and pause to catch our breath. We nod to each other, then zip around the corner and duck behind a Volkswagen-sized steel gas tank set up on bathtub feet so its base is held about five inches off the ground. I can lay my cheek to the sidewalk and peer out into the open spaces of Fort Farley. Sergeant Wily, invigorated by the run, his tongue waggling, crouches down next to me and waits for orders.

Most of Fort Farley is an open cement playground made for tank practice: bumps and dips, ramps and trenches, all with smooth sides. The terrain has the undulating effect of an empty swimming pool. Abandoned for years, it is now heavily spray-painted, unpoliced, and frequented by skaters, who own it by squatter's rights. The place is way skatable, extremely grind-able terrain. It is entirely surrounded by various cement structures, overseen by a distant geodesic dome. I am on the edge of a huge circle.

At this moment, the middle of this vast playground is entirely empty.

Except for a man on a motorized wheelchair.

Forget him for now. I scrutinize the buildings all around, which appear utterly abandoned. Of course, I know they are all teeming with a dozen subcultures, each bloodthirsty minion armed and waiting for me.

The first group I spot off to my left—how could anybody miss them?—is the media: satellite dishes, unwieldy cameras, boom microphones, huge lights mounted on giant praying-mantis skeletons, and Ken-doll robots with paste on their faces rehearsing their colorless intros. Bloated network vans are being torn open from behind and disemboweled of their electronic trickery by sniveling media hyenas. The electric emotion radiating from these myth manufacturers is not fear, but excitement. They got the red lens going, hoping to catch some blood splatter. Behind me to my left, a dozen bystanders, who are drawn like moths to cameras and guns, are smiling like celibates at a witch burning.

Also to my left but further along the circle is a posse of about twenty skate rats: Hoofin' Mouth and crew, looking deeply concerned.

Everybody else who should be here by now—cops, Italians, Chinese, Spit musicians—is invisible.

Denny bumps and bops over the frozen waves, very conspicuous and being filmed, a curious sight to the invisible gangsters, an outrage to the unseen lawmen who are certainly recognizing him and planning on arresting him as soon as the shoot-out is over. Denny crosses and recrosses the open space, peering behind buildings and moaning theatrically.

He's got a thousand guns pointed at him, and he's showing off. Christ, he is an idiot.

He should know my location. I hoist my walkie talkie. "Come in, Infospore."

Denny speaks into his headset. "Welcome, Dinkleberry. All elements present or accounted for."

"That was not the code name we agreed upon, Infospore."

"Apologies, Douchebag. Prepare for coordinates. Pigs to your direct right, on ground and on roof. Tiananmen Square boys directly across from you. To their right are more Tiananmen Squares with mixtures of Mussolinis. Lensheads, being subtle as ever, should be obvious to you. A sorority of bystanders is forming behind the lensheads and directly behind you. No sign of Princess Leia just yet."

"Thanks, Infowhore."

Looking to my right, I see nothing but buildings curving along the perimeter. But when I look up, I freeze. I see SWAT boys quite well, none of them facing me, all of them on one side of the roof, with guns pointed at Denny. On second consideration, I suppose they are aiming over Denny's head towards the cement bunker across the way which makes a perfect fort. That must be where the gangsters are.

Imagine this great circle as a clock, with me at six o'clock. On my left is the media at seven o'clock, the skaters are at eight, the gangsters are directly across from me at high noon. The cops are to my right at four o'clock. Denny is in the middle, cruising around the face of the clock like a fly everybody is afraid to swat.

I'm looking at a stalemate. Everybody is afraid to move, mesmerized by the presence of the TV cameras. The tension in the air is so heavy, I can barely lift my check off the cement.

Bored cameramen, who don't recognize drama unless it is exploding in bloody clots in their faces, turn their attention to the skaters. The skaters, hanging as only they can hang, assemble around a trench in the cement, twelve feet deep, which forms a perfect half-pipe.

Skate punks and cameras. Hm. What do you think happens?

Somebody pops in a Public Enemy disc and punches the selector button to PE and Anthrax in a ball-kicking rendition of "Bring the Noise." Aaaaaaah, sweet. White kids in pink and green mohawks are airborne, carving out totally bizotic nose ollies, eggplants, Christ Noldairs, and frigid airs. Gravity is dead. The air is alive with flying wizards. Deserted children on a deserted landscape, they swoop above the ruins, a flying orgy, a rainbow saturnalia, an ecstasy of soaring poseurs, punks, and wiggers, who consecrate their youths to a scorned and ancient vocation: to transcend their mortality, to wrest one moment from eternity and soar above the defeated earth. Rip, shred, tear, and slash. I am witnessing the Triumph of the Punks. My eyes mist up.

Okay, so maybe skateboarders ain't so bad.

I jump as a familiar funkadelic song starts up to my right, minus the bass line. Spit is playing out of the back of Chugger's van, which is suddenly parked prominently along the circle between the cops and the thugs, at two o'clock, directly across from the skaters. I'm sure the Spitsters are ignorant of their vulnerable position, intent as they are on not letting the plankers steal the media attention. Cameras swivel, dials spin, lights crane, media leeches trample and scramble for position.

I spin Denny's scanner to one of the cop frequencies, tape down the thumb button on the mouthpiece, slide my live Paddy Reilly tape into my music box, and blast Irish folk songs through their sliver of bandwidth. From the roof, I can hear cops cursing and trying to shout out suggestions for alternative frequencies.

That should paralyze them for a minute or so. Cops are about as crafty as blowfish.

I shout over my walkie-talkie, "Sending message, Infodork."

I pull out the first bottle rocket, the one which trails my prewritten note: "Start Ho walking across the lot, and the next missile will send you the safe-deposit key." I stab it in a crack in the cement and lean it towards Chen's army. I light the fuse, Wily cringes as the sparks fly, and up it shoots.

It lofts over no-man's-land in a trail of aurous stars, hanging a visible paper message, and touches down in China. After a moment, it pops like a puny blinking mockery of the firecrackers that may be next. I can't see if someone is picking it up. Spit finishes their first song.

Silence. Smoke unpleats into the sky like an untangling braid of hair at the bottom of the ocean. The suspense is excruciating. Wily is becoming agitated.

Something emerges from the bunker. Something fuzzy. Something blue.

Is it?

It bobs behind a cement undulation in the terrain, slowly rises to reveal a head and shoulders.

Some of the skaters stop soaring. "Hey! It's Ho!"

My heart surges in my chest, clogging my vision.

The cameramen, sensing a dramatic moment, jostle, elbow, and hockey-check each other. Ho dawns like a blue supernova, emerges into full view, and continues her walk towards her fellow thrashers like a punk rock Jesus across the choppy waves. I won't fire the next bottle rocket until I can see the roots of her hair.

She is walking very stiffly, as if she knows how much firepower is trained on her. Behind her, where the bottle rocket landed, a ribbon of unspooling smoke is lariating into the sky.

A gunshot resounds. All the skateboarders instantly wipe out. TV folk cringe and duck. The surrounding structures reverberate menacingly.

It was fired into the air. From the Chinese camp, as if prodding me, "Show yourself, or we ice her."

I wipe my sweaty hands on my hip pads. Okay. Now is Chet Griffin's moment of truth.

Plan? I have no plan. I hoped that by arranging this musical of motley elements, frozen under the scrutiny of the media, I can make my trade. Chaos is infinitely more robust and adaptable than any order. This bumpy terrain is Chet's even playing field.

The media is my insurance. It's my one pin holding Chet's Five-Ring Circus above a collapse into violence. So long as other copies of the evidence exist, they will have to bargain with me.

But what about the cops? Are they going to save her? Or will Gina shoot her? I spin my scanner to a second police frequency.

"Seven Charles Three. Report of robbery in progress at FedEx at 211 Montgomery Street. Subjects two Asian males in blue suits and ski masks. Weapons displayed. They are in shipping room at rear of building."

"Clear."

"Seven Charles Five. Report of robbery in progress at Bank of America at 223 Montgomery Street. Subjects four Asian males in blue suits and ski masks. Weapons displayed. They are in safe-deposit vault."

"Clear. Request backup."

"Seven Charles Nine clear for backup."

I feel myself snap out of my lifelong hacker fantasy. My last vestige of innocence breaks off and spins away in the typhoon of reality.

Why do I believe that documentation will save me? Information power is meaningless because there are still assholes with guns. Violence, the tried and true ancient means to power, is still master.

I feverishly peer underneath the steel tank and watch Ho slowly walking across Fort Farley. Why haven't the mafia shot her? If they've got all the disks, why don't they just kill her?

My question is answered by the unique standpoint I possess with my eye to the floor. Through the periodic drainage slits that run along the base of the walls on either side of the gangster bunker, I espy the chopping feet of what must be the Chinese stormtroopers. They are fanning out in both directions at once. Someone spotted where the sparkling trail of my bottle rocket led back to, and they are sprinting around both sides of the circle in two simultaneous charges. Apparently, they are bold enough to weave through the buildings behind the cops on my right side, and behind the skate rats and news crews on my left, and sandwich me between two deadly pincers.

I am struck in the face by a realization the size and mass of a wrecking ball: Ho is not a trading chip. She is a distraction. She is meant to draw me in while the bloodlusting shock troops come from either side to annihilate me.

Once they get me, nothing prevents that bullet from splitting Ho's skull. The glimmering rumor of my life is what keeps a thousand bullets from gang-raping my beloved's body. They have decided not to let the cameras intimidate them. Our extermination takes priority.

Two brains with the damning knowledge. Two brains that need to be crushed. Both brains are here. Now is their moment, and they know it. About fifty professional killers, intent and myriad, race around the circle with one function: Kill Chet Griffin.

Naturally, I shit.

I turn my back and flee—as always, instinctively heading towards the convenient group of gawking innocents.

Wily dashes out into the open space. I stop dead, spin.

Oh no . . .

The cameras pick up a fluorescent blue dog, galloping towards the punk chick like a lover through a field of wheat.

Half the cameras swing in Wily's direction. I can hear newscasters chanting spontaneously composed expository.

The entire Fort Farley population—skaters, cops, media, bystanders, musicians, and gangsters—is frozen as this renegade blue rottweiler gallops feverishly towards his master.

Everybody, that is, except Ho. Ho has not reacted.

Wily makes it to within fifty feet of his paramour when Ho hears his bark and spots him out of the corner of her eye. Her iron face blossoms, she shouts, *"Wily!"* her arms extend for an embrace, her toe pivots.

A rifle crack. Ho's head explodes in tufts of blue.

I fall to the floor as a volcano erupts in my brain. It feels like an atomic bomb rocking the ground, sending a whiplash through the cement earth and raising sheets of dust from the cracks.

It's the cops. Over my head, a thousand tons of lead are being hurled at the cement gangster fort, which spits dust and smoke like Fort Sumter.

I peel my wet face off the concrete and stare into the center of the cement field. Ho's still body is splayed on its stomach. Wily, oblivious to the whole world, is bent licking at her head, surrounded by a pentagram of scattered blue hair.

"No . . . not Ho."

Wily is all alone out there. The media is more concerned with attaining dramatic angles, the Chinese hit men are rapidly tightening the vise around me, the SWAT army is hurling lead into the fort, the Spit musicians are reeling beneath the firepower being sent over their heads. Nobody is moving into no-man's-land to retrieve the fallen angel.

Nobody except the skate rats.

They charge forward en masse, a tight phalanx of draft dodgers beneath the overhead hurl of bullets. They gather around Ho and Wily in a big bunch. I can hear nothing over the racket.

Cameras eat videotape. Everyone with a steady salary is cringing behind a barrier. I can feel the Chinese killers closing in on every side. There is no place to run.

I'm about to die, and suddenly I don't care.

I did this to her. It was my problem, and I dragged her in.

To my right, I hear the drumming of a hundred feet.

An explosive surge of adrenaline bolts me straight into the middle of the circle. Nitro boiling in my blood, I am slicing the radius towards Ho and the skaters. Beyond them lies the besieged fort of the killers.

The cameras are on me. As I bionic over the undulations and jump pitfalls, the gaggle of skaters moves back towards their half-pipe in a tight huddle. Wily follows behind, yelping without sound. I see no Ho. I'm muttering feverishly, "Please, Ho. Please."

And now the ultimate nightmare is thrust upon me: I, the man whom every armed gunman in this battle wants to kill, am out in the open beneath a firefight between those most eager to do it.

I swiftly turn left, gun towards the half-pipe where the skaters are lodging, and shred directly across the line of sight of the mafia bunker, whose gunmen are too busy reeling from the barrage to fire back. I stumble, hit a shoulder roll, keep going without breaking momentum. No cop bullet hits me in the back of the head.

"Oh God, don't let this be real. Please."

As I career towards the half-pipe and the bright hairdos swell in my vision, I see no Chinese legionnaires sprinting between the far buildings. My broken heart pumps golden elixir. I'm going to make it.

Then the point man in a long brigade of Chinese hit men comes into view.

My heart clenches and stops.

They continue to pass directly to my left, a long snake of gunmen intent on finding me in the ruins straight ahead.

Eventually, a mercenary glances towards the besieged bunker he was just dispatched from, and spots a rollerblader streaking across the bumps and sinks of no-man's-land. He grinds to a halt and swings the flaring nozzle of his AK-47 at me.

For the first time in my life, I intentionally do a faceplant.

That's right, I do a Pete Rose headfirst dive straight down onto the cement and skid to a stop behind a cement bump which explodes with the impact of lead, covering me with spurts of hot gravel and dust.

I didn't just dive flat out; I mostly dove sideways onto my Rectors: wristguards, kneepads, hip guards, and elbow pads, getting only slight pizza where my forearm touched the searing concrete.

Splayed like a swatted daddy longlegs behind this shrinking obstruction, I roll over and peer through the rain of dust at the roofed policemen, half of whom swivel their muzzles from their target across the way and point them straight at me.

My mouth opens, my vocal cords shred, but I never hear my last scream. Each muzzle flares a nova of constant spray, but I do not spout hot gushers of blood, because the coppers are firing over my head at the second wing of the Chinese killers, which lessens the impacts vibrating through this cement monticle and rattling my bones. But the shift of noise is almost seamless, moving directly through my skull from one ear to the other.

That's when I realize what Denny said must be true: Not every cop is in on this conspiracy. They are just innocently following the orders from their corrupt lieutenant, Gina Corlini. They are ordered to arrest me, not kill me on sight. That's for some paid-off prisoner to do. Right now, I think they are downright trying to save me. They keep the fire going, covering for me, giving me a chance to gun the last fifty feet to the half-pipe.

I roll into a cougar crouch and catch my breath. Nobody is shooting at me—at the moment. I brush the shrapnel off and peer up over the chewed top of this little hill.

Three splayed Asian men, ribcages blooming, sleep the big sleep, automatic weapons clattered through the splatter. The rest, I assume, have scrambled for cover behind that brick wall spouting jets of red dust like planet Mars under a meteor shower.

To my right, the men in the Chinese bunker, seeing the barrage suddenly halved, muster their courage and begin firing back at the police. Some of the cops stop firing over my head and start firing back at the bunker. Then, shots fired from the ground police show me that the other wing of Chinese shock troops, not finding me, have come up behind the cops and begun laying down a vicious locust-plague of bullets. The cops are surrounded on three sides.

Where's Denny? Is he shot?

A quick scan of the battlefield reveals no overturned wheelchair, unless he is lying dead behind one of the cement acclivities, or down in one of the sudden dips.

The wing of killers to my left is still reeling from the shock of bullets that killed three of their compadres, but the firepower aimed at them is down by two-thirds. I don't think I can make the race to the half-pipe before they peek their heads up again and spatter me with lead pellets.

Down on my face, I can peer past the lip of the half-pipe and see skaters soaring into the air one by one. They're jumping a tall wall in order to get behind it. One guy climbs to the top of the wall to scout ahead of the jump and coach the other skaters on where to let fly, since they are all jumping blind. I recognize him. His name is Gumby, after his oddly shaped head.

"Yo! Gumby!"

He is surprised to hear his name called. He looks around doltishly until his eyes finally level on me.

"Where is she?!" I scream. "Call an ambulance! Is she dead?"

At that moment, Ho soars against sky, with a mighty furrow parting her hairdo straight down the middle.

I scream with joy as Ho triumphantly rips a totally raging 360 judo air. I see her set in relief against the white geodesic dome, like E.T. and Eliot against the moon: foot kicking out, spine tweaked, board held sideways at her thigh, arm behind her in a backside grab of the griptape, an airborne goddess. Even killers must at some level appreciate beauty, because for a half-second, everyone—gangsters, cops, camera crews—freezes in awe. Everyone except Data.

Data?

Data leaps from a moving Bronco truck and hits the ground running. He does a kamikaze linebacker blitz straight through the skaters, barrels them down like bowling pins, catches Ho, and keeps running downfield towards the moving flatbed of the Bronco. He's turning this interception into a TD run.

But wait! There's a blue rottweiler after him! Bronco, Data, Ho, and Wily zip by me, heading back to where I just came from.

Fuck fear. I simply get up out of my puddle of blood and join the—

Puddle of blood?

Standing like a statue, allowing a clear sniper shot to my skull, I stare down with horror at the blood on the 'crete. My eyes send a full-color fax straight to my brain stem, which doesn't know exactly what to file this under. I squint at the ground.

A small puddle. Not even a puddle. A smear.

Relief washes through me. The scrape on my forearm! I'm okay!

But my hesitation will kill me. I can't make the trek back across the terrain I just crossed before the mercenaries come out from behind their brick wall. I need speed, tremendous speed.

SuperDenny catches air off an incline, lands five feet away, and spins a *Dukes of Hazzard* skid-out to swing the back of his chair to me. The rubber handgrips stick out from Denny's shoulder blades like the stumps of clipped wings. I grab them.

"Punch it, Denny!"

A spraying wake of dust and pebbles sizzles up from my heels.

Data hurls Ho into the flatbed of the truck just as Wily sinks his teeth into Data's suit pants and leans back. The edge of the truck moves away from Data as Wily wears his smoking toenails down to stumps. The driver of the truck, seeing the trouble, begins to slow down. Data, dragging Wily like a freight train, begins to catch up. As do me and Denny.

Ho stands with an expression on her face that makes me fear for Data. It says "woe to the macho pigs." She swings her borrowed board, and—*whap!*—her magnesium Thunder trucks bash across Data's eyeball.

Bye-bye Data.

Data reels hugely and stops just as we're gunning up behind him. Denny swerves to avoid a collision at the exact moment Wily of the I.Q. Point swings his ass in front of us.

"Yarp!" notes Wily.

Now a smelly blue dog is sitting on Denny's lap. We gun up past the flatbed of the slowed Bronco, not sure exactly what we should do, when a flying angel ollies over our heads in a soaring backside boneless. Wonder Woman touches down on the other side of Denny, knocks me off one of the handgrips, and attaches herself.

"Kick it!" she shouts.

Denny jams his joystick and guns us past the Bronco. The driver can finally see us, and he stomps his accelerator in an attempt to drive straight up our asses.

I throw my free arm around my beloved. "Ho! I love you!"

She shoves me back. "Fuck you! This makes me sick that you get to rescue the helpless chick at the end! I was just escaping by myself, until you came along and stole the glory!"

"Fear not, fairest maiden! I havst rescued thee! Now you're supposed to swoon."

"Swoon this."

"Can't I at least carry you? Don't you want to be whisked away?"

"I don't want to be whisked. I am not a dairy product. Back off!"

My chest is swollen with the purest liquid of manhood fulfilled. Cameras are rolling, cops shooting, bystanders screaming. The Chinese in the bunker across the way to my left are so covered in tear gas and smoke, and so intent upon the cops on the roof, they haven't noticed us out in the open. Yet.

Luckily, the woman next to me has blue hair, and the dog on Denny's lap is blue, and the four of us are riding one wheelchair, so there's no reason we should stand out or anything.

The Bronco steadily gains on us. The windshield is dark.

The invisible spirit controlling the machine sees both his targets on one cockamamie vehicle and is just going to grind us into sausage. The growling chrome grating gets close enough to steam my ass with hot breath. In five seconds, Ho and I will be a pair of bumper stickers.

Denny is heading us straight back to where my hiding spot was. What's he planning to do?

Denny barrels recklessly into the ruins, crashing through trash and covering the Bronco's windshield with our squirrel's tail of dust. It's like pressing the "smokescreen" button on our Batmobile.

The Bronco actually has to slow as Denny, commandeering a much smaller, albeit more laden vehicle, veers in and out of a couple buildings and spiked rusty obstructions appearing from nowhere. Denny is making madcap swerves, going up on two wheels, scaring me worse than the bullets.

Just when I'm about to disengage and take my chances with the Bronco, Denny tears into the bombed-out plane hangar wherein resides the Gate to the Netherworld.

My voice vibrating so much I sound like Johnny Cash with a vibrator stuck up his ass, I yelp, "Denny! There's a stack of mattresses at the bottom of this hole!"

Denny, with balls of steel, never hesitates. He grips squirming Wily with his free arm and bends his joystick towards the hole while the Bronco crashes through the wall behind us and hits ramming speed.

A second huge vehicle crashes through the tin straight ahead, swerves around the gaping hole, and hurtles straight at us on a collision course. The four of us will soon be cold cuts in a steel sandwich. Me, Denny, and Wily shriek like girls. Ho doesn't even quiver.

"It's Chugger!" she shouts.

The Spitmobile guns right past us, Chugger yanks the wheel to the left, and the back end swings around to collide climactically against the front end of the Bronco, sending a precious shrapnel of bouncing snare drums, splintering guitars, squirming black cables, and jury-rigged electronics.

Now Ho is shrieking like a girl. *"Aaaaaagh! The instruments! The van! The cost!"*

Just when I think Denny's going to hit the hole too fast and jump clear of the invisible mattresses, he slams on the brakes, my sinuses interface with the back of his skull, we skid to the lip of the hole, teeter, and plummet.

Boy-yoing!

Five mattresses bounce Denny's quarter-ton wheelchair in a careening somersault. Me, Wily, and Ho are catapulted in three different directions. Denny grips his arm rests as the chair somersaults once—dumping his entire utility belt of Bat-tools all over the floor—rolls over the lip of the mattress pile, and lands on its tank treads.

Wow.

"We did it!" shouts Den. "We escaped!"

Ho moans, "Ooooooh, my head."

I leap to my knees and grab her waist. "My God! Is the pussy okay? Is it damaged at all?"

"I think I have brain damage."

"The pussy, Ho! The pussy!"

"The pussy is fine."

"Whew! Thank God! So what were you saying about your brain?"

"Man, you are a feminist's dream!" She hugs me.

I hug her back. "I love you, Ho."

She squeezes me harder. "I know you do."

"Would you guys knock it off and come on!" shouts Denny. "*First* comes the rescue, *then* comes the sex!"

The Bronco has not approached the lip of the hole, which is curious. We can hear something grinding along the ceiling, like somebody dragging a slab of iron across the cement floor. As a great shadow passes across the hole, some broken guitar necks with frayed strings and the hand-painted Spit logo slide over the lip of the hole and land among us.

"You guys just go ahead," moans Ho. "I might as well just let them kill me now. I have nothing to live for."

I grab her hand, thrust it against my cock, she says, "Oh, yeah," and we start scrambling out from beneath the hole. At that moment, the crumbled remains of the Spitmobile come crashing down like the wrath of Zeus, shooting up tufts of wool stuffing and splintered wood in a bowl-shaped cloud. We all duck as freed mattress springs ricochet and spark off the walls. When the van's wheels catch floor, the van abruptly guns backwards five feet and brakes. Chugger must have had the van in reverse upstairs, grinding futilely against the Bronco, which steadily pushed him into the hole in an attempt to crush us.

"I'm not dead!" shouts Chugger, with sincere amazement.

"Well, come on!" I shout. "Before they start shooting down at you!"

I can hear the Bronco upstairs reversing and pulling back a good distance from the hole. Chugger opens his driver's side door six inches until the upper corner chucks against the arc of the pipe. He looks at us with a teary face that says, *Oh shit*.

I hear the Bronco's tires squeal as it hurtles towards the hole.

"Drive forward off all that stuff!" I yell.

Chugger bends the car into drive and his vehicle limps forward. Just when he gets out of range of the overhead hole, what should pounce down into the darkness but the demon-possessed Bronco, blaring its headlights, snorting and seething with animal rage. It hits the floor with wheels spinning and rams the back of the Spit van, which crumples like a beer can to half its length. The Bronco slows, but its stubborn wheels churn up steam like The Little Engine That Damn Well Knows It Can, and soon the whole mess begins to grind forward like a zombie shot twenty times but refusing to die. The Bronco's headlights are protected behind its bumpers, and they reflect off the crumpled back of the Spitmobile, casting stabbing beams and ghastly shadows over the refuse inside the tunnel. Chugger's eyes are as wide as the headlights, and he bangs the van into reverse, to little avail. The black windshield eats all light cast at it; we can't see who's driving. The chewed Spitmobile slides forward and gains momentum; the tires peel like kiwi.

Me, Ho, Denny, and Wily ululate in four-part harmony like

the Andrews Sisters on PCP. Wily is on Denny's lap in a moment. Me and Ho grab for the wheelchair handles. Denny slams the joystick without ever making sure we're aboard. The wheelchair explodes forward, nearly pulling me and Ho's shoulders out of our sockets.

We are followed by a spitting, grinding robot, the Bronco and the husk of the Spitmobile pursuing in an unholy union. We pull ahead of the abomination at first, but the Bronco's infinite horsepower churns up momentum and gains on us.

Crystal beams slice about the tunnel like siren lights as the pulverized Spit van clashes back and forth off both walls, wriggling and writhing in a slow snake dance as it is plowed before the thunder and lightning of godlike wrath. Poor Chugger, nimbused before the twin-eyed glow of the Bronco, sits trapped inside the nose of this undulating steel worm.

We are regurgitated rodents, escaping out through the belly of the snake that ate us. We splash through digestive juices, chasing our long shadows cast out on the littered floor before us. A small rat's eyes glow red, and he emits a mini-shriek as he scurries to the side.

Ahead, I can see the first arc of azure, hanging a wrinkled skirt of heliacal light. The tunnel's mouth is still a thousand yards beyond. We'll never make it.

The moment before we pass through the burning omega sign, Denny's wheels hit the corresponding cleft in the floor. His chair chunks down and thunks up, then skids sideways. We hit a water slick, hurtle into a topspin, and I am catapulted up the side of the pipe.

The tunnel behind me explodes. Ho disappears. I am covered in white sparks as drums and amps bounce loudly past me. I carve a tight arch up one side of the pipe, then the other, almost scraping both ears on the ceiling as Denny and Wily zoom by, spinning like a top. Twisted metal slides to a stop at my heels. I scramble for balance, boomerang into a turn, and see nothing but carnage.

The Spit van's front tires had thunked down, hit the edge of the pothole, then bounced high enough for the left and right corners of the roof to strike the ceiling and send sparks raining all over us. Chugger's reaction to this was to yank the emergency brake, which bent his vehicle slightly sideways. His front left wheel and back right wheel climbed opposite sides of the pipe, so the van was actually lifted two feet into the air, spraying sparks from both sides and making an unholy sound like a thousand metal fingernails scraping along a chalkboard.

The Bronco did a similar chunk-thump and ceiling scrape, but whoever was driving the truck never hit the brakes. The front end ground into the back left corner of the Spitmobile. Now both axles are torqued entirely out of wack, and the great Bronco beast, wearing the chiseled mask of the Spit van, grinds to a halt.

The last image I see in the battery light is Wily dizzily climbing off Denny's lap and crossing all four legs as he tries to walk up the side of the pipe. Denny's eyes are pointed in two different directions, and his face is green.

The headlights flicker and die.

Everyone, on instinct, remains quiet. Denny does not move for fear of emitting his characteristic buzz. I won't even breathe.

We skidded a good hundred feet. The wreckage blocks the crack of sunlight behind the Bronco. It's pitch black. I'm closest to the bad guy.

Where the hell is Ho?

Then, sounds. Sounds of movement. Grunts.

Somebody is climbing out of the debris. Pieces of metal twist aside. He splashes around the front of the Spit van and silences. He is ten feet from me.

"Well, Cannonball," smiles the voice of Spock. "We meet again."

MAJOR FUCKED-UP SHIT

Good to see he's not grown tired of clichés or anything.

"You know, Chet, the first muzzle flash will tell me where you are."

I'm holding my breath. I won't move.

"And you're thinking the first muzzle flash will show you where *I* am!"

He chuckles, radiating confidence. He's been in situations like this a thousand times. Meanwhile, I'm struggling not to let my knees and teeth rattle out a staccato percussion duel.

"I bet you've wanted to kill me since the first time you met me, Chet. When I was pinching your cheeks and showing you around Chen's old place, you just wanted to bust my ass, didn't you? I could see it in your eyes. Baby punks like you always think they can take a real man like me. You think tattoos and rollerskates make you tough, Chet? They don't. They make you look like a fucking pansy."

Not until the silence pounces in on us do I realize how comforted I am by his voice. His words don't terrify me like his silences. At this moment, I feel that I am alone. Alone with him.

"I'll tell you what, Chet, my boy. I'm putting the gun down. I ain't worried about your crippled friend or your bitch. As far as we're concerned, it's just you and me down here. C'mon. Let's see you take a swing at me, Chet."

Shyeah, right. Like duh.

"Chicken? Figures. You were always a weenie, Chet. A little faggot. You and that other rollerskate fudge-packing boyfriend of yours I wasted on the street."

Something hot and red sears through my terror. My finer

feelings blot out. My attention sharpens into the tunnel vision of rage.

"Yeah, that was me," Spock resumes. "Three bullets straight through his melon. Bang! Bang! Bang! Just fills you with outrage, don't it? That I get to kill him, and then you, and then your brother and girlfriend? Damn! That must hurt! Well, you won't have to suffer long, Chet, my boy. I got a little surprise for you. I'm gonna count to three. One . . ."

I can't make a grab for him. With the echo, I can't even tell exactly where he is. All I know is that his voice is getting closer. Any second, he could bump into me.

"Two . . ."

But I can't defend myself. I'm blind. We're all blind.

Then a faint growl to my left tells me we're not *all* blind.

"Wily!" shrieks Ho.

The entire tunnel flashes and stamps a permanent image on my consciousness: Wily leaping, Spock turned away from me and firing, the twisted face of the Spit van, the momentary flash of red eyes. Then darkness eats us again.

The sound waves bounce down both ends of our hellish subway in rumbling diminuendo, leaving behind one sputtering bleat: Spock's laughter.

"I think I know where your girlfriend is!" Spock manages to spit. He slowly ties down his joyous cachinnation and gets ahold of himself. "You're making my day, kid! Three bonuses in one week!"

I'm frozen. One of us is shot. He is going to pick us off one by one, and there's nothing we can do about it.

I saw where he was. He's five feet away. If I fell forward, I could bite his ankle.

My eyebrows almost hit the ceiling when a voice starts to speak from beneath me. A talking roach? No, it's electronic. It's the police frequency. The scanner is still strapped to my hip.

Passing through walls of concrete, the radio waves eerily move from static to silence and back into static again. A voice pours through clear as spring water for a moment, then cuts off as it begins to give out my bank's address.

Spock starts his bronchial cackle again and spits. I feel a hot globule hit my knee. "Boy! That sucks, huh? All that work for nothing! Is life a bitch, or what?"

His voice is close to my face. Our breath is mixing. I want to take a step back, but I'm afraid to make a noise. He might touch me at any moment.

"Gee, let's see. Should I kill your girlfriend first?"

The ice-blooded reptile rises, eyes aglow. I twitch when his fingers snap inches from my face.

"Oooooooh, yeah! I almost forgot! My surprise! Let's see, I had counted to one, and I had counted to two, so that just leaves—"

"—three."

The lighter flashes in Spock's hand. The split-second is stretched out like taffy: Our faces are one foot apart, his gun is pointed directly over my shoulder. He is swinging his gun toward my face.

Both of us are about to learn why you never corner a terrified animal.

I leap forward, beyond the nozzle of the gun, and grab his skull. Before I can even think, my teeth have sunk into Spock's cheek at the exact moment Wily, who must have crawled forward, sinks his fangs into Spock's rear. The holler of his larynx gurgles so close to my ear.

I hear the gun clatter on the floor. His fingers dig into my squinted eyes. Backpedaling, his calves strike Wily, and he totters and falls, howling. The shock against the floor knocks my bite loose, but I still have his head in my hands. Losing control to a manic side of myself I never knew existed, I lift his head and smash it down onto the concrete. I do it again and again and again, like a jackhammer.

Even after the blood is streaming out his ears and nose and I feel his skull break like a cantaloupe in my hands, I cannot stop. I keep hurling it down until it stops going crack! crack! crack! and just goes mush, mush, mush. I keep slamming until I am certain every speck of his brain is pureed.

I stop, exhausted, my open mouth hanging jump-roping streams of saliva. My hands are sticky with blood and brain fluid. I look at Spock's broken face in the yellow lighter glow. The vision bypasses the beast and speaks to the buried angel in me, who asks, *Who would do such a horrible thing to a human being?*

I pull myself over into a corner and vomit copiously. The horror in my stomach is expelled. My consciousness is split, the cleft halves straining across some psychic corpus callosum.

In a puddle of dirty water, I see my face, my blood-smeared hands. I break the reflection into widening circles and fever-ishly scrub the blood off my hands.

I look at my hands, the hands that make love to Ho.

I stomp out the lighter.

A whisper nuzzles through my delirium. "Where is he?"

It's Ho. The whisper of Ho. I feel like I have not heard her voice in ages. I realize my fever has been floating on the sound cushion of an animal whimpering and a woman keening qui-etly into his ear.

"I—" How do I tell her? Did she see? "I think I . . . no, I'm certain I killed him."

"Are you *positive*?"

"Yes."

Only the tiniest heartbeat of a pause. Then, "Can we get some light in here? Denny? Are you there?"

Denny burps. "Yes."

"You okay?"

"All functions focused on trying not to hurl," says Denny. Wily yelps.

"Oh, honey honey honey," croons Ho. "We got to get Wily to a hospital. He's going to die. I know he is."

From the direction of the Bronco, a needle of white stabs into our eyes. We scream.

"AAAAIIII!!"

"Chill!" shouts Chugger. "It's me!"

We all pant with relief.

"Where's that dude?" asks Chugger. "I'm tripping! I can't

believe he just walked right past me! I—ugh!"

I throw my backpack over Spock's face. "Don't look at him!"

"God *damn!*" exults Chugger. "Did you do that, Chet?"

"Shut up."

"Let me see!"

"Shut up!" I roar. "And turn off that fucking flashlight!"

Chugger obeys. My deed disappears. Now I can believe it never happened.

Then Denny's voice. "Chet, you better chill out. Chugger, go point that thing at Wily."

Chugger takes a few steps away from me before he clicks on the light. Then the image flashes.

"Oooooh, fuck," says Chugger.

Ho's bravery breaks down into sobs.

Scissored inside the white triangle is the pietà image of Mongrel in the Arms of a Ho. My crippled friend is behind them, looking on like a shepherd. Inside that tiny triangle of light, set alone in the infinite sea of blackness, is everything that is sacred to me.

"Denny," I plead, "we have to get Wily to a doctor or something. Let's get him on the chair."

Chugger puts down the flashlight and steps forward to help. The poor animal twitches with excruciation as we lift him, but he stays stoically silent. He only whimpers when he loses physical contact with Ho.

I struggle not to touch the round circle of hamburger. There is no exit wound.

The monster in me is dormant again, asleep. He leapt forward, a ghost of my ancestors, the demon living inside all descendants of murderers, and went back to his coffin. But tonight, humanity's curse was my salvation.

Tonight? It's not even ten A.M. yet. But down here, it's always night.

Ho seizes control of Wily's welfare, and Denny waits patiently while she arranges Wily's limbs, strokes his fur, and croons wordless sounds in his ear.

"Chugger, my man," I say, "think you can walk out of here on your lonesome?"

Chugger shudders, his eyes run along the cobwebs, but he forces himself to act macho. "No prob, dude. I ain't bugging. Here, take the torch."

"Nah, you take it. You're on foot. We know our way out of here."

"Cool. Good luck."

I look at him for a moment, then, "You're all right, Chugs. I'm sorry I yelled at you, man."

"Hey, forget it, Barnacle."

We jackhammer fists, slap hands, clasp thumbs, and hug.

When we separate, Chugger slaps my shoulder. "You better jet."

Ho has Wily secured on Denny's lap. Denny already has blood all over him. Ho gets on her borrowed board behind Denny. I mount up, then look over my shoulder at the man we're abandoning.

"By the way," I say. "I don't want to dwell on trivialities or anything, but thanks for risking your ass and throwing away your livelihood to save our lives today."

Chugs glances over his shoulder at his junked capital, then looks at me and circles the flashlight about his ear. "Drumming makes you tap-happy, dude."

Denny guns the chair. We spray off. As we pass beneath the first crack hanging an ethereal veil of light, Chugger disappears into the throat of the pipe.

I killed someone. With my bare hands.

We exit into daylight. By the time we can stop squinting, Wily has ceased making noises. His eyes have stopped blinking. He is foaming at the mouth, a red, white, and blue dog.

The supergrips on the treads of Denny's chair churn us straight up the steep angle of the cement trench, and we double back towards Fort Farley, where smoke rises and the guns have silenced.

We enter straight up behind the media in their makeshift village. The smell of tear gas makes our eyes water. Ambulances are parked at skewed angles. We beg them to take Wily, but they are too busy saving wounded gangsters.

Most of the cops are out scouring the battlefield. A huge contingent of them seems to be entirely absent. But three or four are standing around a single squad car. Nobody is arresting us.

Handcuffed thrashers are sitting around on the ground chatting amicably in skatespeak. Skateboarders get arrested all the time. Skating is basically against the law, especially if you have purple hair and a safety pin stabbed through your eyebrow. One of them notices me, points to my wound, and comments, "Pretty splendiferous forearm steak."

I recognize Mr. Hair Helmet—that polyester who muscled his way into my *Blazing Bladers* slot—intoning into a camera with a surrealistically icehearted sense of drama.

Ho spins on Denny, a disturbing vibrato to her voice, "Den, you have to get Wily to my vet. Here's his address."

She hands him a business card. Guess she carries that with her everywhere she goes.

"Tell him to spare no expense. You're the fastest among us. Please do it fast, Denny. Please."

Denny nods, says nothing. Ho bends to kiss her dying animal, but Denny guns off before she can clasp his face in her hands.

We are left staring after them.

Sweaty Ho is walking in circles and holding her board at her side like a holster. Still riding off the adrenaline, she turns to me and growls, "Let's double back and bust ass on that dude who tried to shoot me."

"Are you *bent*? We just escaped!"

"That son of a bitch shot my hairdo. Nobody fucks with my hairdo."

"You could have been killed!"

"Trying to kill me is one thing, but fuck with the hairdo or the wardrobe, and you incur the wrath of Megabitch."

"Let's be thankful for what we still have."

"Quite a long view coming from a man whose only concern was my pussy."

"Well, that numbers among the things we still have, doesn't

it? How can you compare something so vital to my happiness to something so trivial? Besides, your hairdo looks ultra-fucking-hype now."

She flutters her lashes. "You think so?"

I roll my eyes.

"Well, now that you're my man," she goes, "you have to get blue hair, too."

"Ho, you will *never* see a real man like me with blue hair! Pink, maybe! But never blue!"

Ho smiles at me, backhands me on the stomach. "Opf!" I say, then backhand her back. She laughs, then breaks down and punches her head into my collarbone. I hold her.

She sobs like a child. Jagged spasms of sound. My heart rips open.

"Is he going to die, Chet?"

"I don't know, Ho."

Her muscles are twitching. She's still pumped. I want to use this adrenaline in her. I put my hands beneath her ears and lift her face to me. I wipe her tears away with my thumbs.

"Ho, we can't let those bastards get away with this. They're on their way to my old apartment right now to destroy the last of the evidence. We have to get there before they do."

"They have a head start."

"But we're skaters. In this city, we can move faster than the traffic."

She looks at me hopelessly.

"Please, Ho. I need you."

Out from under the cement structures of Fort Farley, the police frequency comes in through my portable scanner clear as liquid silver. Our ears are strafed with a sandstorm of squad car numbers, crime codes, and outright panicking. Every two minutes, five more squad cars are called away from Fort Farley to Mission and Seventh—isn't that where Chen is? The jittery reports coming back contain gunshots. The gangsters are engaged in a civil war. The firestorm sounds so thick, the cops won't get involved. They're trying to contain it on three sides to allow the in-fighting gunmen an escape route. Then I pick up some cop chatter:

"They got away again? Corlini's gonna shit the pan."

"Didn't you hear? Lieutenant Corlini's been arrested. Halcott is in charge now."

My beeper tweedles. I don't need to look to know the number.

We turn a corner, blow a stoptional sign, and nearly collide with a single policeman on foot, sent down here to stop traffic from coming within bullet range of the fort. Ho swerves at the last second and accidentally knocks the policeman's cap off his head. The chubby five-oh pivots, shakes his fist, and furiously writes a detailed description of Ho's buttocks.

Ho looks over her shoulder at the scrambling Keystone Kops. "We're not even being chased!"

"They're being called away to something bigger."

"Something *bigger* than what just happened at Fort Farley?"

Rollercoasting over the endless undulations of San Fran, we pass not a single police car, which are normally ubiquitous in this part of the city. If the criminals want to go on a crime spree, they better start now. Prime time to start a grocery riot. We soar right past the mini traffic jams bunched up behind red lights. Thankfully, we do not cross paths with any gangstermobiles racing to my home.

As we sprint through the front door of my apartment complex, we are confident nobody has arrived yet. I just have to grab the disks and go.

We burst through Denny's door, and find him awkwardly packing up computer disks by himself.

"Chet!" he shouts. "The FCIC are on their way here!"

"Are you shitting me?"

"The phone was ringing when I rolled in. They analyzed your programming signatures and figured out that Snakebyte is MacHack. They've been driving around the city all night with a cellular-free directional antenna, and they followed the signal to this building. They know you're operating from inside your confiscated apartment. They're getting the Secret Service boys together with the local cops and making a raid on your place in like five minutes."

"Fuckin A. Out of the frying pan."

Ho shouts, "Did you drop Wily off?"

"Yes. I had to tell them you were heiress to a million dollars, and they knocked him out and started operating. They told me he probably won't make it."

"Oh, God," moans Ho.

I stalk past Denny towards the bathroom. He follows. "Chet, let me take the heat for this one."

"No fucking way. I seduced you into this scheme. We're both repeat offenders."

"But my first offense isn't on the books! Besides, a cripple's jail isn't as bad as the one you'll be going to! One of us has to take the fall, so it might as well be me!"

"Forget it, Denny. It's my ass; I'm taking the heat."

"They can't punish me like they can punish you! I'm disabled! Plus I can show that I did good things with my computer talents! What can you show? Nothing but crime. Don't forget, I was a cyberlawman, bringing in dangerous hackers by the dozen!"

"Denny, there's nothing a jury hates like a cop gone bad."

"But Chet—"

I march through my bedroom door and stop dead as I stare into the imperturbable face of Data.

"AAAAAAAUGH!" we all carol.

Data smiles, clamps my shoulders between his viselike mitts, and hurls me bodily across my room. I hit the wall and crumple to the floor like a marionette. Ho swings her board to give Data a second black eye, but it snaps in half over Data's forearm as he backhands her into the opposite corner. Then he very intelligently karate-kicks Denny's joystick, which propels Denny straight back through the bathroom. Data slams the door, then drags my half-ton filing cabinet in front of the entrance.

He looks at me as I struggle to stand. He pushes a hanging chain light out of his face. Again the smile.

I dizzily get in a boxer's stance and face him down. "All right, you thyroid freak! You want me? Come and get it, monkey-boy. I'll kill you just like I killed your friend Tweedledee."

I jump forward and take a swing. Data weaves his chin back and his hair whishes slightly from the breeze of my enthusiastic attempt. I immediately kick my rollerblade towards his nuts, but he catches my foot, raises it into the air, and kicks me between my anus and prostate.

Oochie.

I'm balled up on the floor snorting lint from the rug. Ho jumps him from behind, but he saw it coming. He catches her in midair and uses her momentum to spear-chuck her over his shoulder. She lands on top of me.

He laughs again. Not a joyous laugh. Just one snort. His eyes are dead. He looks like a suburban boy dismembering a beetle.

I stand, catch my breath, waddle forward, say with a hoarse voice, "All right, chucklehead. Let's rock."

Data's single eyebrow Vs into fury. He explodes forward

with a freight train's speed, battering-rams his fist straight into my face. His ham-sized fist cracks against my cheekbone with a howitzer's force. I never have time to bend to the blow. My head never lolls. I just take it straight on, my whole skull and spine absorbing the full force of the clout. It stuns me momentarily, but when I open my eyes, I am still standing. I have not moved. I blink, my eyes slowly focus.

Data's unibrow has pulled up into an arch. He is wearing an entirely different expression. It's like the look of wide-eyed shock you see on a toddler immediately before he howls after being stung by a bee. His mouth is open, his eyes are milky, his cheeks are chubby. He's holding his arm in a funny way.

On the end of his arm is what looks like a hand. But it's surreal, like the rubber clocks in Salvador Dali paintings. It looks like a bag of broken glass. A thousand little bones in his hand snapped in different directions, and he is trying to hold it very still. Data's voice vibrates, "Ah-yah-ah-yah-haaah . . ."

My face throbs, but feels perfectly intact.

A shrieking Ms. Piggy *"Hi-ya!"* emits from over my right shoulder. Ho is leaping through the air, one leg snapping forward like a lead pipe shot from a crossbow. The ball of her heel interfaces with the center of Data's face. His nose pops and explodes like a raspberry hit with a hammer. He topples backwards and crashes down on my very expensive boa cage.

Glass shatters into the air, and a green tentacle envelops Data's torso-sized neck with terrifying efficacy. His face instantly turns purple and looks ready to pop. Me and Ho stand in weighty silence as my snake, without betraying the slightest ounce of passion, or even evidence that his heart rate has risen, squeezes the life out of his first human, a creature much too big for him to swallow.

Data thrashes horribly, his bulging mammalian flesh seemingly so soft and mortal compared to the cold scales armoring the undulating muscles of the snake. There is no hate, no mercy, just machinelike efficiency. I can feel my spine twitching with ancient terror, but me and Ho are frozen. We don't help him.

For five long minutes.

When Data's bloodshot green eyes glaze over and his face becomes inanimate, my snake, so intimately attuned with Data's glimmering and then extinguishing life, immediately lets go. Data flops forwards, his face strikes flat on the floor like a cinder block. My snake slithers around his cage for a moment, curls into a comfortable position, and stills. Utterly calm. The shambles of his home, and the big hole through which he could escape, do not interest him.

Data is dead. Dead and in my bedroom.

Denny is knocking on the door. "Chet! Ho! Are you guys dead yet? Hello?"

Me and Ho spend a full minute shouldering aside my filing cabinet. Denny wheelies in and stares.

"Damn! That's two people you killed in one day, Chet!"

"I didn't kill him. My snake did."

Data's dress shirt is open. On his chest is Bobby's tattoo of a spider.

"Anyway, as I was saying," goes Denny. "I should be the one to take the blame so I can be a political martyr. They'd never believe you did it by yourself anyway."

I stare blankly at Denny. Ho slaps me on the shoulder. "That was quite a shot you took, bud."

My checkbone glows hot and hums. "I don't understand why my skull isn't caved in."

Ho smirks. "You ain't been in enough fights, Chet. Everybody knows a skull is harder than a fist. Hands break ten times more often than faces. The fistfight is a TV myth."

Ho has kicked many an ass, so I don't argue with her.

"Let's drag him onto your futon," says Denny.

Me and Ho grab him by his collar and drag him towards my mattress.

"Jesus. He is one heavy slab of meat," complains Ho.

"You know, it amazes me," I grunt. "I feel not one ounce of remorse about this. The only thing I feel is relief."

"You shouldn't feel remorse over this scum," goes Denny. "How many people would this guy have raped and murdered before he died of old age?"

We roll him onto my futon, pull the covers over him, tuck him in.

"Do you think he has a mother?" I ask. "Kids?"

Denny looks at him, shrugs.

Ho looks at her watch. "I'm so glad you sensitive males are respecting the dead with this moment of silence," she goes, "but don't we have, like, *thirty seconds* to destroy evidence?"

Me and Denny meet eyes, then spasmodically pounce on my computer. I sit down, boot up, let the memory wind up, and prepare for the self-destruct command.

My hands freeze above the keyboard. Nobody moves.

Ho says, "If you destroy the evidence that you're a hacker, you destroy the evidence that puts Wozniak and Levy away!"

"What should I do?" I lament. "If I let the FCIC get hold of all this, me and Levy will be cell mates."

"Either you both go to jail, or neither of you do," says Den. "Make your decision."

My beeper beeps. I roll my eyes.

"Call it back!" shouts Denny. "Maybe you can make a deal."

Denny clicks on my speaker phone. I punch the number and hold Ho's hand. It picks up immediately.

"Hello, Chen."

"You're alive?!!"

"And I've got my chick back, too. How about that? Thanks for not peeling back her fingernails." I kiss her fingers.

"Hi, Chenny!" shouts Ho.

Chen takes his mouth away from his phone and shouts some orders in Chinese. There's a ton of noise going on in the background. People shouting and running. Is that static or gunshots? Then he gets back on.

"Griffin, call this number!" He frantically reads me some phone number and hangs up.

"What was the number, Denny?"

Denny repeats it. I dial it. A familiar voice comes over the speakerphone.

"Hello?"

"Michael Levy?"

"Chet Griffin." His voice is quavering with terror. "If you burn the evidence, I will give you ten million dollars."

Dead silence. We all stare at each other, telepathically trading fantasies. Ten million dollars. Ten. Million. Dollars. My eyes dilate, my sight contracts into tunnel vision.

"Think of it, Chet," croons Levy. "Ten million dollars."

"Stick it up your ass, Levy. I'll see you in prison."

The front door splinters open. My fingers reflexively hit Alt-Ctrl-Shift-@. A flood of suits raids my home. An endless loop starts eating up my whole hard drive.

"Unplug it!" shouts a man in a beige suit.

A blue-suited man in sunglasses makes a headfirst dive for my electrical outlet. I pin his wrist to the wall with my foot.

A hairy fist grabs the back of my collar and yanks me backwards onto the floor. I am rolled over, a knee goes into the back of my neck, and I am cuffed. My computer is unplugged, which aborts my endless loop. Denny is yanked from his chair to the floor. He doesn't have the coordination to break his fall, so he just lands on his teeth. Ho stupidly puts up a struggle, gets locked in the notorious choke hold, and is cuffed facedown on the floor.

A gun is needlessly pointed at the back of my skull.

"I sure am getting a lot of guns pointed at me today."

The amusement begins as a Secret Service spook barks, "Nap time's over, saphead!" and yanks Data out of bed. Data lands—*clomp!*—like a side of beef, smearing a streak of snotty red across my sheets. The SS tough guy screeches like a daisy girl.

"Eek! This guy's dead!"

BUSTED

"**Who is that?**"

"That's a dead guy," I go.

"I know it's a dead guy! Who killed him?"

"Uh, I don't know."

"What do you mean, you don't know?"

My voice is muffled by the rug smushing my nose. A film of dust is on my tongue. Why didn't I ever vacuum?

"Uh, he was here waiting for me—because he was with Chen—and he tried to kill us—and we were fighting, and he just keeled over dead."

A uniformed cop is inspecting him. "No bullet wounds. No blood, except for his nose. Somebody crushed his hand in a vise."

They pull me up off my face and slam my ass down on my chair. Denny is back up in his wheelchair, nursing his front lip. Ho is handcuffed to my radiator . . . looks kind of sexy, actually—mmm . . . anyway, most of the cops gather around me—me being the able-bodied white male.

A local cop smiles at me, then gets in a boxing stance. "You punch this big galoot in his nose?"

"*I* busted his nose," declares Ho.

None of the cops—all male—know how to react to this, so they go back to talking to me.

"Jesus, look at this place!" yells a uniformed cop, staring at my Giger and Minera posters. "It looks like a nightmare in here!"

"I'm all ears for any cut-rate interior decorators you happen to know," I say. Captured heroes are supposed to make smart-ass quips, you know.

"Sorry, fella," retorts Clancy McGee, glancing around at his comrades. "But you don't get no interior decorators in jail!"

Hardy har har. My room is thick with bristles and testosterone. It comforts me somehow. Nice little offset to Ho totally Hoifying the atmosphere with all her clothes. The windows haven't been opened since she left, and I can still smell her sexy funk.

A pair of uniformed cops are taunting Ho.

"How did you get your hair like that?"

"It's natural," says Ho.

"Was that your dog out there?"

Ho turns her head away and says nothing.

The cop who put his knee in the back of my neck looks me over. "Recognize my voice?" he asks.

"Sergeant Halcott!" I cry. "Congratulations on your promotion! Nice to finally meet you!"

"This is the way I hoped we'd meet, too."

"C'mon, I'm the one who got Gina's bust for you. I'm the innocent victim in all this."

"My ass you are," he snorts. "If you're such an angel, why did I get the order to raid this place—which happens to be police property—with the goddamn United States Secret Service? This is a first for me! I can't *wait* to find out what this is about!"

The beige-suited straight plugs in my computer and sees an endless message, saying, "nyah-nyah-nyah-nyah."

"Very funny," he says to me. I grin.

Beige Boy gestures towards Denny, apparently afraid to talk to him directly. "Who is this guy, and how is he involved in all this?"

"I am MP Phred," declares Denny, pounding his chest like Tarzan, "hired by Wozniak and Levy, and it was *I* who broke into their banking system and stole the information contained on all these disks! I'll have much to tell the world at my trial!"

The cops, of course, don't understand him.

"He's just a pawn in my scheme," I say. "I used him to borrow computer hardware and scout Fort Farley for me."

Denny is instantly livid. "That's bullshit! I masterminded the whole thing! *I* was the one with access to Wozniak and Levy's bank accounts!"

The cops look to me for translation.

"Denny, I know you must be upset that I manipulated you so easily!"

"*I'm* not the dumb one! *He's* the dumb one!" he shouts, spraying drool on the cops. "I am solely responsible for breaking and entering and burglary! Read me my rights!"

"Now he's telling you to string me up for taking advantage of his small mind."

"Small mind, my ass! Dammit, you stupid cops, listen to me! I'm the one who should be going to jail! It was *my* idea, and I executed it! Chet Griffin couldn't hack a celery stick with a machete!"

Denny is waving his hands around like a cockroach. I look sorrowfully at the cops.

"Sad, isn't it?"

"Chet, I'm gonna kill you."

Me and Ho are led to the door. Ho refuses to move, and has to be dragged on her back. Sliding across the carpet, she smiles up at me.

"I always wanted to do this. Passive resistance, man."

I roll my eyes as they walk me out after her.

Denny shouts after me, "You haven't won this one yet, Chet! I'll be in jail before you can blink!"

"Sorry, Denny. Have a nice decade being free!"

"*You'll* be the one spending the rest of your life *not* behind bars, Chet! *I'm* getting all the blame for this one! And don't try to stop me! You hear me, Chet?! Cheeeeeet!"

"**Chet, my** name is Detective Gambill," the beige-suited man informs me. "I run the Federal Computer Investigations Committee. I'm sorry we left you in your cell for so long, but my colleagues and I had a lot to discuss. It's been a long time since I've personally gone on a raid—not since the last time we arrested you, in fact. But I decided to make an exception in this case."

I don't recognize him. About twenty cops arrested me last time. My internal bogometer, which measures the degree to which something is bogus, tells me this dude has a high bogosity ratio. That gleaming white smile is emitting a steady stream of bogons. He continues.

"You see, I've made my climb up the law-enforcement ladder since I was out handcuffing criminals like you. And in that time, I see you've made your way up your own dark ladder— and haven't exactly made a killing for yourself, if you don't mind my saying."

There are no local cops in here. Just Gambill and two handsome Fed eunuchs in sunglasses with tongues removed. We're in a white room with obvious one-way mirrors. I still have not been read my rights. I'm trying to figure out why I was placed in a private cell.

"I remember your parents well. Very loving, very upright folks. You seemed to be a promising young man at the time, with only one mischievous hobby. It's a shame you didn't honor their memories by kicking that one dangerous habit. Instead, you let it consume your life."

He offers me a cigarette. I decline. He doesn't seem to note the irony.

"You've come a long way since you were MacHack. We always feared what would happen if some teenage cracker never grew out of electronic trespassing and got a real job. If someone can learn so much as a teenager, imagine what they could do if they stayed in the digital Underground for ten years?"

He sucks his cigarette for effect. Think I'll continue giving him the bunny eyes. Should get me some more information.

Gambill resumes. "He would become a hacking specialist, a Ph.D., if you will, of breaking into other people's computer systems and stealing private information. We always feared his coming, because we knew how difficult it would be to catch him. But here you are, caught and floundering in our fishbowl, and we can do what we want with you. It's an exciting day for us."

"What's going to happen to my friends?"

"Ho will be released. So will your friend Denny. When those disks are analyzed by the state prosecution, and the press get their hands on this, they'll be heroes. But the information we get from your disks—especially the disk we found in the pocket of the deceased—makes a pretty complete picture, unfortunately for you."

He watches for my reaction. I make none. So he drives the nail home.

"We have enough to put Wozniak and Levy in jail for a little while—and more than enough to put *you* in jail for a *long* while. Home burglary, breaking and entering police property, tampering with evidence, hijacking a bus and kidnapping fifteen citizens, vandalism, conspiracy, phone fraud, almost every conceivable electronic crime—and possibly murder."

I nod. So this is how my life goes. I find myself smirking.

"You look as if you always knew this day was coming."

"Yup."

"And you accept that?"

"Nobody did it to me but me."

"But you brought down some of the biggest criminals in the city. Some will say you should be rewarded."

"I'll get three square meals a day. I won't have to make rent. Instead of pimping myself out in traffic, I'll pimp myself in jail. The only injustice would be Denny or Ho being hurt. If they get off scot-free—"

"They get off scot-free."

"Then I have no complaints."

"That's it?"

"That's it. Might as well take me back to my cell now."

"Think you could ever go straight someday?"

"Become MP Phred Two? After I've done my time and been pleasantly rehabilitated?"

"If there was a salary of—say—ninety thousand dollars a year? To start?"

"Fuck you, Gambill. Me hacker. You Fed."

"Yeah, yeah, yeah. We have a fundamental difference in our ideologies, right? You believe in freedom of information.

I believe in national security. You call me Big Brother. I call you anarchist."

"We don't need to discuss it. We're not going to change each other. Prison is not going to make me go straight."

"Who said you're going to prison?"

"You did."

"I never said that. I said we have enough evidence to put you in prison."

I sigh and wait for the punch line.

Gambill likes his significant pauses. Thus the cigarette. He takes a long drag, exhales, then spits his mind.

"How would you like to work for me? Starting right now?"

Of course I told the FCIC to suck my socks, but that doesn't mean I didn't sell out.

If a police officer gathers evidence through illegal means, the evidence is thrown out of court. But if a citizen collects evidence through illegal means, the court has a party. All my stolen computer files, audiocassettes, and printouts were used by the prosecution to burn Gina Corlini, Michael Levy, and Marc Wozniak. The question of my computer theft was considered another matter to be settled at another trial.

Since we were putting rich folks in jail, the media actually gave a shit. Every time me and Ho ran up the court steps, cameras and microphones were in our faces. I told them I was a rollerblading cybersamurai named Chet Griffin, but my fellow elite call me "Ultimate Badass." On TV four hours later, they showed my face talking, and, to our hysterics, subtitled across the bottom of the screen, "Chet Griffin, known among his bike messenger friends as The Ultimate Bad Ass." I could just see those "friends" yodeling with rage.

Ho read somewhere that the odds someone will remember what you say increase exponentially each time you repeat it. Reporters would ask her how she managed to stay calm during all the time she was kidnapped, and she would answer like, "Well, working with my band Spit, I learn a lot about remaining calm but alert under pressure. See, Spit is a Bay Area band, and when we would play at the Padlock, charging fans only six bucks, there was a lot of pressure for Spit to sell out. And when I was kidnapped, just like when I play with Spit, I used to say to myself, Ho Pixie, playing bass with Spit as you do—" Most of this drivel was edited out, but Ho never said six words without one of them being *Spit*. When the TV showed her on the witness stand, the caption beneath her face read, "Ho Pixie. Bassist for local rock 'n' roll band Spit."

The TV loved us. We refused to wear anything but skate outfits, and the attention-hungry prosecutors decided it was a great idea, and suggested we appear in court with sunglasses. The prosecutor's assistant coached us how to convey as much attitude as possible on the stand. Like we needed lessons. The youth culture of San Fran ate it up. We became, for our allotted fifteen minutes, the emblematic couple of the Crazy City.

Of course Gambill prosecuted me to the full extent of the law, but it was a circus. The jury was influenced. They didn't understand the subtleties of computer crime. All they saw was a renegade vigilante, single-handedly bringing down a notorious conspiracy of stock criminals and corrupt cops, saving the stockholding citizens of this city hundreds of millions of dollars. These young punks pull off what the cops were too chicken to try, and now the cops want to put them in jail? I heard the second sweetest words ever spoken: *We find the defendant not guilty of all charges.*

The sweetest words ever spoken are *I love you.* I hear that every day.

Neither of us had to pay a dime in legal fees. The checks came in like leaves in a hurricane, almost surpassing the record still held by the Miracle Man, who, incidentally, has also been acquitted. But I suppose fate found him guilty; he's paralyzed for life.

In any case, we didn't cash the donated checks. The sleaziest lawyers in the city, hungry for media light and hoping to run for office someday, volunteered to represent us free of charge. Ho told one particularly persistent attorney he could only have the job if he barked like a dog. He yipped enthusiastically, then Ho threatened to tell the authorities he was chasing cases and slammed the door in his face.

Cameras in your face every day drive some people to suicide. Denny, of course, was in his element. CFED, Citizens for Economic Democracy, could not have gotten more press.

The fact that Denny was disabled, a talented computer hacker and techie, and a smartass made him popular with journalists—though TV played him as some kind of renegade Stephen Hawking. Their technology didn't do well with Denny's speech style. While the newspapers quoted pages of his political expounding and snide jokes, the TV edited down his expositories to single-sentence paraphrases and ran subtitles across his chest. While he said, "First I busted open the banking scheme with a superhack. Then I turned the evidence over to authorities, but I didn't wait around for them to make an arrest. I went straight to the famous Fort Farley Firestorm and scouted around in the open, risking death on all sides, so I could save Ho and my sidekick Chet"; meanwhile, the white words across his chest read, "I helped my skating friends with computer technical assistance, then acted as their scout during the Fort Farley Firestorm!"

Boy, was Denny pissed about that one. Now me and Ho call him "Scout."

The other night, Noam Chomsky gave him a call and asked him to do some research. Denny threw himself from his chair and prostrated himself before the speakerphone.

Freed from indentured servitude to Wozniak and Levy, Denny acquired a high-paying job in Silicon Valley, where he immediately relocated. Elana said yes. I'm supposed to be best man. I miss him more than I've ever missed anybody.

It turns out Ho sustained a mild concussion. The doctor gave me the rundown:

"She'll have to stay in bed."

"No prob."

"She'll suffer from fairly serious headaches for a while."

"She can hack it."

"She can't partake in any strenuous physical activity."

"Whoa-whoa-whoa! Rewind, doc! I thought *she* was going to be doing all the suffering!"

She was supposed to be all better in a month. She was out of bed and skating in a week. We were dorking the shit out of each other in two days. I think she finally let me in her pants because she figured a post-jackhammer headache was better than listening to me whine for another day.

All the adrenaline involved in the effort to save Ho and the media excitement that followed has completely cured me of my hacker plummet. One day I woke up and realized I had gone fourteen days without surfing infospace. My rising addiction is cured. For now.

Somebody counted thirty thousand bullets fired in the well-documented Fort Farley Firestorm! There were four dead, and ten wounded. Three gangsters were killed in the first volley of police gunfire that struck a charging wing. A criminal known as Spock was killed by a bizarre auto accident in an abandoned drainage pipe. Four gangsters were wounded by friendly fire. No policemen were killed, but six were wounded: five from their own guns or from the guns of their colleagues, one from ricochet.

Some of the media people are rumored to have actually orgasmed with glee.

The cops cuffed every single skate punk, reasoning that they'd look up something to charge them with later. Except for the wounded men, not a single gangster was arrested, nobody who was arrested was charged, nobody was held overnight.

After a ten-hour autopsy, the coroner determined that Data was killed by a fast-acting powder that paralyzed his lungs after it was surreptitiously deposited through his anus. Cutting-edge DNA technology determined that it was Lee Harvey Oswald who administered the insert.

Gina Corlini was the only police officer ever prosecuted. They got her on a host of crimes ranging from stock market cheating to conspiracy to commit murder. There was lots of media light on her. She is a childless unmarried female in a position of power. The jury deliberated for two minutes. Ten years in a maximum-security prison. Bye, Gina.

Sergeant Halcott was given Gina's job.

Mr. Hair Helmet was fired after he called the Fort Farley Firestorm! the "Fort Fiery Fartstorm!," a classic to be included in many a blooper show. A newsman can refer to all the rape and castration he wants to, but say the word *fart,* and you're off the air.

The Wozniak and Levy trial lasted a year and a half. Buckets of money were spent to tangle it up in red tape. Eloquent speeches were made to Wozniak's golf partner, Judge Amos, about how vital Wozniak and Levy's investments are to businesses that provide American jobs. For stealing eighty-eight million dollars from stockholders, they were each given a one million dollar fine and a six-month sentence. They went to federal prison, where they continue to run their business through computers in their private cells. They should be out in a few months, where their millions are waiting for them. Michael Levy has already received a job offer to teach business ethics at UCLA.

Reginald Andrecht of Andrecht's Futons was the only small-time business owner who was prosecuted. By sheer coincidence, a major thread of my electronic money tracking went straight through him. Andrecht has five kids, three of whom are in college. His trial lasted a grand total of twelve hours. For stealing eleven thousand dollars from stockholders, he was given two and a half years in federal prison, where he is allowed to have visitors once a month. His bank account of seven thousand dollars was seized, as was four thousand dollars worth of business capital. He spent fifteen grand on lawyer fees, all of it borrowed. His wife runs the futon business now, which has so far managed to hover above bankruptcy. The innocent guy who worked there part-time was laid off, and his fiancée refused to marry him. Andrecht's daughters have started working as waitresses and have gone deeper in debt, but they are still in college. Andrecht had served fifteen months before Wozniak and Levy were even convicted. He should be released soon, based on his angelic behavior.

No connection was ever made between Michael Levy and Chen.

Chen was killed by his own men. The newspapers went to great lengths to research the story of this "well-known drug kingpin" (who was never arrested in his life) and publish it on the day of his extravagant funeral, which was attended and paid for by the guys who butchered him. Somebody else runs his operation now.

The price of crack on the streets vibrated momentarily, then stabilized. The Drug War totaled forty-four arrests, half of whom were minors. Ho identified eight in a lineup. No high-ranking drug dealer was ever prosecuted. The deaths caused by this drug crackdown are hard to separate from the average run-of-the-mill murders that occur every month in our local poor neighborhoods, so nobody bothered to make a calculation. It's much more exciting to count scattered bullets at Fort Farley.

No New York Italian mafioso was ever convicted. Michael Leone was indicted, but the recording I made of him speaking for Rocky Rachino and openly considering murdering Chen was mysteriously thrown out of court. He never even had to appear.

I don't know whatever happened to the six bike messengers who suddenly found their means of survival yanked out from under them. Probably scrimping along, getting evicted, crashing at each other's pads, sharing ciggies, scanning the dusty cracks of gutters, reminiscing about Spider, too busy hustling to whore their bodies to dwell on me and Ho or their assassinated employer and torched workplace. What keeps them going is the brotherhood I was never a part of. All they got is adrenaline and each other. And you expect them to respect your sidewalk?

Spider's daughter, Ariela Tori Fulghum, was taken from her crack addict mother after her father's death. Ho used her influence with her old daycare employers to oversee Ariela's eventual placement with an affluent family in Contra Costa Christian County. Ariela just turned three, and she's white, so she found people to love her fast. She will probably never remember her daddy, who died with her name on his lips.

Someone told me Apollonia Corlini is still alive at eighty-one. She ran away from Sicily to America to give her family a better life. She lived to see her only son murdered and her only daughter sent to jail. She is left with no grandchildren.

Ho's moms claims to have "foreseen" her daughter's success. Ho's dad changed his contracting name to "Spit and Shine General Contracting."

Ho, famous for having been kidnapped by the criminals she eventually brought to justice—not to mention her double-oh-seven work breaking the insider trading ring through a single-handed gathering of evidence—was made a sort of poster girl for the Bay Area.

Her band was signed immediately.

The first thing Ho did with her fame was take out a loan against her future earnings to get Wily a ridiculously expensive vet. Wily had to have one of his hind legs amputated, but the loss doesn't seem to register in his nugget-sized brain. He hops around sniffing a great variety of teenage nuts. You can trace his progression through a crowd of thousands by the chilled yelps. It's like he's keeping inventory of the Spit fan base. We call him Tripod. When his back leg gets tired, he rests his haunches on a wheeled dolly and drags himself around that way. Now he's a skater. Denny is jealous and looking into getting a disabled pet of his very own. I suggested getting a fish with no fins, so you have to shake the bowl like one of those Christmas snow globes to watch him swim. But Denny wants a paralyzed ferret. God knows why.

I still ain't told you the best news of all. Bobby joined a rehab program of his own free will. It's five months and eighteen days since he took a hit so far, and still no relapse. I call him every night, and he sounds great. He promises that if he ever feels the call too hard, he'll call me on my brand-new shiny cellular phone. He knows I'll drop everything and go to him. He even has a *girlfriend* now. With no crack expense, he's riding the current tattoo wave like a bitchin surfer.

And that's all I'll ever need.

Last I saw Bobby, he did a number on my back with his tattoo pen. My beast, reptile, and angel became integrated into one circle. He converted the crown of thorns wrapped around my heart to a garland of flowers. To cover the name ANNA, he did a totally phat portrait of Ho's face.

*   *   *

Right now, we are on tour, opening for the opening act of a one-hit wonder who used to open for Hole. My official job title is "roadie."

It's time for Spit to brandish the material they've just recorded for their debut album, *Loogie*. Ho stalks on stage, puts the microphone somewhere in the vicinity of her sinuses, snarls back a long rattling chain of mucus, and hawks up a bubbling gargle of phlegm. The band hits with a speed metal number at the exact moment the ptooie is supposed to fly. That unique count-in basically sets the mood for the night.

After the concert, Ho and her skate buds, recently hired as roadies, ascend their portable half-pipe. Teenage idolaters, budding punk rock feminists who worship Ho and have read the *Spin* article ten times, gladly pay the four bucks to watch the skate show. It's midnight. Nearby bonfires give the giant wooden contraptions a hellish aura. I put on Jaco Pastorius's *Word of Mouth* and blast it through the giant speakers to confirm the pagan mood. The male skaters, dressed like peacocks, strut their stuff and defy gravity in front of the flashing cameras and gasping spectators. Then the orgy is saddled with a moment of silence.

Everyone is waiting to see what Ho, girl of the hour, decides to rip. Everyone holds their breath as she climbs the lip. For dramatic effect, Ho wets her finger to test the wind. She launches, descends, carves up and down the U to build momentum, then breaks the tension with a total goof move. Ho does the rare Clothespin Invert, more commonly known as the Pervert, which is an invert where you soar up the ramp, do a one-handed handstand on the lip of the coping, place the board between your knees, squeeze and hold, then grab the board and re-enter. It looks totally dorky, especially when a chick does it, so everybody laughs. Every skater, that is.

Ho slices the slope and lands on top of the opposite coping. She raises her board in the air by one hand and stands like a little warrior. The fans cheer.

After Spit moves through any town, skate equipment and nose ring sales skyrocket, and female punk bands sprout up in many a garage. In the heavily lingoed skate circles, there has always been a stubborn resistance to the inclusion of females, who are called "Sheilas," "Board Bettys," and "wenches."

Ho has a great comeback. When some ignorant skate rat calls her "wench," she says, "I'm not a wench. I'm a Ho." Then she usually nails a totally smokin Melon Grab Les Twist, which tends to silence the pig snorts.

And me? No change, really. Except that ever since I became a player in this top-heavy economy, I've magically gotten over my tendency to brag.

"Ready?"

"Ready as I'll ever be."

We both stare down the only hill in Kansas. The landscape below looks like a frameless Frederic Edwin Church painting. Great place for falling in love and shit.

Ho is styling big time. She's wearing a cheerleader's outfit she picked up in some second-hand store. Mismatched sneakers. She's pulled her pink hair up through the two slits in her skate helmet and tied it with a bone, a dried cow vertebra in fact. She thinks it looks bitchin, but I think she looks like Pebbles Flintstone. She says that's why it looks bitchin. My snake and Wily are in attendance. Wily scampers around excitedly, intuitively rooting for Ho, then gets tired and falumps onto his square skateboard. In his glass cage on wheels, my legless boa stares at his own tail, not giving a shit.

"You know the stakes, right?"

"Sure. This is for head."

"I hope you shaved, motherfucker, cause I don't want no razor burn on the inside of my thighs. And no beating around the bush."

"You just better keep them throat muscles loose, baby."

She chuckles and scratches the scruff of my pink mohawk. "This is a pointless bet."

"Ready? . . . Set . . ."

Ho sticks her hand up my skirt and yanks my boxers. "Waitaminute, studmuffin. How come you get to do the ready-set-go?"

"Okay, we'll do it together. Okay with you, babe?"

"Sure, toots."

I borrowed Ho's skirt, and I have a giant woman's symbol painted in lavender across my bare chest.

We both chorus, "Ready . . . Set . . . Go!"

Instant hyperspeed.

This is what life is, man. You can have your crucifixes and your handguns and your porches. My talisman will always be nigger Yin and honky Yang, forever moiling in a 69 embrace, each smiling his ass off.

That's the ultimate rush.

Peace.

I heft my bike up the six flights and dump it by my scuffed rollerblades. Fucking sixteen deliveries today, all of them up-hill, piddly-ass pay. The eighteen-year-old studs who used to idolize me are now twenty-year-olds with casts. The new eighteen-year-olds want my job, and my knees are starting to sound like Rice Krispies. The Legend won't carry me much further.

I step into the stench of mildew, the taste of dust. Two or three of my roommates wiggle their noses and scurry around the corners. Their eyes flash red like digital signals, recognize me, then flash off. They get back to sniffing. The creatures I once fed to my reptile now claim rights to my space.

No sense showering. The water will be brown until the tenants downstairs use the showers tomorrow morning. Ho won't be back from her Good Vibrations job until after mid-night, because she's in charge of dusting the dildos.

The Spit tour ended. After the initial attention generated by the trial, record sales fell off. A good album is irrelevant with-out a catchy single. There has been no second record deal. Ho received her last royalty check eight months ago. I sold my cellular phone for two tickets to San Francisco, then sold my snake for the deposit on this place.

Me and Ho got a place in the Mission. We argue a lot more. Mostly about money. The sex arguments haven't started yet, thank God. But Ho rolls with the punches, she works long hours, she makes her own clothes, she inspires me to tough it out. No matter how down we get on each other, the issue of us splitting is never even in the cards. Me and Ho are tight.

Which, two years into it, gives you more staying power than love. And a sense of humor doesn't hurt.

Believe me, I need it. Ho and Wily threw themselves into an ecstasy of grief when Wily relocated to Berkeley to live with Ho's "dadums," who actually owns something so old-fashioned as a backyard. Ho blows a lot of bank on BART trips across the Bay to cuddle and slobber with the amazing three-legged two-neuroned rottweiler. Me, I'm never going near a BART train again.

Through my cracked window, I can see the shimmering obelisk of the Transamerica Building, looming like a pyramid over sinking Atlantis. Levy gets out of jail-camp tomorrow, and he'll buy one of those top offices with a shaving from his pinky fingernail. A square foot of that building is worth more than I am. But it has an Achilles heel: It needs bike messenger nerves; it needs electronic blood.

I sigh, strip naked, and eye my only possession. A gift from Denny.

A guilt gift. Denny fell on the other side of that great iron curtain that descends between married and single people. He gratuitously invited me to Elana's baby shower, and then got all embarrassed when I showed up. He's sitting there nibbling finger foods and drinking Postum with his pinky stuck out, telling computer jokes with his dweeboid work colleagues, all of them pushing their glasses up their noses and gasp-laughing like Darth Vader having an asthma attack, and here this dark-side hacker shows up with tattoos, a shaved head, and a dyed black goatee. We couldn't even talk shop. Everything I said was cause for much internerdulation among the dick clique. Me and the straights don't speak the same technical language. They create. I steal. They program. I jury-rig bits of trash. Every time I invite Denny up to SF, he tells me, No thanks, me and the wife are going to stay in and peruse flatwear catalogues. Denny grew up on me. The crack in his integrity that created MP Phred has spread like a fungus to consume him. Denny is a straight.

It's one hell of a dumbass gift for a friend to give an ailing friend. Would you give a junkie a needle? A terrorist an Uzi?

But I would have one anyway. I would steal to get it. Maybe he knows that, and that's why he gave it to me.

I'm bored, broke, friendless. I tried to stop. I really did. But it's the only thing in the world I'm good at.

I sit down at my throne, a plastic milk crate. I hold my brain in my lap and flick the red switch on its side. A trillion nerve-roots burrow invisibly through the soft underbelly of the global plutocracy. I type the codes that make monoliths tremble. Hackers across the datasphere freeze and listen, knowing that only a resurrected digital demigod could wield such power.

I type out my decree.

"Tremble, pharaohs. Arise punks. I am Phoenix. I have returned."

ACKNOWLEDGMENTS

Special thanks to Mart Trenor, who wanted Chet to be a stuttering sexually deviant professor of biology ninja who is incredibly handsome, brilliant with computers, and has a three-foot penis; to Elle Trenor, who wanted Chet to be a female jazzercizing Tolkien expert who knows karate, volunteers to teach adults how to read, and has a not-quite-so-cocky husband; to Nathan Newman and Anders Schneiderman, who both said Chet should be a government-overthrowing socialist ninjew who gets laid all the time and is much cooler than his sidekick partner with whom he is in cahoots to make the world a better place; and to Jonna Hervig, who said I could make my hero into anything I wanted him to be, though I might want to consider making him a sexy viola-playing mother of two who nurtures injured animals and never allows any violence in the novels in which she stars and believes the only true test of a truly enjoyable story is if you cry during the entire thing. I hope I have managed to land Chet somewhere in the middle of all this.

Every writer out there should join a writers' group and shut the hell up for once while other writers criticize his life's work to his face. Immeasurable thanks to my comrades with unsheathed pens, especially Mir Tamim Ansary, Bill Falcone, Tracy Slein, Jennie Dorman, and Jeff Zittrain.

Also writers Marlene Lee, Wendy Frey, Gail Ford, Don Anderson, Gary Turchin, Vaughn Phelps, Gary Aldrich, Beth Glaser, Janine Freedman, Dave Barry, Stephanie Strand, Joe Sutton, Michael Sheahan, Peter Wong, Tony Tepper, Erika Mailman, Bryna Stevens, Eva Miller, Phil Downey, Aaron

Hamburger, Dorothy Lefkovits, Ethel Mays, Ilse Sternberger, Steve Cassal, Nancy Peterson, John Greene, Leonard Irving, Annie Soo, David Mensing, Jan Lord, Henry Wong, Bonnie Anderson, Andrew Miller, Tom Quontamatteo, Jeff Black, Larry Beresford, Rose Mark, Joyce Hendrickson, Carrie Burgess, Christyne Sisk, Adam Sills, Lexy Mountjoy, Sarah Dewitt, Ben Clarke, Adele Kearney, Bill Howton, Ed Wolfe, Michael Pauker, and Mike Ruggio.

Since moving to the artists' haven of America, the Bay Area, I've learned that the best music is not on any CD, the best people don't get noticed, and the best novels don't get published.

Thanks to the team of Ph.D.'s who read this and offered advice without the narcissism of your average fiction writer: Nathan Newman, Anders Shneiderman, Paul Reitter, Andy Carpenter, Tim Lynch, Suz Rivera, and Daphne Anshel.

And skaters Pat Rock and Tim Quirk, thanks for stoking me.

Anything stupid about this book is entirely their fault, and I take credit for all the cool stuff. And I get the money, regardless.

And a second dedication belongs to a talented editor, agent, and angel on earth, Frances Jalet-Miller, who supported my writing without pay for eight years. Love you, Frances. And God bless you, Molly Friedrich, agent extraordinaire, for taking me under your wing.

Tremendous credit belongs to David Szanto for astute editing, boundless enthusiasm, a great sense of humor, and working long hours. And may good fortune rain upon the visionary head of Rob Weisbach.

I never really thanked Leo Simon, Paula Messengil, Alex, Lindsey, and Shadow for giving me a free laser printer and paper.

And immense gratitude to the man who is destined to get a hundred books dedicated to him, Clive Matson, the teacher, poet, and hub of the unofficial Bay Area writer's network, to whom I owe my literary ass for dragging me out of isolation, hooking me up with other writers, donating printers to me, and single-handedly galvanizing the disjointed miasma of lonely scriveners into that rare and magical thing: a community.

TURN THE PAGE
FOR AN EXCERPT
FROM COLIN HARRISON'S
EXCITING NEW NOVEL,
AFTERBURN—

AVAILABLE SOON IN HARDCOVER
FROM FARRAR, STRAUS & GIROUX . . .

SEPTEMBER 7, 1999

He would survive. Yes, Charlie promised himself, he'd survive *this*, too—his ninth formal Chinese banquet in as many evenings, yet another bowl of shark-fin soup being passed to him by the endless waiters in red uniforms, who stood obsequiously against the silk wallpaper pretending not to hear the self-satisfied ravings of those they served. Except for his fellow *gweilo*—British Petroleum's Asia man, a mischievous German from Lufthansa, and two young American executives from Kodak and Citigroup—the other dozen men at the huge mahogany table were all Chinese. Mostly in their fifties, the men represented the big corporate players—Bank of Asia, Hong Kong Telecom, China Motors—and each, Charlie noted, had arrived at the age of cleverness. Of course, at fifty-eight he himself was old enough that no one should be able to guess what he was thinking unless he wanted them to, even Ellie. In his call to her that morning—it being evening in New York City—he'd tried not to sound too worried about their daughter Julia. "It's all going to be *fine*, sweetie," he'd promised, gazing out at the choppy haze of Hong Kong's harbor, where the heavy traffic of tankers and freighters pressed China's claim— everything from photocopiers to baseball caps flowing out into the world, everything from oil refineries to contact lenses flowing in. "She'll get pregnant, I'm sure," he'd told Ellie. But he wasn't sure. No, not at all. In fact, it looked as if it was going to be easier for him to build his electronics factory in Shanghai than for his daughter to hatch a baby.

"We gather in friendship," announced the Chinese host, Mr. Ming, the vice-chairman of the Bank of Asia. Having agreed to lend Charlie fifty-two million U.S. dollars to build his Shanghai factory, Mr. Ming in no way could be described as a friend; the relationship was one of overlord and indentured. But Charlie smiled along with the others as the banker stood and presented in high British English an analysis of south-eastern China's economy that was so shallow, optimistic, and full of euphemism that no one, especially the central ministries in Beijing, might object. The Chinese executives nodded politely as Mr. Ming spoke, touching their napkins to their lips, smiling vaguely. Of course, they nursed secret worries—worries that corresponded to whether they were entrepreneurs (who had built shipping lines or real-estate empires or garment factories) or the managers of institutional power (who controlled billions of dollars not their own). And yet, Charlie decided, the men were finally more like one another than unlike; each long ago had learned to sell high (1997) and buy low (1998), and had passed the threshold of unspendable wealth, such riches conforming them in their behaviors; each owned more houses or paintings or Rolls-Royces than could be admired or used at once. Each played golf or tennis passably well; each possessed a forty-million-dollar yacht, or a forty-million-dollar home atop Victoria's Peak, or a forty-million-dollar wife. Each had a slender young Filipino or Russian or Czech mistress tucked away in one of Hong Kong's luxury apartment buildings—licking her lips if requested—or was betting against the Hong Kong dollar while insisting on its firmness—any of the costly mischief in which rich men indulge.

The men at the table, in fact, as much as any men, sat as money incarnate, particularly the American dollar, the euro, and the Japanese yen—all simultaneously, and all hedged against fluctuations of the others. But although the men were money, money was not them; money assumed any shape or color or politics, it could be fire or stone or dream, it could summon armies or bind atoms, and, indifferent to the sufferings of the mortal soul, it could leave or arrive at any time. And on this exact night, Charlie thought, setting his ivory chopsticks neatly upon the lacquered plate, he could see that although money had assumed the shapes of the men in the room, it existed in differing densities and volumes and brightnesses. Whereas Charlie was a man of perhaps thirty or thirty-three million dollars of wealth, that sum amounted to shoe-shine change in the present company. No, sir, money, in *that* room, in *that* moment, was understood as inconsequential in sums less than one hundred million dollars, and of political importance only when five times more. Money, in fact, found its greatest compression and gravity in the form of the tiny man sitting silently across from Charlie—Sir Henry Lai, the Oxford-educated Chinese gambling mogul, owner of a fleet of jet-foil ferries, a dozen hotels, and most of the casinos of Macao and Vietnam. Worth billions—and billions more.

But, Charlie wondered, perhaps he was wrong. He could think of one shape that money had not *yet* assumed, although quite a bit of it had been spent, perhaps a hundred thousand dollars in all. Money animated the dapper Chinese businessman across from him, but could it arrive in the world as Charlie's own grandchild? This was the question he feared most, this was the question that had eaten at him and at Ellie for years now, and which would soon be answered: In a few hours, Julia would tell them once and forever if she was capable of having a baby.

She had suffered through cycle upon cycle of disappointment—hundreds of shots of fertility drugs followed by the needle-recovery of the eggs, the inspection of the eggs, the selection of the eggs, the insemination of the eggs, the implantation of the eggs, the anticipation of the eggs. She'd been trying for seven years. Now Julia, a woman of only thirty-five, a little gray already salting her hair, was due to get the final word. At 11:00 a.m. Manhattan time, she'd sit in her law office and be told the results of this, the last in-vitro attempt. Her *ninth*. Three more than the doctor preferred to do. Seven more than the insurance company would pay for. Good news would be that one of the reinserted fertilized eggs had decided to cling to the wall of Julia's uterus. Bad news: There was no chance of conception; egg donorship or adoption must now be considered. And if *that* was the news, well then, that was really goddamn something. It would mean not just that his only daughter was heartbroken, but that, genetically speaking, he, Charlie Ravich, was finished, that his own fishy little spermatozoa—one of which, wiggling into Ellie's egg a generation prior, had become his daughter—had run aground, that he'd come to the end of the line; that, in a sense, he was already dead.

And now, as if mocking his very thoughts, came the fish, twenty pounds of it, head still on, its eyes cooked out and replaced with flowered radishes, its mouth agape in macabre broiled amusement. Charlie looked at his plate. He always lost weight in China, undone by the soy and oils and crusted skin of birds, the rich liverish stink of turtle meat. All that duck tongue and pig ear and fish lip. Expensive as hell, every meal. And carrying with it the odor of doom.

Then the conversation turned, as it also did so often in Shanghai and Beijing, to the question of America's mistreatment of the Chinese. "What I do not understand are the American senators," Sir Henry Lai was saying in his softly refined voice. "They say they *understand* that we only want for China to be China." Every syllable was flawless English, but of course Lai also spoke Mandarin and Cantonese. Sir Henry Lai was reported to be in serious talks with Gaming Technologies, the huge American gambling and hotel conglomerate that clutched big pieces of Las Vegas, the Mississippi casino towns, and Atlantic City. Did Sir Henry know when China would allow Western-style casinos to be built within its borders? Certainly he knew the right officials in Beijing, and perhaps this was reason enough that GT's stock price had ballooned up seventy percent in the last three months as Sir Henry's interest in the company had become known. Lai smiled benignly. Then frowned. "These senators say that all they want is for international trade to progress without interruption, and then they go back to Congress and raise their fists and call China all kinds of names. Is this not true?"

The others nodded sagely, apparently giving consideration,

but not ignoring whatever delicacy remained pinched in their chopsticks.

"Wait, I have an answer to that," announced the young fellow from Citigroup. "Mr. Lai, I trust we may speak frankly here. You need to remember that the American senators are full of—excuse my language—full of shit. When they're standing up on the Senate floor saying all of this stuff, this means nothing, *absolutely* nothing!"

"Ah, this is very difficult for the Chinese people to understand." Sir Henry scowled. "In China we believe our leaders. So we become scared when we see American senators complaining about China."

"You're being coy with us, Mr. Lai," interrupted Charlie, looking up with a smile, "for we—or some of us—know that you have visited the United States dozens of times and have met many U.S. senators personally." Not to mention a few Third World dictators. He paused, while amusement passed into Lai's dark eyes. "Nonetheless," Charlie continued, looking about the table, "for the others who have not enjoyed Mr. Lai's deep friendships with American politicians, I would have to say my colleague here is right. The speeches in the American Senate are pure grandstanding. They're made for the American public—"

"The *bloodthirsty* American public, you mean!" interrupted the Citigroup man, who, Charlie suddenly understood, had drunk too much. "Those old guys up there know most voters can't find China on a globe. That's no joke. It's shocking, the American ignorance of China."

"We shall have to educate your people," Sir Henry Lai offered diplomatically, apparently not wishing the stridency of the conversation to continue. He gave a polite, cold-blooded laugh.

"But it is, yes, my understanding that the Americans could sink the Chinese Navy in several days?" barked the German from Lufthansa.

"That may be true," answered Charlie, "but sooner or later the American people are going to recognize the hemispheric primacy of China, that—"

"Wait, wait!" Lai interrupted good-naturedly. "You agree with our German friend about the Chinese Navy?"

The question was a direct appeal to the nationalism of the other Chinese around the table.

"Can the U.S. Air Force destroy the Chinese Navy in a matter of days?" repeated Charlie. "Yes. Absolutely yes."

Sir Henry Lai smiled. "You are knowledgeable about these topics, Mr."—he glanced down at the business cards arrayed in front of his plate—"Mr. Ravich. Of the Teknetrix Corporation, I see. What do you know about war, Mr. Ravich?" he asked. "Please, tell me. I am curious."

The Chinese billionaire stared at him with eyebrows lifted, face a smug, florid mask, and if Charlie had been younger or genuinely insulted, he might have recalled aloud his war years before becoming a businessman, but he understood that generally it was to one's advantage not to appear to have an advantage. And anyway, the conversation was merely a form of sport: Lai didn't give a good goddamn about the Chinese Navy, which he probably despised; what he cared about was whether or not he should soon spend eight hundred million dollars on GT stock—play the corporation that played the players.

But Lai pressed. "What do you know about this?"

"Just what I read in the papers," Charlie replied with humility.

"See? There! I tell you!" Lai eased back in his silk suit, running a fat little palm over his thinning hair. "This is a very dangerous problem, my friends. People say many things about China and America, but they have no direct knowledge, no real—"

Mercifully, the boys in red uniforms and brass buttons began setting down spoons and bringing around coffee. Charlie excused himself and headed for the gentlemen's restroom. Please, God, he thought, it's a small favor, really. One egg clinging to a warm pink wall. He and Ellie should have had another child, should have at least tried, after Ben. Ellie had been forty-two. Too much grief at the time, too late now.

In the men's room, a sarcophagus of black and silver marble, he nodded at the wizened Chinese attendant, who stood up with alert servility. Charlie chose the second stall and locked the heavy marble door behind him. The door and walls extended in smooth veined slabs from the floor to within a foot of the ceiling. The photo-electric eye over the toilet sensed his movement and the bowl flushed prematurely. He was developing an old man's interest in his bowels. He shat then, with the private pleasure of it. He was starting to smell Chinese to himself. Happened on every trip to the East.

And then, as he finished, he heard the old attendant greeting another man in Cantonese.

"Evening, sir."

"Yes."

The stall door next to Charlie's opened, shut, was locked. The man was breathing as if he had hurried. Then came some loud coughing, an oddly tiny splash, and the muffled silky sound of the man slumping heavily against the wall he shared with Charlie.

"Sir?" The attendant knocked on Charlie's door. "You open door?

Charlie buckled his pants and slid the lock free. The old man's face loomed close, eyes large, breath stinking.

"Not me!" Charlie said. "The next one!"

"No have key! Climb!" The old attendant pushed past Charlie, stepped up on the toilet seat, and stretched high against the glassy marble. His bony hands pawed the stone uselessly. Now the man in the adjacent stall was moaning in Chinese, begging for help. Charlie pulled the attendant down and stood on the toilet seat himself. With his arms outstretched he could reach the top of the wall, and he sucked in a breath and hoisted himself. Grimacing, he pulled himself up high enough so that his nose touched the top edge of the wall. But before being able to look over, he fell back.

"Go!" he ordered the attendant. "Get help, get a key!"

The man in the stall groaned, his respiration a song of pain. Charlie stepped up on the seat again, this time jumping exactly at the moment he pulled with his arms, and then *yes*, he was up, right up there, hooking one leg over the wall, his head just high enough to peer down and see Sir Henry Lai slumped on the floor, his face a rictus of purpled flesh, his pants around his ankles, a piss stain spreading across his silk boxers. His hands clutched weakly at his tie, the veins of his neck swollen like blue pencils. His eyes, not squeezed shut but open, stared up at the underside of the spotless toilet bowl, into which, Charlie could see from above, a small silver pillbox had fallen, top open, the white pills inside of it scattered and sunk and melting away.

"Hang on," breathed Charlie. "They're coming. Hang on." He tried to pull himself through the opening between the wall and ceiling, but it was no good; he could get his head through but not his shoulders or torso. Now Sir Henry Lai coughed rhythmically, as if uttering some last strange code—"Haa-cah . . . Haaa! Haaa!"—and convulsed, his eyes peering in pained wonderment straight into Charlie's, then widening as his mouth filled with a reddish soup of undigested shrimp and pigeon and turtle that surged up over his lips and ran down both of his cheeks before draining back into his windpipe. He was too far gone to cough the vomit out of his lungs, and the tension in his hands eased—he was dying of a heart attack and asphyxiation at the same moment.

The attendant hurried back in with Sir Henry's bodyguard. They pounded on the stall door with something, cracking the marble. The beautiful veined stone broke away in pieces, some falling on Sir Henry Lai's shoes. Charlie looked back at his face. Henry Lai was dead.

The men stepped into the stall and Charlie knew he was of no further use. He dropped back to the floor, picked up his jacket, and walked out of the men's restroom, expecting a commotion outside. A waiter sailed past; the assembled businessmen didn't know what had happened.

Mr. Ming watched him enter.

"I must leave you," Charlie said graciously. "I'm very sorry. My daughter is due to call me tonight with important news."

"Good news, I trust."

The only news bankers liked. "Perhaps. She's going to tell me if she is pregnant."

"I hope you are blessed." Mr. Ming smiled, teeth white as Ellie's estrogen pills.

Charlie nodded warmly. "We're going to build a terrific factory, too. Should be on-line by the end of the year."

"We are scheduled for lunch in about two weeks in New York?"

"Absolutely," said Charlie. Every minute now was important.

Mr. Ming bent closer, his voice softening. "And you will tell me then about the quad-port transformer you are developing?"

His secret new datacom switch, which would smoke the competition? No. "Yes." Charlie smiled. "Sure deal."

"Excellent," pronounced Mr. Ming. "Have a good flight."

The stairs to the lobby spiraled along backlit cabinets of jade dragons and coral boats and who cared what else. Don't run, Charlie told himself, don't appear to be in a hurry. In London, seven hours behind Hong Kong, the stock market was still open. He pointed to his coat for the attendant then nodded at the first taxi waiting outside.

"FCC," he told the driver.

"Foreign Correspondents' Club?"

"Right away."

It was the only place open at night in Hong Kong where he knew he could get access to a Bloomberg box—that magical electronic screen that displayed every stock and bond price in every market around the globe. He pulled out his cell phone and called his broker in London.

"Jane, this is Charlie Ravich," he said when she answered. "I want to set up a huge put play. Drop everything."

"This is not like you."

"This is not like anything. Sell all my Microsoft now at the market price, sell all the Ford, the Merck, all the Lucent. Market orders all of them. Please, right now, before London closes."

"All right now, for the tape, you are requesting we sell eight thousand shares of—"

"Yes, yes, I agree," he blurted.

Jane was off the line, getting another broker to carry out the orders. "Zoom-de-doom," she said when she returned. "Let it rip."

"This is going to add up to about one-point-oh-seven million," he said. "I'm buying puts on Gaming Technologies, the gambling company. It's American but trades in London."

"Yes." Now her voice held interest. "Yes."

"How many puts of GT can I buy with that?"

She was shouting orders to her clerks. "Wait . . ." she said. "Yes? Very good. I have your account on my screen . . ." He heard keys clicking. "We have . . . one million seventy thousand, U.S., plus change. Now then, Gaming Technologies is selling at sixty-six even a share—"

"How many puts can I buy with one-point-oh-seven?"

"Oh, I would say a huge number, Charlie."

"How many?"

"About . . . one-point-six million shares."

"That's huge."

"You want to protect that bet?" she asked.

"No."

"If you say so."

"Buy the puts, Jane."

"I am, Charlie, please. The price is stable. Yes, take this one . . ." she was saying to a clerk. "Give me puts on GT at market, immediately. Yes. One-point-six million at the money. Yes. At the money." The line was silent a moment. "You sure, Charlie?"

"This is a bullet to the moon, Jane."

"Biggest bet of your life, Charlie?"

"Oh, Jane, not even close."

Outside his cab a silky red Rolls glided past. "Got it?" he asked.

"Not quite. You going to tell me the play, Charlie?"

"When it goes through, Jane."

"We'll get the order back in a minute or two."

Die on the shitter, Charlie thought. Could happen to anyone. Happened to Elvis Presley, matter of fact.

"Charlie?"

"Yes."

"We have your puts. One-point-six million, GT, at the price of sixty-six." He heard the keys clicking.

"*Now* tell me?" Jane pleaded.

"I will," Charlie said. "Just give me the confirmation for the tape."

While she repeated the price and the volume of the order, he looked out the window to see how close the taxi was to the FCC. He'd first visited the club in 1970, when it was full of drunken television and newspaper journalists, CIA people, Army intelligence, retired British admirals who had gone native, and crazy Texans provisioning the war; since then, the rest of Hong Kong had been built up and torn down and built up all over again, but the FCC still stood, tucked away on a side street.

"I just want to get my times right," Charlie told Jane when she was done. "It's now a few minutes after 9:00 p.m. on Tuesday in Hong Kong. What time are you in London?"

"Just after 2:00 p.m."

"London markets are open about an hour more?"

"Yes," Jane said.

"New York starts trading in half an hour."

"Yes."

"I need you to stay in your office and handle New York for me."

She sighed. "I'm due to pick up my son from school."

"Need a car, a new car?"

"Everybody needs a new car."

"Just stay there a few more hours, Jane. You can pick out a Mercedes tomorrow morning and charge it to my account."

"You're a charmer, Charlie."

"I'm serious. Charge my account."

"Okay, will you *please* tell me?"

Of course he would, but because he needed to get the news moving. "Sir Henry Lai just died. Maybe fifteen minutes ago."

"Sir Henry Lai . . ."

"The Macao gambling billionaire who was in deep talks with GT—"

"Yes! Yes!" Jane cried. "Are you sure?"

"Yes."

"It's not just a rumor?"

"Jane, you don't trust old Charlie Ravich?"

"It's dropping! Oh! Down to sixty-four," she cried. "There it goes! There go ninety thousand shares! Somebody else got the word out! Sixty-three and a—Charlie, oh Jesus, you beat it by maybe a minute."

He told her he'd call again shortly and stepped out of the cab into the club, a place so informal that the clerk just gave him a nod; people strode in all day long to have drinks in the main bar. Inside sat several dozen men and women drinking and smoking, many of them American and British journalists, others small-time local businessmen who long ago had slid into alcoholism, burned out, boiled over, or given up.

He ordered a whiskey and sat down in front of the Bloomberg box, fiddling with it until he found the correct menu for real-time London equities. He was up millions and the New York Stock Exchange had not even opened yet. Ha! The big American shareholders of GT, or, more particularly, their analysts and advisers and market watchers, most of them punks in their thirties, were still tying their shoes and kissing the mirror and soon—very soon!—they'd be saying hello to the receptionist sitting down at their screens. Minutes away! When they found out that Sir Henry Lai had died in the China Club in Hong Kong at 8:45 p.m. Hong Kong time, they would assume, Charlie hoped, that because Lai ran an Asian-style, family-owned corporation, and because as its patriarch he dominated its governance, any possible deal with GT was off, indefinitely. They would then reconsider the price of GT, still absurdly stratospheric, and dump it fast. Maybe. He ordered another drink, then called Jane.

"GT is down five points," she told him. "New York is about to open."

"But I don't see *panic* yet. Where's the volume selling?"

"You're not going to see it here, not with New York opening. I'll be sitting right here."

"Excellent, Jane. Thank you."

"Not at all. Call me when you're ready to close it out."

He hung up, looked into the screen. The real-time price of GT was hovering at fifty-nine dollars a share. No notice had moved over the information services yet. Not Bloomberg, not Reuters.

He went back to the bar, pushed his way past a couple of journalists.

"Another?" the bartender asked.

"Yes, sir. A double," he answered loudly. "I just got very bad news."

"Sorry to hear that." The bartender did not look up.

"Yes." Charlie nodded solemnly. "Sir Henry Lai died tonight, heart attack at the China Club. A terrible thing." He slid one hundred Hong Kong dollars across the bar. Several of the journalists peered at him.

"Pardon me," asked one, a tall Englishman with a riot of red hair. "Did I hear you say Sir Henry Lai has *died*?"

Charlie nodded. "Not an hour ago. I just happened to be standing there, at the China Club." He tasted his drink. "Please excuse me."

He returned to the Bloomberg screen. The Englishman, he noticed, had slipped away to a pay phone in the corner. The New York Stock Exchange, casino to the world, had been open a minute. He waited. Three, four, five minutes. And then, finally, came what he'd been waiting for, Sir Henry Lai's epitaph: GT's price began shrinking as its volume exploded—half a million shares, price fifty-eight, fifty-six, two million shares, fifty-five and a half. He watched. Four million shares now. The stock would bottom and bounce. He'd wait until the volume slowed. At fifty-five and a quarter he pulled his phone out of his pocket and called Jane. At fifty-five and seven-eighths he bought back the shares he'd sold at sixty-six, for a profit of a bit more than ten dollars a share. Major money. Sixteen million before taxes. Big money. Real money. Elvis money.

*   *   *

It was almost eleven when he arrived back at his hotel. The Sikh doorman, a vestige from the days of the British Empire, nodded a greeting. Inside the immense lobby a piano player pushed along a little tune that made Charlie feel mournful, and he sat down in one of the deep chairs that faced the harbor. So much ship traffic, hundreds of barges and freighters and, farther out, the supertankers. To the east sprawled the new airport—they had filled in the ocean there, hiring half of all the world's deep-water dredging equipment to do it. History in all this. He was looking at ships moving across the dark waters, but he might as well be looking at the twenty-first century itself, looking at his own countrymen who could not find factory jobs. The poor fucks had no idea what was coming at them, not a clue. China was a juggernaut, an immense, seething mass. It was building aircraft carriers, it was buying Taiwan. It shrugged off turmoil in Western stock markets. Currency fluctuations, inflation, deflation, volatility—none of these things compared to the fact that China had eight hundred and fifty million people under the age of thirty-five. They wanted everything Americans now took for granted, including the right to piss on the shoes of any other country in the world.

But ha! There might be some consolation! He pushed back in the seat, slipped on his half-frame glasses, and did the math on a hotel napkin. After commissions and taxes, his evening's activities had netted him close to eight million dollars—a sum grotesque not so much for its size but for the speed and ease with which he had seized it—two phone calls!—and, most of all, for its mockery of human toil. Well, it was a grotesque world now. He'd done nothing but understand what the theorists called a market inefficiency and what everyone else knew as inside information. If he was a ghoul, wrenching dollars from Sir Henry Lai's vomit-filled mouth, then at least the money would go to good use. He'd put all of it in a bypass trust for Julia's child. The funds could pay for clothes and school and pediatrician's bills and whatever else. It could pay for a *life*. He remembered his father buying used car tires from the garage of the Minnesota Highway Patrol for a dollar-fifty.

No such thing as steel-belted radials in 1956. You cross borders of time, and if people don't come with you, you lose them and they you. Now it was an age when a fifty-eight-year-old American executive could net eight million bucks by watching a man choke to death. His father would never have understood it, and he suspected that Ellie couldn't, either. Not really. There was something in her head lately. Maybe it was because of Julia, but maybe not. She bought expensive vegetables she let rot in the refrigerator, she took Charlie's blood-pressure pills by mistake, she left the phone off the hook. He wanted to be patient with her but could not. She drove him nuts.

He sat in the hotel lobby for an hour more, reading every article in the *International Herald Tribune*. Finally, at midnight, he decided not to wait for Julia's call and pulled his phone from his pocket and dialed her Manhattan office.

"Tell me, sweetie," he said once he got past the secretary.

"Oh, Daddy . . ."

"Yes?"

A pause. And then she cried.

"Okay, now," he breathed, closing his eyes. "Okay."

She gathered herself. "All right. I'm fine. It's okay. You don't have to have children to have a fulfilling life. I can handle this."

"Tell me what they said."

"They said I'll probably never have my own children, they think the odds are—all I know is that I'll never hold my *own* baby, never, just something I'll never, ever do."

"Oh, sweetie."

"We really thought it was going to work. You know? I've had a lot of faith with this thing. They have these new egg-handling techniques, makes them glue to the walls of the uterus."

They were both silent a moment.

"I mean, you kind of expect that *technology* will work," Julia went on, her voice thoughtful. "They can clone human beings—they can do all of these things and they can't—" She stopped.

The day had piled up on him, and he was trying to remember all that Julia had explained to him about eggs and tubes and hormone levels. "Sweetie," he tried, "the problem is not exactly the eggs?"

"My eggs are pretty lousy, *also*. You're wondering if we could put *my* egg in another woman, right?"

"No, not—well, maybe yes," he sighed.

"They don't think it would work. The eggs aren't that viable."

"And your tubes—"

She gave a bitter laugh. "I'm *barren*, Daddy. I can't make good eggs, and I can't hatch eggs, mine or anyone else's."

He watched the lights of a tanker slide along the oily water outside. "I know it's too early to start discussing adoption, but—"

"He doesn't want to do it. At least he says he won't," she sobbed.

"Wait, sweetie," Charlie responded, hearing her despair, "Brian is just— Adopting a child is—"

"No, no, *no*, Daddy, Brian doesn't *want* a little Guatemalan baby or a Lithuanian baby or anybody else's baby but his own. It's about his own goddamn *penis*. If it doesn't come out of *his* penis, then it's no good."

Her husband's view made sense to him, but he couldn't say that now. "Julia, I'm sure Brian—"

"I *would* have adopted a little baby a year ago, two years ago! But I put up with all this shit, all these hormones and needles in my butt and doctors pushing things up me, *for him*. And now those *years* are— Oh, I'm sorry, Daddy, I have a client. I'll talk to you when you come back. I'm very— I have a lot of calls here. Bye."

He listened to the satellite crackle in the phone, then the announcement in Chinese to hang up. His flight was at eight the next morning, New York seventeen hours away; and as always, he wanted to get home, and yet didn't, for as soon as he arrived, he would miss China. The place got to him, like a recurrent dream, or a fever—forced possibilities into his mind, whispered ideas he didn't want to hear. Like the eight million.

It was perfectly legal yet also a kind of contraband. If he wanted, Ellie would never see the money; she had long since ceased to be interested in his financial gamesmanship, so long as there was enough money for Belgian chocolates for the elevator man at Christmas, fresh flowers twice a week, and the farmhouse in Tuscany. But like a flash of unexpected lightning, the new money illuminated certain questions begging for years at the edge of his consciousness. He had been rich for a long time, but now he was rich enough to fuck with fate. Had he been waiting for this moment? Yes, waiting until he knew about Julia, waiting until he was certain.

He called Martha Wainwright, his personal lawyer. "Martha, I've finally decided to do it," he said when she answered.

"Oh, Christ, Charlie, don't tell me that."

"Yes. Fact, I just made a little extra money in a stock deal. Makes the whole thing that much easier."

"Don't do it, Charlie."

"I just got the word from my daughter, Martha. If she could have children, it would be a different story."

"This is bullshit, Charlie. Male bullshit."

"Is that your legal opinion or your political one?"

"I'm going to argue with you when you get back," she warned.

"Fine—I expect that. For now, please just put the ad in the magazines and get all the documents ready."

"I think you are a complete jerk for doing this."

"We understand things differently, Martha."

"Yes, because *you* are addicted to testosterone."

"Most men are, Martha. That's what makes us such assholes."

"You having erection problems, Charlie? Is *that* what this is about?"

"You got the wrong guy, Martha. My dick is like an old dog."

"How's that? Sleeps all the time?"

"Slow but dependable," he lied. "Comes when you call it."

She sighed. "Why don't you just let me hire a couple of strippers to sit on your face? That'd be *infinitely* cheaper."

"That's not what this is about, Martha."

"Oh, Charlie."

"I'm serious, I really am."

"Ellie will be terribly hurt."

"She doesn't need to know."

"She'll find out, believe me. They always do." Martha's voice was distraught. "She'll find out you're advertising for a woman to have your baby, and then she'll just flip out, Charlie."

"Not if you do your job well."

"You really this afraid of death?"

"Not death, Martha, oblivion. Oblivion is the thing that really kills me."

"You're better than this, Charlie."

"The ad, just put in the ad."

He hung up. In a few days the notice would sneak into the back pages of New York's weeklies, a discreet little box in the personals, specifying the arrangement he sought and the benefits he offered. Martha would begin screening the applications. He'd see who responded. You never knew who was out there.

He sat quietly then, a saddened but prosperous American executive in a good suit, his gray hair neatly barbered, and followed the ships out on the water. One of the hotel's Eurasian prostitutes watched him from across the lobby as she sipped a watered-down drink. Perhaps sensing a certain opportune grief in the stillness of his posture, she slipped over the marble floor and bent close to ask softly if he would like some company, but he shook his head no—although not, she would see, without a bit of lonely gratitude, not without a quick hungered glance of his eyes into hers—and he continued to sit calmly, with that stillness to him. Noticing this, one would have thought not that in one evening he had watched a man die, or made millions, or lied to his banker, or worried that his flesh might never go forward, but that he was privately toasting what was left of the century, wondering what revelation it might yet bring.